STREAMS OF BABEL

OTHER NOVELS BY CAROL PLUM-UCCI

The Body of Christopher Creed

What Happened to Lani Garver

The She

The Night My Sister Went Missing

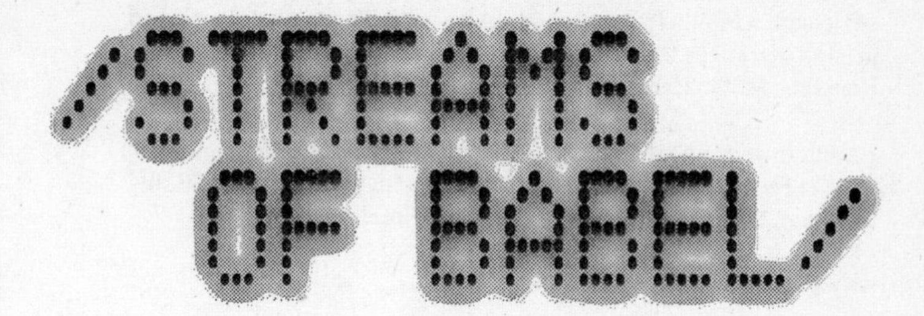

CAROL PLUM-UCCI

HOUGHTON MIFFLIN HARCOURT
BOSTON NEW YORK

 Published in the United States by Graphia, an imprint of Houghton Mifflin Harcourt Publishing Company. Originally published in hardcover in the United States by Harcourt Books, an imprint of Houghton Mifflin Harcourt Publishing Company, 2008.

www.graphiabooks.com

The text of this book is set in Minion.

The Library of Congress has cataloged the hardcover edition as follows:
Plum-Ucci, Carol, 1957–
Streams of Babel/Carol Plum-Ucci.
p. cm.
Summary: Six teens face a bioterrorist attack on American soil as four are infected with a mysterious disease affecting their small New Jersey neighborhood, and two others, both brilliant computer hackers, assist the United States Intelligence Coalition in tracking the perpetrators.
[1. Bioterrorism—Fiction. 2. Terrorism—Fiction. 3. Communicable disease—Fiction. 4. Computer hackers—Fiction. 5. Espionage—Fiction. 6. Interpersonal relations—Fiction. 7. New Jersey—Fiction.] I. Title.
PZ7.P7323Str 2008
[Fic]—dc22 2007026503

HC ISBN 978-0-15-216556-7
PA ISBN 978-0-547-25873-7

Printed in the United States of America
DOM 10 9 8 7 6 5 4 3 2
4500220716

To Rick and Abbey—
thanks for putting up with me.

"We have slain a large dragon. But we live now in a jungle filled with a bewildering variety of poisonous snakes. And in many ways, the dragon was easier to keep track of."

Former CIA director James Woolsey,
on acts of terrorism

TRINITY FALLS,
NEW JERSEY

ONE

CORA HOLMAN
THURSDAY, FEBRUARY 28, 2002
6:13 P.M.

I SAT VERY STILL, waiting for the police and ambulance to arrive. If I dropped my gaze from the living room window, I could see my mother's body on the couch from the corner of my eye. So I stared out at the oak trees and silhouettes passing under the streetlamp. A girl's voice rose, with a couple of guys adding whoops and shouts.

"...gonna win tomorrow! Go, Trinity!"

My wish wrenched my insides—to be that carefree girl out on our pretty street, with sports and guys to worry about instead of this. I had assumed, like anyone would have, that my mother had just overdosed.

I call my mother Aleese. She had walked into my life for the first time when I was twelve. She was an addict then and got worse, but fortunately, she didn't make public spectacles of herself. Even so, I'd always feared a visit from the police, and the moment had arrived. A minute after the singing died away, flashing red lit up the house like a fire.

I sat in the chair beside Aleese, gripping a glass of water. I knew from my grandmother dying three years ago that the shock doesn't hit you right away. I couldn't look at Aleese on the couch, but I could say things in my head, like *She has died* and *I am alone now,* knowing the shock was about four days off.

I thought there might be some way to keep Aleese's drug habit from looking so awful. If the paramedics got suspicious that we weren't particularly close, I could mention that Oma, my grandmother, had raised me. I should remember to refer to Aleese as "Mom." I could make her sound a little respectable by saying that she had at one time been a freelance photographer. I knew that was true. I had the camera to prove it.

But there was no getting around the worst of this. I had always hoped that if Aleese accidentally overdosed, it would be while she was buying her drugs in Atlantic City, her one inspiration for leaving the house. I would *get* the phone call instead of *making* the phone call. Now the police would see how we lived.

"Come in?" My voice squeaked as I sat frozen.

Our little ranch was suddenly full of people. Four officers, four paramedics, a man in a suit and tie. Nobody ever came in our house, so it was like being hit by a tidal wave. Loud voices and gnarled replies from walkie-talkies filled the air, and footsteps echoed through the walls. They made me want to curl up in a ball, but I sat up very straight.

"Hey, Cora. Are you all right?"

My eyes rose to see Rain Steckerman's dad. He was the man in the suit and tie. He had been the local FBI director for years, then right after Christmas he'd become something bigger. He was now some South Jersey supervisor for the U.S. Intelligence Coalition. *USIC.* I recalled the name and that he had been on television a couple of months back, but I couldn't remember why. And I couldn't understand why someone who tried to catch terrorists would be here with the police and paramedics.

I realized he was out of breath. And I put it together that he would have seen all the flashing lights from his house. He had run up here trying to be nice.

I didn't want to hear nice. Especially since his daughter went to my school. Rain Steckerman was perfect and had more friends than anybody. *Lord, don't let him feel sorry for me. Don't let him tell Rain about this so she can pity me even worse.*

"Uh...hypodermic in the couch, belt under the coffee table," an officer recited the news. Mr. Steckerman's face was between his and mine. He was looking at me intently, so he couldn't miss what I couldn't help: My eyes were rolling.

"What was in the vial, hon?" the policeman asked.

"Morphine."

I wished Mr. Steckerman would back away from me. He was making me want to cry. He looked like he *expected* me to cry in front of all these people. But a voice rang loudly from the kitchen, drawing my attention away from the men surrounding the couch.

"...used to be, like, a...newspaper photographer in Beirut or somewhere, and a bomb went off, destroyed her shooting arm. I think that's it. She's been a recluse and a drug addict for years."

I was stunned that the paramedic knew all of this, but he'd just recited it into a cell phone. I had never said it to anyone, and my mother had never been arrested. Her morphine addiction had been Our Big Secret. At least, I thought it had been.

Maybe other people have always known, and I've been too stupid to realize it. I had imagined that we'd kept the secret so well, and some strange part of me made one last stab at keeping the secret now.

"She...had a strange flu," I admitted loudly. "I have it, too! It was making her nose bleed. It started bleeding about half an hour ago. She suddenly...stopped breathing. I tried CPR, but I've only seen it done on TV." I trailed off quickly, wanting only to forget how my pushing on Aleese's chest did little more than send small gushes of blood out her nose.

"She snort something?" an officer asked. He was young, couldn't have any kids in my school. Not that it mattered, with this room full of people who probably did.

"She never snorted anything. She only took injections."

"Does she have a prescription?"

I just rolled my eyes again. My own questions fired off in my head. Why couldn't my mother have said something heroic in her last words? Why couldn't she have finally told me she loved me?

"Take a picture of me."

"Don't be crazy, Aleese! I'm calling 9-1-1 this time!"

"Take a picture of me first."

"Just keep that ice on your nose, and—"

"I know you love that goddamn camera you stole from me. When was that? Ninety-eight? Are you going to learn to use it? Now is the time."

"9-1-1, please state your emergency."

"Um... my mother has the flu and she's been complaining of headaches, and now her nose won't stop bleeding."

But she sure could talk. And be rude, and terrify me as always with her surreal, drug-induced comments. Do some things never change?

The paramedics had started to move her already. They were putting her on a stretcher behind two policemen, so I couldn't see much.

I decided, *Things that never change can change in an instant.*

"Where are you taking her?" I asked. It seemed I ought to know.

"It depends on whether your family wants an autopsy," the paramedic said, and I glanced at him. He looked familiar. Football games...a face in the stands. *Oh, damn. Football dad. Whose dad?* What did it matter? Nothing mattered.

"Cora, what extended family is coming to stay with you?" Mr. Steckerman shook my shoulders slightly. "I know your grandma passed away when you and Rain were freshmen, but is there someone else?"

You and Rain. Like we were best buddies because we lived a dozen houses apart. Like I had something in common with Rain Steckerman except that we breathed the same air at school. I swallowed. "I have another grandmother in California. She's coming."

I knew I couldn't get away with that lie for long. I wasn't sure seventeen was old enough to make funeral arrangements or sign papers or anything that might need to be done. I just wanted to get him out of the house for now. I needed my house quiet. I needed to think some more, and he was too important to be in here.

In a blur, the business in January that had put Mr. Steckerman on the television news floated through my head. Trinity Falls and bunches of other communities between here and New York had to test their water supplies—terrorist threat. The tests had come back negative even before the television stations found out about it. So Mr. Steckerman had been the local hero who got to announce that. Now he was in my living room—a man who had been on television. Thinking of him as a man who lived in my neighborhood gave me an even more bizarre feeling than when I'd watched him on the television.

He backed off into the kitchen, but I could hear his murmuring clearly. "...file a recommendation for an autopsy. Kid says the woman had the flu, and the kid looks like she has the flu, too."

"A mild flu can kill a drug addict, Alan. I don't see the point," the paramedic replied.

"It's just that I haven't heard of any flus going around that cause people to bleed out through the nose and ears."

"Touché," the paramedic said. "But what are you suggesting? Do I need to start rooting through my mountain of memos on emerging infectious diseases? Or do you need to start rooting through your mountain of bioterror threats?"

"Neither, I'd say. But why take a risk when it's in the hospital's budget to do an autopsy?"

"Because it's a busy night, and I don't need the paperwork hell." The paramedic sounded a little defensive, but Mr. Steckerman must have made some face, because he went on. "Fine, fine, I'll file a rec. And how's this? I'll even check out the kid before I leave. This house doesn't look like it comes equipped with medical insurance. It's a goddamn mess."

Mr. Steckerman agreed. *He's going to tell Rain what the inside of my house looks like.* I was horrified. Suddenly, the paramedic was in front of me, cutting off my circulation with a blood pressure cuff. Then he stuck a thermometer in my mouth.

"Have you ever done drugs, Cora?"

I spoke to him around the thing. "*Mm-mm!* Never! See?" I showed him my elbows and patted the backs of my knees just below my skirt line. I would probably have showed him between my toes just to prove it, but Mr. Steckerman was back, squatting down beside him.

"I'm sure what she's saying is true," he told the paramedic, and I died a thousand deaths. *Rain must have talked about me. He knows you have to have friends even to smoke pot.*

"Honey, what's your birth date?" Mr. Steckerman asked.

I sensed the importance of the question, though it took me a few moments for the reasons to come clear. As the paramedic read the thermometer, I spit out, "I'm eighteen."

My life was a chronic secret, and yet I don't ever remember a real *lie* coming out of my mouth too many times before tonight. I've always managed to keep secrets by not getting so close to people. It had been important to me, for some reason, not to have to keep track of lies.

"Your temperature is just over a hundred." The paramedic offered half a shrug. "Have any nausea? Vomiting? Diarrhea?"

I shook my head on the first two and nodded on diarrhea, not looking at him. I hadn't looked closely at any of the paramedics. First, it would have meant looking at Aleese. Now it would have meant looking at them to say I'd spent most of today in the bathroom.

I finally looked when the paramedic who had come up behind Mr. Steckerman said, "My mom's got the stomach flu, too."

I am hallucinating. Just let me die, too. I prayed for this face to change into one I didn't know so well. Scott Eberman was cracking gum, looking somewhere around my waist and not my face, thank god. I had been worried about somebody's dad showing up, not somebody who graduated my sophomore year, and certainly, beyond all people, not one of the Ebermans. He had a brother, Owen, in my grade who was even taller—and better looking if you listen to the way most girls carry on. I'd always thought Owen was just sweeter.

An image flashed of marching band, my first game freshman year, lining up to go on the field at halftime while the team was coming off. Scott Eberman pulled his helmet off his sweaty head about fifteen feet in front of me, and my jaw dropped just at the sight of him.

Another halftime, I was so busy staring at him that I forgot to move with the band. So he bumped into me in all this heavy equipment, took me by both shoulders, and moved me, saying, "Sorry, excuse me." Only he kept looking right over the top of my head and talking to the running back. He never even saw me. I don't think he even knew he touched me. But I walked around for three days, rubbing my shoulders in a haze, saying, "Sorry, excuse me."

Even now, Scott Eberman was not seeing me—just my stomach or knees or something, while he was thinking of his sick mother. I could feel my eyes filling up, finally. An Eberman in my house was too much.

"Phil, take some blood from her," he told the older paramedic. "I took some from my mom last night...keeps saying she's too busy at work to go to the doctor, so I have a choice between kicking her in the butt to go there or nailing her to the chair just long enough for me to take blood..." and so on and so forth. I was trying to rub tears out of my eyes before they spilled. It was another bizarre attempt not to attract any more attention to myself.

This Phil was pulling a vial and a needle out of some orange case, quietly joking about how it was still illegal for Scott to take blood. I was grateful for their idle chatter about Scott only having half a year to go in paramedic training, and what the lab doesn't know won't hurt anything.

I endured the pinch without moving as this needle pierced my arm. I played Invisible Girl pretty well until Phil muttered, "What the hell..."

I glanced down and could see a purple spot grow quickly to the size of a dime under my skin. He pulled the needle out and pushed down on a cotton ball, having captured only a few drops.

"Strike one." Scott squatted down in the space Mr. Steckerman had left when he went to the kitchen again.

"I never miss," Phil said. "That's weird."

"You know what?" Scott pressed on the purple spot, now about the size of a quarter. He jerked the rubber tie off my bicep. "This is why my mom wouldn't go to the specialist this week. The nurse in Dr. O'Dell's did this to her arm last week."

He wrapped the rubber tie on my other arm and started pressing on the crook of my elbow. He still hadn't looked at my face, thank god, because now I could only think, *He's touching me. Why can't I wake up?*

The older paramedic made praying hands in his rubber gloves. I couldn't tell whether he was joking or not. "You don't have to trust this man," he said, and I thought his eyes were smiling a little. "This *boy*..."

"Boy, schmoy. I'll be twenty. One of these months." With a smile, Scott finally looked into my eyes. For a moment, I was a person. Not a vein, not a stuffed dummy on the sidelines, flute in hand. He said, "Not to worry. I didn't gouge my mother, and I won't gouge you, either."

He took new supplies from Phil, stuck me with a new needle. The tube started filling up, and my skin stayed flesh-colored this time.

"Voilà," he said to Phil, who was grumbling about beginner's luck as he opened a Band-Aid.

He pulled the needle out of my arm and pressed a cotton ball on it as Phil wrote something on the vial. I glanced up to see Scott's brown eyes cutting right through me again. They were the worst of his great features—small and round. But they fit perfectly with his chiseled face, elflike nose. I looked away, but he didn't.

"So. Do you still play the flute in the band?" he asked.

"How did you know I was in the band?"

He stuck the Band-Aid on and pulled one side of his mouth up funny. "What do you think you are, the invisible person?"

For lack of something better, I nodded.

"It's a special gift of his," Phil put in, "along with finding dead center of a small vein. This kid never, ever forgets a face or a fact. It's ridiculous."

I could not think of a more logical reason for Scott Eberman to remember me. But he cast the guy a dirty look over his shoulder, dropped to his knees, and drummed the arms of the chair on either side of me. I couldn't meet his eyes anymore, and it seemed the longer I stared into my lap, the longer he stared back.

"You know what I wish?" he asked. "You know my mom, right? Well, she's got the flu, too, which means she's contaminated already. Probably my brother and I are, too, so...I wish you would come over to our house and sleep there. She would like the company. Honestly."

"Oh. No...," I stammered. "Why would I...barge in on you and your sick mother?"

His eyebrows shot up in two perfect arches while he looked sideways for a second. "Uh...maybe because you've just had a death in the family?"

"Well, my mother, she..."

"Your mother, what?" he persisted.

"She...didn't do much but sleep. At least not when I was here. Which wasn't much. I work in the Acme after school. My grandmother pulled some strings and got me that job right before she passed away..." *Do we have to do this?* He wasn't moving, and logic reminded me he was just trying to be nice. My rehearsed line flew into place and saved me from being rude. "I didn't even live with my mother until I was twelve. One day she just...showed up on me and Oma. That was my grandmother. She died three years ago."

He said, "When I was a kid, Mom and I used to walk our dog past your house, and if she was trimming the hedges or something, your grandma would talk it up with Mom. I remember her saying a few times that she'd have have had ten kids if her husband hadn't died right after—"

"—right after Aleese was born." I felt myself unwinding the slightest bit. I remembered when Oma died, people were very awkward around me. It seemed only the funeral director, doctors, and nurses—people who were used to death—knew that stupid conversations like this are all right, that they really do help.

But his normalcy was taking him places that, in this case, were not normal. "Last time I saw her, your grandma also said that your mom hurt her arm in an accident?"

"Um..." I had already lied about my age. Feeling so achy and tired, I just spilled the truth. "I'm not sure how it happened. There was an accident overseas, maybe an unsuccessful surgery, and that's when she got addicted to painkillers. She just...never got unaddicted. I wish I had something less selfish and more interesting to say than it was easier to go to school all day and work all night. I've got a lot of money in the bank. Guess that's one good thing. Ha ha."

"That makes one of us." He didn't laugh back. "And that's not selfish at all. Morphine addicts can be extremely violent, among other things."

"You have no idea."

I forced my mouth shut by pinching my lips with my fingers. And Scott Eberman was drumming his fingers again. I could not believe he wasn't looking at me weird.

"You know what my mom does? For a living? She's a lawyer, and she wastes too much time in court with women who come crawling to her from the Rescue Mission, who need a divorce from their drunken, abusive husbands and some cashola to help raise their kids. I keep telling her, 'Mom, I could give you five personal injury clients a day with high-paying accidents,' but she won't listen to me. Consequently, I'm in paramedic school instead of medical school, and that's why our house looks like crap."

The pressure from holding in tears probably made me laugh harder than I should have.

"It's clean, real clean, but that's because of me. We got clean sheets. Come on." He stood up, put his hand down to me.

"No. No thank you."

"Yes. Come on." I could see his fingers waggling in front of me, like he wanted me to take them, and I drew back automatically from such a surreal sight.

"I don't want to!"

"I'm telling you to. Come on..."

I realized I was curled up in a little ball, peering at his waggling fingers from over the tops of my knees. His hand dropped to his work pants and he patted his palm against his leg twice.

"If you don't come with me now, my mother will show up at your door in about half an hour. If she's well enough tonight. Good days and bad days. I think it's been three weeks now. You shouldn't be alone with this thing, Cora Holman. It's not easy to get rid of, Cora Holman, who plays flute in the Trinity Regional band."

He handed me back my glass of water, which he'd put on the floor. I watched him move backward. She might come in half an hour. I needed half an hour just to be alone, to hear the normal loneliness of this house, to gather my normal thoughts.

After an eternity, it seemed, he was gone; they were all gone, and the silence hugged around me.

I circled around the living room, staring at that couch. There was a thin line of blood that had dripped down the side.

I hadn't noticed Aleese's ear bleeding, but Mr. Steckerman must have been right, because I had wiped her nose after my CPR failed, and none of the blood made it to the couch.

I stared at that dark stream before going off to my room, crawling on my knees to the back of my closet and feeling around for the Nikon my mother had referred to in her last words. She wasn't so smart. She'd known I had it, but she hadn't known that I used it quite a bit.

I had gotten this strange compulsion last fall to start taking pictures around Trinity Falls on Sundays. It kept me out of the house on my day off, for one thing. For another, it made me feel like I belonged to the place instead of like some squatter, some daughter of an addict. Through a lens, the most beautiful parts of Trinity came clear. Azalea gardens in bloom in spring. Trees that lined streets in perfect, royal arches. Lawns as thick as Persian carpets and green as Ireland. People hung American flags off porches and trimmed real hedges around their swimming pools in Trinity.

There was something serene about taking pretty pictures, and that's all I had ever liked to take. Maybe it was the fever, but something possessed me, or shot into me, something that felt...evil, or like anger, or dark knowledge. Desperation of some sort. *My mother is inside of me right now.*

It was a violating thought. But the moan that came out was very much mine—small and squeaky, not like the bowels of hell that had moaned out of Aleese when she was coming off a high. I raised the camera to my eye, zeroing in on that red line, thinking of Aleese's final words.

"*Take a picture of me.*" She had always loved to make me squirm when some crude thought struck her. But she had already been in and out of consciousness when she had said it. I wondered, confused, if there wasn't something sincere about it, and I replayed the words in my head, trying to hear her tone. "*Take a* picture *of me.*" "Take *a* picture *of me.*" As if, maybe, she thought there was something worth capturing in truth, no matter how ugly, that made it valuable—as valuable as scenes from a quaint New Jersey town.

I looked at that thin line of blood through the lens, though I couldn't believe I was doing it. After a moment, it looked like a red tear. One red tear, silent, permanent, so symbolic of a sad life, a sad ending, a failure, a *truth.*

I snapped the picture, and the flash brought me back to reality. *Cora, your mother just died, and you're sitting in the living room taking pictures of her blood. That is beyond sick. It's the fever. Go to bed.*

One of the paramedics had left some pills—Tylenol or something—but I forgot to take them. I crawled into bed in my room, shivering from chills. Mrs. Eberman never came.

TWO

OWEN EBERMAN
THURSDAY, FEBRUARY 28, 2002
7:14 P.M.

JUST BEFORE LYING down to play couch commando for the night, I pressed my face to the living room window. I was trying to see through the dark, far into the next block. I had noticed my brother's ambulance beside some house down there about half an hour ago. Usually, if Scott was just helping to check out an elderly person with palpitations, he would stop home afterward with his squad. They liked to hang out long enough to down a pitcher of Mom's mint iced tea and suck up a couple of sports highlights on ESPN.

But the street was dark, the ambulance gone. I flopped down on the couch, feeling relief that I wouldn't be faced with the noise of a squad. Call me selfish. Mom would always get mad when I called myself selfish, and yet there I was, feeling relieved, when some calamity may have happened down my street.

I reminded myself of the one time Mr. Shumaker, our neighbor, had three buddies over to play blackjack while their wives went to cavort at the casinos. The fathers were watching all the kids, and Scott said these young, hotshot attorneys were twenty hands in and three sheets to the wind when the Shumaker three-year-old took a nosedive down a flight of stairs. Scott said his squad prevented a lot of people from driving drunk when their kids needed a stitch, and it came with the territory.

It could have been anything, I told myself. The explanation fit my mood best.

I get in these moods I call "my moods from hell," though my mom is more cheerful and calls them my "need-to-regroup times." Maybe they weren't so terrible as all that. I mean, I didn't sit here in the house thinking that I wanted to annihilate people. I was just slightly off my gourd about how sometimes the world is a confusing place. And sometimes I feel like I don't belong here.

These days always hit me the week before the South Jerseys in wrestling and in November, too, if we made the football playoffs. I'd be pushing it to the max along with everyone else, until one day I'd just decide, *I don't want to hear one more locker slam. I don't want to hear one more dumb dirty joke. I don't want to feel one more person tugging at me—and that goes for the girls, too. I'm tired of smelling my own sweat, and the sound of the phones could make me psycho.*

All the guys on wrestling were gearing up for the time of their lives. I guess I was, too, but still. I felt like I would love six weeks on a deserted island, though Mom always said a weekend would balance everything out.

I reached for my two-liter of Dr Pepper and a bag of pretzels, grabbed the remote, and put my feet up on the coffee table, which always killed Scott, because he kept it clean with Windex. But he wasn't home, so I could relax without any guilt fest. Everything was cool, until the phone started in.

"I'm not home!"

My mom picked up. "This is Janice... Hi, Stenger. Nope, not home, hon. Try Bob Dobbins's house. I'll tell him to call you when he comes in, okay?"

She hung up, and I couldn't have counted to five when my cell phone pitched in. It was in my backpack, tossed by the front door. I glared at the light that flashes green all the way through my backpack, then I went back to ESPN and hockey. Mom walked over to fix the drape I'd left cockeyed, reached a hand in the pack, and checked out the caller ID.

"It's Myra." She made a sour face.

I just shook my head. Myra McAllister broke up with me last week, and all this week she was having seller's remorse. But the memory of her words cut two feet into me sometimes. *"You know what your problem is, Owen? You're a freak of nature. I have never seen anybody who can do so many things so well, and your heart is not in any of it. Including going out with me."*

I said, "Myra, that is so not true." But I knew it *was* true.

The whole argument started after the coach pushed me up to this officer from West Point after a Horizons assembly for seniors. The officer already knew my name somehow. Well, Myra was still upset that I hadn't jumped into the lap of a Georgetown football recruiter the week before, so when I told this West Point officer, "I still don't know what I want to do,"

Myra told me I would end up shucking clams off the Atlantic City beaches. There wasn't too much I could say back.

Mom was holding my cell phone and bleeping through my caller ID. "Before that it was... Dobbins, Jon Dempsey, Adrian Moran. Where's the party?"

I grabbed the remote again and climbed through the channels, away from the sports. Thirty-seven, thirty-eight, thirty-nine, AMC. *Lawrence of Arabia.* I recognized the first five minutes scrolling before my face and thought, *Very, very cool.*

"Dempsey's," I muttered.

"Why is he having a party on a school night?" she asked.

"It's not a school night. Teacher Development Day tomorrow," I reminded her.

"I take it you're not going." She came over behind the couch, bent over, and kissed me on the face. "You know, you don't have to play all these sports, Owen."

"It's not that." I pulled away from her.

"Then, what is it?"

I didn't know. Just *noise.* I never talked about my moods from hell, because who would get it? I figured I could just sit and watch something very cool like *Lawrence of Arabia* and not be a jerk in public.

The phone rang again as Scott came in the door. He was closer to the cordless than Mom was.

"I'm not home!" I shouted again.

Mom was tousling my hair now, which was normal, but she'd gotten even more touchy-feely lately, it seemed. Ever since she got sick a few weeks ago. "And if you want me to tell the coach to quit throwing recruiters at you, it's no problem."

"No! Just gimme ten feet. Sorry, Mom, but—"

"He caught Mom's flu. Lying down," my brother said into the phone, and I shot an evil glance at him through the kitchen doorway. "Nope, not coming. Call him tomorrow."

He hung up, parked his paramedic jacket on a hook behind the kitchen door, and came into the living room.

"Do you have to tell them I'm sick?" I griped. "Sounds wimpy."

"Sick in the head." He swatted my hair on his way past and plopped down beside me. "If I tell them you're not here, they keep calling back every five minutes. I'm not your...lying social secretary, dig? What's up? That douche bag from over on the Gold Coast get to you worse than you're letting on?"

He grabbed my bag of pretzels, stared at the TV.

"She's not a douche bag."

"That's generous of you."

Since I couldn't exactly deny anything on Myra's long list of my weirdness traits, I sat there trying to decide why I didn't feel all that upset. She had some problems of her own, maybe that was it.

"She's all right, she just...gets drunk. You ever been at a party with a slurring, giggling, drunk girl who totally stinks of tired booze?"

"Mm-hm." He sent his eyebrows up and down a few times. "They get even better after the party."

I grunted. "That's romantic."

He kept watching me, crunching on his pretzel way too loud. "You know, if you don't get over this notion that you're holding out for love, I'm gonna have to call up Candy Cane, have a bunch of your buddies tote her over here."

Candy Cane is this hooker from Atlantic City who had been

hired by the crazier guys for parties when Scott was a senior. My friends hadn't done the Candy Cane routine yet. *Whew* on that one. For the most part, stuff like that had all the appeal of sticking my face in a bucketful of other people's spit.

"Yeah, yeah, yeah." I grabbed the bag of pretzels back. "I'm a freak of nature."

"No, you are not." He slapped my knee and swung it from side to side. "You are... *extraordinary,* and don't forget it. Hey. Wanna watch *Superman*?"

I bit into a pretzel, smiling. I used to watch the movie *Superman* when I was around eleven and totally related to this gigantic, spazzy kid who dropped into this perfect little American town, where everybody's great—and yet, he just can't get comfortable. And it was kind of easy for me to dream up strange ideas, like our dad was a superhero. Mom used to avoid questions about who and where our father was by joking that we came from a bolt of lightning that dropped from heaven. I used to actually hope it was true. When you're five-ten in sixth grade, already kicking field goals from the thirty-yard line—*but wishing you were off in the woods with your dog*—it helps to think of yourself as some mutated version of a Clark Kent.

Fortunately, I quit growing last year—at six-four. I won the South Jerseys in wrestling at 189 after pinning two guys, one from Ocean City and one from Toms River, and then I overheard a *Press* reporter telling another that "Owen Eberman probably just peeled ten thousand off that kid's scholarship" to some school I can't remember. He was laughing. I guess anyone else would have thought, *Oh well.* But I was like, *That sucks... why am I doing this?*

"Nah, no *Superman,*" I said. "You wait. Now that my phone's not ringing, somebody's going to walk through the door any minute, and then we'll have to explain why we're watching *Superman.*"

He tossed the remote in my lap. "Your call, bro."

He got up. I could hear him in the kitchen, chasing around behind Mom with the third degree. "Did you take your temperature? Why not? Did you pick up the results of your blood work, or do I have to do everything around here?"

"No, you don't have to do everything, hon. 'Fever of Unknown Origin.'"

That didn't make Scott look too happy, though it was a relief to me. I had started getting scared that Mom had leukemia or something. She had looked fine today, but for almost a month it had been three good days, two bad days, two good days, three bad days. Scott took three tubes of blood from her, after she refused to see a specialist, and left them at Saint Ann's lab. She's just not a doctor person.

"...only thing I had today was a headache," she was telling him.

"You take anything?"

"Yes."

"Did it go away?"

Silence.

"Well, why don't you go lie down? Go watch a movie with Owen? He'll give you the remote."

There went my night in front of the tube. I glanced down at this big envelope under my ankle and froze, like I did every time I noticed it. Mom had tossed it at me last week when I was complaining about all these recruiters being up my shorts already. I don't know how long ago she'd gotten it, but it landed in my lap and she said, "You're not ready to think about this now. But if I had any betting money, I would bet that in a few years, you could happily end up here."

I stared at the return address again in its dark, thick typeface. *Princeton Theological Seminary.*

Scott was making her sit in the kitchen chair while he took her temperature. This is what I didn't get: For all my brother probably hopping on Candy Cane and whoever else was drunk enough, and for all his foul mouth and domineering attitude, he was far less selfish than I was. He always came in here thinking about Mom first thing, and I was too wrapped up in my own noise-and-mauling damage. And she'd been talking about telling the coach to give me some breathing room, and having brochures sent to me from Princeton, like she had the time.

She never stopped working for people who can't afford to pay her, and she never had a dime extra, which explained why we only had one TV. Scott agreed with her about me and Princeton. I just didn't get it.

"Here, Mom. Watch what you want." I held the remote out to her as she zoomed away from Scott's evil paramedic meddling. He went rooting for a cold pack he'd said he would crack for her headache.

"I'll watch what you want, Owen."

"No. I'll watch what you want." I had to force it out, but the major sacrifice got me feeling somewhat in their league of unselfishness.

"I finally rented *Joan of Arc,* thinking you'd be doing homework."

Joan of Arc. A Mom special. A female-superhero-superdeluxo-the-woman-saves-the-day chick flick. Double, triple, quadruple damn. "That's fine, Mom."

Then, there was a knock at the door, and I lost it. Took the Lord's name in vain, which makes Mom really unhappy. And just to make me feel worse, she said to Scott, "And whoever it is, we have finished lying tonight. I can't stand lying, even to keep my boys out of a party, where surely there is trouble to be found. If you don't want to see somebody, Owen, don't run up to your room and think I'll tell somebody you're not here."

Mom patted my cheek on the way past, and I could feel her hand was all too warm, now that I was paying attention. I just chucked the envelope back on the table, listening to Scott peal off with the truth to the person at the back door.

"You don't wanna come in here, Rain. He's in one of his moods. Yeah, one of those watch-TV, don't-touch-me, don't-talk-to-me, I'm-not-home things."

"Oh, he'll talk to *me*." Rain's ski jacket rustled as she tried to push past him, and I shut my eyes.

Rain Steckerman lived kitty-corner to us, and if you were in the mood to see no one, she was about the last person you'd want to have over. Rain was a captain on two of her four sports, was the life of every party, and never had my social breakdowns. She had a car but couldn't drive it half the time because her dad was chronically taking the keys from her for breaking curfew. She didn't do much wrong while she was out, but she just couldn't stand to leave a party until it had fizzled down to the loadies, herself, and whomever she drove.

Fortunately, she knew about my moods and never busted

my stones. I think she was so popular because she didn't know how to pass judgment.

"Owen?" she shouted in the door. "Please let me in. I won't touch you, I promise. It's an emergency, and this time I really mean it!"

"Emergency" meant she still didn't have a date to the prom, and it was nearly March.

"At your own risk," Scott muttered, and she came barreling in as Mom put the video in the machine.

"Hey, Mrs. E, sorry to bust in when you're sick, but I didn't know where else to come." She threw off her ski jacket and flopped down beside me. Her hair was still wet from swimming, and her cheeks were all red like she'd lost her car keys again and walked it from school.

"You're going to catch pneumonia," I lectured. "You got individual championships tomorrow, right?"

"Right."

"You gonna do us proud?" I asked as she put a hand on her chest, out of breath.

"It's in the bag. Fifty yard, at any rate. I was losing air on the butterfly, which is a truly frightening experience if your nickname happens to be Iron Lung. Listen to this wheeze."

She breathed in, and I stuck my head closer to her neck. Definitely a wheeze. "How'd you get sick at a time like this? Danny Hall keeping you up all night?"

"We had a fight on Monday. He told me I'm domineering, which is so not true. I haven't talked to him since. Can't blame this on him."

"Well, this time you kept a boyfriend for... three weeks?

Maybe you're getting a little handle on that domineering thing, Rain." I cracked up.

She balled up her fist at my humor. "Mrs. E, I said I wouldn't touch your son, so don't let me hit him!"

I put an arm up, just in case she came through.

"You probably caught it from me," Mom said, and Rain dropped her fist, distracted.

"This is bad, Mrs. E. Dad won't let me swim if he hears my death rattle. He's got those FBI detective ears, you know? I know I can talk in front of you. You've covered for us before, right?"

Mom groaned and dropped into the chair with her hand over her eyes.

Rain turned to Scott. "Dude, I need a miracle drug and a place to lay low until it kicks in. Can you guys help me out?"

He laughed, cracking the cold pack and holding it up as he moved toward Mom.

"Does this look like a miracle drug?" He laid it on Mom's forehead and held up his hands, waggling his fingers. "These are just...normal hands, darling. Take two aspirins and go to bed."

"I can't go home! All the lights are on, which means my dad's over there. I'll never get past his eagle eyes. And I know I said I wouldn't touch you, Owen, but check this out."

She took my hand and laid it on her forehead. That's when I realized her red face wasn't from walking home. She was burning up. I made the hatchet sign on my neck and raised my hands helplessly at Scott.

"We're looking at two medals down the toilet, bro," I pleaded with him. He felt her forehead and then let out a laugh.

"How well do you know the pope? Know any television evangelists?" But he pointed to Mom's chair at the dinette table while griping about how many people in the neighborhood do this to him. "And it's not like people around here don't have money to go to the doctor. They're all rolling in bucks except us. It's *time* they can't spare. Nobody has the time to go to the doctor, so they impose on *my* time."

"You don't look so busy to me," Rain argued as he pulled his white backpack with the red Saint Ann's Hospital insignia on it from behind the door. He listened to her back through a stethoscope and continued to gripe. "Tell that to the DOA we picked up tonight and the baby I delivered in the ambulance this afternoon."

She spun to look at him. "Wow, you can deliver a baby already?"

"Shut up and breathe."

She wheezed and shut her eyes, like she was praying.

"It's not in your lungs. You sound like Mom. Bronchitis... flu of some sort."

"Whew. I'm swimming, no question. So, you delivered a baby?" She tried again.

He was over at the sink washing off the digital thermometer and laughing at her. People think when you work on an ambulance squad, all you do is either drive or sit there and tremble.

"It's easy," he said. "We call it 'playing catch.' You just plant yourself down by mom's knees and you... *catch.*"

"Yeah, but... you look at *naked ladies*?" She cracked up, and I did, too, watching the disgust bloom on his face. My brother was born old.

"Children, children..." He stuck the thermometer in Rain's mouth.

"What about the DOA?" Mom asked. "Anybody we know?"

"Well, sort of. Since we're not lying anymore tonight, there's a kid involved, lying about her age. I had to leave her alone in the house when we took away the corpse, which was killing me, but hell, I couldn't pick her up and carry her out."

"What are you saying?" Mom sat up totally straight, holding the cold pack so it wouldn't drop. "How big a lie are we talking about? Three months or five years?"

Rain stood up beside him, watching the digital reader cross-eyed until it beeped.

"Hundred and one. It's not a death sentence, but you really shouldn't be swimming tomorrow, Rain."

"We'll get it down! You got Tylenol?" She handed the thermometer part back to him. "Mrs. E? You got any antibiotics you can spare?"

"Great. Lies, cover-ups, now drug peddling...what kind of a mother do you think I am?"

"The *best,*" Rain assured her, going over to the TV.

"I'm not giving you any medicine Scott says I shouldn't. Scott, what about this DOA?"

He was reaching in Mom's medicine cabinet with a finger to his mouth to help him think. "It's not a big lie. Who knows, she might be eighteen; she just looked like she was lying to me. I never miss a detail, ya know? Upperclassman at Trinity Regional. Senior, I think. And that's all I'm telling *you.* If you think I'm going to inspire you to go flying out of here when you're feeling like this...I'll tell you tomorrow."

"No, no, no, no." She moved a few steps toward him. "We don't leave minors alone in houses after picking up a DOA. What on earth were you thinking?"

"About the corpse, Ma! That's my job. Cops were there. Rain's dad must have seen the lights on his way home, because he was there, too. Somebody'll work it out. She's got a grandmother coming in from California tomorrow. California, *hmm*... There's an off-the-top-of-your-head ring to it if you think about it. Probably a lie, too."

"Give me a name. I'm your mother."

"No. Beat me. The answer's still no." He was pulling out a pill bottle and he stopped to look at her. "Will you please think of yourself for a moment? Do you want to stay sick forever? Mr. Steckerman will handle it, I'm sure."

"Well, I'm going to call him and make sure."

"Tell him I'm here, but don't tell him I'm sick!" Rain begged, curling up on the other end of the couch. She put her feet on me for a moment, stuck out her tongue, and then mercifully pulled them up under herself. I think she missed hearing the "upperclassman at Trinity" part to describe this daughter of the DOA, but I didn't.

"Bro, just tell me it's not someone we hang with."

Scott handed Rain a handful of pills, probably aspirin, vitamin C, and whatever penicillin Mom was trying this week.

All he said to me was "No, definitely not someone you hang with."

So, I left it at that. Mr. Steckerman would handle it. Scott had a glass of water, but Rain said, "I need a bigger one. You know what? That's what we should all do while we're sitting here. We should each try to drink a quart of water. I can flush anything in twenty-four hours just by drinking, drinking, drinking water."

"That's probably not a bad idea," Scott said, though back at the spigot, he was grumbling about being a cocktail waitress. Mom had him fill up her Evian bottle under the tap while she called the Steckermans', got the voice mail, and just said, "Alan, please call me back."

"Huh...He didn't say he was working tonight," Rain mused, but she didn't get up to leave. Never let it be said she would hang out alone when there was some other option.

So, we sat there watching *Joan of Arc*, Rain and I drinking from these huge German beer mugs and Mom nursing an Evian refill like she did every night. Rain whispered every once in a while that we needed to get a water filter because our water tasted like metal. She drifted off to sleep. Mom just got glazed, watching Leelee Sobieski, alias Joan of Arc, take some huge spear through the shoulder that was threatening to make her bleed to death—until Saint Catherine showed up. Scott vacuumed the bedrooms, folded wash on the table, did the dishes.

I went back and forth between watching Leelee Sobieski's decent blond hair get shorter and more snarly, and Rain's miraculously long blond hair dry. Somehow, even during swimming season, Rain managed to keep it shiny and silky, and it dried around her shoulders like she'd brushed it a hundred times. While she was sleeping, I picked up a strand of it, flicking it this way and that.

We had never gone out. It probably had to do with us living too close for comfort in anything but the friendly sense. We had that next-door-neighbor, best-buddy, can-I-borrow-your-gym-socks-mine-are-dirty thing going pretty well. About twice a year I'd go over there and collect half my T-shirts off her bedroom floor. The buddy thing was for the best.

I called her my relationship counselor. I would get a heart attack going for some hot girl. I would realize after a few weeks this hot girl had a vicious streak that didn't sit well with me. Rain would wander over to my house, and I would dump on her, and she would give me fifty ideas for send-off lines that left nobody hurt. That is something you don't take for granted, and you don't want to ruin it by kissing.

As for Leelee Sobieski, aka Joan of Arc, this was not a chick flick after all. And she was very cool, surrounded by these gnarly soldiers, who were trying to use her to win a war against the English. Finally, the English guys caught her and shoved her in some birdcage to humiliate her, and you got the idea they were going to burn her at the stake.

I whispered to Mom, "How old was she?"

"Teenager. Around your age." It took Mom a minute to answer, and when I looked she was squinting a little. The ice pack was in her lap.

"My age. And all this really happened, Mom?"

"Yes."

"And they're going to burn her alive."

"Yup."

"That must have hurt."

I kept watching, remembering Leelee Sobieski had heard the voice of Saint Catherine at the beginning, telling her to be good and she would have a really meaningful life. And yet here she was, a teenager, hung up in a birdcage, about to be burned at the stake.

I thought, *God, what kind of a deal is that?* But there was something about her situation that made me first twitch, then grow annoyed, then feel disturbed, and finally, it left me with some blooming revelation. In a strange way, I was jealous.

To have some belief in your life so meaningful that you would die for it? What would that feel like?

Then it struck me about all this sports stuff, all these parties, all these girls I decided I liked and then didn't like. It was all a big bore. I was *bored,* not schizoid.

I watched this bunch of British priests tie this girl to the stake, and I was feeling really sorry for her, but at the same time I was asking these questions that were, like, coming out of nowhere. *God, how come you gave her something so heroic to do with her life? Did she try extra hard, or did you just like her better than me?*

By the time the British lit the flames and they started eating away at Joan of Arc's feet, I definitely decided I was not jealous anymore. I was all *How long do you stay conscious while you're turning to London broil?*

I pressed on my eyes with the balls of my hands. "That's perverted. Tell me they're not going to show it."

"You can look. In fact, watch her face. She's going to look up, and Saint Stephen is going to come down, sweep her off, and prove to her that it was all worth it."

Mom was slurring a little, and I figured she was tired. Sure enough, the directors did this very cool shot from over Leelee Sobieski's head, like from Saint Stephen's perspective. In the next shot, it was from her perspective, looking up, and coming down from heaven was the shining white light, and in it was a horse and some guy, obviously Saint Stephen, and she said in relief, "Thank you."

Nobody wants to die young and in a disgusting way. But I was asking myself, *Which is better? To have a shelf full of sports trophies that your kids won't even remember to bring down out of the attic? Or to live a life so meaningful that people would make movies about you five hundred years from now?*

The credits were rolling. Mom had turned out the light at some point, and that's why I didn't see her stand up. I switched on the lamp and saw she was putting on her coat.

"Where are you going at this hour?" I asked.

"I really wanted to see the ending." She sniffed like her nose was full and sounded like she was slurring worse. "I don't want you to alarm your brother. But go upstairs and tell him very calmly that he needs to drive me to Saint Ann's. This sinus headache is really out of hand. I think... something's wrong."

Scott called his unit instead of driving her, just because if my mom asked to be driven to the hospital, it was way serious. They brought in a stretcher, which freaked me out beyond words, despite that she refused to lie down. Her nose had started to bleed.

Last thing Scott said before he left with them was to Rain. "Don't forget, you got germs. Keep your face out of his." I realized Rain was beside me, rubbing my face with her hand, whispering in the side of my head that everything would be all right.

THREE

CORA HOLMAN
THURSDAY, FEBRUARY 28, 2002
10:31 P.M.

I SWITCHED ON the living room lamp and stared past the couch, seeing the blood streak only out of the corner of my eye. I really didn't know what had driven me out of bed with these chills.

My eyes fell on Oma's cordless phone, and shame wafted through me over how little I had used it. *Maybe... twice in the past four years?* I couldn't remember if my avoidance of the phone had been sudden, upon Aleese's arrival, or learned after a few embarrassments. My memory felt clunky, half asleep.

Maybe I had dreamed the phone was ringing. Maybe I had just wanted it to ring. Maybe Aleese had become a form of company over the years, and without her groans and rambling nonsense, I was feeling new depths of *alone.*

I blinked at my watch... 10:31. Aleese was still alive some four hours ago. I had slept restlessly for three hours.

Instead of seeing the huge mound of Aleese's laundry on Oma's TV chair, I saw Oma, watching her shows and smoking her cigarette, one leg tucked under her as always. I saw myself at five, playing Barbie at her feet. I wanted badly to remember Oma's and my good times, but *I'm snapping Barbie's tight, blue skirt. I like my Barbies to look perfect, but it's hard to snap.*

"Oma, do I really have a mommy?"

"Are we going to start this again?"

I don't like the silence that follows Oma's trail of smoke. There's something dark in it, something that seems to say…

"She doesn't like me."

"She doesn't know you, Cora."

"Why doesn't she ever come here to visit me?"

Silence.

I get Barbie's suit perfect, but she still looks messy. It's her hair. I start brushing it with my own hairbrush. Long, smooth strokes.

"When did you see Mommy last?"

"Two days after Christmas last year. Remember, you stayed with the Blumbergs next door, and they gave you homemade ice cream every night? She was in New York for a three-day layover."

I don't want to ask why I can't go, too, when she sees my mom. Oma never answers. Barbie's hair is free of knots. I twist it up in a swirl to clip with a bobby pin.

"Would Mommy like me if I had blond hair?"

"Come up here." Oma pats her knees. I climb into her lap, despite that she's smoking a cigarette, which makes her cough a bad smell.

"Now, you know I don't lie to you about anything, Cora. Right?"

"Oma is not perfect, but Oma never lies." I repeat what I hear often, and I'm thinking Barbie needs a handbag.

"So, it's like I've said. Your mother doesn't have a lot to say about her daily life. But she's a photographer. She works far away. She's very smart... too smart. If I'd have had my ten kids, and they were all that smart, I'd be set for life."

"But you told me she's poor."

"She's... financially stupid."

These conversations never make sense. They're never pleasing in any way, and so I don't get this twitch to inquire often.

"At any rate... I love you from here to the stars and back, Cora, and you just have to accept that as enough."

She means that my mother will never love me. My mother is wild and crazy and financially stupid. I slither down again, deciding it's time to find Barbie shoes that match a handbag. I like my Barbies perfect.

I jerked toward Oma's chair, and despite my achy joints, I picked up the mountain of Aleese's dirty clothes. I decided it was the mess around here making me sick—who wouldn't be sick? I lowered my eyes behind the mound, so as not to see the little stream of blood down the couch. Maybe I just decided to wash her clothes because they seemed more approachable than the couch.

In the laundry room, I separated out the lights from the darks and added bleach, so that when I decided on a charity, they would get the nicest package possible. Busyness—it had always kept me safe. And busying myself brought the needed memory to the forefront: *I know why I got out of bed.*

I started the wash load and slowly retreated to the living room, back to the couch. Often Aleese left her crusty spiral notebook full of poetry and thoughts on the floor beside her, but that night I would have to raise that bloody cushion to get to it. As I leaned slowly toward that stain, I felt my mind floating conveniently backward, away from the dried stream, to the first time I ever saw the notebook—

The front door slams and draws me out of the bedroom, and Oma's standing in front of her television chair. This woman with short black hair and beautiful peachy skin is standing between her and the television.

"Hi, Mom. I'm broke again. But this time in more ways than one."

Just a cardboard box and cheap suitcase lie beside her. The final thump is a backpack she lets fall off her thumb, and it lands at her feet. It's huge, covers her knees, but she's rubbing her left arm, which is bandaged from the shoulder to the tips of her fingers.

"I just finished six weeks in a rehab hospital in Israel, trying not to end up here, but their charity only goes so far."

"What happened, Aleese?"

"You still run around town saying you never lie?"

"Absolutely."

"Then I can't lie to a nonliar. Uh... two years ago my evil lover got carried away and tried to drag me off to his cave by the arm. Does that work? I've tried hospitals on three continents. But all the king's horses and all the king's men..." She takes a peacoat off her good arm, drops it on top of the pack.

"Aleese, you've been telling me you hurt your arm... Why didn't you tell me it was this bad?"

"Denial." Her voice is loud. "Except for the fact that it hurts like hell, I got no feeling in it. Nor will I, according to the last idiots at Mount Sinai Hospital. They ate my last cash. Got any room?"

Oma's eyes swim over to me. I can barely see her mouth move as she mumbles, "You've always said you wanted to meet your mother. Well..."

The woman comes toward me, stops, leaving three feet between me and her. She's not big. I'm just about as tall. Despite that she's petite, she swaggers, like a beautiful pirate, like somebody fearless. Her eyes are deep brown, so much like mine. But she's far prettier than I am. Her nose is sharper, her jaw is more squared and determined, her thin lips are redder. I feel... diluted or vague or something. Her black eyes glare. At first I think it's fear. Then I decide it's something worse. Contempt?

"So, this is Cora." Her eyes run down my legs and up. "This is my brat."

"Oh my god..." Oma rests her forehead in her fingers with her eyes shut, but one corner of my mother's mouth turns up.

"Don't mind my sense of humor, kid. It's rough. I'm Aleese."

I wonder why she's sticking her tiny hand out for me to shake instead of hugging me. "Please call me Aleese. We'll get along far better that way—"

And out of her backpack had tumbled a fat, spiral notebook, the kind with the five dividers and lots of skinny-lined pages. It was big, and it hit the floor with a thud. It had been an angel of mercy, pulling my stunned gaze from the pirate eyes that were too strong, too weary, too angry, too apologetic for my normal existence.

I had seen the notebook a thousand times since then, as it was never far from her. Once, she'd caught me trying to scoop it up while she was sleeping, and she got me in some sort of death grip by the neck. Her strength seemed to gather when she was drugged.

"The devil lives in my books, brat. You want to loose the devil all over your precious little Trinity Falls? Go ahead. Open it." Her dilated pupils bulged into the dark brown of her irises.

"Lie back down, and don't ever touch me like that again." I have learned not to fear her, to believe she won't hurt me. She's never gone past pulling my hair, and only when she's so blitzed that she's speaking in Middle Eastern languages.

She lets go. I heave a sigh and vow not to let her dictate my movements.

I had opened the notebook occasionally when she was in the Land of Nod. But she'd always left it facedown, and I could only ruffle the back few pages without risking awakening her. I hadn't seen much—blasphemies I wouldn't care to repeat, nonsense laced with bitterness, things akin to "All work and no play makes Jack a dull boy."

If she had *long* been a drug addict, had *long* been mean and spiteful, I could have done without that information. I could have done without it now. I still flipped to the back.

Dated February 27, just yesterday, she had written this:

Jack and Jill went up the hill to catch the perfect photo. Jack fell down and broke his crown, and Jill... gets gangbanged by a goddamn bunch of rabid, fucking goons.

I plopped down in Oma's TV chair in disgust, pulling myself into a ball to ward off deeper chills. I remembered Oma telling me a few times how all Mother Goose rhymes had hidden meanings. She had even mentioned the Jack and Jill poem, something like Jack had been a King John of some European nation, and he had led his army into battle. He died fighting, symbolized by "fell down and broke his crown," and his country, "Jill," surrendered shortly thereafter.

But applying kings and queens to my mother's life seemed too surreal. I could only flick my wrist, turn the huge clumps of dreaded pages, now stiff and crackly with writing. I couldn't remember the date Aleese came here to stay, but I knew the month had been September, the year 1996. There were only a couple of entries that month, toward the beginning of the notebook.

After the date "9/12/96" was "Somebody Tell a Joke."

I'm the sad orchestra playing in the end of an epic classic. I'm the oboe solo saved for lovers torn asunder, for child victims of the London plague, for stale smoke rising after bombs leveled German villages.

God, you're maudlin today, Aleese.

Skeleton walks into a bar. Skeleton sits on a stool, says to the bartender, "I'll have two beers...and a mop."

Where's the stewardess with the scotch? How'd I get the goddamn middle seat on a transatlantic goddamn flight? If I cry, I will fall prey to my foes on either side. The perky pregnant lady on my right might try to hug me, and I'll have to strangle her. The stone-faced Pakistani on my left might roll his eyes and crumble into my well-kempt sling, not that I would feel it.

Where's Jeremy?????

Jeremy Brandruff Ireland. September 1, 1957–September 10, 1996.

Oh Jeremy.

Oh my god.
Why didn't I just die in Mogadishu?
Oh Mogadishu...

I glanced back up at this man's name, this death date, which apparently was just days before she wrote it. And I heard the echoes of Aleese's mournful, incoherent cries from one night in her second year home. It was the only time I'd heard her mention a place from her wanderings.

"*Oh... Mogadishu...*"

"*Oh... Mogadishu...*"

"*Oh... Mogadishu...*"

She'd groaned it so soulfully and sadly, as if it were a lost lover's name. But I'd never asked her what the word meant. She had woken herself up muttering too loudly, and the next night when I came in, she was asleep with a sweat sock stuffed in her mouth.

Mogadishu... *somewhere in Africa?* In elementary school, when a teacher showed us a map of the world, I would wonder where on it my mother was instead of Trinity. It had inspired me never to want to think of places outside Trinity. And now *Mogadishu* dissolved conveniently into the silence again as I stared at "Jeremy Brandruff Ireland," and two dates.

I had always associated myself and my roots with Oma, all the while knowing that this picture was inadequate. But with a mother so mysteriously estranged, how much chance did I have of knowing about my father?

As I stared at this name, the hair stood up on my arms, as though the air created a draft to signal his significance. If

September 10, 1996, was a death date, how did he die? Had Aleese come home beaten down by this grief, too? Did she simply have no feelings left?

I should have felt interested, having perhaps discovered my father's identity. But it was exhausting to stare at the name. Written so mournfully, it implied that Aleese had been capable of love. So her attitude toward me was even more stupefying, and like I did every so often, I saw clearly the inconceivable horror I always worked so hard to ignore: *Even bad mothers love their children. My mother should have loved me.*

It was the morphine. I'd relied on the morphine to explain so much—and except for a bad week here or there, her morphine had been able to kill *my* pain as well. It seemed strangely like it had been my addiction, too, and now that she was beyond its powers, so was I.

My eyelids suddenly seemed to weigh a thousand pounds as the memory struck me of the box Aleese had brought home with her, the one that was near her feet when she shook my hand and implied that I should never call her "Mother." *It had been full of videotapes.*

I felt the reverb of it calling to me now from somewhere. Attic? Crawl space?

I choked as an ambulance passed by the window again. The hulking shadow was silent this time, except for splashing through that huge gutter puddle out on the curb and sending a great wave of orange dots dripping down the screen like tears. They filled the room yet again with red, and reddish orange tears dripped down the screen, forcing a vivid flashback of earlier tonight.

"We got clean sheets. Come on."

Why hadn't I gone with Scott Eberman?

The reddened walls and reminders of death doubled my aloneness, which I never dreamed I would have felt back when I used to predict that Aleese would eventually overdose. I didn't know what to make of myself without her. I should have felt relieved. But I felt so very alone.

The truth bled through with the crazed red flashes of the silent ambulance: *I could produce enough idle chitchat in school to earn myself a shiny trophy. But I had zero relationship skills. All my energy has gone into preventing relationships, not creating them.* To go with Scott Eberman would have been like flinging myself out of an airplane without any skydiving lessons. I would have crash-landed in the bramble of my own klutzy, panicking awkwardness.

I stood to make a dash for my blankets. But I managed to grab the phone out of its cradle and take it into the bed with me. I knew no one would call. I didn't want anyone to call. I think I just wanted to sleep with the phone.

FOUR

SCOTT EBERMAN
THURSDAY, FEBRUARY 28, 2002
10:59 P.M.

I ACTUALLY LIKE being inside Saint Ann's Hospital. I like taking my shift breaks in the emergency room nursing station, watching the medics fly around, hearing the ring of oh-so-many phones. But tonight, I didn't feel that sense of control over an out-of-hand universe that usually comes with being in the ER. I paced away from Mom's cubicle, back to Mom's cubicle. And the fact that I know all these doctors and nurses didn't help as much as you'd think.

They were probably more sympathetic to me when I brought Mom in than they would have been to your average Charlie. But when they couldn't get Dr. Godfrey in here immediately, and they couldn't kill her pain immediately, my toes curled and uncurled as I paced. I was resisting temptation to start kicking my fave nurses' anklebones. Familiarity does not breed solutions, and somehow that came as a shock.

Mom waved me away from her after almost an hour. I could tell this headache was still giving her hell, but her sinuses had stopped bleeding, and her vitals were normal. Dr. Godfrey was Saint Ann's allergy and infectious disease specialist, and I'm not sure whether it was Mom's reputation in the community or my employment here that got him to say he was coming at this hour, but I felt relieved.

"I don't need a babysitter while I pee in a cup and get the third degree, hon," she murmured, holding a cold pack over her right eye. "Go find your buddies and show up for the bottom line."

I actually raced down to the break room to see what the paramedics on night shift were up to. Before I could reach them, I almost clanged heads with Alan Steckerman, who was coming out of the elevator. I was surprised to find him here.

"Scott, I would have come up sooner, but the dispatch is all garbled down in the basement." He sighed in relief, like he'd been looking for me. "How is she? They said what? Strange sinus infection now, too?"

I shifted around. "And we'll probably be in drumroll status for the next twenty-four hours. I'm not looking to piss off half this town, but tomorrow I'm taking her up to a good research hospital in Philly if I don't get some answers fast."

"You do whatever you feel is best, but um... don't panic. It's got to be a coincidence."

By "coincidence" he was talking about Aleese Holman bleeding out through the facial orifices, versus my mom's bloody nose. He could be right, I knew. I surely hadn't freaked to see a DOA with the same flulike symptoms as my mom. But when my mom's nose started to bleed like my DOA's? I gave the squad a Priority One call. I still wasn't ready to relax and admit I had panicked.

I looked down at my watch and saw it was quarter to midnight. The obvious question finally rapped me on the head. "Alan, what are you doing here at this hour?"

"Besides yawning?" He strolled along beside me toward the break room. "USIC's got me doing all sorts of stuff that the FBI never did. I have to clock in forty hours of forensics and human anatomy before September. If a terrorist threat actually came to pass, USIC might have to work closely with physicians and pathologists, or so its policy manual reads. So, Johnny Gallagher has been... very patronizing, poor guy."

Johnny Gallagher was Saint Ann's head coroner. We moved into the empty break room and collapsed into a couple of chairs.

Alan yawned again and rolled his stiff neck around. "Gotta do something with my nights, being that there aren't any Cinderellas breaking my door down."

Mr. Steckerman's wife had been killed in a six-car pileup outside the Shore Mall when Rain was only three. The man had been up to his gizzard in sexy, flirting divorcées since I could remember—though he rarely took anyone out. I kept watching him because, in spite of his shrug-it-off tone, I sensed some tension. Being that my mother's presence here was taking my brain apart, it took me a minute to draw up obvious question number two.

"So, what the hell is Johnny Gallagher doing here at midnight? Couldn't this wait until tomorrow? It's not like he's got the mayor on his slab."

He shrugged. "He had to scrub to a Level Three, being that she was a needle user. Maybe he doesn't like to waste so much time during the day."

I almost missed the way his eyes dropped from mine when he spoke. They didn't dart like most liars' would have.

"That was pretty good, Alan. Nice try."

"What?"

"Come on. Did USIC call Johnny in to work on that corpse?"

"*Mm...*," he moaned, like a guy finding himself in check in a game of chess. "Your powers of observation have amazed me since you were about six."

I watched as he put his feet up on the seat, and I said, "If there's anyone you guys should trust, it ought to be those of us who pick up the sick and the dead. What's going on?"

"Probably nothing. I called Washington tonight to tell them I was putting this autopsy on my tab, under my training budget. They called back half an hour later and said to send any samples to the Centers for Disease Control in Atlanta."

He shrugged again, and this time I sensed more sincerity, though the news disturbed me. The CDC is where all the paramedics' memos came from on emerging infectious diseases. And Mr. Steckerman had his own mountain on symptoms of bioterror. Welcome to the year 2002. The dust of the Trade Center falling couldn't reach into South Jersey, but the world seemed more panicky now. My supervisor, Phil, was always shaking his head at our memos and saying, "Strange times, strange times." The emerging infectious disease awareness had actually struck the summer before 9/11, but it was after 9/11 that we noticed our mail slots at work filled beyond what we were able to read on the job. Add terror intrigue to science, and you've got Mount Memo.

"Probably the CDC discovered extra space in its Strange Sinus Phenomena refrigerator, blathered that to the bosses, and we're just being good, contributing Americans. That's the assumption I'm working with at any rate. Even if Johnny Gallagher jumps when I mention the CDC. Generally, these things turn out to be nothing, Scott. *No-thing.*"

Even if it was *no-thing,* my head went a little nuts. I envisioned Washington telling him some terror cell was trying to blampf us with the Ebola virus. Ebola kills with 90-some percent accuracy, and its deaths come equipped with bloody noses. Rumors flew that some sicko terror nations had gotten their hands on a few Ebola samples and had tried injecting it into soda cans as part of their fun-and-games curriculum.

I would have laughed outright at my own imagination, but one's version of reality shifts a little when one's own mother lies down the hall—with a strange flu and accompanying nosebleed.

I leaned forward in my chair as my mind for detail suddenly fired off a useful yet slightly nauseating image. "Alan, I'm sure you're sick of hearing the words 'water tower' after what you went through in January. However. You know that puddle in front of the Holman house has been there for weeks. I wasn't thinking of it too much tonight, except that it forced us to park the ambulance in the middle of the street. But if we're going to sit here and talk about USIC intrigue...I'm thinking of it, okay?" I laughed uncomfortably. "I don't know how water towers work and all, but...it's just funny, that puddle. It hasn't rained in over a month, and there's no sewer in the middle of that block to back up, so..."

"So you're imagining some...what? Some poison in the water so strong that it could eat through a pipe? Leak into the street?" He laughed, too. "Think of it. If a germ was that strong, we'd all be dead."

"Well, don't snicker at me for trying too hard."

"Actually, I'm laughing at myself! When we were doing the testing, I asked Leo Stetson over in the Utilities Department about that puddle one day. He and I were driving to my house. It looks funny—like it doesn't have a source. Stetson assured me that puddles in streets have nothing to do with the water towers in question. There's just a leak in the vein somewhere near Shore Road, though he did say if it were in front of the Blumberg or the Endicott estates, it would be fixed by now. That part is a shame. We gotta make sure to look after that little Holman girl."

Right now, I'm looking out for my mom, I reflected, though I said, "Yeah."

"They're a good bunch, down at the CDC." Alan shifted around, his face growing serious. "They ran all sorts of tests for the water; the whole thing amazed me. There are tests to tell them if the water is suspicious—even if they can't name the substance making it suspicious. Trinity's towers came up pristine; same with all the townships I supervise. It was an expensive exercise, but the CDC and Washington are sparing no expenses this year. I think that's why they agree to pay for random autopsies here and there."

I still hoped if anything bizarre showed up in an autopsy, it might be found in USIC's pile of memos—certainly not in mine. My memo mound from the CDC on emerging infectious disease symptoms was growing, despite my attempts to keep up with it all: West Nile virus, E. coli, mutations of the common cold, hoof-and-mouth, blah blah. For whatever reason, Saint Ann's had decided that paramedics need to know this stuff, too, so I wished I had a computer chip for a memory.

"No matter what, I'd rather have my job than yours," I muttered. I remembered after the media discovered the water-tower check, he said on television that they'd tested all water supplies because of some "chatter" they'd captured online.

"One thing I would hate about your job is having to acknowledge a threat as real that was found in a chat room. A *chat room.* It just sounds like smoke and mirrors. Like you're chasing Captain Hook, ya know?"

He nodded. "I was always a phone guy, a face-to-face guy. Maybe it's my age..."

"It's not your age," I assured him. "My buddies e-mail me something, and if I have something to say back? I pick up the phone. I'm pretty good at picking up on people's thoughts. But it's from watching faces and motions and expressions, and from hearing the clicks in people's voices...you know. It's the only way to do things."

"For *us,* maybe. I'll tell you something interesting. It's not exactly a secret—it was vaguely referred to in a January issue of *Newsweek.*"

I don't have time to read *Newsweek.* "Go for it."

"The reason we tested all those water towers was that a Pakistani informant had captured a lot of related chatter over a few weeks' time. This Pakistani informant, he's sixteen years old."

That was younger than Owen. "You gotta be kidding."

"No. Supposedly he's an ace hacker, and he writes programs that help the intelligence community find spies online. USIC just calls him the Kid. Of course, that age thing may be an idle rumor. I don't ask any more questions than I feel I have to. But I've seen copies of the chatter he captured, along with the notes of his interpretations."

"Really? Does he sound sixteen?"

Alan laughed. "He's not saying 'kewl!' and 'f-this' before all the chatter he sends us. He sounds... invisible. Truthfully, I only remember the chatter."

"What'd it say?"

He sighed like he was exhaling the many hours of nights not slept. "'*Waters will run red in Colony One... Waters will run red three hours from Home Base in December... They will drink in December and die like mangy dogs in April.*' Isn't that sweet?"

"What's 'Home Base'?"

"The agents were thinking Home Base was the headquarters of some terror cell. They were checking water supplies in Yemen, Jordan, Ethiopia... But the kid thought Home Base was New York, for reasons I wasn't privy to. So along with all other supervisors within three hours of New York, I decided to test the water."

"You mean to tell me... our government spent all that money testing water, based on the theories of a sixteen-year-old?"

Alan shrugged, looking weary again. "Sixteen or fifty-two. It's simpler than it sounds. You get a dozen scripts of chatter like that, and you have two choices: You either investigate or you ignore them."

"Well... he was wrong," I said, feeling somehow victorious. The idea of a kid younger than Owen steering some sort of rudder on American intelligence—that oiled my puke factor.

My brother couldn't even remember to keep his feet off the coffee table.

"In the case of the Internet, we're grateful for what we can get, Scott. It's a vast, dark galaxy of hiding places. But we got a double whammy on that water supply threat, because anytime someone mentions waterborne agents of bioterror, it's a punch in the gut. You know..."

Yeah, I did know, but I let him say it anyway. Our towers had come up clean, so it was merely interesting.

"A potential water attack is different from a mustard gas attack or a subway bombing—where knowledge of the crime and the display of symptoms are simultaneous. In the case of waterborne agents, people don't drop like flies. The three germ agents we studied during my training took weeks, even months, to build up in the human body before people became symptomatic. Therefore, with water threats, intelligence has to jump on things like chatter, which, in and of itself, feels like smoke and mirrors. But we can't afford to wait around for symptoms, or for the crime scene to be compromised many times over. There are just a thousand and one problems with water threats."

There's nothing much to say to that glurt of tasty news. I shuddered. He took the reassuring high road.

"There's nothing...nothing to hook up the Holman woman with anything I'm aware of," he said. "But you tell me what you would do if you walked into a DOA that was the slightest bit suspicious—and your desk was covered with the types of memos that are covering mine."

"I'd dot all my *i*'s, sure. So, what was Johnny Gallagher saying about the corpse?"

"Not a lot. I watched him start the autopsy from the observation deck so I wouldn't have to superscrub. All looked fine to him from the neck down. She didn't even have the enlarged heart of a morphine addict, considering the number of collapsed veins. All her organs looked healthy. He said she probably built up an amazing immune system, waltzing through every disease in Asia and Africa while working as a photographer."

"That's where she was a photographer? Asia and Africa?"

"So the rumor goes."

"Shooting pictures of *what*?" Growing restless, I got to my feet and pulled him by the arm. "I'd like to take a quick peek at the corpse, listen to Johnny ramble for a couple of minutes. Maybe by that time Dr. Godfrey will be finished with his late-night shit-shower-shave routine and I'll find him with Mom."

Alan walked along beside me down the corridor to the basement elevator, telling me his lump of Holman gossip, being that he had known the grandmother, Natalie Holman. "Aleese was freelance. I heard she worked on a newspaper in Beirut for a while. But I think most of her freelance jobs were for charities. Feed the Children, Peace Corps, stuff like that."

"You're kidding."

"Nope."

I scratched my head, remembering that sweet little Holman babe hiding her face when I had mentioned a morphine addict's tendencies toward violence. "*You have no idea,*" she had said. "How the hell does a photographer for Feed the Children end up addicted to morphine and beating up on her kid?"

He pushed the elevator button. "I remember Aleese Holman from when she was in high school. She was always...a little different. You know how some parents run around saying their kids are too smart, and that's why they don't do well in school?"

"You mean, ye ol' they're-just-bored routine?"

"Yeah. Natalie Holman was the song leader of that tune. Not that the kid ever did anything horrendous. She got arrested a couple of times, but it wasn't for drugs or boozing. It was for..." He chuckled as the elevator door opened and we stepped in. "I had just gotten on the FBI down here when she and a couple of kids from the student newspaper broke into the, um, Not-So-Humane Society and let all the dogs loose from the death row pen."

I snickered. The girl sounded like a cop's nightmare, but a part of me wanted to say, *Nice going.*

"Another time, she got arrested for lying across the doorway to that old abortion clinic on New York Avenue in Atlantic City. When the cops showed up, all the protesters moved amicably to the curb—except for her. In either case, most picketers would have been happy to carry a sign around on the front sidewalk. She was, um..."

"A determined little prick," I finished for him as the elevator delivered us into the basement.

"Crusade rider, that's for sure. I'd imagine her over in Beirut, either siding with the extremists or picking them up by the throat and hurling them into the Wailing Wall. It's hard to say what she did over there, because I think she was a morph addict already when she came home five years ago. All Natalie Holman ever said was 'She's home, she's injured, and it's sad.'"

We turned the corner of a long hallway. The morgue is buried deep, down near the back entrance.

He went on. "Johnny looked at her arm, the old injury, just

for curiosity's sake. He dug in with a scalpel just below the shoulder and stopped... said if he went even halfway around her flesh, the whole limb would have landed on the floor with a splat. Hell of an injury. The muscle and cartilage were 90 percent severed, hanging mostly by veins and scar tissue. It's a wonder she didn't get gangrene."

"Wonder how she got hurt in the first place," I muttered, remembering Cora Holman's claims not to know herself.

"Johnny said the only time he'd seen an injury like that, right at the joint, was in a guy who'd had his shoulder run over by a truck. Only in her case, none of the bones had been broken. Looked to him like somebody just tried to wrench her arm off—just kept twisting and twisting, back and forth until—" He stopped himself with a cough and a sour face. Even I was struggling with that mental picture. "At any rate, gangrene might have been a blessing. An amputation and an artificial limb would have been a better deal, though it's neither here nor there now."

"So, did Johnny examine her brain?"

"He was just getting out the buzz saw when a guy from your night squad bumped into me in the men's room, said they'd brought in your mother about an hour back. I shot up here. I ought to call Rain—make sure she's not out cruising—"

"Rain's at our house," I told him casually. "She dropped in to see Owen after swimming and fell asleep on the couch. She woke up when the squad came in to pick up Mom, but she's with Owen."

"She was sleeping before midnight?" He slowed again, watching me. "Is she all right? She has a cold... thinks I don't know. I'd hoped it wasn't caught from your house."

I didn't feel it was my job to bust Rain yet, though I watched him sympathetically. "Alan. Don't freak. Your kid does not have an emerging infectious disease."

The door ahead opened, and Johnny Gallagher appeared in fresh scrubs. I wondered if he was just taking a needed break. I knew doctors don't like to work on potential AIDS autopsies for long periods without a break. The theory goes that they can lose their concentration and get careless with the scalpel. He rubbed Mr. Steckerman's shoulder as we came up. "I don't think you want to go back up there. She, um, looks a bit strange."

Strange...that was an unusual term for our normally precise coroner. "What, you still got her face down under her chin? Sew her back together so Alan won't puke, and let us on the deck. What's the story?"

"She's sewn up. She, uh...bled out into her skull," he said. "Brain aneurysm. I'm certain the lab results will show she was loaded up on morphine, but aneurysm is the cause of death."

Nothing contagious. Nothing I hadn't seen before. "What do you mean, she looks strange? She looked fine when I picked her up. For a corpse."

"Her features are...let's say...without their usual dimension." He spoke more to Alan than to me. "The problem is that aneurysm usually just bleeds out into the skull. It doesn't penetrate the sinus cavity and exit the facial orifices. Passages to the ear, nose, and throat are not easily compromised, but some of her tissue samples were like cooked noodles, and her sinuses were like Jell-O. They had started to crystallize before I even opened them. I sewed her back up as fast as I could, but I needed the samples and had to follow protocol. Personally, I've never seen tissue compromise quite like that before. I could have written my name in her sinuses with a blunt pencil."

I suddenly wished Alan and I had not just been heaped in conversations about the CDC. Sometimes there's a thin line between thinking of the worst that can happen and letting your imagination run wild, especially when your work involves the more colorful aspects of public service.

But I changed my mind about seeing this corpse and backed away slowly toward the elevator. Alan didn't try to stop me, but we locked eyes as I pushed the elevator button. The eerie chat-room blather he'd mentioned was stuck all over my head: *Waters will run red in Colony One... Waters will run red three hours from Home Base in December... They will drink in December and die like mangy dogs in April.* I tried telling myself all sorts of reality, like that of all the places on the globe to be terrorized, it just doesn't happen to your hometown, and also that the water towers had come up pristine when they had been tested.

But I kept seeing the image of Mom sticking her worn-out Evian bottle up to the tap several times a night. And the sicker she got, the more she'd try to flush it by drinking the water.

I didn't want to make myself nuts. I just felt like I ought to go see her again and make sure she was okay.

FIVE

CORA HOLMAN
FRIDAY, MARCH 1, 2002
4:59 A.M.

I WOKE AGAIN toward dawn to actually find myself in Oma's room, pulling boxes off her closet shelf. The line between sleeping and waking had been that thin for many hours, so I was not exactly stunned.

But I couldn't remember what I had been rooting for, until boxes lay strewn around me and I had the item in my grip, pulled from a box of my fourth-grade Girl Scout projects.

Baba.

"Cora, how can you put that crusty lamb under your face? Give it to me. I'm gonna wash it—"

"Oma, you can't put Baba in the washer! He'll drown!"

"Just so you know..." Oma waves her cigarette toward Baba, so I cover Baba's nose. "...that lamb is full of five years of kid drool. And the terry cloth might as well have gone through chemo. Oh, what the hell. God bless America, where kid germs are sweet as honey."

I sniffed Baba warily. And as if I had smelled the sweet aroma of comfort and security only yesterday, I squashed him into my neck like I used to and stumbled back down the hall.

As I waited for sleep in the dark, I noticed my mother's notebook on the nightstand. I couldn't remember bringing it into my bedroom. Had I walked in my sleep earlier? It seemed to me I woke up one other time to find myself at the window—staring out at Shore Road as if I were waiting for some car. But I couldn't remember bringing that journal in here, and now it had a strange hue, as if the pages in the binding were glowing neon.

The room had turned from black to an ashen gray. Outside, the blackbirds were already calling. *Sunrise is causing that glow.* But I had no intention of reading Aleese's blather—not when I felt so weak and chilled after my trip down the hall.

"Jack fell down... broke his crown... Jill... gets gangbanged by a—"

I cleared my throat just to wipe out the crude echoes of Aleese's humor. It made me cough, which made me realize my left eye had been throbbing for some time. It seemed hard to pick out one particular ache when I ached all over, but now it was strong enough that I couldn't control where my mind went.

"... by a goddamn bunch of rabid, fucking goons."

My mother sounded like some bizarre combination of *Alice in Wonderland* and *Boyz N the Hood.* Oma's words returned, about Jack and Jill and kings and queens and countries losing wars.

Was Aleese "Jill" and my father "Jack"? Was this Jeremy Brandruff Ireland "Jack," and some sort of a great leader? *Was my father royalty?* Had he led Aleese to take pictures of a battle?

I enjoyed a number of possibilities until echoes of Aleese's moaning filled my head again. *"Oh... Mogadishu!"*

I remembered something... A bunch of guys from school had seen a movie, *Black Hawk Down,* and they came into physics one Monday talking in disgust about the Somali people in the city of Mogadishu, either... eating American soldiers alive... or dragging them alive through the streets until they died... I hadn't been paying enough attention.

Obviously, Aleese had been in Mogadishu at some point, though that information, like most concerning her adult life, had died with her. I knew she had not been in the military and could not have been involved in the *Black Hawk Down* violence, which had occurred in the midnineties. Putting anyone I knew at the events that sparked a movie seemed almost impossible—and with my mother, it seemed almost laughable.

"It wouldn't kill you to pick up after yourself once in a while. I'm not your nursemaid, Aleese."

I'm just back from singing in the choir's holiday show. I'm picking up socks, beer cans, used tissues that have been thrown at the television screen, at yet another depressing documentary. I realize I've kept my posture very straight while picking things up, squatting with my legs turned sideways instead of stooping or bending. It's part of me lately, this perfect posture, along with reaching for perfect, proper English. It sets me at odds with Aleese, assuring me that I don't have to end up like her.

"You don't know what dirt is, brat. You have never seen dirt."

"I've seen you, and I would say that is plenty."

"Yeah... I guess I'm pretty scurvy anymore. Sorry about that."

It sounds almost sincere. She can sound very sincere for a mo-

ment or two. I wait for her to explode into some deplorable punch line, but she doesn't this time.

"Why don't you get some help, Aleese? Why don't you go to a rehab clinic?"

"Because." She picks up her jelly arm and lets it flop down again like she sometimes does to amuse herself. "Did you know that even if I came up with the money for an amputation, this would still hurt? Did you know it would hurt all the way down to here?" She makes a swiping motion at her hip.

I feel a stab of pity and continue around, picking up whatever she had dropped, thrown, or left around that week. She's manipulative. Oma had always whispered that. I had to be careful not to get sucked in to her pity parties.

"There's got to be something you can do so that you're not always—" I stop. I was going to say, "so horrid. You're like a person possessed by the devil."

She sits up, and at this point I do get scared, because her dark eyes blacken, like they can when she decides to fly at me. She's always stopped short of hitting somehow, but she gets me in death grips—by the arm, the neck. She can be amazingly strong, even with one bad limb.

"So that I'm not always what? What, Cora! So I'm not always bothering you? You have no idea how good you have it! You were raised so goddamn spoiled, you need to visit a few other countries. And do you know how easily I could have had an abortion?"

I smooshed Baba tighter under my chin and wished for sleep, but my mind refused to shut down. Jeremy Brandruff Ireland. September 1, 1957–. I reached for the notebook again, to stare at this name, to see if the air still spun when I thought,

"My father." My eyes glazed over, unable to focus enough to read, though I was pretty certain that if the name Jeremy Ireland had passed by my eyes, I would have noticed. But one half-interesting fact came clear: You could tell when Aleese was needing her drugs, because her pretty, rounded handwriting would turn squarish and jagged, and her sentences became twisted and full of embittered words.

I'd heard enough of that in five years, so my eyes sought a passage that was rounded and pretty. Very few at the end were, but toward the beginning, they were about half and half. I stared at one dated just a few days before the first one I'd read...it looked like she was also on an airplane. My eyes zeroed in, maybe because it was melodious, almost rocking me and Baba...

> *It's as if this airplane is soaring upward, upward, upward, through the reaches of space, presenting the grand overview of our troubled planet as the sun sets behind it. I think of the wars and the rumors of wars, and I see little pinpricks of orange blink and bulge on the Dark Continent, as the blazes of war snuff out dozens more lives before returning to black.*
>
> *Then Asia flickers—first Palestine, then Iran, then Jordan, then Iraq, then back downward to the Nile again, and over Africa. I can hear a million voices—victims on tenor, terrorists on bass, soldiers on baritone, civilians on alto, children on soprano. As we used to say in school choir,* "God, somebody's off!"
>
> *We are, all of us, conjoined in sad song, committed to our marriage of bad harmonies. We're linked as closely to those whom we hate as those whom we love. Film and photo*

and e-mail and planes—they pull our faces together as tightly as beads on a string. A hand waves in North Africa; a wind ripples in America. A gun designed in Virginia, with metal purchased from China, sends its bullet through the guts of a foot soldier in Somalia. The hateful collide with the loving; the wise collide with the foolish; the loving are sometimes hateful; and the simplest of people often seem to be most wise. And as I've already proposed, the dead collide with the living, and if I'm not proof of that, then nothing is.

I'm returning to America, because I want to die there, because for me, there is nothing left. Nothing except some memories, and One Nation under God, which, in spite of all its little hypocrisies and ill-bred boorishness, still appears to have Providence on its side. It's the one place where, from up here, I don't see the orange flickers of civil unrest, political upheaval, or invasion. America has managed to keep its dignity. Even though I have not, I want to be part of it again. I want to die in my own backyard, where dignity persists, like the wildflowers that bloom regardless of what men can do…

And that was it. Just a thoughtful passage. It was hauntingly prophetic as concerned her, and yet so very strange—reminding me in its poetic language of what I had tried so hard to sound like while trying not to sound like her. I didn't know what to make of that.

I snapped the book shut. Aleese had been coming home to America—probably knowing she was coming to Oma and me—and she never mentioned me at all. I didn't know why that should hurt me at this point. I had never dared to love her.

The book fell out of my arms, and I realized, as sleep hazed in, that my headache was gone and the chills of fever had turned to a clammy, drenching sweat. I threw the blankets off and tossed Baba down the mattress so we were joined only by my fingertips. And I enjoyed a moment of feeling that at least my body barometer was working right again. I hoped my bout with sickness was going away for good.

I prayed for that, picking at Baba's belly, until sleep took me away from sad thoughts, away from sickness. Suddenly, I was the one flying in a plane, looking down on our planet at dusk and seeing, instead of deadly orange flickers, an endless trail of beautiful white dots, as if one person were joined to the next, holding candles with tiny flames that flickered and glowed, ending in America and extending backward across the ocean, and to the farthest corners of the world, away from Trinity....

KARACHI,
PAKISTAN

SIX

SHAHZAD HAMDANI
FRIDAY, MARCH 1, 2002
4:30 P.M. KARACHI TIME

IN MY VILLAGE near Karachi, the sun comes up red. Before my parents died, I loved to watch it while walking to school, before the bazaar opened and all the yelling and traffic began. I had to walk for an hour on gravel road, past the Arabian Sea, to school. Wild grass and bits of dune protected the fishing boats on the beach that looked like oxen asleep. I would look from the peaceful beach ahead to the sun rising red over the brown clay roofs of the city.

I would look at the sun and say, "You are all mine; you belong only to me."

Then, three years ago, I was introduced to some phrasing that has become central to my very existence: "*Computers have blurred the line between child and adult, because in the land of computers, children are the men, and the men are the children.*"

My father spoke those words when I was thirteen. At that time, I left school and went to work at his and my uncle's

Internet café in our village. I did so because my father decided to go to "school," and someone needed to help Uncle. My father trained to become a Middle Eastern technology specialist for the FBI in New York. This is a spy who understands computers as well as many Asian languages. It is a rare person.

I am sixteen and a part owner of the Internet café, and that has been rewarding and part of my pride. But much tragedy has struck. Lately I feel like a giant cross wire with crackling circuits, and my asthma bothers me all day. I think my brains and chest are turning into a World Wide Web.

I watched on the Internet six months ago as the World Trade Center toppled, not knowing if my father, mother, and brother were safe, living just nine blocks away. My chest filled with relief when I found out they had not been injured. But then, just two weeks later, a gas line broke in their apartment building, claiming the lives of all eighteen tenants. Uncle Ahmer calls the loss of my family an act of God, and I know this to be true. But I feel the building's gas lines were compromised when the Towers fell. I have trouble sorting the two tragedies out.

Today, I told visitors to the café that my family died inside the World Trade Center. I could feel Uncle Ahmer stare at me, though I did not recognize my error until he turned me by the shoulder, pushed me toward the door, and said, "Go to the sea and clear your head!"

So, I walked the beach and watched the late afternoon sun, and after a while the facts in my mind returned to their normal positions. I had hoped to see the sun again as I had at thirteen, at my last times of saying, "The sun is all mine. It belongs only to me."

My mind roared, instead, to the programs I'd left open on

my hard drive and to the extremists gathered around terminal five. They were seated just one row in front of my workstation. Pakistan hosts many wanderers these days—both harmless and dangerous. When extremists come to the café, I often capture their screens, script their chatter, and sell it to USIC, as my father had sold intelligence to the FBI in Karachi, back when he was a policeman.

My mind roars also to Hodji, a USIC agent seated at terminal nine pretending to be Egyptian. I am letting Hodji down while I am out here trying to be a boy. I hurry back in embarrassment.

At my terminal, I realize that I still have my earpiece in place. Hodji's terminal is away from the rest, in the back. I do not expect him to whisper his American humor and complete my humiliation.

"Hey, kid. Shahzad. You work too much, ya know. In America, you'd be going to school and playing football and going to parties with hot babes."

He is pretending to read AlJazeera.net. He only has to mutter, and it fills my whole head. I cannot speak back to him. The Americans have only given me an earpiece, no hidden piece for my voice. They are afraid I will forget myself and speak too loudly to them. They think sixteen is not a man yet.

I appreciate Hodji's humor, despite that he sometimes says dirty words like "hot babes." His joking makes these extremists around terminal five seem like just other guys, not natural-born killers who would be happy to saw off my limbs if they knew what I was up to. Americans use the term "terrorist" to describe such men, but Americans are far more terrified than most people. "Extremist" suits my culture's thinking.

Safely behind them, I still have their screen captured on my terminal, and I watch the extremists' chatter. For the moment, they are merely joking with a contact in London about how you can buy and sell amazing things on eBay if you live in Europe or America. The London contact bought blue jeans for a dollar and sandals for two dollars. It is not interesting yet. So I send an instant message to Hodji:

> You Americans, you treat your children like sacred cows.
> SEND.

I smile as his chair suddenly squeaks. He is not expecting me to be so brazen, to lay a message right on his screen, what with these extremists right under our noses. It is enough that I have their screen captured on my screen. I am myself again—puffed up and exhilarated like the American cowboy.

If I send Hodji more messages, he will tell Uncle Ahmer, who would later smack my lungs loose or grab my hair for a lecture. He helps the Americans because he likes the money and gifts. He feels no sense of loyalty to them as my father did.

But I can't resist my own urges sometimes. Hodji's constant lectures about what I *should* be doing at sixteen, they seem condescending. He acts like America sets all the laws in this world. I must straighten him out. I start an e-mail to him in scramble mode.

> You treat your children like sacred cows. Of course, I would very much like to go to school and play football, but I like my job very much more, thank you. If you are correct and I am the best programmer/hacker you have

ever met personally, why do you protest to my doing it? Here in Pakistan, people don't care so much that I am sixteen. I don't want to go where I am not a man, thank you. No more than you would like to go back to school pants and vars...varsh...

I cannot remember the word they had tried to tempt me with, last time they offered to send me to live with my aunt Alika and cousin Inas on Long Island, New York. Hodji says my father made him swear to do this if something happened to him, and Hodji is now torn. He is an honorable friend to my father—but he needs me as a spy right now. Americans will not let minors spy, not on their own turf. So, if I went, I would have to become an American schoolboy, and it is hard to find informants with both computer skills and knowledge of many languages. Hodji doesn't want to lose me yet.

And I do not want to go. You don't swap your manhood for appealing trinkets, no matter how good they are—like flat-screen monitors and education and Wendy's Double Double Cheese Cheese and yarsh...varsh...

...varsity letter sweaters. It is very ironic, Hodji, but for me to become American, I would lose much liberty. As you in your eloquence have stated: "Americans would shit themselves before letting a teenager spy on their turf." So, I will have my fun over here where the rules are not so rigid, and rely on you and Roger to bring America to me with your tempting gifts, thank you. I am a v-spy, now and forever.

V stands for virtual, and v-spy is what online informants like me are called.

As part of my reward, Hodji's boss in Karachi, Roger O'Hare, sends me gift boxes of American things. He cannot come to our village often, because he has blond hair and would make notice of himself. I have only met him twice, late at night, but I sometimes awaken to find a sizable box by my bed with no note. In the last were two fat Starbucks coffee sacks, a Snoop Dogg CD, a Red Sox cap, Nestlé Crunch bars, Instant Quaker Oatmeal, Oreos, video games *Doom* and *Doom II,* a John Grisham novel translated to Urdu, and Slim Jims.

What I really want I cannot have, which is Gap jeans and Prada sneakers. In this village, expensive clothing might imply we are doing enormous favors for Americans, and considering some of our clientele of late, I would not like to wear them at my funeral.

I send my message scrambled, which will drive Hodji crazy upon receiving it in Karachi when he returns to his office late tonight. He will think I have important news and unscramble it to find only my eloquent speech. I find this quite funny. It is a serene afternoon. The extremists are not stirred up.

I switch screens because I hear them grow quiet, which means they are no longer looking on eBay. Sure enough, they are watching reverently as screen name StarFind, who USIC has discovered is a high school mathematics teacher in Hamburg, chats away about Americans decreasing certain gifts to Israel. It makes the listeners grunt with satisfaction. I have read it all before on many of the sites where I seek intelligence to sell to Roger and Hodji.

I check upward in their chatter, just to be sure I have not missed anything. Then I plug keywords into one of the search engines I initially designed for my father: "Colony One," "vinegar," "rivers," "run red," and click GO.

I have been strategically put by Uncle Ahmer to find chatter containing these words after Hodji paid eight hundred dollars for one scripted conversation I sent them last November. I had seen chatter posted by a log-in VaporStrike, though I could dig up no information as to his identity. It read, *"They will anoint the waters with Red Vinegar—rivers will run red in Colony One."* As it sounded like a threat, I flagged it, translated it from Arabic to English, and sent it to Uncle Ahmer, who sent it on to Roger and Hodji in Karachi. Hodji showed up within twenty-four hours, with the eight hundred dollars and specific instructions for Uncle Ahmer to keep an eye out for further chatter containing these terms.

Roger and Hodji know that Uncle Ahmer does not hack or v-spy. He is nothing but a voice box for my computer skills. But the USIC officials cannot get past my age. They always approach him, not me. He is content with this arrangement, because he gets to keep most of the dollars that way. I don't care about dollars as much. I care more for my adrenaline rushes.

My program automatically searches not only this chat room but 217 others I have recorded because extremists have been known to chat in them. It searches them in both Arabic and languages using the English alphabet. The agents tell me very little, but I can figure out much just from my own searches.

It is obvious to me that "anoint the waters with Red Vinegar" is a terroristic threat, possibly to do with poisoning a water supply. Another post, to VaporStrike by an Omar0324, read, "*Waters will run red in Colony One... Waters will run red three hours from Home Base in December... They will drink in December and die like mangy dogs in April.*" Hence I know that probably somewhere on this planet, people are drinking poisoned water that is slowly compromising their health, and they may not become aware of it until April. I don't believe the chatter is a hoax, but finding the flesh and blood behind these log-ins is a problem. Omar0324 hides behind a Yahoo! address, which is untraceable even to me, same as VaporStrike. These extremists and Colony One could be anywhere on this planet.

I know USIC has searched in Africa for Home Base because another chat room I scripted had this English in its chatter: "*American intelligence agents took three of our comrades in for questioning in the Sudan yesterday and tested six wells. They almost fell in, pfwaa!*" I don't know what led USIC to the Sudan, but because of another post, I believe Colony One is in America. VaporStrike told two online cronies on December 29, "*Waters ran red yesterday on the Dark Continent, three hours from Home Base.*" Home Base would be the location of the terror cell headquarters. And granted, the Dark Continent means Africa, but I have been v-spying on VaporStrike for weeks, and I know he has a love/hate obsession with America. I believe he is being coy.

I nagged and trumpeted my deep sense that Home Base was New York, and Colony One therefore was within three hours of it. I sent them other e-mails from VaporStrike, referencing America as that "Dark and Unruly Habitat." In January, USIC was formed, and almost immediately the new supervisors decided to test all these water supplies. After all the towers came up clean, Hodji's nickname for me was "Expensive." I did not care. My instincts are not given to misinterpretation of so much chatter. A few weeks later, I sent Roger link after link to news pages of a strange outbreak of illness in California. *Check this! Many alarms! Colony One???* I repeatedly nagged.

"Yo, Expensive! We can read the online newspapers ourselves, thank you," Roger finally e-mailed to me. He says to stick to my chat rooms, to the *gathering* of intelligence, and not the *interpreting* of it. I am insulted.

But next, I am humiliated. The Centers for Disease Control confirmed that the California illness was linked to E. coli—bad spinach at a fast-food salad bar. *Oops.* Hodji says they knew this, even as I flailed e-mails to them. "Expensive" wore off, but "the Kid" has remained.

I won't look foolish again. I keep to myself these days that I think Colony One is in America.

Only one hit on "vinegar" has downloaded. When I chase it, I find only an antidote for the bite of an Angolan fruit fly. Very serene afternoon. The extremists are so content that for a few moments, the only sound in here is my normal asthmatic wheezing. When they make a few comments among themselves, Hodji takes occasion to mutter into my earpiece.

"Did you know there are three hospitals for every square mile in New York City? Did you know they could find the right asthma drug for you just by watching your lungs on a laptop for half an hour?"

He is in rare form today. I am not wheezing badly now, though that is unusual since my family died. Several weeks after their funeral, Hodji saw me get so bad as to collapse. Once I faint, fortunately, my chest opens up normally again. I simply got up and resumed working, but it scared the life out of Hodji. He sent to Karachi for medicine, but it doesn't work for me. I need many tests, and thus his references to New York City hospitals.

My screen suddenly goes to black. I roll my eyes, listening through the *sssssst* of the power loss. I glance over to the gruesome threesome. Their screen has gone to black, too, and they make groans of disappointment, despite that StarFind's rhetoric contained nothing new and exciting.

Uncle Ahmer comes out and stands behind them, scratching his head. I assess that he has rigged the crash to get rid of the extremists. He must want to tell us something important.

He holds up some cable wire and speaks in Arabic, in which they had been conversing. "We crashed this morning, also. I must rewire again. I'll try to have it done for tomorrow. You will come back?"

Their disappointment causes them only to drop some rupees beside their keypad and stalk outside with their Styrofoam coffee cups. Uncle Ahmer locks the door, puts up his closed-for-servicing sign, and moves for their money.

"Good men! They leave a tip!" He tosses one coin to me, pockets five or six himself, then drops the fake cable wire into Hodji's palm. "Roger is coming. He e-mailed half an hour ago."

I look out the window. It is almost dark. It is highly unusual that Roger will bring his blond head here before midnight.

"He says it's important," Uncle Ahmer tells us, and I can see opportunity flash in his eyes. When the Americans say it's important, there are usually larger payments coming. He turns to me. "But first, Roger wants to know if you found any more chatter today on 'Colony One' or 'Red Vinegar.' "

I shake my head, humiliated. "Why does he ask this every day lately? To disgrace me? I've seen nothing since the chatter I gave you three weeks ago—about the devil."

The chatter had been between Omar0324 and VaporStrike: *"Red Vinegar is a roaring devil so treat the devil with respect... or it will suck your brains out through your face, also."*

I had sent Roger and Hodji so much chatter on this mysterious target Colony One, and this substance Red Vinegar, that USIC inquired of me more and more—even after my New York water tower and California E. coli embarrassments—implying they do not think it is an idle threat or a hoax. Then, the second week in February, almost all chatter abruptly ceased.

"I ran my search every twenty minutes today," I say. "They have either contrived a new chat room on a site I have not found yet, or they're simply not discussing this threat."

My insides feel eaten. I don't like knowing that people's lives could end if I miss information. That is much weight to carry, to think of other sixteen-year-olds like me, who may live without their father or mother as I do now, if I don't continue building my searches. In that sense, Hodji is right. My job is too old for me.

But at the thought of Roger O'Hare coming, I force my spirits to bounce back up. Roger promised when next he comes to bring Drake's Apple Fruit Pies, Kit Kat bars, and Cracker Jack. I will make a huge pig of myself, and he will rub my hair and tell me what an idealistic and honorable man my father was and how I should move to America soon.

I won't tell him what I really think: Americans make lazy offspring, and I would not fit in over there. The Internet shows me this. Their teenagers go to school, and then to shopping or a party or barbecue or a club and leave a huge mess for their mother or father, who make the wash and cook and clean and earn all the money. To behave like this, I would insult myself.

But there is something inside of Americans I feel I must not be seeing—at least the bighearted ones like Roger and Hodji. I know I am very important to these agents. I read gratitude in their faces when I give them intelligence. And I read torment, too. They want to fulfill promises made to my father back when they were FBI and he was a Karachi policeman looking to go to America. He made them promise to make sure I got my American education if something were to happen to him. Yet, as "Americans would shit themselves before letting a teenager spy on their turf," they would lose me as an information source.

To me, it is more important to be a v-spy, and besides, who wants to go to live in a place where one's parents died? I need to find some important intelligence so that I can prove my value here and now.

My computer has rebooted. I try my search one more time: "Colony One," "vinegar," "rivers," "run red," and click GO. I click into the chat room that has produced "Colony One" and "Red Vinegar." My eyes almost pop out of my head.

It is an Arabic post from Omar0324, who is chatting with VaporStrike in a room recorded in my search engines but not used by them recently.

Omar0324: A woman died in Colony One tonight. As best as I can determine she was a drug addict. Not of much value to our goals. But it has started.

VaporStrike: Her brains bled out her face, I suppose? Pwfaa. Forgive my irreverence.

Omar0324: Forgiven. I have not gotten close to the hospital. Too risky. I have only Catalyst's hacking skills and my eyesight to prove things as of yet. Catalyst said she was DOA, and from the symptoms delivered across their handheld radios, I feel they will assess the cause of death as brain aneurysm.

VaporStrike: I thought we established that Red Vinegar would not rear its ugly head until April.

Omar0324: The weak succumb first. Two hours ago, an ambulance visited another house and took away another female. Symptoms I captured included only flu and severe headache, but I feel we will see—

I don't scream for Hodji. I want to stick the script under his nose accompanied by my humblest good manners. He will never call me the Kid again. I chase around for a few minutes but can only determine that VaporStrike is chatting from a U.S. server. It belongs to a café near New York City that I know well, called Trinitron. This probably means he is somewhere near that server, but the truth is, he could access it from anywhere on the globe. About Omar0324 I can determine even less. He has managed to hide the embedded codes of any server at all. I don't focus any disappointment on his tricks, to which I am accustomed. If Hodji and Roger are correct, and the location of Colony One is in Africa, then he is somewhere on the real Dark Continent. I am focused on my good luck. This is a very, very frank conversation, which is unlike them. They generally speak in codes that force me always to read between lines and suspect innocent chatter.

However, my luck evaporates as quickly as it came. I open

a Word file swiftly to script the chatter, but to my amazement, when I switch back to the chat screen, only their names still show, but with blank spaces between. I know what I just read, and have never seen chatter not be where it was ten seconds ago. To my deepest shock, the blank spaces between their names indicate that their speeches are, like them, able to come and go via the black holes of an endless galaxy called the Internet.

They log off and are gone. I will catch them later, but for now I am stumped, and I have no script to show off to Roger.

SEVEN

SCOTT EBERMAN
FRIDAY, MARCH 1, 2002
6:30 A.M.

THE SUN WAS barely up when I returned to the hospital after a sleepless night. I felt something was terribly wrong as soon as I walked into the ward where Dr. Godfrey had put Mom late last night. I knew he would be here starting rounds already, but nobody was in the nurses' station, despite that the phone was *ring-ring-ring*ing. I automatically flew to pick it up but never got farther than the "hell" in "hello" when I saw the medical convention outside my mom's private room.

I wanted to run toward it, but it was like one of those nightmares where the bad guy is chasing you and you're moving in slow motion. I could hear Godfrey's voice sounding off with something indistinguishable and nurse extraordinaire Haley Gibbs exclaiming, "—walked in here two minutes ago, and she was like that!"

Another nurse turned, put her hand on my shoulder, and pushed me back. "Scott, don't go in there."

Dr. Godfrey came flying out, still muttering, with Haley following on his heels.

He saw me. "Don't go in there."

It's like someone telling you not to surface in a swimming pool. But Godfrey's gloved hand replaced the other nurse's, and he pushed against the middle of my chest.

The Code Blue squad was in the cube. The all-too-familiar beeps and bumps and honks ground through my head.

"What the—" I froze, staring down. Godfrey's hand had left a perfect replica of itself in the middle of my T-shirt, dripping red in blood.

He tore off the gloves and dropped them into Gibbs's hand.

"Get him a scrub shirt," he said to her, which ought to have been the least of his worries, the least of my worries. But I'd seen this before, when my mind was focused on something medically horrible and complicated. My brain would flip, only for a nanosecond, to something less important, almost like a swimmer taking a gulp of air between strokes. I whipped off the T-shirt and flung it to Haley, who was unlocking the linen closet. And as I chased, bare-chested, after Godfrey I gave that bloody T-shirt one final look, sensing it was something I ought to keep as memorabilia for my children and grandchildren—or at least for myself and Owen.

Letting it go was like an admission that this situation, whatever it was, could resolve itself. It ain't over till it's over, we always said in the ambulance. Hell, we could even keep a Code Blue alive for hours, or days if we needed to, until we could think of something to bring it back to life. I turned my face from that T-shirt, sensing I would never see it again. But since I wouldn't be needing any memorabilia from this strange scene, chasing after Godfrey was far more important.

EIGHT

SHAHZAD HAMDANI
FRIDAY, MARCH 1, 2002
5:30 P.M. KARACHI TIME

ROGER LAYS HIS gift box on my chair, but I cannot think of it yet. I have ranted my entire story in Urdu, which Roger does not understand. I don't even realize it until Uncle grabs hold of my forearm and translates to English.

"Omar0324 has just posted that a woman has died in Colony One. Her, um, brains bled out her face. Another is ill—"

"Let me see the script." Too calmly, Roger removes the head covering from his thick blond hair as Hodji runs around closing blinds. Roger's height alone is enough for people to make note of him if we are not careful.

"He doesn't have it. He says the chatter disappeared before his very eyes," Uncle finishes, raising his eyebrows like I may be a childish idiot.

I trudge on in English, despite that my spoken English is horrible. If you wonder how one's English can be horrible in today's world—especially for a person who knows many obscure Asian languages—the answer is simple: With a click of a mouse, almost any English translates to Arabic, and this is impossible with lesser-known languages. Because of its popularity, English is the easiest language in which to become lazy, and in my panic tonight, my tongue goes thick and awkward.

I stutter, "VaporStrike makes to be near the café Trinitron. That café near your New York, only... subhuman."

"Suburban," Roger corrects me but fails to smirk or call me Kid. I detect he is interested.

"Omar I no can make to be somewhere."

"Bet he's in Africa," Roger mutters. He looks at Hodji, who has returned to his side, and repeats my statement: "A woman has died in Colony One. Her brains bled out her face. And a second woman is ill or dying..." Roger's blue eyes light in hope. "*Mmm,* lots of meat in that. Lots of clues."

"You feel you can find Colony One—based on that one statement?" I ask, having known the Americans too long to show much amazement.

Hodji does not have to remind me, but he does. "You gave us a script on StarFind when he said there was a fire in his school the night before, set by a bunch of unruly teenagers. Remember that?"

"Yes." They had no idea where on the globe StarFind was or who he was, but with that one tidbit, USIC located him. He's been under surveillance ever since.

I am wheezing badly, but I do not realize until Hodji starts to rub my back and he bangs on it just once. "Go look in Roger's gift box. Don't think about disappearing chatter right now. Take a break—"

"But you don't believe me!" I steer my face away from the Frost Glacier Freeze Gatorade he waves before me. Normally, with the athletic suck top, it is a favorite gift.

He holds up Drake's Apple Pies. I take them and stare at the packaging, wondering whether to devour them now or save them for more peaceful times. I look in the box as the three of them retreat to Uncle's office.

I can hear Uncle's here-come-the-dollars tone float out as I calm my chest by munching what I have found on top—Kit Kat bars.

I see the bright orange word PRINCETON, and pull out the black cap. I take my time straightening the brim and studying the plastic adjuster. I put the cap on my head, hoping I look sufficiently bored as would befit a man.

A few of Uncle Ahmer's words float up. "...not for less than fifty thousand American dollars," he is saying in Arabic.

Fifty thousand dollars. I whisper into the air, which seems at times so filled with my father's kind and idealistic spirit. "Father...Uncle's ambition has exceeded his honesty again and is ferociously working his jaw. We have nothing to give the Americans worth even a tenth of that amount."

I have two new programs half written, which Uncle could sell for about a thousand dollars each. One would search through known extremists' chat sites in Russian and translate their chatter to English. I have written other such programs for translating Arabic, German, French, or Spanish into English. These are the languages most extremists use on the Internet. Roger first called these programs Shahzad's track 'n' translate gems, and finally just TNTs. USIC loves the TNTs because a downfall in American intelligence has been Internet spying.

Once I finish these programs, their agents will be able to track chatter in yet another language without actually knowing that language.

Still, Uncle Ahmer has never asked the Americans for more than fifteen hundred dollars for one of my TNTs. Such is equal to one year's wages for both him and me.

"No less than forty thousand."

Forty thousand dollars. "Uncle is making mischief for money, Father."

My father thought of America as the end of the rainbow, the place of free education, democracy, liberty, artistic freedom, pursuit of dreams. Of course, he was not so above it all, and he spoke of the material enjoyments, too. In his e-mails he frequently would send me digital photos of himself and would write the photo captions in his own lazy English:

"Her I am etting my Kentucky Fry YUM YUM YUM it will be yor favrit."

"Her I am in my new tommy hilfrigger jacket I look lik reel american yes?"

"Her I am at Yankees go Yankees go soriano! I eat oscar meyer weiner today...pleeze don't tell your mother since meyer is jew."

My father spent many hours reading Arabic translations of American classics and history and idealism, yet he enjoyed nothing more, I think, than a roller coaster. One time, he e-mailed me his own screams from the Scream Machine at Six Flags Great Adventure, New Jersey. I miss my father's silliness as much as his wisdom.

Uncle Ahmer, on the other hand, does not love or hate the Americans, nor does he love or hate those who hate America.

He provides Americans with intelligence only for the payments. And he provides coffee and tea and uptime for their terrorists. He takes their money without thought, even when I have not successfully scripted their chatter. He sees no hypocrisy in this and says with much glee, "If I have the sun, the sea, and a fat wallet for my family, it is a very good day. It's none of my business what another man does."

"Ahmer, forty thousand is not realistic." Roger's voice rises slightly. "We should not pay that much to do *you* a favor."

I don't understand their prattle, and beneath two CDs, an Eminem album and the *Les Misérables* sound track, are two more Gatorades. I remove them, but then tear the Drake's pies package open, forgetting to look uninterested.

"No deal for less." Uncle Ahmer's voice stands firm, and I sense this time there is something very earnest in his tone. "I want assurance of years of wages for Shahzad and me if you bring this thing to pass."

I freeze, the pie only three inches from my mouth. I understand this to mean only one thing: *For some reason, the Americans want to buy the café.* But that makes little sense. We have always given them intelligence at fair prices. Their "owning" us can in no way improve the job I have been doing for them.

"Shahzad...come in here," Uncle's voice carries through at this most embarrassing time. I have both pies shoved in my mouth, with my lips spread as wide as the equator. Their staring embarrasses me, and then I can't swallow.

Hodji comes around, guffawing at my humiliation. He grabs a Gatorade, opens it, and gives it to me. As I drink, I realize I have forgotten to savor the taste of the pies for future reference, and they are both gone now, blobbed into mush in my throat by Gatorade.

Still, I address my uncle in Urdu, which the agents don't understand, swiping at what crumbs must be on my face. "Uncle, we must keep the café at all cost. It makes up our pride."

But Uncle Ahmer starts chuckling at the agents, and he sidles up to me, which means I am in danger of being pinched if I say the wrong thing.

"Shahzad, these USIC agents are confused." He laughs, too casually. "Did you know, Shahzad, that all this time, these men think you are *sixteen*? I tell them you are *eighteen*, and they want to see your birth certificate."

I cannot process so quickly his scheme. These agents know I am sixteen; they know everything about me from years of friendship with my father. They are looking at each other, not me, as if they are questioning how far they will carry an ill-begotten scheme of my uncle's.

"Please go over to the house and ask your aunt Hamera to find your birth certificate," Uncle says, nudging me sideways.

My real birth certificate will say I am sixteen. He means for me to go up the street to our less-than-honorable neighbor, Aman Somadi, pay him twenty American dollars, and have a birth certificate made to reflect eighteen years. I don't understand why Uncle would want me to lie about my age, or why the Americans are not objecting to this stupidness.

His suspicious behavior intensifies as he speaks very slowly, too casually. "Shahzad. Do you know what an *internship* is?"

I do. It means you work for a wealthy Karachi businessman for nothing. I already make money and don't see why I would give away my valuable skills for free.

"I don't know why these agents never mentioned to me before that you are eligible for an *internship*, Shahzad. I think it is because they perceived you have never attended high school. While you're at it, go dig up your latest report card."

So, I will need forty dollars. If I object, Uncle Ahmer will pinch me until I bruise, or stand on my foot until Drake's pie plasters the walls. But I don't want any USIC internship, especially since, gauging from the price Uncle Ahmer is holding to... *this internship is in New York and not Karachi.*

My uncle is not bargaining for our café, I realize. He is bargaining for my life. I do not like this.

"Is anyone going to ask me what *I* will do? Being that I am in charge of my choices?" I ask. This is a very American argument, I have learned. Americans seem to back down if you imply they are infringing on your rights to choose.

Hodji does sigh but doesn't back down. "Shahzad, first and foremost, there is your health. You need American medicine—"

"I am healthy! I have bad asthma attacks maybe once a month!"

"You have them once a week! You only pass out once a month. That is *not* normal."

"A terrible thing, yes," says Uncle Ahmer with too much drama, since he is very accustomed to seeing me pass out. The sympathy behooves his position.

Hodji plops down in Uncle Ahmer's chair and looks weary tonight. "Look. You need an American hospital, American tests."

I shake my head. "You always say that if ever I go to America I can no longer be a v-spy. I don't suppose that has changed?"

They are quiet for such a long minute that I am stunned.

The way American culture protects its young, I do not conceive of how this could change.

"If you're eighteen, there is *one* allowance for what Americans would consider work in ... the Hot Zone," Hodji stumbles. His fingers rake through his dark hair. "If it were Twain, the answer would be no, no, no. But Twain has my health benefits and a five-dollar co-pay for whatever might ail him."

Twain is Hodji's son, who is my age. He goes to private school in Manhattan and makes good marks. Sometimes Hodji slips and calls me Twain, usually when I am in the throes of asthma and he is panicking.

I realize the "Hot Zone" of which he speaks. I repeat my father's oft-spoken words: "Computers have blurred the line between child and adult, because in the land of computers, children are the men, and the men are the children."

"Correct," Hodji says, though he will not look at me. "But I'm out of my comfort zone here. It's one thing to pay a Pakistani kid for v-spying in his backyard. It's another to put him on an American payroll to do it on Long Island."

See, he knows my age to be sixteen. He is pretending he doesn't know, probably because this internship would get me some medical benefits. One reason for the start of USIC is that it can do faster work, because it will not take years to check credentials, as do the FBI and CIA. I now see Uncle's motivation for the false documents, though I do not have any such motivation myself. My father would not want huge buildings falling on me, or for me to accidentally drink the very poisoned water I seek out. Roger can think that Colony One is in Africa all he wants. I do not.

"Things have changed since my father spoke of his hopes for me to follow him," I remind them.

Roger ignores this fact. "It's actually a safer situation for you, Shahzad... if we can make USIC see it that way. It's nothing you haven't done over here in Pakistan. It's actually the same thing, only in an Internet café on Long Island. If you are on the payroll, at least we could get you adequate protection, whereas over here, you're wide open. One mistake, and we could all be chopped liver."

"USIC owns this Internet café?" Uncle asks.

"No. We pay them not to ask questions," Roger says. "The managers know we've been using their intranet structure to capture the screens of several well-known subversives who chat from there regularly."

"Trinitron," I hear myself say.

Roger grins as if my guess is remarkable, though it is nothing. Trinitron is the Internet café on whose server I have just found VaporStrike. I often find VaporStrike using terminals with Trinitron's embedded codes. He has two friends who visit the café, also, known only to us as log-ins Catalyst and PiousKnight.

So... Trinitron is serving as a spy trap for USIC, I realize. They want me to work there, doing very similar things to what I do here. Somehow, I do not think it will be as much the same as they are leading me to believe.

Roger continues, "Thanks to Trinitron, other v-spies have picked up quite a bit of intelligence. Still, we can't arrest VaporStrike or either of his friends. We can't even bring them in for questioning."

"Why not?" Uncle asks.

"If we alert them to our interest in them by arresting one, we'll end up shutting their mouths tighter than a steel drum," Roger says. "Better to give them enough freedom so that they don't know they're on a leash. We've found out a lot about VaporStrike, Catalyst, and PiousKnight since you first started sending us chatter, Shahzad."

I don't allow my eyes to jerk to his. While I have been unable to turn up any information on their identities, I have sensed that USIC had some luck via other sources. I pretend only mild interest as Roger reveals some intelligence.

"We know their names, aliases, travels, educations, criminal histories—all that good stuff. We know they were not involved in the 9/11 attacks, at least not directly. But VaporStrike and PiousKnight were in Yemen in 2000 when the USS *Cole* was bombed, and Catalyst was in Kenya in '98 when the U.S. Embassy was bombed. Now they're all together online, sending god knows what around the Internet on a daily basis. Coincidence? We don't think so. Of course, we could arrest any of them tomorrow, based on the chatter you captured." He jerks his head toward me but turns his eyes to Uncle, who makes an emphatic statement.

"Get out a hacksaw. Start taking off their heads. They'd do the same to us soon enough, if they'd any clue what we're up to." He strikes a match hard and lights one of his foul-smelling Pall Malls. Fortunately, he turns to gaze into the crack of fading light between the shade and the window and sends his smoke away from me.

I see fire smoldering behind Roger's restless eyes. "If I loved living outside the law and had the stomach for inflicting pain, I'd have gone CIA instead of FBI. Nah. God made me to uphold the law."

"Me, too," Hodji agrees, as if they have talked about this many times.

"You're stuck with us." Roger sighs, but there is resolve in it. "As far as we're concerned, these things have to be handled delicately. We're not pulling them in yet—especially considering that we're not going to drill healthy teeth to try to get information or set fires under their chairs. We're going to wait and watch them until they tell us some critical things. First: Who are they working for and what are they about? We can't find an association to any known terror cell. Second: What kind of poison is in Red Vinegar? Is it really infecting people, or is it a hoax? And finally: Who is Omar? Where is Omar? I think if we can find Omar, we'll find Colony One, we'll find the exact nature of Red Vinegar, and we'll find a sleeper cell that wants to kill lots of innocent people."

After my thoughtful silence, I return us to the point of the conversation. "It doesn't take a genius to capture their screens and script their chatter," I remind them. "I can continue doing that from here."

"The chatter won't script." Roger smiles knowingly. My story to him about disappearing chatter made more sense than he was letting on. "USIC had an agent in Trinitron last night, trying to script VaporStrike and a crony. He says they're using some homemade program that has a double whammy. First, it makes chatter disappear. He saw it himself. The chatter appears, and within thirty seconds the monitor blinks. Then the page reads like it was never there."

So he believes my story of VaporStrike and Omar0324.

Hodji continues, "Apparently, all the publicity of the 9/11 terrorists making their plans on the Internet has scared them.

The terror cell has this one way to continue communicating without detection."

I examine the concept of disappearing chatter, frantically searching my head for the programming sequences that could bring this to pass. It is like Internet disappearing ink. I think of a few possible lines of programming, but *is the command with the sender or the server or both?*

Even virtual chat rooms create a temporary script that lasts until the speakers exit. I can capture much of that with my searches, which I run up to twenty minutes apart. To capture chatter that erases from the script as soon as the intended eyes behold it? I would have to be everywhere at once, constantly.

"All chatter about Colony One appeared to cease the second week in February," I mutter. "But it hasn't ceased at all, if this is true."

Hodji chuckles without smiling. "It's true. We're being outsmarted."

Roger continues, "That's only problem number one. I said they've got a program with a *double* whammy. The chatter that's posting and disappearing is not usually in either English or Arabic. The other v-spy said that sometimes what they post is in our alphabet, sometimes in...god knows what alphabets. It looks like they're sharing a massive translation program."

"Of some lesser-known languages," I mutter in awe. "Probably translating to lesser-known alphabets...which makes a keyword search of chat rooms impossible."

"That's what we think. Because we can't script it, we need somebody on-site who can look at any number of languages and get the gist of what these guys are saying on the spot."

I groan, thinking of people somewhere in this world drinking the water about which VaporStrike brags with such audacity. I ought to be willing to do anything.

Uncle Ahmer tries to pull me aside, but I shake loose from him in a panic. "Tell Trinitron to just send me the hard drive. I will find the stupid program! Even if they ran it off a disk, the evidence of its behavior will be in the activity. What have you over there? A smattering of idiots?"

This time Uncle Ahmer is not so gentle. He tosses me into the now-dim café, though he fans his hand in front of my face, as if this will help at all. He whispers in a gentle tone.

"Shahzad, listen to me. Get rid of your asthma before you give your aunt Hamera a heart attack and I suffer another loss. Get the American education that your father wanted you to have. You can live with your aunt Alika and cousin Inas, go to school with Inas, and work at night, when the extremists come out of their holes. I will send you money regularly."

For once I see in his face something like affection. He does not often show this. I would think this was about the vast fortune USIC is implying he will get, except for this rare look in his eyes.

But I have not seen my aunt Alika or my cousin Inas since I was three. And I am mindful of one of Uncle's favorite sayings: *The devil you know is better than the devil you don't know.* I am familiar with my uncle, with my daily routines, with asthma, even with entertaining dangerous extremists under my own roof.

Yet America is something quite different. I read online once that Americans see Vietnam as a war and not a place. Well, I see America as falling buildings and broken gas lines. It is a series of terrible news photos that have haunted my home page for months and remind me constantly of my family's loss.

Roger comes to me. He reads my eyes and tries to keep our thoughts focused. "It's been the tradition for subversives to speak in code and make only vague allusions to their schemes online, Shahzad. But with them sharing some weird software and feeling this much protection, who knows what they're talking about. What we're missing."

I try to swallow, but I have no spit. Only a sore and rattling chest.

"We've been fruitlessly searching Africa for Colony One and have turned up nothing. You still think VaporStrike's Dark Continent is America and not Africa? I don't believe that, but would you like to prove us wrong? Here's your chance."

"So I can go there and die myself?" I turn from them to glimpse the setting sun.

Uncle says in Urdu, so they won't understand, "You're being a small boy with a wild imagination. Go get a birth certificate before I kick a second crack into your ass. Get a transcript also that makes you to be in high school. Take two twenty-dollar bills from the coffee can in the house. Go."

So, I am to go to school and do this internship at night. VaporStrike, PiousKnight, and Catalyst have been called by Hodji "night crawlers" who only chat after dark, so it would work out—for USIC. My heart is troubled.

I decide to argue this out later when my head is clear. I go to pay for false documents, but only so I can enjoy taking deep breaths under the cover of night. I don't like having to watch the Americans gloat.

NINE

CORA HOLMAN
MONDAY, MARCH 4, 2002
1:15 P.M.

I SAT IN MR. GLENN'S law office, watching him shuffle through paper after paper. I was glad to be out of the house again, having spent four nights by myself. That isn't to say I had spent three days utterly alone. Neighbors, teachers, and coworkers who heard the news rang the doorbell, dropping off food and offering kind words.

I'd ask them in but would find myself sitting at the edge of my chair, though I was far more comfortable than I would have been if I hadn't scrubbed the entire house from top to bottom after I got better. The mysterious flu finally left me at dawn the day after Aleese died, but I would use tiredness as an excuse if visitors started staying too long. People left after ten minutes or so, probably mystified that I wasn't completely falling apart.

"Again, Cora, let me say that you don't have to sell the house yet if you're not ready." Mr. Glenn gathered the papers into a stack that I was supposed to sign.

I still felt oddly at peace. Maybe it was the fact that I had on stockings and a black suit, with my hair twisted up in the French knot I usually save for concert choir. Maybe those things helped me finally feel older, more ready to make decisions.

"It's all right, Mr. Glenn. Really."

I had overheard the words "the wrecking-ball house" and "that Holman eyesore" a few times around town. It totally stung. I wanted it torn down as badly as the next person, and I'd had no idea how much the property alone was worth until Mr. Blumberg, my next-door neighbor, had mentioned it when he and Mrs. Blumberg stopped over the morning after Aleese passed, putting homemade ice cream in the freezer.

It had not been a tactless conversation with the Blumbergs, by any means. In fact, I had brought up selling the house, stating a longtime fantasy of owning one of the little condos down in the meadows. We ended with Mr. Blumberg saying that when I was ready, he would buy the property and add twelve thousand dollars to the market value to make sure I would "have enough." He was a stockbroker, ridiculously wealthy, Oma had always said. And the fact that he couldn't wait to get our little ranch shoveled away to extend his property didn't seem offensive to me. I understood.

I signed for Mr. Glenn. Paper after paper. First and foremost, I signed emancipation papers proclaiming me an independent for the three months until I was eighteen, so I could legally make decisions concerning Aleese's cremation, my finances, and the future. I read the fine print of most of the documents and understood more than I thought I would.

"Mr. Blumberg says to make sure you understand you can

stay and finish the school year. Take your time. Find a condo or something you really like. I will help you. He will help you."

I watched Mr. Glenn, curious about his doe-eyed look. I noticed that all the people who stopped in for brief visits at the house had had this same gaze, as if they were feeling something I couldn't quite understand.

"I'll...um...keep in touch about my search. I'm definitely staying in Trinity Falls, so...," I babbled, signing the last page. I could imagine the little condos quite clearly because I'd dreamed about having one all to myself since I was about eight years old. I took long walks to watch the construction and the young couples move into them. They were probably expensive with their view of the islands, but our property value was more than enough to buy a condo, even if all a new owner wanted to do was knock down the "eyesore."

I could go to college, too, at Astor College, fifteen minutes away. All the while, I could be a part of this Trinity Falls I had attached myself to through a lens. I could do it as a person with a clean house, as a respectable person. No matter who was to hear stories about Aleese from the police or the paramedics, I could prove I was different. That had become important while I was cleaning.

"Great. Well, let's go to the service," he said, standing up and looking at his watch.

"Oh! Um..." I shot up. "You don't have to come. It's just... me and the minister. It's private. I mean that's nice of you, but um—"

"Not what the newspaper said," he mumbled, grabbing a copy of the *Atlantic City Press*.

I hadn't called any newspaper. I'd had one conversation with the coroner's office about a "straight-to-the-crematory" and one conversation with Oma's minister, whom I had called. *Must have been the minister,* I decided, staring at this obituary. It said some things I didn't even know about Aleese, like that she had attended the University of Missouri. I had only heard Oma refer to her as "a dropout who couldn't even stay long enough to find a husband and have me ten grandkids." It contained the exact name of the newspaper in Beirut she had worked for, but not the dates. It seemed to me Oma had mentioned that Aleese had only kept a full-time job for six months of her adult life, "because she was out of her element, should have been having kids." Oma had always been a little nutty about her own missed dream of ten kids. Oh well. The obituary made Aleese sound respectable.

At the bottom, sure enough, were the time, day, and place I'd arranged with Reverend McNaughton at the little Methodist church on Main Street that Oma and I used to go to sometimes. It said nothing about the service being private, and I realized I had not mentioned that to Reverend McNaughton, not that it would matter.

"May I keep this?" I asked Mr. Glenn.

"Absolutely."

"And don't worry about coming. Honestly. In spite of this…it's private." *No one would come.* I agreed to let him drop me off, so I wouldn't have to walk the ten blocks.

One time back in freshman biology, Owen Eberman and I were paired up for an entire period to watch bacteria changing under a microscope. I was more in love with his brother than I was with him, but I still found myself tongue-tied. He talked when he had to—not a lot, but not nervously, either.

He laughed a couple of times at something he did that wasn't right. When I did something wrong, he didn't laugh. He was nice like that.

The most surreal moment of my life was seeing them come walking into this church—Owen and Scott. It's just a little white church with one aisle up the center of the pews. I was standing there with Reverend McNaughton, and they were coming right toward us. They had on shirts and ties and goose-down jackets. The floor started falling out from under me.

I froze. They kept coming, and each of them hugged me.

"You guys, you don't have to be here!" I said. Scott was wearing sunglasses—the mirrored kind, which meant I was faced with my own astonished expression. Owen wasn't wearing glasses but looked half-in-there, staring up at the rafters like they were interesting.

"How are you feeling?" Scott asked.

"Fine. Great. Got over it by the next morning."

He heaved a sigh of relief. "And so, you've had four days now...no fever, no bronchitis, no digestive tract problems, no headaches?"

I could not believe he even remembered.

"Yes, um...how are you?"

"Been better. Ya know..." He lifted up his glasses for a split second so I could see his eyes were all swollen and glassy.

"You guys, I am so, so sorry." I was ripping in half between wanting to back away and wanting to hug Scott, who looked like he needed it, and my better judgment won out. I could feel the same aloneness and terror wafting off him that I'd felt when Oma died, and my hand flew to the back of his head when I hugged him. I heard him sniff the same time I did, and I let go quickly.

He just shoved his glasses to the top of his head, wiping his eyes with his hands. He didn't look too self-conscious, maybe because I was wiping my eyes with my thumbs, feeling his anguish.

"Hey. We'll be here for you today, and you be there for us tomorrow. Deal?"

"Sure, absolutely." Like they needed me to be at their mother's funeral, like there wouldn't be three thousand people.

I put a hand on Owen's arm. "You guys shouldn't be doing this. Not now. This is too nice of you."

"We know what it feels like," Owen said. He knew what it *should* feel like. My life with Aleese had been far different from theirs with their mother, though I didn't attract attention to it.

Scott fumbled around with words that probably would have come easier in a home, without the echo in the rafters.

"...results of the autopsies...cause of death on your mother's death certificate will be aneurysm, nothing about morphine, as it looks to them now like she hadn't ingested enough to overdose or to facilitate what was going on in her brain."

I sighed in relief, thinking of the lessened potential of embarrassment. But I was still confused. "So...morphine had nothing to do with this?"

"Nothing except it might have masked pain and symptoms of illness. Do you have any idea how long she had been sick?"

I shook my head, ashamed at having not given her more of my attention, now that it had come to this. "I'd say she'd been blowing her nose for a few weeks. She complained of nausea, but that's a side effect of morphine, so that was normal. It's hard to say."

I shrugged helplessly, but his nod was mercifully understanding. "Some of her and Mom's blood and tissue samples have been sent to the CDC. Two brain hemorrhages in town with flulike symptoms in two days, that's *Twilight Zone* material. Plus, there was some, um, unidentified bacteria in the sinus cavities. They'll be looking at that. Your blood was sent, too, just to be really safe, you know? We're hoping that we're not looking at some strange, new emerging infectious disease. God, I hope not."

I felt glad that Reverend McNaughton put his arm around me and shook hands with the boys. I figured he could talk to them and I could sit down. But when I looked beyond Owen's huge frame, other people had come into the church. Mr. Steckerman. He had Rain with him. A couple of my old English teachers were behind them. I grabbed hold of the pew and leaned against it. I had not wanted other people to be here. I had wanted my own space, my own little silences to say goodbye to Aleese, to tell her I was bitter about nothing, and to pray for her while an assuring man's voice droned on.

In came the Blumbergs, followed by Mr. Bennett, director of the marching band, and two of the girls I talked a lot to in the flute section.

I was sure the real story about Aleese was out by now, if it hadn't leaked out over time. *What are they doing here?*

The first one to reach me was Mr. Steckerman. My eyes were filling up, so I couldn't see beyond him, but I could smell Rain. She had this head of blond hair that's always full of shampoo smells, and she's always tossing it carelessly like it's nothing more important than a dollar-store baseball cap. He touched my elbow, and I hoped to god I found the presence of mind to say, "Excuse me for a moment."

I went rushing into the choir room, and Reverend McNaughton followed.

"I didn't want this!" I cried after he shut the door.

"Didn't want what, Cora?" He looked confused, though the issue was plain to me.

"My mother was a...a mess!" I tried to keep it low. We'd had this conversation on the phone. He, too, had known about Aleese's addiction and asked point-blank about whether it had gotten worse or better after Oma died. "All she ever did when I was at home was lie on the couch! She never even moved into bed at night! I didn't want all these people here. What are they doing here?"

"Cora, they're here for *you*."

I looked for the silence to be filled with something...a thought...a revelation of how that could be true.

All I could think of was *Why?*

I let him lead me out to so many people I couldn't count them—though I was suspicious that many of them were here in memory of Mrs. Eberman, as if my mother were somehow connected to her now in people's kindnesses. The fact was, the two of them had nothing in common except, perhaps, some terrible germ. I hugged people back until the skin on my arms tingled. The last time I'd been hugged by anyone was at Oma's funeral. The sensations were different now. At Oma's funeral, there had been no consoling me. Nothing could have put less distance between a hopeful thought and myself. Aleese had not been there, hadn't come out of her stupor, and I had been glad, glad to speak in prayer with Oma, without having to worry about what Aleese might hallucinate or commentate at a public service. This time, as the service droned on, I felt kind of... bruised... limp and mushy, like an overly ripe pear.

"Let us pray."

I bowed my head automatically. This was the part of the service I had wanted. The part where I could sit quietly by myself and tell Aleese that I hoped she was happier now and that I was not the type to nurse a grudge.

But Mr. Steckerman was seated beside me. He was holding my hand, and it was making me feel stiffer, especially since he had his fingers laced through Rain's on the other side. It gave me a strange feeling of being joined with her. I didn't deserve it any more than my mother deserved an association with Mrs. Eberman, and Rain knew it as well as I did.

She was another one like Owen Eberman whom I admired from my little space in the school corridors, the sidelines of the cafeteria.

"Yeah, I lost my mom when I was three," she had said to me a few moments before the service started, like it was perfectly natural for the first lines of conversation between us in years to be preceded by a hug, in a church, and not preceded by a "hey" in school.

"That's a shame. I'm really sorry."

"You get used to it. It'll be different for you. You'll have memories, at least."

One hug, two lines based on misinformation, and now I was in some twisted way attached to her via her father's touchy-feely ways. She wanted to be sitting a few rows back with the

Ebermans, "her buds," as I'd overheard her calling them in the corridors, as if they were just normal guys and not legends around here. Then again, she was a legend herself. But she was stuck with me, with my pretense of sadness that, fortunately, was supported by tears of dizziness over all this hugging, and by the fear of what the minister might say. The prayer was ending. I had missed my chance to tell Aleese anything fair, true, or even merciful. The best words to say about Aleese that I could think of came from the minister, not from me.

"From the dust of the earth we come, and to dust we return again. This is the will of the Lord..."

TEN

OWEN EBERMAN
MONDAY, MARCH 4, 2002
2:20 P.M.

"AMEN." I BLESSED myself, noticing that the teachers in the row in front of me didn't, and hoped that was okay. This wasn't my Episcopal church. I couldn't remember what was right, or anything except one fact that kept me going.

It was that Mom could have picked any of a thousand movies to watch on the last night of her life. Since one of the last things she saw was Joan of Arc taken away by Saint Stephen, it was like a sign from above that she, too, had been taken up by a white stallion and a saint in bright lights. It helped to think of Mom as someone who was sacrificed, who couldn't get better because she was too run-down from serving everyone else. The thought helped *me*, at any rate.

Scott was a different story. All he wanted to do was yell at doctors and dish out orders, and have them explain how two women from the same neighborhood can have brain aneurysms on the same night. He wasn't very impressed by their answers, which amounted to "We're working on it."

I looked up at the church rafters. I just wanted to see or hear something miraculous—a light, a flash, half a word from either Saint Catherine or Saint Stephen, Saint Joan, the Lord, or my mom. If it sounds crazy, I had no idea what I would wish for when my only hope would be seeing a miracle.

My brother's profile slumped forward and drew my gaze downward. Scott was bawling quietly again. He had enough tissues packed in his pocket for me and him. Problem was, I hadn't needed them yet. I felt like a wimp next to him. I would get to thinking about Mom too much, and it felt like a dam that's going to blow…and it scared the hell out of me. It was easier to watch Cora Holman, watch the minister…

"…have two great pictures Aleese's mother, Natalie, gave me when Aleese first went overseas," the minister was saying. "I want to show you what's in the heart of a person who wants to use her talents to promote charity and world peace."

The first picture was poster-sized, mounted on something that made it stiff. I'm not a photo guy, but it looked like any number of pictures you'd see on a Feed the Children ad on television. Maybe a little better. She managed to click when this little black girl's eyes were perfect—full of hopelessness, confusion, and maybe acceptance. She had one of those bloated bellies and was wearing only an undershirt, sitting in mud or wet clay or something. The photo was black and white.

My eyes moved to Cora, whose shoulders were squared. Her posture was just as good as if she were sitting in English class. I figured that she must be so used to seeing her mom's work that she could see it at a funeral and hold herself together. *So strong.* We'd all heard about her mother's addiction over the years, little dribs here and there that fell out of grown-ups' mouths. Her mother had been some awesome photographer who lost the use of her shooting arm after an accident, and she was too depressed about it to ever get off her pain medication.

I guessed we'd have felt sorry for Cora, but it's hard to feel sorry for someone who's always got her collective act together. My friends have nicknames for everybody, and we'd come up with a few for her—Audrey Hepburn, Miss State Senator, Little Miss Perfect. She never had anything to do with our crowd, probably more to do with the dorky crowds, though I couldn't call her a dork. Dorks looked kind of bad, and she never had a hair out of place. She wasn't shy, really. Just... aloof. Above it all.

I watched her as the minister pointed at little details in this photo. Cora was as unmoving as marble—as if the perfect child would just expect to have a really talented mother. And don't all artistic geniuses end up addicted to something and reclusive? It was forgivable. I just wished I had Cora's... *dignity.* Unless I thought about it, I spent every minute of the past three days slumped like an overgrown bear.

Rain was turning ever so slowly to look back at me. I could read her lips. *Are you okay?*

I nodded.

I love you.

Love you, too. I wished she were sitting back here so I could smell her hair and punch her knee, and she could punch mine, and maybe I wouldn't feel so... detached... numbed... paralyzed.

"And this photo is a little harder to take, but it's a truth Aleese felt the need to share." The minister put down the black-and-white photo and held up a huge colored one. An audible groan lasted only a second, but a few disgusted gasps echoed.

This giant photo was of a black man. I didn't know what country it was taken in, but he was dressed in nothing but a pair of cheap pants without a belt, and lying on muddy ground. It reminded me of *Black Hawk Down,* this horrifying movie I'd seen about Mogadishu with Dobbins and Moran. The barrel of a rifle lay over the dead man's palm. He was riddled with bullet holes, but his eyes and mouth were wide open. A line of blood ran from his mouth into his ear. I didn't know which was worse, that an expression of horror had lingered after death, or that part of his intestine had popped through his pants and lay on top of his stomach.

I remembered the recruiter at school from West Point. My girlfriend Myra was pissed at me when I didn't fall all over the guy. My thought of him tied in so well with this picture: *What, you think I would ever want to pick up a gun and stick it in somebody's guts and fire? You got the wrong person, bud.* It was a disgusting picture, and I wondered if the minister hadn't pushed it way over the top by showing it here. But then again, it made me want to slap the photographer on the back and shout, "Good one!" I studied the dead man's eyes, and for whatever reason, wondered, *Did he see Saint Stephen?*

I looked up at the rafters again. It was the wrong thing to do, because the picture boiled over inside of me, bringing me into that some-other-world I felt half in, and my head started pounding from the kind of garbage that could get me all upset, all screaming on the inside... *No, no more wars, sickness, death...*

no more poverty, burnings at the stake, tortures, murders, hate... Why is this world so gross? That's why I only let myself get half into things before wanting to chill out at home again. If you got too close, you didn't just feel the good stuff, you felt the bloody, fly-eaten leftovers of whatever violence made the news, and you ended up doing things like wanting to scream.

It just flew out of me. Bawling, not screaming, thank god, but it was loud, and it brought up flashes of standing in my mother's hospital room just after she died. They wiped the blood off before I got there, but they forgot to shut her eyes. Scott shut them.

He was passing me a tissue, then three. The minister stopped, and I was all, *Dude, will you shut up? How can you be selfish enough to stop a service? How can you come apart, and the lady's own daughter has more self-control?*

A shadow moved from the front row, and Rain dropped beside me. Cora had not moved a muscle, not even deserted like that—humiliated, because I couldn't shut up.

The minister was speaking again, and I was trying to listen, but at first I could only hear Rain whispering.

"Hey, bud... make it through this..." She had a hold of my face in that way Mom used to, pulling at my cheeks with both hands when she wanted to make a point.

Then I heard Scott whispering, "Get your face out of his. You got germs... never good with that sort of photo."

This sick feeling in my stomach went a little crazy, turning hot, then cold, then sending icy streams to my head and down my arms. I wondered if Scott's lecture on germs had come too late. It felt like that twenty-four-hour flu thing you get maybe every couple of years, that hits you like a brick, flattens you for a day, and then disappears again. But this one was more like three bricks. *You're not sick; your stomach is just upset over that sickening picture. It will go away. You don't have what Mom had.*

I turned my face up to the rafters and repeated all that maybe five times, but when these chills broke like a waterfall, I stopped praying. The only words in my head were *Something's wrong. Something horrible.*

ELEVEN

SHAHZAD HAMDANI
TUESDAY, MARCH 5, 2002
2:45 A.M. KARACHI TIME

THE NIGHT AIR is thick. I cannot sleep but only stare at the silhouetted clump of my packed bags. We leave for the airport at seven thirty. This thing is happening so very fast. I know the seriousness of USIC's need, and I don't begrudge them the desire to put someone very multilingual in the Trinitron café quickly. But I fear I will lose more than I will gain, ironically, if I make this trip.

Hodji has been lecturing me for three days on what it will be like. "In America, the intelligence agents play on a team. You stay on your base. You have to do as you're told and not ask questions. They will not share things with you like Roger and I sometimes do." Of course I understand the American baseball and playing your particular base. But I also wonder what will happen if I see leads that I could chase for them.... Will they let me do it? Will they tell someone else to do it, and I will never know the outcomes of my own accomplishments?

My time is all but gone for working freely. I get out of bed, tiptoe around my bags, and head silently across Aunt Hamera's garden over to the café. I can see my computer blinking in the dark as I put the key into the lock. I rarely shut down. For some reason, it makes my asthma worse to see my screen dark and not reaching out to the world at large. Hodji says it is a form of claustrophobia. He jokingly calls it in English "computero-phobia."

I glance down the street to the boardinghouse before entering the café. A light is on in the last second-floor window—in the room Hodji had taken for his fake job as a "traveling salesman of paper products." Last night he went to Karachi to take care of business. Possibly he was checking in with other v-spies.

The light means he came back in the night—he plans to accompany me to America—and he is not sleeping, either. I suppose his other v-spies didn't turn up enough to inspire him to relax. I switch on the light in Uncle's office, knowing Hodji will see it. Perhaps he would like to come and see my new program jump through many hoops.

And Roger's words, calling the extremists' program a "double whammy," have been in my heart since he said them. I have been counterprogramming, finding ways to combat a translating and a disappearing chatter program.

First, I have pirated many obscure translation programs and have worked them into my search engines. Hence, my search programs will hopefully hunt for keywords like "Colony One" in two dozen more Indo-European languages.

And last night I finished an auto-search component that will search chat rooms constantly instead of manually—even as I sleep. It should automatically script any chatter that contains my keywords in any of those languages.

I approach my terminal anxiously, as if it contains a snake. And what do my eyes behold but a wonderful sight: The whole top half of the screen is filled with alerts, at least nine of them, looking like this:

ALERT: VaporStrike is Online: www.trinitrononline.com/chat/hodgpog-hall/%729.36.24%/ Enter2:07am Exit2:27am.
ALERT: PiousKnight is Online: www.cheezyfriez.com/chat/nonames-hall/%617.92.18%/ Enter2:22am Exit2:28am.

I glance joyfully down the list, reasoning quickly that VaporStrike has been online twice with Omar0324 and once with their other extremist comrade, PiousKnight. And Omar0324 has been on once with several other unknown log-ins, and these I might be able to trace.

I click tentatively, remembering Uncle's favorite saying: *Life is never so easy.* The text file that was supposed to copy the chatter is empty. This can only mean that their chatter has disappeared before my program found them.

The café door opens, ringing Uncle's cowbells and making me jump.

"What are you doing? You're supposed to be getting your beauty rest. How's your asthma?" Hodji's voice rings too loudly for this hour. "Ready to get rid of it for good?"

I have more pressing priorities. I go to the second ALERT link, and find that again I have a chat link but no scripted chatter.

"You oughtn't wear that cologne," I mutter against my disappointment. "Smells too expensive."

"It's just ordinary Old Spice. You can buy it anywhere."

"Smells American."

"Well, that's surely not the same as expensive. You're offending the French and the Italians. What else are you doing?"

I explain my success in devising alerts and my failure in scripting chatter. It makes him stare for a moment. "Shahzad. You found these guys chatting while you were sleeping? *Are you serious?* You could sell that program for a million bucks in America just the way it is."

My chest rattles when I sigh. "You Americans... always thinking about money."

"No, thinking about *opportunity*." He points to my last ALERT. "Look at this one. It has no exit time yet."

I click on it quickly, as it states that VaporStrike is online with Omar0324 in an Arabic chat room.

VaporStrike and Omar are idling, and I scroll up in their chatter to see many white blanks, though I do see again the rift in their erasing-chatter program: It leaves their names but only erases what they say. If I cannot catch them while chatting, I will at least know when they are up to their tricks.

Hodji goes to make coffee, and I drum my fingers on the keypad, thinking I will feel much better when I have my two cups. I have been drinking coffee since age nine, as it is the best thing around here for asthma. It will wake my brain. I am not prepared to see this phenomenon unfold on-screen, but suddenly, here it is:

Omar0324: You may ask your questions. I am much obliged to finally discuss this with you at liberty.

VaporStrike: Will local doctors figure out the contents of Red Vinegar?

My neck snaps at VaporStrike's frankness, which is both offensive and elating. They must feel very confident with this new program.

Omar0324: You give the medical community too much credit, my friend. They will not figure it out this year—or next.

VaporStrike: How can you be so certain?

Omar0324: Red Vinegar is not a known biochemical agent. It is a mutation. Even the CDC has not ever seen it before.

I am too stunned to say *bingo!* I don't realize at first that I am reading Sindhi, one of the Indian languages. And before I can wheeze, the text is gone.

"Hodji!" I call. "Come quick!"

As he gallops to me, I spit out quickly, "Red Vinegar is not a natural agent of bioterror, but a mutation of something the CDC knows. These terrorists think the CDC would not recognize it."

I don't have time to script the chatter before it disappears. But here comes more.

VaporStrike: I don't understand your sciences, nor do I want to. I did think, however, that we would see more deaths in March, being that the affluent use more water, washing sometimes several times a day.

Omar0324: If you see more deaths in March, it will be because of weak immune systems, not because of compulsive scrubbing. You can rub Red Vinegar in your eyes, mix it with soap, and wash your hands in it. Your little cuts and pimples are safe. You have to drink it—glass by glass—over many weeks.

I give this news to Hodji while he sits at a terminal beside mine, muttering, "'*You have to drink it... glass by glass...*' That's disgusting. We need to write it if we can't script it."

But I am busy watching and verbally translating languages in which I have many gaps, all off the top of my head. Hodji rushes to switch on another terminal and type. Omar and VaporStrike are translating their little secrets however they wish—and probably the recipient translates it again if he can't understand what is sent. With some multilingual translation program only a click away, they are like children with a big box of crayons.

I see fresh chatter fly up in Pashto, a primary language of Afghanistan.

Omar0324: Red Vinegar weakens the immunity system. The cause of death is usually other infections. Its only signature is the weakening of tissue such as that found in blood vessels. Through fluctuating fevers over many weeks or months, it turns veins and arteries to overcooked egg noodles. They burst, rip, clog, causing stroke, clots, aneurysms...

I repeat the rest as best I can, and Hodji is typing furiously. He exclaims, "Maybe it's a hoax."

We have discussed this possibility many times, and this chatter brings the idea back again. Most secret chatter is posted by philosophic extremists, not scientists. They are well versed in bomb making and violent schemes of bloodshed, but this talk of mutated agents of bioterror is scientifically based. They say it is nothing USIC has ever seen before.

"Spit it out!" Hodji nudges at me in excitement as a new post flies up.

"It's Punjabi," I say in my native tongue, which allows me to recite it easily.

VaporStrike: Will you tell us if any local newspaper implies the deaths are not natural, so we can download the articles?

So...Omar has access to local newspapers. I announce to Hodji that we now have more proof that Omar is living near Colony One, wherever it is. Omar's answer is even more critical.

Omar0324: Whatever appears in the newspaper will be strange and unintelligible. USIC is looking for a poisoned water supply. That we could strike at a vein or a smaller portion and not infect a whole city is not in their thinking.

I stammer in confusion, "They've hit...a street. A...neighborhood. One side of a mountain or a part of a village...just a part—"

"How in the hell is that possible?" Hodji asks.

"They do not say."

Hodji mutters again that it's a hoax.

"But who would go to all this trouble to translate and erase hoaxes?" I point out, and he does not answer. Anything is possible, but I do not want to think I have been chasing down a hoax for four months.

Who is this Omar? *Where* is Omar? I feel we will have the location of Colony One if we can find this elusive player. Is he a businessman? A scientist? A doctor gone mad? On which continent?

Omar and VaporStrike are idling.

"Did Roger find any place yet where two women have died of brain aneurysms?"

"Yes, several." Hodji nods. "But it's a big world out there. I'll see if I can get cell reception and call him... He needs to know about this chatter, pronto."

Hodji dials a three-digit number that will put him through to Roger anywhere on the globe, if it is a good night for cell reception over my village.

"Where is he?" I ask.

"You don't need to know that," Hodji answers, to my annoyance. "We have to practice being in America now. You can't ask questions on your new squad and expect to get an answer."

"But..." I feel my chest tighten with panic. "This says Red Vinegar is very real and very dangerous, and it would be hard to detect. He may be drinking it, for all we know—"

"Not your problem," he mutters, refusing to look at me.

"Shall I search for agents of bioterror that are known to be most easily mutated?"

He waves the phone in the air, as that sometimes helps find reception. "I think the CDC can handle that... once Roger gets ahold of them."

"But *I* want to know."

"Ringy dingy," he says with relief and puts the phone to his ear. "Then, search now, because I can't promise what they'll let you do in America— Roger? It's me. Turn on your e-mail...I don't care what meeting you're in. We've got a red-hot *bingo*."

Both Omar and VaporStrike log off suddenly, and I wonder if it is because I have been in there as an invisible log-in, which means I am not entirely invisible. I do not show up as a log-in in the chat room, but if they are cautious, they will see "number of guests: 3" when they are the only two present.

Hodji sees them leave and turns to his screen, rubbing his eyes. He did not come here with his contact lenses, I suppose. "We have to tell Roger what we got. He says he can't get to his secured e-mail for a couple of hours."

I study Hodji's scramble of notes. "Red Vinegar is a mutation of a biochemical agent...you cannot be harmed by washing in it—you have to drink it. We have that it will weaken the immune system, and often other germs are the cause of death."

It is hard to think, as Hodji is repeating all this approximately two words behind me the whole time. "Red Vinegar, it weakens veins and arteries, turning them to..." I hunt for Omar's exact words. "...to overcooked egg noodles. It causes strokes and aneurysms."

I have no more memory space available in my head, and his notes, in English, are too full of typos. Hodji sticks his face right up to the screen. "We have that only a small piece of Colony One was hit, not its entire water supply. We have no clue how they did that, but we know Omar lives nearby. This is a gold mine."

I just sit dumbly, watching the printer kick and begin to print out all that he has typed. "Do you want a fax or an e-mail?"

Hodji asks, and then says, "Good, because the fax machine works as well as the cars, telephones, and ATMs in this god-forsaken village."

I suppose that means Roger wants an e-mail. I translate Hodji's notes to Arabic so that I can fill in the sentences correctly and not fill my head with English on top of all these other languages. While they take wild guesses at potential biochemical agents, I wonder with sudden hope if this major *bingo* means I can continue working from Pakistan.

Hodji puts his cell phone back in his pocket finally, and I ask as much.

He does not look enthusiastic. "Look, what we just went through, kid. You can use the intranet structure at Trinitron to your advantage, maybe. You can cache the screen faster than you could script the chatter...and using the intranet, they won't have any of the usual signs that someone might be watching."

My father went to America and died, and I will get my foot in some trap as well.

I try telling myself I will be much safer in America than in a small village on the outskirts of Karachi. I tell myself that Roger is in Africa because he's traced the two dead women to an African community, and not to the shores of the land my father loved. I try. But there is a sinking feeling inside my ribs. It has to do with how it is late in Africa, and even important people need to sleep. Yet Hodji just interrupted Roger in the middle of a meeting. It is likely that Roger is not in Africa....

"Let's just say...wherever Roger is, you helped put him there. Okay?" Hodji mutters anxiously as I express my anxieties one final time. "You've done a great job for us here, Shahzad. All good things have to change."

"Can I call you? Once in a while?" I ask. I do not like his silence, how suddenly he seems overwhelmed in something unspeakable, something relevant to his safety and my safety and the security of operations. He looks like he does when he speaks of Twain. Only now, he is saying nothing and looking at me.

I put my fingers to the keypad. I will download any articles I can find on agents of bioterror that have been successfully mutated to unrecognizable forms. I want to use my final hours wisely and not get caught up in sentimentality.

However, I want to save an hour for myself—to walk the beach at dawn, gaze at the Arabian Sea, and think of my carefree boyhood one last time. Perhaps then I will feel more ready to put my feet on the soil where my family died.

TWELVE

CORA HOLMAN
MONDAY, MARCH 4, 2002
4:10 P.M.

I FOLDED MY ARMS across my woolly sweater as I paced into my living room and tried rubbing the chills out. The sweater was never worn before. It had been one of Oma's last gifts before she realized I no longer liked to wear oversized clothing. Despite the turtleneck beneath, the wool itched, and the rubbing didn't stop my teeth from chattering. This relapse of flu came over me during Aleese's service, about the time Reverend McNaughton was showing off her photographs. And while it hit me quickly and furiously, I could only think that Scott Eberman sat three rows behind me, and it was my solemn duty not to give him anything else to worry about. I don't think I let myself move a muscle until the service had ended.

Now I stared out my living room window, maybe half an hour after the Blumbergs dropped me off. Cars were parked all the way to the corner. Every spot was taken, except the one where the huge puddle spread outward in front of my house.

All the people were mourners. But they were all down at the Ebermans'.

Are you proud of yourself? Congratulations. You're alone again... and sick.

I knew I had sent out a thousand little "messages" at the service to those who wanted to come here afterward—thank you, but no thank you. It had all been an autopilot routine, easy as crossing my legs, and at the moment, autopilot was all I'd had.

A couple that had just parked at the corner walked by on the other side of the street in nothing but light sweaters. *It's like summer out there. What's wrong with my body? What in hell killed Aleese?*

All my intense staring was not helping my headache, and I moved toward the kitchen. On the windowsill, I saw the sample packet of Tylenol the paramedic had left with me four nights ago. I had put it there when cleaning, not really having a place for medicine. Oma and I simply never took any. Aleese always referred to her morphine as a "cure-all," and anything of lesser strength as "a fart in a windstorm."

I tore open the packet and swallowed the Tylenol with a large glass of water from the spigot, then went more slowly to the living room. Reverend McNaughton had given me the photos he'd shown at the service. I had perched them on the couch in the same place where Aleese had lain, without really thinking about what I was doing. The little child stared soulfully at me... *Stunning shot. Where did Aleese get her nerve—to love this strange child enough to capture her aura and immortalize it, while I was forever the brat? Was I born with cloven hooves?*

The eyes of the dead foot soldier seemed more focused on

Aleese than me—toward heaven. My amateur photographer's mind couldn't help seeing the situation needed to take this photo. My mother had run through some third world battleground. She had stopped by this corpse, perhaps many others, and she studied this one long enough to relive the man's last moments. She smelled the blood, heard the buzzing flies, maybe even endangered her life by not running. But she had felt instinctively for the sun's angles, moved until they were across the corpse's face, raised the camera, and focused. *She probably bent over with one foot on either side of this corpse's left knee. The smell must have been unbearable.*

She had loved this dead man, too. That she couldn't love me was both ludicrous and factual, and the only answers drifted into my mind in the form of a box full of videotapes—somewhere in the crawl space or the attic.

I found the box fifteen minutes later, having crawled all the way to the back of Aleese's closet, which covered the length of the room. I staggered back to the living room and dropped it with a thud, though I knew it would be anywhere from fifteen days to fifteen years before I could look at these tapes. I sensed some deep, black horror built into what secrets they held. And I didn't know what had possessed me to drag the box out while my head was splitting. I pressed my palms to my temples as the pain grew worse, and I stumbled to the window again, reaching out for the glass.

Oma had died in the street. Aleese made her Profound Statement of the Year later that night, and now it rushed through my head like a hissing snake: *"Even the steeliest nerves will flail for a hand to grab on to when they sense death coming. That's why she ran outside."*

Three blurry figures were coming around the corner, walking slowly, going to the Ebermans', surely. I pressed my palm hard on the cold glass, feeling the urge to break through it and yell.

But when the three got close, I stepped backward out of view. I stared from behind the drape as the Eberman brothers and Rain walked slowly toward my house, on the far side of the street. They must have walked home from the service—getting some air or relief from the crowds in the Eberman house. Rain had her shoes in her hand and walked along in black stockings that were run badly. *Her father probably made her wear a dress to my service... heels hurt her feet... I'm an annoying nuisance... Almost warm enough for bare feet, thank god...*

Owen walked in the middle, his arms around their shoulders, his face looking down. He was bent over in something different from anguish. *Physical pain?* My eyes went to Scott, his firm hand on his brother's shoulder, his determined jaw working up words obviously meant to assure him of something. A part of me wanted to run out there to get some of that reassurance, also.

But if I ran outside, I would *die in the street,* too. I backed away and eased down in Oma's TV chair, somehow deciding that it was more important to make a liar out of my mother. If I died in the chair, Oma would come for me, and maybe Jeremy Brandruff Ireland would be there, all smiles, saying, "Hello there, Cora. I'm your father..."

THIRTEEN

OWEN EBERMAN
MONDAY, MARCH 4, 2002
4:22 P.M.

THE WALK FROM the service didn't clear my head, and I couldn't wait to be home and get comatose under a blanket. I guess that catching some flu less than a day before my mother's own funeral ought to have made me insane, but it only made my numbness worse. I remembered hearing Mr. Steckerman talk sometimes about when his wife died. He would say, "My grief was *complete,*" and I never really knew what that meant until now. It means that you could get smacked by a truck, or your house could burn down, and you couldn't possibly feel any more messed up. Whether I felt like throwing up or just slightly poisoned all over, or whether the funeral was tomorrow or in an hour—none of that mattered.

Even being slammed with a nasty reality—I probably had what my mom had—didn't make me feel any worse. It seemed like I had one foot in an old world and one foot in a new, as we walked past Cora's house, and I wondered out loud, "Am I going to die, too?"

Rain's laugh was part of the old world, where nobody dies around here except of old age and car accidents. Her reminder that she'd had an on-and-off battle with this flu and she was still cruising around town—that made me nod. *Mom died of a strange flu because she was run-down and overworked. Rain and I are in the prime of our health.*

With the exception of where the huge puddle was in front of the Holmans', the rest of the street was lined with cars. Most were familiar, and the owners of them were probably at my house. There had been at least fifteen people there since about twenty minutes after Mom passed away—to make us feel better, and to make each other feel better, *even when we weren't there.* If you think I tend to be a recluse when I'm well, you haven't seen me when I'm sick. I stopped dead in my tracks, then pulled Scott and Rain behind the Endicotts' hedges.

Rain read my mind. "Just smile and say hi, and you'll be in your room with the door shut before you know it."

She was rubbing my arm to encourage me, but with chills it felt like thorns on my skin, and it shot more visions into my head of being accosted by ladies trying to feel my forehead and forcing me to eat this or drink that, all in my face with forks and spoons. I held on to my gut as an imagined plateful of lasagna turned to hairy spiders and cockroaches.

Now my grief was complete. "I can't," I said.

"You got a headache?" Scott asked. He'd already told me that people in shock run fevers, and that he'd expected me to feel like hurling after seeing that bloody foot soldier in the photo. I'm not a blood person. But still, he was making me jumpy.

"No! But one might start if I have to sit with a thousand people and fake normal and eat casserole, and..." I stopped, realizing how I sounded. "What is wrong with me? Why can't I just feel normal in a crowd of nice people who are only trying to help?"

Scott mumbled something about no one liking to be around people when they felt sick. But he'd already told me to savor each moment of our house being full of people, because in about a week, this level of compassion would be gone, and we'd be expected to get a grip.

Rain tugged on my arm, and it caused an "equal and opposite reaction," according to Newton's laws of motion, and I jerked away from her and started walking back up the street.

She caught up. "Where are you going?"

I halted briefly, staring at Cora Holman's house, and that's when I knew I was having a nervous breakdown, the real thing. *The place looked good, inviting.* The fact that the grass was mostly weeds and bald patches with no shrubs, and the house was peeling paint—it helped. The puddle out front almost cordoned it off from the rest of the street, and the place seemed to be calling my name: *Welcome! Come be where it's quiet!*

The girl was aloof, but I didn't think she had it in her to be nasty. She would let me sit in the quiet and be sad with her, and, definitely, she would not impose food and drinks on my baking flesh.

But then, my sanity popped up—or maybe I should call it my small streak of normalcy. I'd had long talks with Rain about my abnormal tendencies, like some days wishing I were home-schooled. She also heard me confess to saying silent prayers before anything and everything—from the top of a football game, to the end of the evening news, with all its murdered, convicted, sentenced, and dying people. In one junior psych assignment, I read about some psychologist guy blathering on about people like me having a "God complex."

Usually, Rain's answer was that I was perfectly normal and to quit worrying about myself, and every once in a while she said something that totally was outstanding. Like before this one college interview, she said without thinking, "Just avoid all your natural instincts and you'll do fine!"

"Come on. You want to go see Cora?" Scott asked.

I walked backward. "No! Why would I want to see Cora?"

I plopped down behind the Endicotts' hedges, trying to ignore my cold sweats. Rain's stockings were now full of holes, because she'd walked from the church with her heeled shoes in her hand. She was going to catch her death.

"This is crazy," I muttered. "I am full-throttle nuts."

"Will you cut yourself a break, please? Whatever you think this week—this month—it's all right," she said.

A sigh sounded above Scott's suede lace-up shoes that he almost never wore. "I always thought the best thing about getting out of high school would be going off to college and playing football. Well, that didn't happen, but it's okay. Because there's something even better about getting out of high school. You quit giving a shit what other people think. You guys sit here, and while you're being utterly petrified of Little Miss Perfect, I will go make sure she is all right."

He strolled across the street, tried to jump the puddle, and missed, cursing over one soggy suede shoe. But then he just knocked on Cora Holman's door. After a minute, she still hadn't answered, so he opened the door, stepped right in, then closed it behind him. Rain and I gawked at each other, and I felt as dumb as she looked.

FOURTEEN

SCOTT EBERMAN
MONDAY, MARCH 4, 2002
4:37 P.M.

TRUTHFULLY, I WASN'T thrilled about trying another can-opener routine on Cora Holman. I was too worried about Owen. I kept telling myself his queasiness and fever could be stress, though I found that hard to believe.

But I forced myself up to the door with the thoughts that were keeping me going lately—keep checking on Rain, make it a point to check on Cora, read all my CDC memos, finally, and figure out what had really happened to Mom.

I didn't want to put off checking on Cora. As I had said good-bye to her at the altar, her please-leave-me-alone shtick had almost lacked the please part. I had gone to hug her, but she had her left hand on my shoulder and her right hand stuck out to me. So, I shook hands and listened to her overly gracious prattle about how nice it was for us to come. She turned back to the minister without giving me a chance to say more than "See you tomorrow."

Owen and Rain had a point: The girl was a prickly pear, coated over with the gleam of magic manners—even when she was sick. My squad doesn't call me Mr. Observant for nothing.

She let a few people hug her *after* me. She didn't want *me* hugging her, probably realizing the too-much-body-heat would register with me. It had registered just from shaking her hand and looking into her glassy eyes.

I could see her plainly through the window, curled up in a chair beyond the kitchen. I had no idea why she didn't respond to my loud knocking, but the door opened easily.

Halfway through the kitchen, I got scared. She was looking right at me, almost through me, and it's not like I expect every person in town to know my name, but I sort of remembered her doing the underclassman doe-eyed look in my general direction at a lot of football games. So, I was a little suspicious of a serious problem when she looked me dead in the eye and said, "Jeremy?"

FIFTEEN

CORA HOLMAN
MONDAY, MARCH 4, 2002
4:39 P.M.

JEREMY IRELAND APPEARED with a face so familiar, it was like I had known him for years. So, transferring the correct name of Scott Eberman to it flung me back to reality with gasps. . . . *I must have called to him out there on the sidewalk in some psychotic moment that I can't remember. How could I do that to him?*

"Cora?" I realized it was the second time he called my name, so I tried to snap to, but I could only sit up slowly and glance at my fingers that, clutching a tissue, refused to let go of the bottom of his jacket, too. "Who's Jeremy? Is that someone I can get for you?"

"No, he's dead." An awful silence swayed in the reverb of my truth. Six of Scott Eberman became four.

"What are you doing sitting here by yourself? Huh? Don't you know that's not good for you?" It was a comforting tone, like Oma's: *"Awww, skinned knees? Let's get them cleaned up."*

"I'm... sorry," I stammered, still thinking I had called to him.

"Sorry for what? Yeesh. After we get you better, we're going to find you a support group. One of those twelve-step things for the, uh, victims."

He yanked on his jacket until I let go, then retrieved a dinette chair, spun it around in front of me, and plopped into it with his hands in his jacket pockets. He stared at my face, then my shoulders.

"Relax. It's just me. Do you always sit like that?"

It's just me... I would have laughed incredulously if I hadn't been pulling from a couple years back to remember how to slouch. It only made me more uncomfortable, more out of breath, so I simply hung my head between us like a puppy dog hoping to get petted.

"Cora Holman, I would love to hug you," he said. "If anyone needs hugging, it's you. But I'm in a quandary here. I'm a paramedic, and I can imagine germ behavior most people couldn't conceive of, so... we're going to be really practical—"

He reached around the tissue for my wrist, rambling about wishing he had gloves. I thought he was checking my pulse, and maybe he had been, but then he was shaking my wrist, telling me to drop the tissue. I had blown my nose into it, so I shook my head.

"... just want to see if we have Christmas colors..."

He put some strange pressure on my wrist that made my fingers open. He pulled a pen out of his pocket and poked the tissue open on the floor rather than touching it himself. The thought roared through me: *I have something serious, I have something contagious, or he wouldn't be acting like this. What killed Aleese?*

A few tears erupted. "Um, what's Christmas colors?"

"Red and green." He stared downward, obviously not bothered by my outburst or my tissues. "But all you have is white. White is good. May all your Christmases be white."

He reached to the box of tissues and handed me another. Then he sat there watching me, his hands stuffed in his pockets again.

"So. What hurts?"

I pointed a shaky finger to my eye.

"Headache?" He reached for my eye, then thought the better of it, putting his hands back in his pockets.

"Yes."

"Bad?"

All this crying actually seemed to have cut the pain way down—or maybe it was the relief of human company. It had been years since I'd been asked to describe something bothering me. I wasn't quite sure what *bad* was, whether I qualified...

"*Bad?*" He asked louder, as if it was important for me to confess.

"Yes, but...I took Tylenol. About twenty minutes ago. Maybe it's starting to help some."

He put his hands up emphatically, like he wanted to pull my face up to his to say something important, but he opted to drum on his knees instead.

"Can I ask for a favor?" he said.

"Sure."

"My brother's outside. Can I bring him in here?"

"Sure..." But my eyes rolled as I went through wrenching visions of trying to hold a conversation. "Truthfully, I don't want to see anyone right now—"

"Neither does he. He's sick, too." Despite Scott's attempt at a casual expression, I saw the fuming hells behind his eyes.

"I've got about fifty people in my house right now for him to contaminate, if Rain hasn't already done so. She's with him. I'd like to bring her in, too."

My eyes flew around. My three-day cleaning job, which had looked so spic-and-span this morning, suddenly showed all its flaws. I hadn't cleaned the windows...Aleese's box of videos was in the middle of the floor.

"Cora, don't stress out. You know how badly you don't want to talk to people right now? Trust me: You'll be in there with the champ. I'll just bring Owen in, and he can lie on the couch while I run down to my house and see if Dr. O'Dell or Tom Hennessey, my boss, is in there and can come look at you guys. I'll tell Rain to keep quiet for once."

And before I could object, he was out the door again. I sat there blinking, relieved that this headache actually did seem better, enough so that I wouldn't be moaning aloud. I knew my heart ought to be slamming—*Rain Steckerman and Owen Eberman in my house?* But the overwhelmed look on Scott's face melted it down to mush. *He's too young for all this...his mother is not even buried yet*...and yet I sensed it kept him sane somehow, this looking out for the sick. Maybe it was good that I hadn't argued.

Owen appeared in the doorway, then Rain, then Scott, and I could sense Owen's anxiety in his huge, stiffened frame. It flared from his blue eyes, but with something else...*relief?*

"Cora, thank you very much," he said, reminding me of Prince William taking the flowers from strangers after his mother, Princess Diana, passed away. It was sincere but awkward, wrapped in grief, that a thoughtful person wouldn't want to spew all over strangers.

"You got one of those bad headaches?" Rain asked, drawing near to me in concern.

I stonewalled her, again trying to decide what "bad" meant.

"I've had two," she went right on. "You feel like you're gonna die, but then it starts going away faster than other headaches I've had. Very, very weird headaches."

"Yes. Very weird." I don't know what drove me to my feet, except that I felt like I ought to do something. "May I get you anything? Would you like tea? Ice water?"

"How about a pair of socks?"

Rain reached up under her skirt and stepped out of her badly run stockings right in front of Owen. She stretched and cracked her toes. Owen didn't seem to notice, and when my eyes met hers, her fingers flew to her lips as if she had done something wrong.

I knew I occasionally had this effect on people. With all my trying not to be like Aleese, I had shot myself in the foot. I made people my age uncomfortable. Rain would have asked my questions entirely differently—*You guys want soda?*—instead of my prissy little tea speech. But it was too late now, so I made my way to the laundry room. I didn't wear sweat socks, but figured Rain would be happiest in a pair of Aleese's that I had just bleached and washed and, fortunately, had not yet sent to Goodwill.

Scott had visited the bedrooms and pulled pillows off my bed. He tossed one to each of them and tossed mine on Oma's chair. He had moved Aleese's pictures over to the fireplace mantel, and Owen was flopping down in her place on the couch.

With a finger still pointed at me, Scott said to them, "Don't let her get you anything. Don't let her be polite. Everybody, go to sleep. I'll be back."

He stepped over Rain, who sat on the floor with a pillow in her lap, and as if his first advice would be lost on her, he said, "You keep quiet."

And he was gone.

I slithered into the chair and squashed the pillow into my neck slowly, not wanting to shut my eyes for fear of looking rude, but not wanting to be the first to speak. Scott surely knew his brother well. Owen said nothing. I could only see the top of his head over the pillow, but I assumed he hadn't fallen asleep that fast.

"You guys want to watch cartoons?" Rain crawled on all fours to Aleese's television set, turned it on, and pressed the channel button until cartoons appeared. I hadn't watched cartoons in years and didn't recognize the characters.

My head still hurt enough to keep me from sleeping, so I just lay perfectly still, stewing in my little hells, the worst of which was that they had found me here alone. Surely, there was no other way to find me, but at the strangest times I could get an all-too-weird outsider's sense of my so-called life. *Cora, you're like the Grinch who stole Christmas: all by yourself at the most inappropriate times.*

The thought could have brought on sleep, just to escape it. But it was like an invisible presence kept shaking my shoulder—maybe Oma, maybe Aleese or my father—maybe five thousand dead souls. Maybe the earth rumbled so far down that the surface stayed silent. I just felt like a megatsunami rolling across the Atlantic, still far from shore but about to make impact with places the ocean had never seen.

If that sounds weird, I cannot tell you how weird it felt to see Owen Eberman's head sticking up from Aleese's usual place on the couch, while Rain Steckerman sat in Aleese's white sweat socks and a black dress. We sat and watched some tiny cartoon kid in huge glasses fight a bad guy trying to take over the whole world. I watched Owen and Rain turn almost to silhouette as the sun dropped low outside.

SIXTEEN

SCOTT EBERMAN
MONDAY, MARCH 4, 2002
5:02 P.M.

I SPOTTED DR. O'DELL right off. He was standing just inside our kitchen talking to Mr. Glenn, an attorney buddy of Mom's. But as I made my way through the living room, I was stopped by neighbors, coworkers, my two entrepreneur uncles who had flown down from New York—they all wanted to hug me. It brought me to life.

But with the idle chitchat, I sensed that everyone thought my mom's and Aleese Holman's similar deaths were a freaky coincidence—and I was not about to tell them otherwise. Until I had some idea what had made this handful of people sick, I couldn't see the point in scaring them half to death. While I chatted it up and lied about where Owen was, I didn't see a single raw nose, hear a single cough, or see a single hand rub a single sore gut. Nobody even sneezed, for Christ's sake.

I finally pulled Dr. O'Dell into the kitchen.

"How are you doing?" he asked.

"I'm okay. My brother's not." I watched him raise his eyebrows, and I supposed my tenderhearted brother might give the impression of needing a Valium. I leaned close. "He's got Mom's flu. And the Holman girl had a relapse this afternoon."

He groaned quietly. "Symptoms?"

"Same as Mom's, only they're split up right now. Owen's got the stomach-fever part. Cora Holman has the fever and sinus headache. And Rain Steckerman's had it all, though it's reduced to a stuffed nose right now."

While he searched his head for a response, I asked, "Have you had any more patients in your office complaining of a flu that couldn't make up its mind between sinus or intestines?"

He shook his head. "Believe me. I've got my eyes wide open for something unusual like that. So does Doug Godfrey, so does..." He named four or five family doctors associated with the hospital. "Considering it's flu season, I've seen very little flu, what with the warm weather."

"Yeah, yeah, yeah..." I rubbed the bridge of my nose in frustration.

He gave the predictable response: "Unless one of these kids exhibits a few symptoms we wouldn't assess as common flu, I don't think we have enough to hospitalize them. We'd have to hear something definitive from the CDC first. That'll be a week from today. Who knows? Maybe they'll all be better by then, Scott."

"Or maybe they'll be worse."

He raised and lowered his eyebrows. "Where are they?"

"Down at Cora Holman's house. Whatever it is they have, if

it's the least bit airborne, I didn't want to risk having Owen down here breathing on everyone."

"I figured you'd have them cordoned off somewhere." He squeezed my arm with sympathy and a sad grin. "That might be the best place for them, given what germs can be around an emergency room this time of year, and I *know* I don't have enough to get them quarantined. How about if I ask Doug Godfrey to stop by the Holman place and get some blood samples and anything else he feels is relevant?"

"Why not?" I muttered. Maybe an extra blood test or two thrown in for good measure wouldn't turn up "Fever of Unknown Origin."

"I'll call Doug," he said. "He's stitching up a car accident tonight—torn sinus cavity—or he would be here now. But I'll get him to stop over on his way home. You get what you think your brother might need to stay put... We'll keep it between us for the time being. God forbid, but if it's some ferocious new germ, I'll shout how you did your part to keep it contained."

"Thanks," I muttered, though heroics were not what I wanted to be known for. I climbed the stairs to our room and found Bob Dobbins and that whole gaggle of Owen's friends stretched out on the floor and the beds, waiting for him.

"Where's the man? How's Cora Holman?" Adrian Moran asked, lying on my bed.

Lest they blab and the town be thrown into a panic, I just said, "He's lagging along with Rain. Cora Holman is... Cora Holman. What can I say?"

"Did she look like a million dollars, even at her mother's funeral?" Jon Dempsey asked as I stepped over him and Dobbins and yanked off my tie. "I'm telling you, the girl's a statue. She's got no feelings."

"She didn't come apart at the seams, though I don't think she's as frigid as you guys make her out to be."

"She had a lot of friends show up, at least?" Dobbins asked. Bob Dobbins was the one among them who seemed most like Owen—most human in his approach to people—and I detected genuine concern in his voice. Before I could say something, Dempsey cast Dobbins a confused look.

"Who *does* that girl hang out with, anyway?"

Nobody seemed able to answer. I stuck a pair of Owen's sweatpants into a gym bag.

"You know what? Maybe you guys should catch up with Owen tomorrow. He's kinda...you know..." I pretended I was tearing my hair out. I didn't feel I should let them wait around for Owen all night.

I was met with a stony silence I pretended not to notice. My brother wasn't loud or the life of the party, but he was more or less the heart of this group, and they'd probably follow him over a cliff. I went into the bathroom and swiped Owen's toothbrush quickly, and Dobbins almost banged into me on the way out.

"What's up?" he asked. "What can we do? Coach even called off wrestling practice today and tomorrow so we could do for Owen like he would do for us. Don't just, ya know, tell us to leave."

I exhaled an apology. Dobbins had replaced me as running back last year on the football team. He wasn't future Harvard material any more than I was, but he had a piercing eye that let you know he was interested in what you had to say, and he wasn't known for spilling over at the mouth. I pulled him along down the stairs and into the laundry room, shutting the door.

"He's not flipping out, is he?" Dobbins asked.

I shook my head, realizing that would be their first suspicion. "He's just come down with something and...it looks a little like what Mom had, that's all."

"So, where is he?"

"Cora Holman's. She's got it, too."

He let out a groan. "Damn. No rest for the weary. Bet it's not serious, dude. Rain's doing okay?"

"Seems to be."

"And sorry about Dempsey's comment on Cora up there. It just isn't the time, but uh..." Dobbins laughed nervously. "He's always had a case for Cora Holman, so he has to cut up, I guess."

I opened the dryer door, liking how easy it was to pursue this line of talk instead of the more serious ones. I joked, "He likes poised and proper, huh?"

"He likes a challenge. We keep telling him he'll have better luck with a member of the British royal family. As for them having what your moms had..." He gestured awkwardly. "Cora's mom was a drug addict, right? Didn't we used to hear that around school?"

"Yeah."

"And your mom's favorite motto was always 'I sleep fast.' I mean, neither one was probably up for fighting terrible germs, right? So...maybe you shouldn't worry about Owen so much. It's not going to get him like that, Scott, if he's got what your mom had."

"You're probably right, but—"

"But you got your paramedic's imagination working overtime, eh?"

My head dipped in half a nod. "It's on a mountain of memos from the CDC, all these emerging infectious diseases we're supposed to be looking out for while working."

"Yeah? I guess nothing matches what Owen has?"

"I read through a stack of thirty-six of those memos last night, though most of them are far-reaching. Ya know... 'There's this tsetse fly in Marrakech that's been biting Africans in the ass. If it hops a plane to Newark, here's what you might see.'"

"You're gonna make yourself nuts." He laid a hand on my shoulder. "Try to relax, man. You're starting to sound like Mr. Steckerman."

"What's he saying?" I had started to reach in the dryer for a T-shirt, but I froze.

"Nothing—lately. We had that assembly in early January when he went over from the FBI to USIC, and he came to school to talk about terror attacks. It was part of the 9/11 razzmatazz, like, a canned speech that was coming from law enforcement officers all over the country."

"Oh." I must have looked wrung out because he kept patting my shoulder until I bent down to get the stuff out of the dryer.

"He told us that as Americans, we have a responsibility to look after our neighborhoods and make sure there's no suspicious activity going on. But then... he wasn't very good at telling us what we were supposed to be looking for. In fact, he got us all confused by saying that as Americans we shouldn't profile."

I pulled out Owen's favorite Steelers jersey and dumped it in the gym bag. "I guess he can't exactly say to look for a bunch of 9/11 poster boys assembling suspiciously in public places while carrying Zippo lighters and dollar-store box cutters."

A laugh blew out his nose, but he muttered, "Don't, man. Tannis is around here somewhere."

Tannis Halib, son of a Saudi heart surgeon at Saint Ann's, was another of Owen's football buddies. I groped around the dryer in a frustrating hunt for two matching socks.

"Shit, I wouldn't have Steckerman's job for all the tea in China," I beefed. "At least I can say, 'Here's a picture of a goddamn tsetse fly. It's from goddamn Marrakech, and if you see one, you better squash its sorry ass.' So, what did he end up telling you? Hell, I'm open." I shrugged. "Might as well look for terrorists while I'm looking for tsetse flies and every other goddamn thing."

"I don't even remember. Something very vague and... *American.* Look out for people gathering in houses on a regular basis where they didn't used to gather. Something like that."

"Ha! We'd all be under arrest in this house tonight."

I found two Wigwams but one had a hole, so I tossed it over my head and fished for another. "Confusing times, as my boss constantly says," I griped on. "*Strange gatherings in your neighborhood,* huh? With my luck, I would end up busting some new division of the local garden club and every lady in town would be pissed at me."

"I saw a strange gathering," Dobbins went on cheerily. "I didn't say anything about it after Mr. Steckerman's terrorism assembly, though."

"Yeah, maybe you should report it to him," I said politely, eyeing up another sock, which turned out to be a short Wigwam, and my first find was a long. Owen wouldn't care, but I had this thing that socks ought to match up. I'm a realist: I don't believe in the black hole in the dryer.

"But it sounds like profiling," Dobbins went on. "I probably would have said something, but I figured it would sound dumb."

One new Wam in the dryer meant another new Wam also was in the dryer. I pulled out a bedsheet, hoping that would help. It was the sheet I'd stripped off Mom's bed and washed about ten minutes before she told me she wanted to go to the hospital.

The bed was still stripped. It's part of the whole run-over-by-a-truck feeling I'd had for three days—bumping into items that remind you of how alive the person was a week ago. I was barely listening to Dobbins.

"...saw a strange gathering while I was parked in front of Buzby's Liquors over in Surrey. You know that discount shoe place across the street?...dozen or so men were in there after hours, popping champagne and drinking forties. It's like they were toasting something, celebrating something. I took a walk over that way, because Ronnie got to chatting with Mr. Buzby, and he didn't leave me the keys to play the radio."

Ronnie Dobbins was Bob's older brother, and I just nodded.

"I walked over to the shoe store, because it looked like they had Asian revenge on Prada in the window, and I wanted to see how close the match was, ya know? Well, they saw me through the window and slithered into this back room—all dozen or so of them—like they didn't want any window-shoppers gazing directly at them. It's a pretty quiet street outside of Buzby's, and it was like they had a second thought about what they were doing when I went up to the window. And this one guy came to the door, unlocked it, and said to me that they were closed, which I knew. It looked like he wanted to get rid of me. And truth be told? His English was for shit. You know how my dad rags on about that. People come here, and they ought to start learning the language before they start soaking our money. Anyway, I thought it was weird because it wasn't New Year's Eve for two more days. I was at this liquor store with Ronnie to order a keg for our party, so it was probably only the twenty-eighth of December. They were toasting each other, like, celebrating something..."

I rose slowly to my feet, rubbing the back of my head where I'd just banged it on the dryer opening, upon hearing that date. I'm good with details, but sometimes it takes me a while to know *why* I'm good with a particular detail. That December 28 date made me jump, and it was only while straightening up that I remembered Mr. Steckerman quoting some e-mail intelligence chatter from the guys they thought were trying to poison water somewhere: *They will drink in December and die like mangy dogs in April...*

"You saw this in December?" I asked curiously. "A bunch of guys in a storefront, speaking shitty English, and celebrating like they'd just accomplished something?"

"Or won something, or did something, yeah."

I thought about this, half shrugging. It could have been a great sale that netted the owner thousands of bucks. They could have been some religion I didn't know—of which there are a hundred in these parts—that started the new year on a different day than we did. The idea that they were celebrating the finishing up of an act of terror seemed truly out there, though I was a little bit intrigued by the image.

"What do you think they were celebrating?" I asked.

"Hell if I know. I didn't think about it at all... Until Mr. Steckerman said to watch out for unusual gatherings of people. But then I decided it wasn't worth telling."

"Why?"

"Because. I don't know if 'weird' means 'suspicious.' But here's one more thing. They were at a party with all guys. Who leaves the opposite sex out of champagne, unless it's one of those cultures that treat women like shit in the first place?"

I looked down, and a newish, long Wigwam lay flopped over one sneaker. I reached for it, annoyed and half confused. "So. We've got a party in a store. No women. Bad English. And paranoia when you start looking in the window."

"Is that suspicious?" he asked.

Hell if I knew. "Crazy times, Jeezus."

"Yeah, and it happened around here. *Around here.* And it was at least two weeks old by that point. Nothing had been blown up, so it doesn't matter."

I got a chill over the memory of Mr. Steckerman's story at the hospital—about certain waterborne agents of bioterror taking months to become symptomatic in humans. I patted Dobbins's bicep, trying to feel sufficient sympathy. He hadn't heard that story.

I slung the gym bag over my shoulder. "The grand overview is that something around here took two lives, and if it's anything dramatic, it's got to be an emerging infectious disease. The only agents of bioterror that could strike in December and kill in March would be in the water. And USIC said the towers are clean."

Dobbins's laugh reminded me to take a reality check. *Mystery of the Terrorists at Trinity.* Sounded like some goddamn latest edition of the Hardy Boys.

"So... can I go with you to see Owen?" Dobbins turned the subject. "If I don't tell the other guys? He shouldn't have to suffer the flu pukes with Rain's motormouth driving him nuts and Cora Holman's frigid good manners giving him frostbite."

I couldn't answer because my mind was all over the place. I couldn't help myself. I had visions of Mom refilling her dented, dinged, three-week-old Evian bottle at the tap every time I turned around. I couldn't see how USIC could be wrong about their testing results, but I was uneasy, remembering how things sometimes happened on my shift—people died in the ambulance, even when you thought you had everything under control, or you were doing the best job that you knew how to do.

"Maybe we could just drive past that discount shoe place and get a look at those guys," I suggested. "Not that you can tell a terrorist just by looking at one, yada yada..."

"Well, you can't see them," Dobbins said. "Here's the weirdest thing about that story. The day after New Year's, I went to take the keg back for my brother. And the discount shoe store was deserted—I mean *gone* deserted, like the windows were soaped up and the place had been shut down, and there was a FOR RENT sign in the window."

Like they'd done something, celebrated it, and then skipped town. I didn't want my imagination to run wild, but I was drawn to this concept like the moon draws water.

"The place was still deserted when we got another keg there after winning that last wrestling match. It's almost like I dreamed it or something."

"But you didn't," I questioned him, "right?"

He shook his head, heaving a sigh. "No, man. I was wide awake and stone-cold sober. You really think I should have bothered Mr. Steckerman about this?" he asked again.

"Who knows? Probably their lease ran out and they were celebrating a year of American prosperity. But I'll tell you. Nothing is helping me more to get through these days than trying to figure out what got Mom. Maybe I could put it on my list of stuff to do to keep from having a nervous breakdown—just to drive past there, maybe look in the windows. You in?"

"Any time, bro."

I looked at my watch. "Owen's probably still sleeping, and I'm just too twitchy to sit downstairs with my uncles, et cetera, and talk about the past."

"I'll drive. But then, I want to see Owen. I don't care what he's got."

I nodded, reaching above the detergent to grope through some extra medical supplies I kept around. I tossed some surgical gloves at him. "Wear these around him. Breathe at your own risk...and don't look at me like that."

His stunned eyes dropped, and he shoved the gloves in his jacket pocket without saying anything.

SEVENTEEN

CORA HOLMAN
MONDAY, MARCH 4, 2002
5:31 P.M.

WHILE OWEN SLEPT, Rain gazed at the television until another cartoon show had finished—Looney Tunes, which I knew. I watched with one eye barely opened and the other shut in case she happened to look over. A conversation was out of the question right now. How long would it be before she got to *Where are all your friends?* Or, *Tell me about your mom.*

But she had been right about her headache predictions, and by the time the fourth Looney Tunes cartoon had run, I felt so much relief that my eyes only wanted to relax.

She turned as the credits rolled. The last little drippings of sun shot strange rays through the window, giving us a slightly orange glow. If I shut my eyes now, she would know I was trying to avoid her.

She crawled over, and I managed to smile.

"How's your head?" she asked.

"Better... thanks."

"Told ya. Very weird headaches. You get the digestive tract parts, too, yet?"

"Yes. On the first day."

Her jaw bobbed downward, but then came up, as if she had decided against asking me if I'd thrown up or had the runs. I would have answered her, I think. But to offer such a detail without being asked—the thought left me muted. She reached up and patted my hand, kind of stroking it awkwardly, but it was a nice gesture. It was outside the "necessity touching," like hugging at a funeral. The sensation went all the way up my arm to my heart, making me wonder if there wasn't something magical about the human touch after all.

But the comforting feeling only lasted until her thought finally spilled out: "Wow, I can't believe we found you here alone."

Ta-da. It took all my energy not to withdraw my hand, and I found the right words with my autopilot.

"I asked people to let me sleep after the funeral, what with feeling like this."

"Yeah, but..." She stopped.

Owen, the angel, roused and sat up. Rain turned, and as soon as she quit petting me, I pulled my fist to my chest.

"Where's the bathroom?" he asked.

"Uh-oh," Rain said. "Which exit door?"

He finally put a thumbs-up around his stomach and gestured to his throat.

"You want some help getting there?"

He shook his head, got to his feet, and even managed a plastic smile before turning into the hall where I'd pointed. I felt agog at the girl's warmth and went slowly to the kitchen, thinking of what to do for him. One of the people who had dropped off food had been thoughtful enough to bring a liter of Pepsi, also, and I had put it in the refrigerator. I remembered Oma from when I'd had one of my few stomachaches. She used to give me Pepsi with no ice and the bubbles stirred out. I put just Pepsi in a glass and then poured another glass for Rain with ice.

I met Owen coming out of the hallway and handed him the glass. "Here. No ice."

He said "thanks" nicely, but as if he was used to people doing things for him. *Prince.* He looked like one, acted like one...He plopped back down on the couch, but didn't lie down. He stared into space.

"Scott said you're not supposed to do anything for us," Rain said, taking her glass as I held it out. She grinned easily, which I thought was courageous, considering her friend looked so despondent. She looked very accustomed to him, as if nothing he did would seem mysterious or confusing. But since I didn't know what to make of him, I looked for something else.

"Owen, would you like a blanket?"

"Sit down!" they chimed, so I climbed back into my chair. Rain crunched ice, and Owen stared past the television. In a minute he popped out of his stupor, and I mean it was a "pop," with a shaking of his head. His gaze jerked my way.

"So, Cora. How are you?"

"Fine. Thanks."

Rain quit chewing, and they stared, though I didn't quite get what I had said wrong. Owen's eyes started to get that far-off look and he popped again.

"So...do you have a dad?"

Ta-da. Rain's eyes went back to the television, too innocently, I thought.

"Um... yes. He lives... in Belfast."

Or should I have said Dublin? Jeremy Brandruff Ireland. *Ireland doesn't mean he's Irish! What if he's from China?* Until I said it, I could not even remember that he had died. And I wasn't even sure he was my father. *September 1, 1957–September 10, 1996.* Well, it was too late to take it back.

"Belfast. S'pretty cool," Owen muttered as I died a thousand deaths. "At least you know where your dad is from. Mom once told me our dad was from Five-Card Stud, and she got all tears in her eyes, so I left it alone."

His honesty gave me a jolting, outsider view of myself. *Why not say I didn't know Jeremy until I read his name the other day? What had I been thinking would happen?*

"When I was a little kid, I used to pretend my dad was a superhero," he went on dreamily.

Rain looked at him, then me, with a raised eyebrow. I opened my mouth to be equally honest in some way. But my head just went blank like... *like most people's might if they were trying to think up a lie?*

"I pretended that he had to take care of the whole universe, and that was more important than us, so... we had to take a backseat."

I forced out, "It's good to think those things. Little kids don't need to be bothered with harsh truths."

"Yeah." He looked right at me. "So... what now?"

I realized again that he thought I was feeling the same mired grief that he was. Out of the shadows, though, came my out-of-control feelings from when Oma passed, so I knew exactly how he felt. The flashback jarred me out of the chair, and I found myself easing down on the couch beside him.

"Don't touch him," Rain muttered. "He doesn't like being touched sometimes."

Owen cast her a little smile and his already flushed cheeks turned deep red. "You'll get used to me. I'm just really weird sometimes."

"Sometimes?" Rain grinned.

"Okay, usually. But...you know what I could go for right now?"

"What?" I asked, anxious to do anything but sit this close to his anguish.

"Cora, did you ever do the 'group hug' thing in your family?"

At least I wasn't too sick to misunderstand the concept. They each put an arm out for me, and I came into them like you walk into a dark fun house, with your eyes half flinched. I got twisted around, trying to fit into the swaying and jostling of two other people, each pushing or pulling slightly to find their gravity center. It was not a great feeling—sort of like your first kiss in sixth grade—and probably that feeling came from this loud thought: *You don't belong here, not in this hug with Rain Steckerman and Owen Eberman...How did this happen? How did they get into your house?*

EIGHTEEN

SCOTT EBERMAN
MONDAY, MARCH 4, 2002
5:31 P.M.

AS DOBBINS DROVE us to the vacated store, I had a couple moments of sanity. *Couldn't I have put this off until after the service tomorrow?* Dobbins looked over at me a few times, and I guess he was wondering the same thing.

The place was in Surrey, the next town over, which was about as quaint as Trinity Falls, only Surrey had a liquor store. Across the street was a small row of storefronts that probably used to be real stores before anyone dreamed up malls. Now they held an insurance office, the former discount shoe place, and an art gallery that probably stayed in business thanks to eBay.

We got there right around sunset, and I stared at the soaped-over windows as Dobbins pulled into a spot directly in front. The place had an ominous feel, with the setting sun reflecting off the soap instead of letting you see in. Maybe any deserted place with soaped-over windows feels ominous.

I opened the passenger door. Dobbins came around beside me, sniffing the air like it might smell of clues.

"I don't suppose you've ever broken into a place," I said.

He didn't answer, which meant no. I wondered lots of things, like who owned the building to rent it to the shoe people, and what in hell a legit shoe store was doing here when there wasn't a mall within fifteen miles. Sometimes an exclusive clothing store can survive away from a mall, I reasoned, but discount shoes are not exclusive. I was assuming it had been open less than a year, because I had never noticed it, and I remember just about everything after oh-so-many ambulance runs.

We skulked around to the back through the narrow passage between it and the art gallery. A back door stood closed, with cracked glass in one of the smaller panes down near the knob.

"Those gloves I gave you, for when you go near Owen... You got 'em?" I asked.

Dobbins pulled them out, and I thought it was very decent of him not to mention the football scholarship he had accepted at Miami of Ohio and what a breaking-and-entering gig would do to that.

I put my pair on, saying, "I'll do the break-in. You just hang back."

"Don't cut yourself" was all he said.

I pulled the sleeve of my goose-down jacket over my fist, realizing how badly I was sweating. I laid a square punch into the cracked pane. It clattered loudly, and three decent-sized pieces fell inward. "You tried to talk me out of it, if anyone ever asks. *Capisci?*"

He put his gloved fingers around one loose shard and pulled. I reached my hand in and worked the doorknob, studying the situation over my shoulder after the door swung open. There were lots of houses in this neighborhood, but fortunately, the back of the store was screened by a row of trees.

Inside was almost pitch-black, but Dobbins muttered about having a flashlight in his glove box, and he went after it. The beam turned out to be not very bright. It threw a dull, filmy glow onto the walls but only fully illuminated patches about as round and small as itself. We decided this back room was completely empty and went through a narrow hall with a broom closet on the left and an empty storage closet on the right.

"They didn't leave a damn thing," Dobbins muttered, spraying the light across the empty shelves.

I actually saw an empty plastic champagne glass—the kind you'd take on a picnic—back in the corner.

We came to the big front display room, which was brighter, lit in a dim orange as the setting sun tried to break through the soap on the windows. The room was as neat as the storage closet and contained only a few shelves built into the walls, which had been wiped clean. A black metal desk sat off in the far left corner, the only piece of furniture there.

"What kind of shoes did they sell?" I asked.

"Just sneakers, I think," Dobbins said. "But by the time I saw the wannabe Pradas up close, some illiterate was staring at me, like 'Leave now, jerk.'"

"Discount shoe store," I repeated, because the situation just wasn't adding up. Sneakers are mostly worn by younger people. Kids would simply go to the mall. They wouldn't think about stores in a small town.

Beyond the shelves, the walls were mostly those dark, plastic panels that are supposed to look like wood. They were pocked with holes from hanging decorations or where more shelves had been added. They shone like they had been wiped down. I focused on the desk itself, which looked kind of new. I brushed my fingers on it and realized it had this sort of gray rubber top to it.

"Top isn't metal," I noted.

"Meaning?" Dobbins asked.

I wasn't sure. I took the flashlight and studied a few pencil scribblings on the desktop. The pencil lead shone but was still impossible to read. It didn't look like English.

Dobbins noted, "Hieroglyphics."

Yeah, it felt kind of like being in a mummy's tomb, what with the soap on the windows keeping the light levels low. But among the letters in some foreign language, I spotted what looked like phone numbers.

"Probably suppliers," I said, sane enough to accept that we weren't going to find the answers to our problems scrawled out in marker on the top of the desk.

Dobbins's gloved hand reached for a drawer and pulled it out. Nothing was inside, not even a penny. He reached for the thicker file drawer beneath. Again, nothing. A pen and pencil lay in the middle drawer. I reached in, felt around the back, felt some sheets of paper, and pulled them out. But they were blank.

A car came down the street, its headlights illuminating the office. We both dropped quickly, and I wondered how smart it was for us to have parked right out front after the other two businesses were closed. The lights dissolved as the car went on. But in the brief seconds of illumination, the rubbery desktop had flashed, and I noticed dents in it.

I put one of the blank pieces of paper down on the spot that would have been right in front of the desk chair. I picked up the pencil we just found and ran it in long, light lines over the paper. The indents from the desk started showing through.

Dobbins watched so closely his eyes got within inches of the paper. I was picking up a lot of gibberish in the indents and hoped, what with the desk looking almost new, that they were from the last owners. I realized, as I colored lightly over the paper, that I was capturing a few more "hieroglyphics." After doing this with all three sheets in different spots on the desktop, I had a few phone numbers, some doodles, and a couple of English words.

One doodle looked like a water goblet, or like the Holy Grail or something. It was surrounded in foreign language characters. A few English characters looked half-baked, like the writer hadn't been scribbling hard enough. Two lines looked obviously like phone numbers. One was followed by the English words "Englewood Dist.," and I gathered the second word was short for *distributors.* Then in the upper left-hand corner came a whole name, Uri Gulav, and an 800 number, wherein I couldn't make out the end. In the lower corner came up the name Omar Hokiem with numbers beside it. Another phone number, perhaps? Only the last four numbers were legible—0324.

Dobbins put his finger under a scratch that could have been the first three numbers and grunted in frustration. Then, he pointed to the doodle.

"What does that look like to you?" he asked me.

"Water goblet?" I guessed.

He kept shaking his head. "Don't you think it looks more like a water *tower*?"

Our eyes met after searching the doodle. Yeah, I supposed it looked like a water tower. There were eight lines running out the bottom of it in a semicircle, and one of them had another thicker line running through the middle of it, as if to cut it in half. That line was really dark.

So then? We both cracked up. This was nuts. I supposed you could make an elephant doodle look like tic-tac-toe if it suited your needs.

Suddenly, I didn't know what the hell I was doing there. I was a responsible older brother. I was a paramedic, or at least I was more than halfway there, and this sort of behavior was not up my alley.

"Dobbins, we're fucking breaking and entering," I noted.

He said nothing at first, but then, "It's for Owen and Rain. Cora, too."

Whatever. I didn't really think, after that sudden burst of sanity, that we would find anything in this scribble except doodles and phone numbers important to any retail store... and the name Omar Hokiem was probably their choice of shoe box distributors.

"Let's get out of here," I suggested. I stuffed the penciled sheets of paper into my pocket, and we beat it through the dark corridor and came around to the car just as the sun set.

NINETEEN

CORA HOLMAN
MONDAY, MARCH 4, 2002
6:10 P.M.

MY EYES WANDERED halfway open. There was Aleese, staring right at me with her black pirate eyes. "It still stinks like garlic and apples around here. Jesus, that's awful—"

I sat up, my heart banging. Aleese turned her gaze and stooped over something—a dead body. I caught the dark silhouette of a man's head beside Aleese but slightly closer somehow. As Rain tossed her hair, I realized I was watching Aleese on television, and Rain must have helped herself to the videotapes in the box.

Aleese was squatting over a dead body lying in some sort of narrow alley. *Had she murdered someone?* My fears of the afternoon came back from when I'd first brought out that box. I'd fought off notions that she had filmed many dark things—she had done it almost compulsively. Her dying words, "*Take a picture of me,*" still haunted me. The camera cut closer to her, and the shot was trembling, as if the cameraman were nervous or disgusted and forgot to be steady.

Aleese looked up again after closing the corpse's eyes with her finger and thumb. "Unfortunately, we can't film a smell, Jeremy. But we're here to report to Georgie: Cyanogen stinks worse than death itself. Jesus Christ..."

A man's voice behind the camera had a British accent. "Well, maybe we shouldn't be in here yet, Aleese. Maybe we shouldn't be breathing this nonsense." *What on earth had they done?* So, I had finally heard Jeremy's voice. *My father?* His formal British overtones would have been lovely without the corpse.

But I was appalled—at Rain for having helped herself to the tapes, at my mother for touching a dead body, at my mother for having been so secretive that I wasn't even prepared to defend her to Rain.

"What's cyanogen?" Rain asked, like I would have a clue.

Owen stirred from the couch, and I realized she was talking to him.

He mumbled, "Remember after 9/11, the history teachers switched things, so we studied terrorism instead of World War II?"

She nodded.

"Cyanogen is total poison. If you breathe in even a drop, you're... no more," he said.

I stumbled to my feet, staring at Rain. I had never told off a person in my life except Aleese, but out of my mouth came a wheezing "Stop it!"

Rain misread both my tone and command. She hit pause. I

was left to see an unmoving shot of Aleese staring at Jeremy's camera—staring at me again—angrily.

Rain and Owen couldn't see my reaction in the dark, which probably allowed the conversation to play out so strangely. Neither of them gasped or jumped up or looked the least bit ashamed that I had caught them.

Rain said, "Gosh. Sure wish we had more footage of Mrs. E. I've been looking at photo albums at their house for three days. I would so love to see Mrs. E moving sometimes... in some of her lawyer adventures, though I wouldn't guess they were *this* good."

I realized they felt that I had left the box on the floor for a show of respect to Aleese. And it was perfectly normal, even polite, for them to reach in and patronize it. I was still thunderstruck, but Owen picked up the conversation, as if my "stop it" remark was to pause and reflect on Aleese's "adventure."

"Cyanogen... that's some of the stuff that Saddam Hussein supposedly used to kill all those thousands of Kurdish families in northern Iraq." He pointed at the screen.

"Your mom was in Iraq, Cora?" Rain's eyes glowed as they turned to me.

The two posters from the church service today were now in front of the mantel. I glanced at them before shutting my eyes. I could imagine this better in darkness. I hadn't had the time or the good health to consider how these posters changed things. I'd always known my mother had been as far as Beirut, but the knowledge had come with some images of her lying on a couch over there, high on drugs, and telling people to bug off in colorful terms. I opened my eyes to make sure the footage was real.

Aleese still stared, frozen in that horribly searing gaze, and the corpse was faded in the background.

Owen said, "They're definitely Kurds. Didn't you see that footage in your history class, too, Rain?"

She shrugged, rambling on about Owen and me and the other "honors geeks... No offense, Cora."

"Look at the head coverings." Owen ignored her. "Roll it, Rain. Those dead people, they're Kurds. Right, Cora?"

I drifted up closer to the TV and as I sat on the floor Aleese stood up, and Jeremy moved along behind her, panning the camera as they walked past a dozen or so dead bodies littering a narrow street.

Aleese pointed at a truck as she scanned the high walls. "If we get shot at, we'll dive under that truck over there."

"If we get shot at, I am on my way home." Jeremy's camera jerked and darted. "I cannot believe you dragged me across the border to do this. This isn't the, um, finance-the-orphanage type of stuff we're paid for, Aleese. Who's going to buy this disgusting footage on which we've spent our last dollar?"

I felt my chest loosening up, my spine relaxing somewhat, to the point where I had to put one hand on the floor to keep my balance. The other hand I brought to wipe away tears—and then cover my mouth, as Aleese exploded in her usual syntax.

"You can go the fuck home and shoot weddings if you're going to be a pin dick, Jeremy. We'll give it to... Human Rights Watch, maybe. As for helping the children?" She went right up to a dead person hanging off the side of the truck she had pointed at earlier and picked the guy's head up. "How old do you think this one is? Fourteen? Fifteen? Bring the camera closer, Jeremy. I got a message for Georgie." The camera zoomed, and the dead boy's blank face did look younger than ours.

"Hey, George. It's me again. Me and my dead friend, here. When inhaled, cyanogens disrupt the transfer of blood to bodily tissue. Symptoms include headache, nausea, chills, vomiting, and labored breathing. But that's all a moot point, because you're dead in three minutes. This...this *boy* is obviously with his family, and they are obviously in this truck because they smelled something weird like apples and garlic, and decided last Wednesday's attack wasn't the usual gift of conventional explosives from Saddam. They decided they better get out of town as quickly as possible, and they may have gotten an eighth of a mile. His family took about as many breaths as the people in the gas chambers at Auschwitz."

She waved her hand in the air, and thirty flies left the boy's head. "Welcome to Halabja, Iraq, Georgie. Today is March 19, 1988, eighth year of the Iran-Iraq War. Let this footage profess: *More Kurds should be brought to America. They need asylum or they will end up like this. Give us their tired, their poor...*"

The screen faded to sand.

The part about Kurds needing asylum seemed new to me. It was not something we studied in history class—not that I could remember. Rain hit the pause button again. Then she slowly turned her head to stare at me.

"Damn, Cora," Owen breathed in awe. "Why didn't you ever bring this footage into school? Do you know how cool that is?" In spite of his illness, he chuckled over each word. "Your mother. Sneaked into Iraq. To film the Kurdish massacre. To help bring Kurds to America..." And he laughed some more.

"Who's Georgie?" Rain added.

"Boss?" I muttered, though I hadn't a clue.

Rain patted my arm for quite some time. My vision turned hazy with what must have appeared to be tears of grief. Maybe they were. I felt grievously ignorant of the world's problems. I also felt a strange calming, a coming together of a confusing universe.

I don't know why I had never dreamed my mother capable of anything heroic. I don't know why Oma had never told me stories of things like this, or why Aleese had hidden them from me. I would have wanted to be proud of her. I couldn't get past my stirring question. *Why didn't she love me?*

I reached into Rain's hand and took the remote. Fever chills had returned, but I just let my jaw chatter. I rolled the tape backward to the beginning and watched it through again, watched my mother's passions run hot for the poor Kurdish teenager and cold for Jeremy's fearfulness, and hot for her little speech about getting Kurds to safety in America.

Rain rooted through the box, announcing the bad news that all the other tapes were beta or "newsroom" format and that we couldn't watch them on VHS. I didn't care. I could suddenly watch a tape four times and not care that two high school legends were watching me do it. I could let my teeth chatter out of control and not want to excuse myself to my room to be alone. I could slouch.

I could feel people coming into my house and not get all agog and unable to breathe. I could feel the floor rumbling under the weight of heavy footsteps, but I merely turned to look. Even when I saw Adrian Moran, Tannis Halib, and Jon

Dempsey staring down at me, I figured this could be a dream, and if it wasn't, it didn't matter so much. I gripped the remote tightly but didn't jump up.

Adrian said awkwardly to Owen, "Hi. We, um, found you."

And before he could think of better words, Jon Dempsey blurted, "So...what are you guys doing *here*?"

I only flinched a little, but then turned my eyes back to the screen, and I enjoyed strange rushes from catching Aleese's eye every now and then as I tried to figure out what every little detail could possibly mean about my mother.

TWENTY

SHAHZAD HAMDANI
TUESDAY, MARCH 5, 2002
5:55 A.M. KARACHI TIME

I WALK ALONG the shore at dawn, watching a few red rays break through the Karachi skyline far ahead. I struggle to remember some of my father's melodious words, which I tried so hard over the winter to forget. Often, he attempted to be funny while not losing his intensity.

"Shahzad, America is the country where one plus one equals nine! There, riches have been created via an influx of the tired and poor! How do they do that?"

His giggly speeches begin to return, though they are a poison to my chest. "*. . . and it is the land where the rights of the individual take precedence over the needs of the whole—and voilà! A miracle! Individuals don't selfishly beat each other all day long!*"

I trudge along kicking at little crystalline sea pebbles, and I pose to myself some difficult questions: Is America the tired and poor? Or is America the rich and haughty? Who is correct? My father or the extremists? The extremists don't think of

Americans as individuals, as my father did. They think of Americans collectively, and as something threatening, though the nature of the threat changes, depending on the group of extremists. But so many people try to get to America—from my country and every other country. What is the goal of the immigrants? To become corrupt and selfish?

Shortly after my father went to Six Flags Great Adventure and taped his ridiculous screams on the roller coaster, he visited Miss Liberty, the great statue. He uploaded with the photo his meager attempts to sing in tune: *"Give me your tired, your poooooor, your huddled masses yearning to breathe freeeeeeeeeeeee..."* My ears almost bled with pain and embarrassment.

Hodji had laughed with me. "Ha ha *ha ha ha.* That is terrible!"

But my father's tone was so sincere. He was trying to sing on key for once, for all these tired, poor people who took the Great Dare.

I was quite small when he made up that terminology. He often said there was no more terrifying experience common to man than daring to change *everything*—to leave all your belongings, your family, your house, your neighborhood, your habits, your family's thousands of years of sameness—to go halfway around the world for things you don't know.

"Shahzad, some people break down in grief and panic while boarding the plane to Kennedy, and some who are weak run off, go directly home again."

So, I wonder why people do not stay put. Why not be content with your neighbors and friends and family?

"Shahzad, it's as if every person on earth is born with a statement in his heart: I am meant to be great. I am the child of some

king. The common man yearns to regain his royalty, and thus, he takes the Great Dare—"

I hear heavy breathing behind me and I turn, thinking I will see ghosts. It is Hodji. I suppose he does not trust me to walk the beach and not end up hiding in the bowels of this village until the dreaded flight has left.

He is quite winded. He enjoys to borrow a Pall Mall from my uncle all too often these days.

"Do you know what America is to me?" I turn my eyes to the sea as the realization strikes me. "It is a blob on this map of the world my father used to download when we first tried the Internet, back in '96. I was ten years old. He would point out America, after this blurred map took six minutes to download. That's what it is. A bad smudge in some ridiculously low dpi."

I hear Hodji's breath run out in a way that sounds tired. He says with a yawn and exaggerated patience, "It can be dangerous down here this time of day."

Considering the work we do, his comment leaves me awestruck. I do not dwell on it. My father's philosophies always "rang" to me, like they should have lutes and cellos playing behind them. "Father said it is a great irony that a union built on trust should succeed, where so many iron-fisted rules had failed." I turn to Hodji again. "It all sounded so very majestic and romantic. Until he failed to wake up one day."

Hodji blinks tiredly at the sea. "So, we're blaming the Declaration of Independence for a broken gas line? Is that it?"

"Don't condescend to me, please." My uncle is not here to smack my hair to the other side of my head. It gives me a sense of power—a freedom to think about what is actually true. "I have had very little time in the past six months to think about precisely why my father is dead. I just know that he is, and I'm feeling it right now."

"Maybe you *should* think about it," he mutters. "I've barely heard you mention your father these past six months. That's not normal. And as hard as you've been working for the Americans, it's a little odd that you can't dredge up one good feeling about going there. You're forgetting the whole point of this. Your aunt Alika called late last night. She's meeting us at Beth Israel Medical Center tomorrow, first thing. Well, in her mind it's first thing. She doesn't know about your meeting with USIC. She thinks you're coming to comply with your father's wishes about your education and that I helped you get a job. But anyway, you have an appointment with the best asthma specialist there. You'll be feeling much, much better from there on in. USIC will pay for the whole thing—"

"Beth Israel? It is a Jew hospital," I breathe in confusion.

"It's a *great* hospital. You have to stop thinking like that. We're all mongrels in America. The Jews will not poison your medicine. Everyone will give you good care. Your health insurance as an intern will pay the bills . . . It's all good. Okay?"

I had not intended to make a negative comment about Jews—only a curious one. I had never met one to my knowledge, and it had been on the top of "My List" to do so when my father left Pakistan. He and I each had a "My List" that I had entirely forgotten about, until Hodji just brought up a Jew hospital.

It makes my lips smile a little more as I remember hazily some things: Visit Disney, see Miss Liberty, and see Yankees were at the top. But there were smaller things we had much fun thinking up: Buy Gap jeans, eat Kentucky Fry, stick our heads in a cathedral and see if the incense really can make you dizzy, walk up beside a Jew and see if they really do stink. This could be my chance to see if some rumors that circulate in my village have any basis in fact. I am curious, not meaning to harm.

But I can't help asking Hodji: "Those doctors... will they smell?"

It is our joke sometimes that Americans, the white ones especially, can smell of something I cannot find words for. Perhaps it is... yogurt.

"They might not think that *you* smell so hot." He lifts his freshly showered armpit and sticks it in my face with his vulgar, American laughter. "Smells like a rose, you see?"

He smells of strawberry, plastic, and yogurt, that is what I think. "They stink like this?" I ask.

"Only it doesn't stink. You'll get used to it."

I don't know. Our village is clean. Our home is ceremoniously clean for the sake of my asthma. I think of my aunt Hamera and her two sisters, and how they fold their garments beneath their knees for pads as they scrub and scrub. But for us, ammonia is enough, and bar soap is enough. We are more simple than what I see on the Internet and what Hodji and Father often described. In America, there is a different soap for everything—one for your hair, one for your skin, one for your shaving, one for your clothes. There is one paper to blow with, one to make with in your toilet, one to put to your mouth while eating. In our village, we have only the toilet roll. Hodji has told me I can use the toilet roll to blow with, but if I bring said roll to the table and wipe my mouth, that is very bad manners. I don't see why I can put roll paper to my nose but not my mouth. I don't see why I should be forced to eat with wiping paper in my hands, as if I were a small child. It is very confusing, and with all these soaps Hodji uses every day, I will stink like a nasty bouquet.

I turn only my eyes sideways to glare at him. He is a big and powerful American who can write his own definitions of normal. A revelation rises up slowly from my feet.

"You say I have been working hard for the Americans lately? I have always worked hard. I worked hard for my *father.* Not for America."

If my father's Internet business with Uncle were to continue operating successfully after my father went to New York, it required my staying. I did not protest. I didn't like the situation, but there was never an e-mail request from my father in New York that I didn't fulfill. If he wanted programs or hacking or v-spying or technical advice, I completed all. He would send me some of his pay for helping him or teaching him. Programming—and hacking—came as naturally to me as breathing and scratching and learning the languages of others.

"I worked for *him.* Even after he died. I just think of that. That and how... I really feel nothing about this place."

Hodji doesn't take it as badly as I think he might. "Well, it's good you're finally thinking about it. You've got nothing to do for a long transatlantic flight but think, and if you want my honest opinion, it's about time. You can't hide behind work forever."

He looks at the rising sun over the red roofs of Karachi. He is Catholic but polite. "Did you come to speak to Allah?"

I feel I would like very much to speak to Allah, and I say yes quickly.

I watch him trudge cautiously across the sand, knowing he will be half watching me. He is probably hoping I will think of the many pictures my father sent me by e-mail that I used to treasure, plus the fun we had looking at the world on our screen before he left the Karachi police force. Our early trips across the Internet were more than just America; my father wanted to see the whole world. Of that, I am triply sad.

Computer screens in 1996 were slow moving. But to us, each download was like a page of a gigantic magazine, filled with all the adventures he wanted to take: *Experience our Italy... stay in our Viennese golden hotel... climb our majestic Swiss mountains... swim in our Mediterranean seas... run with our Australian kangaroos... frolic with our Polynesian fish... taste our rich Dutch chocolate... see Disney!*

"So, what do you have now, Father?" The beach becomes blurry as my eyes fill. I have rarely spoken directly to my father since his death. But I see the truth about my father plainly for once. "Father, you got to see *one* country! You fell victim to the men you chased."

The sun bobs ahead in its red richness, but I do not play up to him.

"And you... you used to belong only to me, and now you are quite selfish!" I don't know quite to whom I am speaking—my father, or this enormous sun of early morning, to which I used to say, "You are all mine; you belong only to me."

I stop seeing my father's favorite downloads of Vienna and Polynesia and Brazil and I see something plainer. Once he got to America, my father's most beloved view—even more than Miss Liberty—was of the busy streets of midtown, the multiplicity of souls who had come to seize back their royalty. People in the photos he e-mailed me of Union Square were "speckled," like many litters of puppies. Brown, yellow, bronze, freckled, red, white... They were tall, squat, pale, dark, bald, bearded, skinny, fat, tired, scared—

"*—and great, Shahzad. They came to the universities, the community colleges, the job placement programs, the classified advertisements. They worked with sweat, strength, grunts, and groans, and always, Shahzad, with their dignity. To be paid fairly for your effort is a magical force, a declaration of your self-worth to a world that tends to shred and devour.*"

I want to say something to Allah, so I face the east. "Perhaps I am a coward, Great Allah," I whisper. "Perhaps I should feel ready to reach past the Internet and mere images of reality. So if you please, maybe I would like to be a bigger part of reality, as my father would have wished. Perhaps I would like to taste a ballpark frank, view a cathedral, use chopsticks, visit a theme park, wear Gap jeans, smell a Jew, go to school, see a good doctor, eat Kentucky Fry, watch the Yankees, own an ATM card, touch a piano, read the Shakespeare in the English...

"I would like to remember my father's dreams without anguish. I would like to find his courage and take up his course. I would like to visit for him the Angolans, Algerians, Nigerians, British... Spanish, South Americans, Icelanders, Swedes... Finlanders, Poles, Norwegians, Russians, Canadians, Texans, Brazilians, Argentineans, Afghans, Australians... Or perhaps you can supply me with the courage to go to the one place on Earth where they all converge. I suppose that in your ironic ways, Great Allah, you have fulfilled my father's every dream when he went only to one country. *Allahu Akbar...*"

I raise my head, but in a trance. The great sun is still not mine, though I sense a bigger truth—it belongs to everyone, which might be why I picture it shining brightly on this far-off bad dpi, which contains the fragmented pixels of courage from every country on Earth.

"Great Allah, my father is a fallen, precious memory. Our dreams are in the recycle bin. But if you would be pleased to recover them... Though there is one other thing: I would like to live to be old. *Amin*..."

TWENTY-ONE

SCOTT EBERMAN
MONDAY, MARCH 4, 2002
6:30 P.M.

AS DOBBINS PULLED into my street, I decided to stop at the Steckermans' to get Rain a toothbrush. I could see a lot of lights on inside their house. In fact, four cars lined the driveway, which I'd have thought were people coming to my house, except for one thing. They were all say-nothing cars—the types so devoid of personality that they have to be airport rentals.

"What the hell..." I stared. "Those cars belong to USIC people. From, like, Washington or..."

I grabbed the door handle as Dobbins parked.

"I'm going in there. You better let me go by myself," I said. Maybe I could find a way to get info if we didn't overwhelm them. "Go over to our house and tell my uncles I'm right behind you. We'll take this night one step at a time."

Dobbins whisked the keys into his pocket and we headed in separate directions. From the Steckerman porch, I saw maybe six silhouettes behind the drapes in the living room. The front door was locked. I banged, and Alan came so fast that I almost clanged my fist in his noggin. He stepped out and asked what was wrong.

Big secret meeting, yup. I was trying to look after his kid, like I didn't have enough on my plate, and he was acting like he didn't want me in the house.

"Rain wants me to get her something to sleep in. What, do I have to know the USIC secret handshake?"

He looked sheepish as he stuck his head back inside. "Friends! I'd like you to meet my neighbor from across the street!"

He spoke loudly, as if it were a warning, and this houseful of people turned quiet as I came in. They were all dressed in suits. I shook hands numbly all around when Alan introduced me, and I accepted their condolences, which let me know that at least the name Eberman was clear in their minds. I counted six faces, heard one or two more voices in the kitchen, and spotted a man sitting at the head of the dining room table, surrounded by papers. He was talking on two cell phones at once in what sounded like a different language for each phone. He had hair that seemed almost too blond for an adult's, so I leaped to the conclusion he was speaking something like Swedish and Swiss. *Sophisticated,* yee.

"Sorry to disturb you. I'm collecting a toothbrush and a pair of sweatpants." I clomped up the stairs, went into Rain's bathroom, and grabbed her toothbrush. But before I could come back downstairs, Alan met me in the hallway.

"Scott, if Rain is asking to stay with you guys again tonight, I feel like I ought to say no. You probably need some sleep."

I wasn't sure of how much to say. "It's fine. She keeps Owen sane."

"Well, some of these people might be here until all hours, and she could actually get more sleep if I just leave her alone. How is she right now? And what's happening over at your house?" A look of concern wafted through his general distraction. But I called him on it.

"What's happening at *your* house?"

"I was supposed to be at a meeting in New York today, but with Rain sick and your mom's service tomorrow, I had them do some flight rearrangement."

My heart melted slightly. *Just a routine meeting.* So, why the frosty reception?

I rambled, "Look. I know next to nothing about your job, Alan. But if you and your, uh, *friends* have any idea how some bizarre sickness could take my mother, bounce over nine houses, get the Holmans, then jump back and make Rain and my brother sick... I think I'm entitled to know."

"Your brother is sick?" Alan forced his fingers through his hair. "Did you see Charlie O'Dell? He said he was going over to your house today."

"He's sending Dr. Godfrey over later, though he's not taking it as seriously as I am. I'm *trying* to think of the half the town that's been in my house for the past three days without even a snivel. I'm *trying* to tell myself that two neighborhood deaths of brain aneurysms with flulike symptoms is a coincidence. And most of the town remaining perfectly healthy—that's the evidence. But... it doesn't make sense."

He put a hand on my shoulder and urged me down the stairs with him. Part of me wanted to take him by the throat, shake him, and scream, *What the fuck are all these suits doing here?* But the presence of USIC, if related, made even less sense than the presence of an emerging infectious disease. Diseases can't reason. They show up where they show up. And if it's true that terrorists are not exactly psycho, then they would have to understand that Trinity Falls would be a goddamn stupid place to terrorize. If they wanted to start poisoning people with slow-working germs, there would be more satisfying targets up in central Jersey, with its dense New York suburbs and huge industries. South Jersey was crude in comparison—little more than the Pine Barrens, beach sand, and meadow grass stubble.

I wandered back to the living room as Alan went to get Rain's clothes. The blond-haired man at the dining room table was exchanging cell phones with a woman in a blue suit, as if he were finishing one of his calls and jumping right into a third. Another man dropped a cup of coffee on the table in front of him. *Sophisticated and important,* my local-yokel mind rolled, especially when the cell phone he'd handed to the woman started to ring, and she answered it, saying, "He's talking to them now overseas."

A man came out of the kitchen who hadn't been out here for my introduction, but whose face I recognized. The guy had been standing behind Alan at the televised press conferences about the water-tower testing back in January.

I said, "Imperial... James Imperial. You're the new director of USIC in Washington."

He shook my hand with polite disinterest. "But we haven't met."

I told him I remembered his face from the television two months ago, and he grinned. "Your memory is that fine-tuned? You want a job?"

I wasn't in the mood to joke around. Alan came back,

handed me a bag of clothes, and said, "James, Scott's mother is one of the two women on the street who died."

He seethed in air through clenched teeth. "I'm so sorry. How are you doing?"

I could only nod before Alan went on. "And I've just been informed... his brother, Rain's good friend, has come down with a flu also..."

James Imperial's Adam's apple bobbed into his necktie so hard that I thought it would stick there. That almost blew me backward. It looked like... guilt or remorse or responsibility... but I didn't have much chance to wonder about it. The guy at the dining room table stood up, held both phones out from his ears, and said something to Imperial in Swiss/Swedish/Whatever.

Imperial turned to me. "He would like to say hello to you and express his condolences, if you can just wait a minute."

He... Mr. Switzerland looked like the center of attention around here. When Alan said he would get Rain's antibiotics from her bathroom, I didn't follow. I watched the man continue to talk on the second phone, though after a few more foreign phrases, he handed that phone to Imperial. Then, he dashed through the kitchen without saying anything to me.

Imperial kept the foreign conversation going through the cell, so I figured I ought to just wait by the door. I'd kept myself focused enough to be somewhat sane this afternoon, but the past three days had taught me that nightfall could turn it all around, and it was already dark. I'd heard this about grief: that it comes and goes without rhyme or reason but you can count on a train wreck at sundown. My train wrecks had lasted well into the mornings.

The blond-haired man appeared from the kitchen and came right toward me. I'd heard him speak every language under the sun but my own. So I was stunned to hear him say in perfect English with a trace of Boston slang, "Potty break. Sorry. I've accepted every bit of ease that comes with modern electronics, but I still can't use the facilities while I'm on a cell phone."

I figured potty humor might cut my tension. "I can't zip up without dropping the damn thing into the toilet. Been there, done that."

"A man after my own heart." He grinned at the woman who had come up to us along with Imperial. The blond man's eyes grew serious above his smile. "How are you doing? Alan told all of us, of course."

"Good. For the moment." I can rarely say how it is that I know what I know, but I sensed it would be seriously in my best interests to appear on top of my stress. I forced a grin. "How many languages did you just speak on the phone?"

"Uh...three," he said. "French, Punjabi, and Arabic. The French was my wife. She knows English, but you know the French...She has to pretend she doesn't."

He laughed easily, *so blasé about his French wife and multilingualness.*

"So, how many languages do you speak altogether?"

While the others laughed, he groaned, like they had some private joke going, and he said, "Not enough, believe me. Did you know that there are over a hundred languages spoken in the Middle East alone?"

I hadn't known that, but before I could ask more, Alan returned with the prescription and dropped it into the bag.

"Scott, this is the USIC director of operations in Pakistan, who's visiting the states this week. His name is Roger O'Hare."

I knew Alan and I had talked about Pakistan recently, but with my memory falling down, I only remembered one interesting thing.

"Pakistan...that's where the online informant is who's younger than my brother?" I asked.

"He's talking about the Kid," Alan prompted him. "I told him about that recent *Newsweek* article that mentioned him."

"Ah, yes. The Kid keeps my life colorful." Roger chuckled, but something seemed amiss. Like his pupils were having a hard time staying on me, and maybe he was going through this small talk as an exercise in discipline or something. I'd say his phone calls were making him nervous.

"So, he's real?" I persisted. "He's really a teenager?"

"He's real, and sixteen. Going on forty-five," he said, maybe too casually. "He loves Drake's, Gatorade, and Bazooka Bubble Gum. And while he's sitting in his uncle's Internet café, busting a gut on Drake's Apple Pies, he'll capture the screen of some bloody, dangerous guys sitting two terminals away from him, and he'll script them for us."

I didn't know what scripting was, but I figured it was some serious part of spying. "Sounds dangerous," I said. "I mean, sixteen and all..." I couldn't help but imagine Owen being in that much of harm's way.

His smile faded. "As Americans, we can't force citizens of other countries to behave in certain ways if they don't want to. If they want to sell us intelligence, all we can usually do is watch their backs as best as we can. But the Kid is being relocated. He's not happy with us, but if he didn't wind up with his head sliced off, his health was about to get him. He's got asthma from hell."

"Asthma?" Why the details of legendary people intrigue us normal folk, I can't say, but sometimes even I am a sucker for it. It was sort of like hearing a locker-room story told by a friend of Shaquille O'Neal's. And I could feel the paramedic in me rising up, too. It makes me twitch to hear about people in third world countries with health problems.

"So... can he come over here? There's a thousand hospitals in this country that could clear up the worst case of asthma. In fact, we've got a specialist right here in Trinity Falls, Doug Godfrey, who was with a team in Rome that operated on the pope. Why don't you send the Kid to us? He could stay at our house. Doug would take care of him..."

I trailed off, as a polite grin came over his face. "Thanks, Scott. He's still working, so we're keeping his whereabouts under wraps. But I'll be sure and tell him of your generous offer next time I see him. He'll be touched by that." O'Hare stuck his hand out and gave me an exit line. "Listen, you're in our thoughts and prayers, Scott. We'll be sure to keep up with you via Alan."

As for leaving, I felt like I was passing up a smorgasbord of info. Yet, I'd lived across the street from Steckerman for years, and I knew how tight-lipped the FBI was about case information. These USIC guys would be ten times worse.

But the concept of give-and-take was right there for me. I figured I'd play my only card. Surely I wouldn't end up in the slammer before my mom's service and with my brother feeling sick.

I pulled the pieces of paper out of my pocket, and let my eyes fall onto the hieroglyphics and the only discernible English words I could make out. "You guys aren't looking for someone named...Uri Gulav, are you?"

I could feel the temperature drop about fifty degrees: *Paramedic student thinks he can help out USIC. Oh Christ, how do we be polite?* A couple of people turned their backs and moved awkwardly to the couch, and Imperial turned and raised his eyebrows in this condescending way.

"No, we're not."

I ignored him, focused on this piece of paper. "You're not looking for an Omar, are you?"

I would have felt utterly stupid, except for one thing: This Roger O'Hare actually stopped dead in his tracks on his way back to the table. His neck did this thing that looked like a one-inch whiplash. He turned around and looked at me.

"Omar..." I looked on the sheet, thinking maybe I ought to shut up, but I couldn't. "...Hokiem. And some phone number. The last three digits are 0324, but I couldn't make out the first three. Must be local, though, because—"

I stopped as O'Hare took the paper from my hand and stared at it. He didn't laugh at the pencil lines running across it or try to call me Dick Tracy. I pointed to the goblet thing with the eight lines running down. They looked almost like an upside-down sunrise from a kid's drawing. And one of the lines was crossed over by a thicker line. I mentioned I thought it looked like a water tower. A few of the agents got interested and came up behind O'Hare and Imperial to look at the thing.

O'Hare finally said something, but it wasn't in English.

Though just from the tone, I'd swear it was "Jesus Christ Almighty."

Fifty-five questions later, I'd told them about Dobbins and the celebration he'd seen at the discount shoe store while ordering the New Year's keg. I'd told them about the soaped-over windows the day after New Year's. I'd told them about me and Dobbins going down there, though I called it "to see what we could see" instead of "breaking and entering."

I was trying for a give-and-take thing that wasn't really going my way. They thanked me with necktie politeness, and Imperial finally gave me "The Speech" on please don't break and enter. I ignored it.

I said, "Right now, I'm watching over three kids who have a very strange flu. If there's anything I should know to keep them out of harm's way, I'm sure you'll tell me."

The room was quiet and even more awkward. "I'm *sure* you'll tell me," I fought on as I grabbed the doorknob.

I figured if there was nothing wrong, one of them—Imperial or O'Hare or my neighbor of fifteen years—would have said something like "Not to worry; we promise there is nothing to tell."

But I left under the same weight of silence that I'd first walked into.

TWENTY-TWO

OWEN EBERMAN
MONDAY, MARCH 4, 2002
6:42 P.M.

SOMETIMES I THINK I don't want to see people, but I can be wrong. A smile crossed my face on seeing Moran and Dempsey and Tannis come through that door. I could have done without Dempsey's stupid remark, "What are you guys doing *here*?"

But Cora still looked absorbed in her mother's tape. I don't think she even heard Dempsey.

I countered his rudeness with "What're *you* guys doing here?"

"We spied," Dempsey confessed, looking more proud than ashamed. "Or, I should say Tannis spied."

Tannis bowed. "Dobbins was just having a convo in the kitchen with Dr. O'Dell. And he was leaving a message for some other doctor to come over here because you three are here with some... flu thing. What do you have? The Ebola virus?"

"Hopefully, all we have is my brother being his usual cautious self. Hopefully...," I repeated, and pushed the smile across my face again. "Rain's had the thing for five days, and it's now down to a stuffed-up nose."

"Well, I ain't gonna French-kiss you." Moran shrugged. "If it's so contagious, how come more people don't have it?"

"No clue," I told him honestly. "Put it this way: If it was highly contagious, I don't see how you guys wouldn't catch it from me before Cora and her mom would."

"We don't care what you have," Tannis said. "You're stuck with us. Food?"

I realized he'd brought in a couple of grocery bags and laid them on Cora's dining room table. I didn't need the smells wafting out to tell me that it was something chicken.

"If it's bland," I said.

"I'm starved!" Rain added, and Cora just kept staring at the TV, engrossed with the foul-language speech her mother was giving this Jeremy person again. I didn't call her out of her daze.

Moran stood behind them, watching the footage. "That your mom, Cora?"

After a couple seconds, she said, "Yes."

"Guess what? Cora's mom sneaked into Iraq," I added, wondering why she didn't brag away. "She wanted to get more Kurds into America, so she filmed the Kurdish massacre to let people know."

"You're shitting me." Moran sat down cross-legged beside Cora and watched as her mom gave the little speech to this Georgie about the effects of cyanogen. Cora ignored him but looked different somehow. Her posture was always so good, but right now, it wasn't the first thing you'd notice about her. I don't know what you'd notice about her except that she was pretty.

Her cheeks glowed, which was probably her sickness, but despite her dropping one tear after another, her eyes didn't swell. She just gazed in that blank way of hers.

"All those dead people, that's the Kurdish massacre?" Moran asked. "Wasn't she scared of inhaling poison gas herself?"

Cora didn't move at first but finally answered. "I can't say there was too much she was afraid of. She also was in Mogadishu, where the *Black Hawk Down* story took place. Did you see that movie?"

Moran nodded. "Totally scary. Who's Georgie?"

"I'm not sure... but I think it was George Bush Sr."

A former president. Her dainty dimples showed up, but more from politeness than bragging. Moran just stared at her. There really wasn't too much else to do—Cora Holman was good at getting you to stare. I wished sometimes I could see into her head, because I'd never seen anyone act like her before. I didn't know what it was like to sit as unmoving as a statue at your mom's funeral, or to announce your mom's presence at the Kurdish massacre. In a sense, I admired her and wished I could have that much... is *control* the word I'm looking for?

Another tear rolled down one cheek as she watched her mom again. But even when she cried, it was weird and very different. For one thing, she didn't make any noise.

TWENTY-THREE

SCOTT EBERMAN
MONDAY, MARCH 4, 2002
6:42 P.M.

I WENT BACK to my house to get out of my button-down shirt, now drenched in breaking-and-entering sweat, and find my jeans. I realized I hadn't ironed a second shirt for tomorrow. Here's how whacked my train of logic was: I had a brief thought I could ask Mom to iron it for me.

I sat on the edge of my bed and had my first train wreck of the night. My uncle Davis came into the bedroom, Mom's oldest brother, and he sat there rubbing on my back, blathering on about how he and my uncle Greg would help us out financially. I hadn't even thought about finances yet.

"Please don't be offering us money," I sniffed. "My financial aid should be pretty good from here on in if you don't mess it up."

He cracked up. For a moment. "And I can stay down here as long as you want. Greg can't, but I'm self-employed and flexible."

Uncle Davis was a stockbroker and could have retired at age thirty if he'd wanted to. I almost said, "Aw, great, stay another week," but my head went over to Cora's where my brother was holed up. My paramedic training decided otherwise. "Thanks, but go on home tomorrow like you planned. We have to, um, get back to normal. If I need anything, I'll call, and you're only three hours from here."

I felt split in half—as a grieving person who didn't want my house to empty out, and as a paramedic who didn't want people to get suspicious. If I confessed that Owen was sick, my mom's brother would panic. A guy with his clout could start a community panic, which could actually end up costing lives by jamming the emergency room with imaginations they weren't prepared for.

He put a hand on my leg, reading my mind, I guess. "Where's Owen?"

I thought fast. "Down at Cora Holman's house with Rain. They're consoling one another."

The truth made sense, under the circumstances. "That's probably good for him. Why don't you get something to eat? There's lots of new people downstairs waiting to hug your neck."

I followed him and after chatting it up, I headed into the kitchen for a couple of aspirins. I couldn't tell if my head hurt from tension, paranoia, or something slightly worse. While trying to be careful, I'd been touching sick people all day. A hand reached for mine as I pulled the glass out from under the spigot and plopped aspirin in my mouth. It belonged to Mr. Stetson from the Utilities Department.

He pointed to a piece of yellow paper tacked onto the refrigerator. "I wouldn't expect you to read notices from the city today, Scott, but for the record, there it is."

IMPORTANT NOTICE TO THE RESIDENTS OF TRINITY FALLS ON THE FOLLOWING STREETS. Mine was one of them. It basically said they were fixing a broken water line at the end of the block and to please not drink the water until further notice, which should come in the next few days. I spit the aspirin into my hand, looked at the glass, and turned it over in the sink with annoyance. Mr. Stetson pointed out the kitchen window. I could see past the woods to a couple of huge trucks, like dump trucks, down at the swamp end of our street with a bunch of night lights on.

"They're the culprits. Struck a vein by accident a couple of hours ago, working overtime to finally get Dr. Chad Mather's new house hooked up. They'll get it patched up quick, I hope."

Paranoid thoughts might have gotten me right away, except Leo was a local. And I would not have expected him to lie. *Dumb-asses.* I wondered if I would have to shower with brown water in the morning and if I ought to run down to Cora's to keep sick kids from drinking squirrel poop juice. I turned the faucet on again, though as I wiggled my fingers under the drip, the water was still clear. It would probably start running brown just as I turned on the shower.

"Did you take this notice to the Holmans'?" I asked.

"I did your street myself, yes. I saved your house for last so I could visit with you boys and your uncles some." And he pointed out two crates of Evian water on the counter that someone must have brought over.

"Whom do I thank?" I asked.

"I think Alan Steckerman walked it across the street maybe an hour ago."

I went to the window and stared at his house, with all its shades drawn and all those airport cars parked outside.

I stood there for a long time, and arm after arm went around my shoulder, but no one said, "A penny for your thoughts." Dangerous question under the circumstances. Finally, one arm belonged to Dobbins.

"Learn anything over there?"

I sighed. "I think I learned more over here." I showed him the notice, which I'd been holding between two fingers.

He read it, then stared at the Steckermans'. "You think they sent this notice and they're covering up the truth?"

My jaw bobbed. "I feel like an idiot thinking that. But I'd feel like a worse idiot *not* thinking that. Last summer, I'd have more easily suspected an alien invasion from the planet Zirmakon. But. We're less than three hours from New York, where every fathomable creature roams. It seems like a world away, but..."

"But if you looked on a map of the world, you'd think we would have felt the vibrations when the Trade Center fell." Dobbins saw my side. "Maybe it's like the cockroach principle. My mom says whoever lives closest to the tenement district is most likely to end up with cockroaches. Doesn't matter if your house is big or small."

That made sense, though not much else did. "Just answer me this, Dobbins. If you can get past the concept that a terrorist group would poison the water here...how the hell would terrorists poison only *part* of the water?"

"Damned if I know."

"Isn't that sort of like eating just the flour in your cake, and leaving the eggs and milk and sugar?"

"I'd say it's more like those summer rainstorms we get sometimes—when it's raining over your house, but not over mine ten blocks away." He stopped short and gripped my arm while not moving his eyes from the Steckermans'. "I just thought of my uncle Ron—the wheat farmer out in Hammonton."

"What about him?"

"I'm just thinking of something I helped him do last summer. He wanted to keep some sort of spider mites out of his wheat crop with this one insecticide. But if it had gotten into the vegetables, it would have made them unfit to sell because they would have absorbed the stuff, whereas the wheat wouldn't."

He traced his finger through the air, like he was trying to remember something. "We dug up his irrigation pipe, the one that only watered the wheat. We didn't even have to shut off the water. My uncle had some special metal drill, and he drilled a small hole into the pipe on some weird angle so that the running water wouldn't gush out of it. He hooked this little red box up to the pipe with this tiny hose."

I was kind of lost. "The red box, what? Had the insecticide in it?"

"Yeah. It was time released. He wouldn't have to refill the box all summer. We covered it up again with soil."

My gut kind of bowed, like I'd drunk a vat of insecticide. "Interesting concept," I managed to say. "But there's a hell of a difference between drilling a little sprinkler line and drilling into a public water line. And that's just for starters."

I was back to thinking about aliens from the planet Zirmakon. But I couldn't stop staring at the Steckermans'.

"There's so much USIC in that house right now, you could choke on it, Dobbins. I gave them the sheets of paper—the ones from the shoe store. Now I wish I hadn't. I thought we might play give-and-take."

"And they weren't giving?"

"Not a fart on a breeze," I said. "I feel helpless."

"Don't. You got Rain, Cora, and your brother to look after."

He offered to drive up and down the five streets mentioned on the posting from the Utilities Department and see if there were any unmarked cars or cops, or out-of-towners digging up any water lines or acting otherwise suspicious. I reminded him that there were strange lights on already in the woods, between our house and Dr. Mather's new construction, and that Mr. Stetson had pointed to that place as the spot in question.

Dobbins was out the door as fast as he could go without drawing attention to himself. It could be that he would only find workers from the Utilities Department back there, cussing a blue streak over a broken line. But he might also see some USIC guys—strangers in ties and suits. That would be a dead giveaway.

I needed to think about my brother and Rain and Cora. I went for one of the cases of bottled water in the kitchen and took it out the back door.

TWENTY-FOUR

CORA HOLMAN
MONDAY, MARCH 4, 2002
7:05 P.M.

RAIN AND JON Dempsey were roughhousing beside me. The noise was happy, at least compared with the noises Aleese used to make, but it was the type of thing I used to stare at from across the cafeteria or down the corridor. It was like movie actors had jumped out of the screen into my house.

Rain tried to push Jon Dempsey away, who was attempting to help her up. "The dress thing... it just doesn't work out for you, Rain," he was saying. "I just saw your underwear."

"In your dreams." She pushed his face.

"Ew, get your typhoid off of me. Typhoid Mary."

"Weirdo."

I forced myself to my feet, also. I'd turned the television off shortly after they'd come in but kept the remote in my hand as I pretended nothing was wrong with a scene like this inside my house. Standing up put me firmly back in their world.

I moved toward the table, toward Jon Dempsey, Adrian Moran, and Tannis Halib, and they turned dead quiet. They kind of stepped back and stared down at me as I walked through the middle of them. What was I supposed to say? I knew that "May I take your coats?" was wrong, but I didn't know what was right. So I busied myself with an aluminum cover on one of the pans that had come from the Ebermans' and ended up in the kitchen by myself.

The blackness out the back door looked so inviting. I wanted to fold into it so I could get my thoughts together in privacy and silence. My headache was gone, but not the chills, and my thoughts were cloudy to the point where I wondered if I had dreamed the VHS I'd been watching. Aleese had fought for something outstanding—protecting more Kurdish people and trying to get them into America. I wondered what else I would see of her life prior to coming here, but it was pointless to guess at that now. I just wanted to say "the Kurds" over and over to myself, and try to link them to me through an act of heroics.

I spotted a yellow paper on the floor and reached for it, figuring it was a pizza delivery menu. A shadow materialized behind it. Scott Eberman toed the door open with his foot, with what looked like a case of bottled water or soda in his hands. Bob Dobbins followed closely behind him. Scott looked past me, muttering to himself.

"Jesus Christ... Why do I try so hard? Hey! Guys!" He hollered over my shoulder, then his eyes found mine. "Sorry, Cora. I should have figured their homing devices would have located Owen and Rain... I didn't mean to turn this into a party house."

Dobbins moved toward his friends, but Scott dumped the

case of water on the counter and took the yellow notice from me, something about not drinking the water. I drank a tall glass when I took the Tylenol, but my stomach wasn't upset. He struggled to stand it up behind the spigot with one hand.

"Would you like a piece of tape?" I asked.

"No. Go sit down. Lie down. Don't touch these guys—Rain! For Christ's sake, will you wash your hands if you're touching all that food?" He left the notice on the counter and stalked into the dining room. He turned her by the shoulders and shoved her toward the bathroom, despite that she was in the middle of a sentence to Bob Dobbins that ended with a laugh and "retard!"

Jon Dempsey was a "weirdo" and Bob Dobbins was a "retard." A longing for Rain's easiness with people hit me so deep that I swayed dizzily, watching Scott play supercommando through the doorframe.

Tannis was clapping Owen on the shoulder and talking to him softly. Scott walked up behind him, pulled him backward by the hood of his jacket, and said, "Don't touch him. Go wash your hands."

Then, he stepped over to my chair, where my dropped tissue was still on the floor, and he picked it up with his pen. He held the thing like a lollipop while Adrian lectured him.

"Scott, chill. Last time I kissed your brother was over a week ago! I ain't hacking, coughing, sneezing, shitting... whatever the hell else Rain's been doing—"

Tannis snickered as Rain reappeared, holding her hands up to Scott.

"Do I pass inspection?" she asked.

"If you pick your boogers, you gotta go wash again, so

mind your manners. Dempsey, put that down." Scott walked toward me, tossed the tissue off the pen through the doorway, and I caught it. Jon Dempsey was holding my tea mug by the handle. I'd left it on the dining room table hours ago.

"It's in my way," Dempsey griped. "I'm trying to be useful and set the table!"

"You and whose mother? Wash your hands, please." Scott pushed him into the kitchen, and Dempsey locked eyes with me before putting the mug in the sink. I managed to smile at him, but only a flash. He'd asked me out last year. I don't know what had gotten into him, except that he has a reputation for asking lots of girls out. He had a dual role going of halfway-decent jock and class clown, but his attempts at romance worked into the class clown part. Whereas some guys might have gotten a reputation as "having asked out half the class," Jon Dempsey was stuck with "half the class has turned him down." I managed to be very nice until the third time he approached me. I walked away when I saw him coming toward my locker, and the guilt had stayed with me ever since.

Now, he turned from my sink, as if he could barely remember my brush-off. "You don't mind us here, do you?"

My only answer was a smile and "Not at all!" though it came out more easily than I might have expected. Fortunately, he got absorbed in the bottles of water, pulling one out and reading the label.

"Evian? My favorite." He broke open a cap with his teeth.

Scott came back. He stared at the bottoms of his jeans, which were soaked. He stomped each of his feet, and I heard squishy noises.

"I stepped in your enormous puddle when I couldn't see in front of what I was carrying...," he mumbled.

"I'm sorry about the puddle," I stammered. "Mr. Glenn said he would have the Utilities Department come and do whatever work was necessary to—"

"Stop apologizing. Do you have another pair of socks?" he asked.

I rushed to the laundry room and came back with another pair, to find him barefoot, sticking his socks and shoes in a plastic Acme bag. He grabbed a tea towel and dried his feet so meticulously that Jon Dempsey and I exchanged glances. I had a sinking feeling, what with his own mother's funeral coming up tomorrow. *Was he losing his sense of reality?*

"Yo. It's just water," Dempsey said. "It's warm as July out there—too warm to catch pneumonia, my man. Don't stress yourself so much."

Scott shot him a sharp, annoyed glance, but no comments followed. He took the socks from me after tossing the tea towel into the bag with his socks and shoes and tying off the top. He shut his eyes as he pulled the socks on, leaving me with the notion that, just for a few moments, he wished to shut out the world. My eyes bounced to that tea towel and stayed there until I could feel him glance at me.

"Cora, what are you doing? Do you want food?"

"Thanks, I'm not hungry just yet," I stammered.

"So then...go lie down. Take a load off."

I felt awkward doing that with all these people here, but I pushed myself off the refrigerator, realizing he was probably giving me an excuse to get away from Jon Dempsey. So, I faked interest in the television cartoons, pretending not to be hypnotized by the conversation going on between Rain and Adrian Moran.

"So, where's Danny? Did you hear we broke up on Monday?" she asked.

"Yep, heard all about it. Hall says you're, um..." Moran trailed off with a grin.

Rain grabbed his arm. "Tell me what he said!"

"I don't get in the middle of this shit. Let go of me. Get your typhoid off of me."

"Tell me!" She put her hands behind her back as Scott came past her. "Danny said I was bossing him around?"

"He says you were trying to grope him, ya know? Cop a feel—"

"You pig!" She forgot and slapped him on the arm. Moran couldn't stop laughing, and I found myself trying not to smile. "He was trying to get in my car, and I know he had at least two joints on him! He doesn't remember who my father is. I was trying to search him before I would let him in my—"

"Yeah, right." Moran snorted, and I laughed silently.

I thought it was silent, but they both looked at me.

"Cora, tell this man I'm not domineering just because I have certain matters of principle."

Moran stared, waiting for my input. Fortunately, Scott stepped in between us, handing me a bottle of water.

"Drink this. Don't drink from the tap, okay?"

I thanked him, wondering again about his sanity. Had he forgotten already that I'd read the yellow notice, too? But Adrian was back to arguing it out with Rain, and I didn't have to think up something clever.

Soon my floor and couch were covered with people eating food off paper plates and talking to each other. I took a piece of chicken and some salad, but I only picked at it. Owen didn't eat more than a few bites, but he smiled a couple of times. I felt like a spectator in an audience, but like I could become the stage at any moment.

It wasn't until most of the plates were empty that the glances my way increased, and I sensed some common question behind their eyes. Finally Jon Dempsey, in his go-lucky way, put it out in the air.

"So, Cora...where's all your relatives?"

I had totally forgotten about the story I'd shared with Scott of having a grandmother in California: "I...have a father, but he lives overseas. His flight arrives tomorrow," I added before realizing the horrible spot I'd put myself in. If Scott intended to keep his brother and Rain here like he had implied, they would see that lie unfold. Scott was staring. I put my head down, praying he wouldn't say anything. He didn't, but Dempsey made it worse.

"So, like, where's your girlfriends? Are they coming over?"

"Dude, you just want more fodder for your collection of shrunken girl heads," Bob Dobbins interrupted him, and turned to me. "Don't answer that, Cora. This is not the time, Dempsey. That was way tasteless."

I pretended to giggle with them, and then made like I had to go to the bathroom. I stayed until my heart quit slamming and I felt certain the conversation had moved to something different. When I came out, Scott was leaning against the hallway wall, and before I could say anything, he pulled me back into the bathroom and shut the door behind us.

He must have noticed me blushing, because he said, "So long

as you don't actually believe yourself about dads and grandmas, I'll let it go for now. We've got more immediate problems."

My eyes floated to his.

"Cora, did your mother drink tap water? I mean...as a habit?"

I spoke quickly to get that last subject out of the air. "A side effect of morphine is chronic thirst. She probably drank...a quart every night."

He shut his eyes with a sigh. "There are so many USIC people in Alan Steckerman's house right now, they're falling out the front door."

I halfway got his implication but muttered in confusion. "But...I thought Mr. Steckerman said...I thought the water towers had passed all the tests."

"They did," he said. "But we've got two deaths on our street under very strange circumstances and a notice from the Utilities Department that the four streets surrounding us shouldn't drink the water. Plus, Mr. Steckerman's holding a USIC convention in his house. Am I supposed to think these aren't related?"

I couldn't think. "How would they be related?"

"There could be something in our tap water. Not the whole schmear, not the water tower. Just one of the veins that breaks off from the water tower."

My hand floated to my throat. "How would somebody do that? Poison just a *part* of the water?"

"There are probably ways. But I went to the Steckermans' to pick up clothes for Rain, and if those agents had acted any frostier, I'd have had to smack them."

"But...how?" I repeated. "And what on earth would a terrorist want with Trinity Falls?"

"I don't have the foggiest. This would be a goddamn stupid place to terrorize. We all imagine that terrorists live in places like... the Sudan, or somewhere exotic. And they probably have arms that reach that far. The world is shrinking, you know?"

I remembered Aleese's strange journal entry about us all being connected, like beads on a string. "I do know."

"Here's the only theory I can put together, on the spot. I could be way wrong, but here goes: If, say, members of some terror cell were working or staying around here, and if they were aware of where the new regional director of USIC lived, they might think it was funny to try a few of their little experiments out on his street."

A flash of resentment toward Mr. Steckerman shot through me, but he'd been so kind at Aleese's service, so I forced it away. The theory was beyond believing, though I didn't want to hurt Scott's feelings.

I repeated, "How?" for lack of something better.

He laughed absently. "I'm a paramedic. Ask me something medical. The USIC agents at the Steckermans' were so clammed up, I doubt they'd have told me the time if I'd asked. They don't want to cause a panic, I guess, though I doubt they're sure about anything right now. It's too soon. I'm willing to let USIC figure out how a terror cell can screw up my universe. I just want to know what's in the water. I think it's gotta be the water, Cora. Especially now that I've heard your mother drank it by the gallon, too."

"And so did I." I felt the room sway, not sure if it was some poison or imagination. I had never liked soda. Caffeine and sugar left me jangled. I'd been a water girl since I gave up Juicy Juice.

He just slumped against the wall. "And so did my brother, and so did Rain, and so did..." He stopped, and I hoped he wasn't about to name himself. "My imagination is running wild, of course, but I should have reminded Mr. Steckerman about some of my memos from the CDC—which state that certain waterborne viruses can *become* airborne once they're ingested into the human system. I'm trying to be as cautious as I can without being a lunatic."

His insistence that everyone wash and not touch us made more sense—though sending Owen's friends out of the house might have seemed overboard. I could understand his judgment calls suddenly, and once again I got the impression he did better while keeping his mind working.

His eyes were lit with a fire, though his speech was firm. "I'm certain USIC has big reasons to suspect the water. That notice from the Utilities Department is too coincidental, no matter what they 'appear' to be doing at the end of our street. It's all a ruse—having trucks and lights set up to make it look good. And if the water contained seepage from some local root rot, Alan Steckerman would be taking care of his own kid instead of leaving it to me."

I had to say the whole thing out loud. "You think someone...somehow...poisoned the water on just a few streets. In Trinity Falls, New Jersey. Of all places on the globe."

He finally said, "Let me tell you something, and this is embarrassing."

"Okay," I said.

"I was at work the morning of September 11. Some guy came in and told me the Trade Center fell, and do you know what? I didn't know what the Trade Center was! I live less than three hours from there, but didn't know. Call me a piss-poor tourist, but it's just not on the top of my list-to-pay-attention-to places because lots of business is done there. I'd visited Chicago once with my mom, and I had it confused with the Merchandise Mart. I was imagining this boxy-looking place, maybe fifteen stories high, and the roof had collapsed or something. I said something dumb like 'Tough break, but shit happens.'"

I smiled sympathetically.

"Some guys had some wild idea that we'd all be sitting around slicing our jugulars with our credit cards if the stock market closed. And if by chance this thing happened here? They probably thought they could whack a bunch of rich, productive Trinity people along with the local USIC guru, and that would be some noble accomplishment. They forget about *bottled* water. I bet your family and mine are the only ones on the street without bottled water in our budgets, Cora. So, they'd end up poisoning a couple of single moms, a few kids—and the rich, successful Americans they were trying to get were off drinking bottled water. If that's what happened, how badly would it suck?"

I couldn't conceive of his thinking right then; I just didn't want him to look so fiery-eyed, so haunted. "Don't worry yourself so much...it could be something else entirely," I said.

"I almost hope it is some Al Qaeda shit-for-brains. I just need to know. Fast. Whatever it is, it's closing in on us."

"What do you mean?" I asked.

He picked up my hand, laid the back of it on his face for a moment, then dropped it again. He was burning up.

"A recent development of maybe the past half hour," he said. "Don't tell my brother."

LONG ISLAND,
NEW YORK

TWENTY-FIVE

TYLER PING
THURSDAY, MARCH 7, 2002
12:35 P.M.

IN THE CAFETERIA fifth period, I watched this new kid ahead of me in the garbage line. He looked pretty typical. Dark, foreign, confused. We get new kids a lot in a school this size that's one tunnel away from Manhattan. Migrating families generally come whenever they can get entrance visas. They can't usually plan around things like "the school year starts in September."

I came from South Korea in late November of sixth grade, and it took me a couple of months to realize that "It's Beginning to Look a Lot Like Christmas" wasn't the national anthem. But you'd think this particular new kid had never been in school before. For one thing, he was trying to special order his public school lunch.

"So... excuse me. Um... Do you have please a *baggle*?" He was smiling politely, which meant he was probably from India.

It's hard to tell the difference between certain types of new arrivals, but the Hindus have a reputation as being a pleasant lot.

"Baggle?" the lady server with the fat arms asked him. "You mean a Bag*gie*? You want a sandwich Baggie?"

"No . . . no sandwich . . . um . . ." He was smiling again.

"This isn't ESL class," somebody grumbled from behind me.

"Shahzad! No, no." Some girl in front of him grabbed his arm. Inas Hamdani. Nice enough girl. Honors geek like me, who told our illustrious jocks and beauty queens nicely to go kiss off when they wanted to copy her math and science homework. "That's a breakfast food! You don't ask for a bagel in the lunch line!"

"He wants a *bagel*? I can get him a bagel." Miss Fat Arms looked troubled but waddled off to get him his bagel. The other server had already disappeared back there for something else.

"Sorry, Tyler! Sorry, guys." Inas smiled at whoever was behind me. What could you say? Inas Hamdani blushes in such beautiful Pakistani maroon. "My cousin Shahzad is obsessed with food right now."

Whatever that meant. And okay, so the new guy is Pakistani. Even I can get things wrong.

I could hear the jocks going off behind me in the garbage line. "Ping, is that you holding up the works? . . . It's gotta be Ping . . . asshole . . . druggie . . . geek . . . asshole . . ."

I turned to look, and I saw a smoldering mound of whiteness. Dark-haired, blond-haired, red-haired whiteness. I was annoyed at Inas Hamdani's cousin, but suddenly he was slightly closer to me in life experiences than they were. Like me, he probably was thrown into this civilization overnight via JFK Airport.

I singled out Todd Coffey, because I'd heard he got benched for Saturday's wrestling match over nailing my face last week. He wouldn't risk getting benched again, whereupon the White Mound of Girls couldn't gaze at his bulging physique.

I flipped him the bird. "Quit thinking about sucking on this, Coffey."

"Oh my god" reverberated from the White Mound, and possibly from Inas, but in another language.

I could have made it worse. I could have threatened to fuck with Coffey's cell phone bill or something. I'm slightly better than your basic hacker, such that I could have Coffey's cell bill arrive with a twenty-six-thousand-dollar balance due if I felt like it. But the point wasn't to scare him shitless. I don't exactly like scaring people shitless. I like being annoying.

"I'll do him this time... hold back and have patience, Coffey."

It came from Bruno Fetalius. *Brutus Fetal Positionus.*

Miss Fat Arms returned, handing this Shahzad guy a sesame bagel.

"Oh! Bagels?" I cast a long glance back at the White Mound. "I would like a bagel, too! My mother never gives me breakfast!"

"So, why don't you make your own breakfast!" Miss Fat Arms did a one-eighty and waddled back into the vast, greasy unknown. The White Mound grew volcanic. I didn't look this time—just smiled pleasantly to myself.

Make my own breakfast. Like, maybe I had made my own breakfast, lunch, *and* dinner since we landed at JFK five years ago. This White Mound of Grunts had something resembling American sandwich-making, dinner-producing mothers. I have Dr. Germ, or the North Korean version of her. Dr. Germ, in case you're ill-read, is the woman who designed chemical weapons for Iraq.

If we're telling the whole truth here? My mother is not in America because she likes the place so very much. I found this out in eighth grade, after thinking for years that we'd come here to be upstanding American citizens, *émigrés elitus.*

But I don't want to make Mom sound more clever than she is. Dr. Germ is the Iraqi scientist. My mother is the North Korean gopher. She's a wannabe scientist with only half a Ph.D., and the most she'll ever be famous for is dropping off and picking up. She drops off to the North Koreans what she rips off from her American bosses at KTD BioLabs in Newark, and I'm not supposed to know any of this, of course, but I'd have to say she's largely responsible for my Cingular hacking prowess. Normal boys must find some way to be close to their flesh and blood, yes?

Inas's cousin Shahzad pulled an even bigger boner. I guess he knew enough English to understand a huge explosion had gone off behind him, and that it erroneously had my name tagged on it, not his.

He pulled his arm away from Inas and walked over beside me, gazing behind me as if this negative energy force from the White Mound was in some way interesting.

"Hi! Um...excuse me. My English leave me when I make stupid."

The mound behind me was silent except for a dull hum of giggles. I actually prayed for the guy—for a split second.

"This *my* baggle. I am sorry. Okay?"

Some asshole was asking, "Can you fit your weenie in the hole?" but the other guys were shushing him. Shahzad should have walked away at that point, I figured.

"I don't understand your saying, I am sorry. I am Shahzad. How to you too."

He held his right hand out to me, first. I shook without actually laughing and said, "I think it's, um, 'How do you do.'"

"Oh! How do you, too!"

He moved back to the White Mound and stuck his hand out again. They were laughing in a way that sounded truly dangerous. A major annihilation fest was brewing.

"Shahzad!" Inas grabbed his arm again. If fear had a color, it would be beautiful Pakistani maroon. I was ready to jump in for her, I was.

"Um...can you just forget about him?" she asked the White Mound. "He's really, really new and...all of that."

There's not much response to Inas, what with all her beautiful blushing and humble heart attacks, unless you can be an even bigger prick than I am.

"Listen to me, my man," one said to this Shahzad. "You don't do a bagel at lunch, unless it's a sandwich, and that's not in the state budget. And don't tell me you've never done a cafeteria french fry. It's the only truly edible entrée on our infamous menu."

I jerked around front, so I wouldn't have to remember which of the White Mound had warmed to Inas.

"Oh, I see many french fry in Pakistan," he said, "but not like those at Kentucky Fry. I eat Kentucky Fry last night. Much very good."

Miss Fat Arms handed me my bagel, too. I was in awe of some people's magical ability to keep from getting annihilated. No such magic ever came *my* way, and the fact was making me want to yell, "Where's my cream cheese?" just to send her back again and keep them waiting longer.

Instead, I pulled a small green pill out of my shirt pocket and popped it in my mouth. I said to Miss Fat Arms, "It's an aspirin, yeah right." Then I turned to a security camera and waved.

I had the thought that maybe if I got busted, my mother would be completely humiliated and sent to North Korea. I've grown tired of trying to scare her out of here with e-mails, the source of which she wouldn't guess in a million years. They said erudite and charming things like "I KNOW WHO YOU ARE AND WHAT YOU ARE DOING IN AMERICA."

Since she's almost completely incognizant of my existence, my triathlon hacking skills are beyond her wildest imagination. My only reward has been to hear her pacing the floor at night behind closed doors and talking on this one new cell phone I haven't figured out how to hack into yet. It was gratifying for a while, but lately her pacing and blathering in Korean half the night have been boring me through and through.

So was the White Mound.

"No, no. Cheese sucks on french fries. Just do ketchup." Todd Coffey, of all people, was warming up to this guy.

"Yeah? Well, excuse me, um. This baggle don't taste much very good."

Inas was giggling. "He, um, just wanted to try Jewish food. He never met anyone Jewish in his whole life."

"Oh yeah? Meet me."

I had to jerk my head around to see Dave Kogan shaking Shahzad's hand, a couple other kosher hands reaching out, voices echoing, "Forget 'How do you *too*,' that is bullshit. You know 'bullshit'?" and showing him five different versions of stupid-American-boy handshakes.

A couple of them went on about lox and cream cheese and tomato-basil cream cheese and all this stuff. *How did the bastard do that? The day I walked up to the White Mound, all "I'm sorry I held you up" and, worse, "Your Jewish food sucks," I would have about thirty seconds to live.*

"Miss Dolores! Get the man some cream cheese! We'll wait," Todd Coffey said.

It was Inas, that's what. Her sweetness could bewitch the worst of the worst.

I turned one more time, and Shahzad had actually turned Kogan's hand over and was looking at it alongside his own, as if he were looking for some sort of differences.

One of the guys in the back said, "Is he retarded?"

I changed the question to distract Inas. "Did your family manage to get him in honors with us? Or is he mainstreamed into normal prison life?"

She giggled fantastically. "Shahzad is a genius. He's in honors, despite his English. He can do anything on the computer—anything. In fact, he got a job at Trinitron after school. Pretty miraculous, yes?"

Miraculous. Shahzad's head slowly turned as the word Trinitron bounced through the air. I figured it was a blast of humility—another thing the Pakistanis around here are good for—but it didn't make me less jealous.

"Who did you know to get *that* job?" I demanded. The

software specialists at the Trinitron Internet café have to double as busboys, but they get tips as well as great wages, and it's the best gig outside Manhattan for high school and college computer heads.

"No one," he muttered, as he hunted for English. "I just send them my programs is all."

Hmm. I'd applied there, sending them my best programming sequences (nothing reflecting my hacking prowess), and got a standard "no thanks, no explanation." Maybe Trinitron read my school disciplinary file. And you *have* to know someone.

I left them without saying good-bye and sat two feet from a proctor. The Xanax I'd taken at the end of fourth period made me more relaxed than a jealousy fit would usually allow. Maybe that second one was kicking in already. I was relaxed enough to look at the crazy facts of my so-called life for what they were. I can do that every once in a while.

When you find out that your mother has brought you here so she can help steal secrets from the parents of school friends, what do you do with your life? How do you hang around with anyone? What strings can you pull to get a great job?

I've been kicked in the head enough times around here in the past four years, and sometimes that's how thoughts strike me. Like a kick in the head. Ker-blam, *Tyler, your life is so goddamn embarrassing that it's pointless to be near anybody.*

Ker-blam, *it's your old lady who deserves to get kicked in the head, so why do you insist on standing in proxy for her? Are you any less embarrassed after your blood is spilled and your eyes are swollen shut?*

I winged the bagel fifteen feet into the garbage can. Two points. I had eaten breakfast already. I always ate it, because I made my mom breakfast every day. I kept thinking tomorrow some USIC agent was going to get wise to her and, who knows, maybe some Hollywood ending transpires—he sticks a gun barrel in her mouth and jerks the trigger. Or she'd get sent to American prison forever and ever, and my last name would be all over fucking Fox.com and MSNBC, and the White Mound could finally lynch me and get off with a misdemeanor. Every morning could be the last time I ever see her, so I make her breakfast, and she answers her voice mail while eating my eggs and... *baggles.*

That Shahzad guy is classic, I have to confess. Computer guru? Computer guru better than *moi*? He didn't have any connections? He had a bad case of the liarooskees.

Anyway, here's what you do when you can't get close. You make friends with information. I would have to find out what this Shahzad was all about, how he got my damn job. Once he decided he hated me, too, I would at least have information.

Ker-blam, *Tyler, what good is information if you never do anything with it? It's not like some babe you can take to the movies. You're like that Jeffrey Dahmer guy. Only you collect facts instead of fingers.*

Hey, maybe you should just take too much of one of your numbing agents, carve into your chest with a razor blade, MY MOTHER IS A SPY. GOD BLESS AMERICA, BUT YOU PEOPLE ARE FUCKING STUPID, *and then slowly bleed to death.* Would that be rich?

What in hell would she do with my body?

TWENTY-SIX

SHAHZAD HAMDANI
THURSDAY, MARCH 7, 2002
7:35 P.M.

AT MY TERMINAL inside Trinitron, I have Catalyst's screen captured on my own. He is one of the many patrons, though I do not know which one. My USIC contact is at a terminal somewhere behind me, just like Hodji often was back in my village. I get most communication from him via instant message, though I have an earpiece if I need it. That much is the same, too.

But everything else is changed. Here in America, I don't know who my contact is. I only know him by the name "Tim," and I don't know what he looks like. I am not allowed to turn around and try to figure out which patron he is. I wait for Catalyst to write his response in a chat room, and it is taking him forever.

As Hodji predicted, I am to do nothing if I am not told. I feel like a computer myself, and I think the Americans like to waste time. It is a busy night, and Trinitron is five times the size of our Internet café in Pakistan, with more than forty terminals. In Pakistan, I could sweep or clean up.

Tim IMs me. "Be patient. He's still eating his brownie..."

I nod slowly, staring at my screen. Tim can see both me and Catalyst, supposedly.

Catalyst is online with PiousKnight, though I cannot make out where PiousKnight is chatting from. There are certain types of servers people can use which do not present an IP address or embedded codes, and therefore we cannot tell where they are. PiousKnight has been at Trinitron before, which means he could be in a city nearby. But technically, he could at this moment be in the Middle East, Africa, or South America. I have not seen VaporStrike or Omar0324 online since the night before I left Pakistan.

My nervousness is largely due to my new asthma medication, which makes me breathe so clearly that the silence is now overwhelming. The side effects make me twitch and have a racing heart. I try to remember how v-spying has always made me feel like the American cowboy.

I look toward the wall and a little over my shoulder, which seems like a safe thing to do. The boy whom I had injured over the bagel incident today is one row in back of me. Tyler Ping. He probably is doing some homework, of which we have so much. He seems busy, watching his screen, and not interested in me.

I understand that the American boys thought he was responsible for the bagel incident, and they were not very nice to him. But he taught me "how do you, too," and never fussed over taking wrong blame. He seemed nice enough.

I turn back, and chatter starts to appear, post by post. It is slow, but I recognize Pashto, a primary language of the Afghans, and cache the screen after each post. I have realized the erasing-chatter function they are employing for secrecy will not work in a copy if it is cached via intranet. I immediately translate it anyway, because Tim is waiting. I type in Arabic, which is easier for me, then run it through QuikTranslate for English, so Tim can understand it.

Catalyst: Have there been any more deaths in Colony One?

PiousKnight: Omar reports only the two women, of brain aneurysms. Be patient.

Catalyst: Is the medical community suspicious, being that they both met the same end?

PiousKnight: I have not heard that. However, Omar has reported some suspicious activity in Colony One. Omar says a notice has gone out to residents on five streets that a water line was inadvertently broken by the Utilities Department affecting them, and people should not drink the water.

Catalyst: Are these among the streets that Omar targeted?

PiousKnight: They are the exact streets.

Catalyst: That cannot be a coincidence. The Americans are a roaming devil. They learn their intelligence by osmosis.

I translate Catalyst's last line and try not to smile. I have been their osmosis—but I do not gloat. For one thing, I personally do not even know the continent of Colony One. USIC obviously has figured it out, and it is one important finding that I have not been central to. Back in Pakistan, I could take this chatter and surf and put many things together, but here, I am only to wait. It is maddening, and it is only my second night working here. Fortunately, some of the homework took all my free time in the school today. I have no chance to dishonor my agreement with USIC by surfing without permission.

I send more translated chatter on to Tim as it appears:

> PiousKnight: Fear not. The damage cannot be undone. The Red Vinegar they ingested will not cease to do its work. Those who are not symptomatic may still become ill, based on their consumption to date. Those who are symptomatic already will not have Providence on their side. You will see more deaths, my friend.

I am not a scientist, so my familiarity with bioterror is limited to what I read online. My fingers itch to surf, though I only translate and hit SEND. I could find out the contents of Red Vinegar based on these clues. I have helped USIC with small clues many times.

But PiousKnight posts again:

> They have their little informants and v-spies, traitors to the Truth, who helped them discover that the poisoning is localized. We will sniff them out and squash them, too, in good time.

I cache and type the translation, trying to focus on Red Vinegar and their implication that its effects cannot be reversed. I don't want to focus on their personal threat. I send it to Tim with a pounding heart but no comment.

Catalyst moves on:

Has the CDC identified the contents of Red Vinegar in the water?

PiousKnight: They may have found the water suspicious by now, but they will never identify this germ. It is unrecognizable.

"Not a known biochemical agent. It is a mutation" is how Omar0324 referred to it in Pakistan.

Catalyst: But the effects will become obvious in April, yes? Flulike symptoms will show up, and people will succumb, correct?

PiousKnight: Omar is confident. He states that he is already developing several new vinegars, from mutations with more fluency in water.

I almost jump as I see this development. I send it to Tim quickly, though my fingers tremble worse.

He curses softly and says in my earpiece, "Get on your own screen and log in to their chat room as BlueSky382. I want you to ask them a question."

BlueSky382...I had seen this log-in and had scripted it often for Hodji and Roger. They never mentioned to me—no one did until today—that BlueSky382 is a USIC undercover log-in. Probably several v-spies in USIC use it to play mole.

I log in as Tim suggests, but my nervous side effects double as I prepare to post, because I have rarely played this type of v-spy. There are actually two types of v-spies. Most are moles, who pretend online that they are somebody else, and they strike up artificial friendships. Then, there are the track 'n' translators, of which I am one of the few. I can use computer searches and translation skills to my advantage more easily than most v-spies, but Hodji did not like me ever to speak to the extremists. It is too dangerous for my age, he said, and therefore I usually entered chat rooms as an invisible v-spy—hacking past the log-in—and they were not aware of my presence.

I hear Tim speak plainly as I hesitate. "Greet them. Then ask if they need more money for funding."

My heart beats loudly. I am not well briefed on BlueSky382. What money term do I use? Dollars? Denari? Francs?

Before I know what keys I am striking, I send an IM to Tim. "You are sure Catalyst is not aware of us?"

He replies, "I'm positive. Why? You nervous?"

I will never admit to this. I force myself to log in, and I greet Catalyst and PiousKnight in Arabic. I pretend all the white space between their log-ins means nothing to me. They idle for some time, then PiousKnight posts back in Arabic.

PiousKnight: Greetings, my brother. How is your weather today?

Tim immediately mutters into my earpiece, "Tell him it's been raining for two days."

Long Island, New York, is sunny and balmy like summer, so I presume BlueSky382 is pretending to be elsewhere.

I post it. They ask about what my new pet parrot has thought to say lately, how my sick wife is. I realize the v-spies have embellished quite a story for this BlueSky382, far beyond what I had been capturing in Pakistan. Each time, Tim knows exactly what to say, and I post it.

I notice the Arabic from Catalyst and PiousKnight has stayed Arabic, and it stays visible on the screen, as if they have turned off their translating/erasing programs just to speak to me. I presume BlueSky is not someone they entirely trust.

"Ask if they need more funding," Tim encourages into my ear. "Use the euro."

So, I post,

> Do you need more euros at this time?

They idle, and I don't like this posting blindly. I had no idea until just now that USIC would either pretend to be a donor or actually send cash, and I haven't a clue what the extremists will say back. I presume that Tim is trying to get an actual mailing address from them. USIC can find out more about the terror cell with it.

> **PiousKnight:** Donations are always appreciated.

I post,

> What address should I use?

without waiting for Tim, as Hodji has mentioned this trick several times as used by his moles.

They idle long over my question about the address, though Tim mutters, "Good, good..." Catalyst posts what I am totally unprepared for:

Where are you now?

My heart-arousing medicine makes my hair stand. And I hear some snorting noise in my ear, which I presume is Tim, who thinks these men are funny.

"We're breathing into your necks, you stupid morons," Tim snickers. "Tell him you're still in Hamburg, Germany."

Hamburg.

I post quickly.

Catalyst: Yes, I forgot. Use our Hamburg address for money orders: Friends of the Orphans of the Lost Cities, Box C-112, Hamburg, Germany, 01-55979.

I think Tim will be disappointed, but he sends me Hodji's word: "*Bingo!*" Maybe in Germany they find post office boxes more promising than in the United States or Pakistan.

But before I can bask in my successes, Catalyst blindsides me with another question:

Do you live in Hamburg proper, or in a suburb city of there?

At the same time, I receive an IM from Tim:

Have to take a phone call...hang steady until I get back.

I can hear a cell phone ringing several rows back from me, but I dare not turn to look. I wonder if Tim has been sending these messages to some USIC meeting, and now the agents want to speak to Tim for clarification. He will have to go outside, as cell reception amid all these electronics is ironically horrible.

I lay my fingers on the keys, then remove them again. I wonder if Catalyst is trying to find out about me, as we are trying to find out about him. I don't want to answer in case other v-spies have given other details. After an eternal thirty seconds, Catalyst posts:

> Are you there?

Before I can think, I post "yes," then realize my error. I was not inclined to stupid mistakes in Pakistan, but I wasn't a visible mole, either.

> **Catalyst:** Well? Where are you located?

Anything but an answer will be insufficient. I type:

> Sorry, phone rang. I am in Hamburg proper.

There is idling, and I glance to the side, hoping to see the silhouette of someone returning to a station behind me. It is approaching nine o'clock, and the patrons are thinning out. But Tyler Ping is still working behind me, and no one is coming back to a workstation.

> **Catalyst:** Last month, you reported moving to Frankfurt. You move around a lot.

My heart goes too crazy. He is mole sniffing, I am almost certain. And I wonder how Tim can be so casual as to take a phone call. I drum on my keys and decide to post,

We are visiting family.

I see no one come back to a station from the corner of my eye, but realize I am craning my neck a lot, and it will make me stand out.

Catalyst: How long have you been where you are?

The post glares with suspicion. I feel like he knows I'm in America, and for only two days, and he wants to taunt me. Tim's IM flashes on my screen:

I'm back.

Whew. I bang out to Tim quickly:

Read chatter! How long has BlueSky been in Hamburg?

His voice sings softly but clearly through the earpiece. "Tell him eleven days. Remind him you and your wife are graduate students visiting from Lebanon."

I post these things, and Catalyst turns to chitchat about the funding for orphanages and him appreciating my past donations. I force myself to post the comments Tim speaks, but my nerves are wearing thinner. I think I should get an asthma medicine with fewer side effects or not take it at all at work. Better to wheeze than tremble and hear my heart bang.

For the second time this evening, some cloddish busboy drops the lid to the huge, metal coffeemaker in the back. It bangs onto the metal counter. I shoot out of my seat, standing straight up. The jump makes me extremely conspicuous, and I turn up the bottom of my shoe, pretending to look at it, before sitting down again. Tim IMs me:

> Something bite you in the butt?

I send back:

> My foot is asleep.

I scroll back up to see if I missed any chatter, thinking how Aunt Alika said to call my doctor back and tell him this "wonderful" American medicine is making me jump out of my skin. But it is not a custom that I can conceive of very well. If you get American medicine in Pakistan, you are considered very lucky, and you put up with whatever comes with it, no questions asked.

I hear the voice of Tim again.

"Shahzad, don't panic. But I'm getting activity readings from your terminal that someone has hacked in and captured your screen. It could be just one of those glitches, but I want you to log off, okay?"

In other words, someone else in the café has captured my activity and is watching it, trying to detect what I am up to. *Someone suspects I'm spying.* They could have seen my IMs to and from Tim.... I feel disconnected from my trained protector after logging off, in spite of the earpiece. I sit looking at nothing but my screen, hearing my heart bang, and feeling dizzy.

"Now go get coffee. Take your time. I just want to see if anyone in here is watching you."

Of course I want to look all around at that point, and he reads my mind when I don't move.

"You're perfectly safe."

I force myself over to the beverage station. I order a cappuccino, my very first. All Uncle Ahmer could get at a good enough discount for our café was Starbucks regular ground coffee. Cappuccino is part of my American "To Eat" list, but my first sip will hardly go down. My throat is tight.

I turn and look at a man down the row from me, the one who I think is Catalyst. Some flash of nerve compels me to see his full face, if only for a moment. His dark eyes had been on his terminal, but when I look, he meets my eyes. After a moment, he smiles and nods. I almost drop my cappuccino, clutching my ear with the microphone and thinking, *He knows, he knows...*

"Don't give yourself a heart attack. I'm thinking he just did that because you're the only other Middle Eastern guy in here right now," Tim says.

Pakistan is not part of the Middle East, and Americans often citing me as Middle Eastern does not inspire my confidence in their knowledge.

As I sit his voice comes through. "Log back on. I think you're okay now. Must have been a glitch."

Yes, a glitch, and that is why a dangerous extremist who poisons people's water just smiled at me. I long for Hodji's and Uncle's courageous presences behind me once again.

I don't log in to the chat room this time, as I want to be briefed on BlueSky's background in case I am ever put on the spot like this again. I think Tim will agree. Catalyst and Pious-Knight are now chatting in Baluchi, a second language of Afghanistan, which means they have resumed their conversation from before I came in. Probably they think I was knocked off, and I cache the screen and begin to translate to Arabic again.

I can see that they have been idling before resuming their chat, and I perceive the reason.

PiousKnight: I just received a message from Omar. He says that the offspring of one of the dead women in Colony One has just been hospitalized.

Catalyst: His brains are bleeding out his face?

PiousKnight: It is a she. A teenage girl. No bleeding yet. Omar expects she may exhibit other symptoms and the cause of death may be listed as something else. This is why he prizes Red Vinegar. It hides behind many masks. Good day, my friend.

I translate frantically, realizing this is the kind of detail that USIC can get great information out of. If they can find the location of Colony One by knowing two women died there of brain aneurysm, then they can verify the location by this detail about a girl.

It is as if her blood runs through me, and suddenly I am chilled and my face feels full of sickness. Hence, I follow up the translation to Tim with this:

Why can't you arrest Catalyst right now???

Catalyst has logged off and now is standing up. I cannot help but steal a glance. He looks almost too young to be involved in killings—maybe in his midtwenties. He has hair to his shoulders, long and dark. He looks like a musician or an artist, and it is impossible to tell whether he is Lebanese, Italian, Egyptian... One culture sweeps into another in this world, and I feel we need to be like God, who judges by the heart and not by appearances, to keep our lives safe. I feel the misery of the USIC agents, trying to judge who is capable of murdering innocents.

Tim replies into my earpiece, "That's what my phone call was about. USIC was saying again that we have enough to arrest him with that chatter. Michael says to wait. We need him to lead us to Omar."

Michael is the supervisor of my USIC squad, whom I met briefly yesterday afternoon in New York. I had jet lag, and his face is a blur. But I remember Roger saying back in Pakistan that if they arrest the Trinitron extremists now, all chatter will cease. It seems a very strange price to pay, to let a person like this run loose.

I wish to start hacking into databases like U.S. Social Security for Omar's only clue of identity, the 0324 that follows his infrequent log-in. But I am not allowed. I have no idea if another v-spy is doing this for them, or if they have tapped Catalyst's phone lines. I am only to do what I'm told and try to sleep at night, with no control over my own life.

I want to type an e-mail to Uncle Ahmer. It strikes me all at once that *he* is the missing ingredient to my nerve here in America. While he does not have the convictions of my father, Uncle has the sense of humor that steels me. When known subversives would visit our café, he would stand right over them and say in Urdu, which they do not understand, *"These men stink worse than my shoe, Shahzad."* He would use a tone similar to "Mop up this floor now, Shahzad." So, I would jump up and mop, and we would have a big contest to see who could keep the most straight face. If I had scripted dangerous men well and they gave a tip upon leaving, Uncle would howl and wheeze over the coins until his laughter became infectious.

Uncle's humor cuts the edge off the darker sides of life. He fears no man. Now I have no one who has any humor. This Tim is just a voice, and the blur of other agents I met yesterday seem equally serious. If I start Uncle an e-mail, Tim will see it on my captured screen. So I pretend to make busy while Catalyst stares until my face is breaking with sweat.

Someone is getting up behind me. I glance over my shoulder, and it is Tyler Ping. He is leaving. I glance at Catalyst and realize he has been looking at Tyler, not me.

It is dark outside, and I am looking through a tinted glass front, but I will swear that Tyler followed Catalyst out. And when they got into the street, Tyler dropped something that Catalyst picked up and handed back to him.

I cannot think of the implications of this immediately. My heart is still banging too hard. I turn quickly around to face a message from Tim. And Tim's IM creates further distraction.

"Go home and watch TV," he repeats. "Be normal."

Normal? In Pakistan, we have less than a dozen TVs in our village, but I never watched much. I do not like images without HTML support. They seem arbitrary and groundless. We would not even have had Internet in our village if Hodji and Roger had not gotten to know my father way back when he was a Karachi policeman. Our whole café is discarded FBI hardware.

Tim was intentionally not at my USIC meeting yesterday, because Michael wants him to remain unknown to me by sight. He must know I am new to this country, though I'm not sure he knows I am here less than forty-eight hours. Agents only know what they have to. He adds into my ear, "You should start with cartoons. My daughter Trish is seventeen and loves *The Ren & Stimpy Show.*"

But if I were in Pakistan, I could fight Hodji on the hacking issue and wear him down until he tried for a hacking warrant. Or I would surf until dawn. I would try to align the flulike symptoms of Red Vinegar with any local health news around the world.

But here, I must do meaningless mathematics problems and write a paper about some book in English. I had looked for it online so I can simply highlight and translate it to Arabic, but as Uncle often says, *Life is never so easy.*

And while reading in English, I will surely reflect on this sick girl who is suffering, and where I should be hacking to find Red Vinegar, this other new poison Omar is developing, Colony One, and Omar himself—

Maybe because it is time to face the dark street, I suddenly remember what Inas and her friend Amy have told me about Tyler Ping. They say he is a computer cowboy, and he can hack like nobody at any age. If my eyes haven't just deceived me, he knows Catalyst... maybe he is part of their group... maybe he hacked into my terminal tonight and will tell Catalyst everything he saw—

I sit back down quickly and type like mad. *"I must talk to someone in person."*

But that fast, I receive the message "Tim is not online right now," and when I turn around, all the seats behind me are empty. The door is slowly closing, and only a shadow cuts the sidewalk outside. I pull the cell phone they gave to me out of my pocket, but it is not yet connected, and they were bickering in my meeting yesterday about which phone numbers to give me for an emergency. I surmise they did not expect me to have emergencies so quickly.

I run outside to look for Tim and do not see anyone. I do not even hear an engine start, though I wait for several minutes. It is like nothing is moving on Long Island. Nothing at all.

TWENTY-SEVEN

CORA HOLMAN
THURSDAY, MARCH 7, 2002
7:50 P.M.

I'D BEEN TAKEN to the hospital around four o'clock, on the very gurney that I knew had carried Aleese away one week ago. I was surrounded by Scott's same squad, same ambulance.

The problem started with such a small accident that I couldn't believe I ended up in an ambulance. I was coming out of the bathroom for the fourth time in three hours when Bob Dobbins banged into me and stepped hard on my foot.

The pain subsided quickly, though Scott put ice on it and kept looking at it. The top of my arch swelled like a football and turned purple. Yet every time he told me to wiggle my toes, I could do so without any pain.

This flu had been bothering him, too, but if he had any symptoms besides the bright cheeks and zombielike conversation, he kept them to himself. But after half an hour, he punched a number in his cell phone and said, "Can you just come get her? This is over my head." He finished the conversation in the bedroom but forgot to shut the door, and I heard "possible blood clot" and "dangerous" and "turn into some weird stroke."

So, five minutes later, I was seated on a stretcher. I let myself cry, loudly for once. But as usual, what tears I shed were mistaken for meaning something else. I was terrified, but not really having thoughts about dying. My thoughts came right from this "sick house" that had sprung up so suddenly. Rain's one clogged sinus and slight earache had become a full-blown head cold yesterday, but she watched Aleese's tape with me a few more times and bragged about her and Jeremy Ireland to Scott. She could still talk up a storm about school, and I liked to listen. Whether she was plotting how she would find a date to the prom or talking about some funny incident that happened at a party, I was hypnotized.

As the paramedics took me, I felt cut adrift. Scott realized this, I think, and taking my face in both hands, he said, "You'll probably be back tomorrow... I'll pop in on you tonight."

"What time?" I blurted.

"After I sleep" was all he said.

And he didn't come that night. It implied that he was much more symptomatic and exhausted than he had been letting on.

After his mother's funeral Tuesday, which we all managed to attend, we were led out a back church door away from the crowds. Scott said it is not the most common memorial practice, but it often happens when relatives are not up for talking to hundreds of people immediately after an emotional service. We were brought back to my house, and we slept on and off, day turning to night without us really noticing. I figured word must have gotten out that we were ill, but I had no clue what Mr. Steckerman had said to keep people from either gossiping in panic about a mystery germ, or showing up at my house to extend more condolences. I can only say that nothing made the local news station except brief coverage of what was said from the pulpit at the funeral. Whatever Mr. Steckerman had told people was not repeated around me, and I only knew that he visited every couple of hours, leaving his house full of USIC people, to invent small talk with us and insist USIC's presence here was routine and unrelated. Dr. Godfrey came twice yesterday and once today to be sure we didn't have symptoms outside the normal range for flu. I was too tired to ask questions.

Bob Dobbins stayed with us all day yesterday and came directly after school today, agreeing to wear a surgical cap, mask, and gloves. If he thought Scott's theory of a waterborne germ becoming airborne was crazy, he kept it to himself. Tannis, Jon, and Adrian found the mask-and-gloves concept either too frightening or too ridiculous—I don't know which—and instead they telephoned every fifteen minutes for Owen. Scott was always snatching the phone and making them swear not to repeat his dark suspicions to a soul. They would swear back that they understood his visions of "community panic," and would not betray him, though perhaps the secret made them feel important, and they guarded that sense of importance as much as anything. It seemed to me that it was a lot to ask of three boys. However, it could be that they thought Scott was insane and were protecting his reputation with the secrecy. I thought that people expected to see us on the street in a few days and, with the exception of Scott, we all felt the same way.

It was the first time since seventh grade, when Aleese arrived, that I'd been so close to anyone, and I liked having houseguests more than I would have dreamed—even as Bob Dobbins stepped on my foot.

Hospital X-rays revealed no broken bones, and I was put in a semiprivate room for observation, though the other bed was empty. They left me hooked to an IV that gave me some sort of blood thinner, and planned to do some minor surgery in the morning to "drain" whatever caused the swelling. With no roommate, a television with an actual remote that worked, and food served up to me on a tray for the first time in my life, I settled into my aloneness. I came out of a peaceful doze around a quarter to eight, when Adrian, Jon, and Tannis came through the door.

They had submitted to the mask and gloves, which the nurses must have given them. But Tannis has one of those smiles that reaches to his hairline.

"The nurse said that if we come see people without a diagnosis, we have to wear these outfits," he said. "We're Batman, Robin, and Spider-Man. We've been ordered by the Incredible Hulk and, uh, Superman to come tend to the Princess."

He held out a marsh daisy he'd obviously picked from a vacant lot on his way here. It was the first flower I'd ever received. So despite the world tumbling sideways over their presences, I found myself smiling and reaching for it.

"I'd have brought a huge bouquet if I knew you could woo the woman with a marsh daisy," Jon Dempsey said, and I supposed they'd walked down on a last-minute decision, probably with Scott or Owen's foot in their backsides.

"It's a *magic* marsh daisy..." Tannis leaned over the bed

bars and held the flower halfway between his masked face and my own. "You know how you blow all the fuzz off a marsh daisy and your wish comes true?"

"Yes." I had blown marsh daisy fuzz with girlfriends when I was in sixth grade, because blowing it off in one breath meant you would catch the boy you liked.

"Well, this one doesn't blow." He blew through his mask and the flower didn't move.

I laughed hard enough that it surprised me. "Thank you... sit down...please..." I gave a typically awkward speech while reaching for the button that makes the bed sit up.

I answered all the usual questions: How are they treating you, how badly does the food stink, when are you getting out...? It was only after fifteen or twenty minutes that a headache struck. I thought it was anxiety.

I was taken by my usual horrors—that they had found me alone. I could have called even one girl from choir or one teacher, just to mention that I was here. Somebody calling or visiting would have been better than having nobody here when the school legends walked in. But everything lately spoke of my lonely, pathetic state of existence.

I figured they would leave as quickly as they came, bidding done for the Eberman superheroes. But Adrian climbed onto the empty bed, grabbed its remote, and started switching around TV channels. Jon sat between us in a chair and became engrossed in an episode of *Law & Order.* I found the sense to ask Adrian about a football scholarship I'd heard he was getting, and he went on and on about the University of West Virginia. I asked questions to keep the talk on something other than me.

But the safety net of their lives could only hold for so long. It broke around eight thirty, with a question from Jon Dempsey, stated in his unabashed way. "So, Cora. Did your dad get here?"

I'd totally forgotten that I'd told them my father lived in Belfast, and he was coming... *yesterday?* I was losing track of the days.

"He's coming," I blurted, and when they cast me confused glances, I added, "He had a layover."

Tannis nodded hard, indicating relief. "You shouldn't be here by yourself, you know."

I'd think of something to cover my tracks by the time they left. Meanwhile, I faked interest in the TV episode, but I was horrified with myself for lying... and for being alone. Both seemed unforgivable and drove me into some sort of weird hot flash.

When *Law & Order* ended, Jon chattered on about the Trinity Falls Utilities Department, mentioning how the water still hadn't been cleared for drinking.

"Scott's convinced that the water is the problem. And ever since his mother's service, he's gotten more and more focused on it. And tonight? Dobbins caught him staring at the faucet in your kitchen, Cora. Just staring and staring. It was dripping a little. He was muttering, 'Looks so bloody harmless, doesn't it? Clear as a crystal lake.'"

I didn't know what to make of Scott's poisoned-water theory, but it distracted me from wondering if my hot flashes were making my face shiny with perspiration.

"I thought maybe he had gotten crazed because he's got that flu, too," Tannis said. "He doesn't like being help*less* instead of the help*er*."

"He's better when he's busy," I forced myself to say. "What can we do?"

"We're trying different things." Jon leaned toward me in his chair. "Dobbins told us about their visit to the shoe place. You knew they broke in there, right? The day before Mrs. Eberman's service?"

I nodded. I got the news from Rain yesterday, though Scott wasn't talking about too much in front of Owen.

Jon went on. "Being that Scott handed over to USIC the scribble sheets he got off the desk, we tried to break back in and get him new scribble sheets. He seems sorry to have given USIC his only copy, since they don't want to include him in anything. We had a pencil and blank sheets of paper all ready to go and went down to that shoe store."

"But something prevented you from going in?" I asked.

Jon cast a glance over his shoulder at Adrian, who shot me a sideways look before staring back at the television.

"You're into it now, trumpet mouth," Adrian said. "You better just tell her."

I was generally grateful for Jon's blurting tendencies, because you knew where you stood.

"When we got there, some guy immediately got out of a car parked across the street, and he came over to us. He asked what we were doing. He was obviously staking out the place. We bumbled some half-truth, and he told us to leave—in this very nice way. Nice and... necktie-ish. I mean, he was in a polo shirt, but he had these city-slicker manners."

"And he was in a rental car," Tannis added. "Definitely USIC. They've been through that place with a fine-tooth comb, obviously."

"So...Scott and Bob Dobbins were right in their suspicions," I muttered, feeling my hot flash turn cold. I wasn't sure if I was ready to think of what we had as anything but a sickness. Jumping to the term *victim* seemed inconceivable.

"Mr. Steckerman keeps insisting there's nothing going on. That is bullshit. They may not know if our water was poisoned yet, but if there's nothing going on, why are nine rental cars still parked at the Steckermans'? And what is that guy doing staking out a closed discount shoe store?" Jon asked.

Tannis went on. "Anyway, we helped Scott re-create his own scribble paper from his memory, and he keeps staring at it... staring at this doodle thing he used to call a water goblet, but now he thinks is the water tower. There were eight lines coming from it that we think might represent, like, the main veins that send water throughout your section of town. One had a thick line crossing it, like...crossing it off, or...pointing out where something was."

"Is there any way to find out if the picture is of the water tower?" I asked. "*Are* there eight main veins?"

Tannis flashed a thumbs-up that went a little sideways. "At my house, we went to the Trinity Falls website. There used to be a Utilities Department page, and we clicked on the link, thinking it might give some info about how the towers flow, like a map or something. But now it leads to a PAGE IS UNDER CONSTRUCTION message. Very coincidental."

"Maybe it's just, you know, more post–9/11 dribble," Adrian muttered without pulling his eyes from the television. "History teacher said today that most every city in the country with info about water supplies or electrical plants or stuff like that has been taking all that off the Internet. I guess what used to be helpful to citizens is now a best-kept secret."

I just shook my head in wonder. You tend to think your country is never going to change—that it was and always will be the same.

Jon finally went on. "Yesterday in school, I caught Dobbins in the library, surfing for stuff. He's just not the 'library' sort. I sneaked up behind him and watched what he was up to."

"He was looking up some guy named Omar," Tannis continued. "He was looking for people in New Jersey named Omar Somebody."

"Omar..." I hazily remembered Scott using my computer to surf for the name a couple of days ago. But the sleuthing didn't help anyone else as much as it helped Scott, and I'd spent most of the last two days either dozing or listening to Rain.

"Hokiem." Jon shrugged. "Omar Hokiem. It was just a name that Scott had on that doodle sheet. So I just asked Dobbins what the sam hill he was doing in the library when we usually spend most of lunch shooting baskets in the gym. He asked me, 'You know any computer droids? I need someone way better at searching for stuff than me.' I blurted a couple of Napster freaks I know, but he didn't look satisfied."

"Wait." Tannis stopped him. "Cora, do you want to be hearing all this? If it amounts to just stupid Trinity gossip, we don't want to upset you with it."

I nodded for them to go on, though a sickening wave rolled through me. It was not the kind that indicates your body barometer is malfunctioning again. I'd had so many strange feelings over the past few days, I decided this was from hearing edgy news. And Jon's continuing story about Bob in the library worsened it.

"Bob just said he might have got very, very lucky is all. He couldn't find anything on Omar Hokiem, though he tried different spellings. And when he surfed for them separately, he got so much stuff that it would have taken days to click through. But the librarian was teaching a couple of sophomores down the row how to search for a site that was launched in the past few days. Dobbins thought, why not? Maybe it'll eliminate so much hogwash. When he finally surfed and plugged in 'Omar' and the four-digit number, he got this site. There were, like, six contact names at the bottom of this very-scary terror-cell document, and one of them was Omar0324@yahoo.com."

"What did it say?" I asked.

"I only saw it for a minute, but this terror cell wrote that its mission is to, like, 'stand strong against the devices of Satan, especially those in Europe and North America.' It called Americans 'mongrels,' I remember that. Something like 'The mongrels have replaced the richness of tradition with the seduction of materialism,' and 'We won't be ensnared by their... their *adoration* of flesh and of trinkets that perish with the wind.' It was creepy."

"But... it didn't say they were going to murder people," I hoped aloud.

"Not outright. But I wouldn't put it past them to try something. *ShadowStrike,* that's what they called themselves. Or that's how the word translated. Their real name is in one of those Indian languages, you know..."

"Arabic?" Tannis asked and rolled his eyes in disgust when Jon nodded. "Arabic is not Indian, brainiac."

"Whatever. I gotta start paying more attention in history and quit fooling around with Rain. But it was one of those pages that gives you the option of reading it in either Arabic or English, and Dobbins had the English—"

"Did you give it to Scott?" Adrian asked.

"Dobbins did," Jon said. "I think Scott gave it to Mr. Steckerman, saying he found it himself or something. I don't think he wants Mr. Steckerman knowing that we're running around on his behalf."

"What did Mr. Steckerman say?" I wondered. "Was he grateful?"

"Dunno," Jon said. "I wasn't there. But Scott beefs as much about those guys being unrelenting in not telling him stuff as he does about his fears of the water. He probably got the 'Don't get yourself worked up, you're sick' speech."

"You okay with this, Cora?" Tannis repeated, and it brought all their eyes to me. Tannis looked at his watch—I saw him from the corner of my eye. I had to find some way to get them to leave or they would be here all night, waiting for some alleged family to arrive.

"I'm okay, but I'd like to see the nurse." I pushed the button, hoping it would send them from the room.

They did leave, but I heard Dempsey's voice echoing from the corridor. "...if you guys want to go, then go. Even if she hurls, I got a good stomach. I can handle this for Owen. D'you hear that disgusting story about when Scott picked up her mother, they accidentally left her alone in the house?"

My experiences lately let me know that muffled sounds become crystal clear when your body temperature rises. Half of me wanted to shut them out, but half wanted to hear what was flying around.

"...and so Scott thought Mr. Steckerman was looking out for her, and Mr. Steckerman thought Scott and the squad was. She was *alone* in that place, sick as a dog, with her mom's favorite couch still warm. You want to leave her alone again? Go ahead. I'm staying until her father gets here."

I rolled my eyes in turmoil as they all grunted in agreement. They planned to stay—until I confessed to lying. As the nurse came in, I complained about the headache. She fluffed up my pillow but gave a speech about no further medication being permitted.

"I think I'd just like to sleep," I said. "Can you tell those boys outside to leave?"

I thought she would agree without question, but to my shock she studied me. "I can tell them to leave the room, but I can't make them leave the floor. Where's your family? Is someone coming soon?"

I didn't answer, annoyed beyond reason at this habit of human beings flocking together in painful circumstances. They were nowhere in the corridor suddenly, and I thought maybe they'd changed their minds about staying. So I wanted to scream as they returned ten minutes later with chips and sodas from a vending machine. The nurse was gone, and I couldn't think of a polite way to tell them to leave again. The only noise was the crackle of snack bags as they watched TV, and I just pretended to sleep. At some point, they would realize I had lied about my father, and they would wonder about that, as well as this story flying around that I'd been alone when Aleese was taken away. *Cora Holman has no friends... The girl. Has. No friends.*

I don't know if I was more awake than asleep when the phone rang. I played possum and let Jon Dempsey answer it, afraid that my head would burst if I sat up.

"She's asleep," he said.

I thought maybe some grand angel had whispered a deal silently in my ear: If I could manage to keep my chin up, he would give me some dignity—and a miracle. Because Jon leaned over the bed until I could see him. "Your father, is his name Jeremy Ireland?"

"Yes," I muttered, wondering if I should add, "but the truth is, he's dead."

Jon nudged me in the shoulder with the receiver. "Because, he's on the phone. He wants to talk to you."

TWENTY-EIGHT

TYLER PING
THURSDAY, MARCH 7, 2002
9:35 P.M.

SO I GOT HOME from my Trinitron adventures around nine thirty and sat in front of my terminal, laughing my ass off. I opened e-mail after e-mail I'd sent myself of these cached screens Hamdani had been looking at. I'd been caching as fast as he had. Oh my god.

Not to sound like I'd been caught totally off guard—I *do* read intelligence news, mostly to see if my mother's spying is about to become public knowledge. So I know lots about the intelligence community. I also know lots about terrorists who make plans over the Internet, and this breed of creature called a v-spy who tries to catch them in the act and script them.

And I'd been in Trinitron several times this year, noticing something about the place—it has independent hard drives at more than half its terminals, which means evil people can upload their own hide-and-seek programs. After 9/11 and the anthrax saga, I used to laugh inside that café sometimes, all *Jesus God, calling all terrorists.*

And I thought *my* house was a three-ring circus.

About twenty files were open, all cached screens, and I was trying to figure out what I had here. Okay, so there's these two guys, Catalyst and PiousKnight, and they're making my mom look like a Girl Scout. I'd had a nice little chat with this Catalyst on the way to the train. He said his name is Raoul (uh-huh, cut me a break). I could probably find out who he really is, and who this PiousKnight is, no problem. But for the moment, I was sucked in by their chatter.

Catalyst's friend Omar is poisoning people's water somewhere, and their goose is cooked come April, though they don't know it yet. Whatever Red Vinegar is, it's about to be followed by "*several new vinegars, from mutations with more fluency in water.*" USIC and the CDC are treading deep into it—but Catalyst doesn't know, ho ho, hey hey.

Inas Hamdani's cousin—*Who would have ever goddamn thought?* Call me a pig because I was not all falling off my desk chair, all upset about terrorist high jinks and people getting poisoned. As far as I'm concerned, it's a cruel world out there, and so long as my mother isn't exactly causing it, it's not my problem. Inas Hamdani's cousin, he was my problem. I couldn't believe a kid who's a junior in high school could get this sort of intelligence gig. *How in hell did it happen?*

I did a little hacking into the school's files, and I saw his records already typed in by the anal-retentive secretary crew. Arrived...yesterday morning...from a village that no one in their right minds could spell, in Pakistan. He's got straight As in high school, and he's eighteen. What the hell is the rush to get him into the American lifestyle? And how did he learn to gad about the Internet like Ghostbusters cleaning up a haunted city?

I backed out of the school's files and did some illegal searching around on my own. Hamdani is a very common name in Pakistan, but eventually I found the Shahzad Hamdani associated with this little village you can't hardly spell, and I saw that one of his several e-mail addresses aligns with an Internet café, of which there are also hundreds in Pakistan. But I saw that this particular Internet café has its own server, which is kind of weird, and it was now active. I wondered if I could break into this guy's former hard drive and see what was on it.

I tried, and hit a firewall. Computer gurus' hard drives aren't easy pickin's, but it was the nature of this firewall that made me sit up extra straight. Every firewall comes with a set of properties, and if you know how to find them, you'll see a registration number. Every business that pays for a firewall has a little sixteen-digit number. I remembered this particular number, because I'd seen it before—several times—when I tried to find out how much intelligence knows about my mom.

Just to be sure, I backed out and tried to hack into FBI headquarters in New York, and I hit the same firewall I always hit when trying to find out about her. It's the same registration number.

Shahzad Hamdani has an FBI-sponsored firewall on his server back in Pakistan. I'll be goddamned.

On that note, I just kind of floated out of my chair until I was staring at one of my many bulletin boards—this one hanging over my bed and titled "Einsteins à la Web." My jaw bobbed downward, and I said, "No way..."

One time I turned around in Bloomingdale's, and there in the ladies' scarves was Hillary Clinton. I've got this thing for sophisticated, upright, famous ladies and wishing they were my mom. And seeing her fall in love with this scarf, I got in line behind her to watch her pay. Then I ran home and had her Bloomie's charge erased from Citibank Visa. If you ever see Hillary Clinton in a blue and red scarf with little gold line-y things running through it, that's the scarf I gave her *gratis* from Bloomingdale's. But don't miss the point: There's famous people all over this world, and being that they don't live in a vacuum, *some* lucky devil gets next to them every waking hour, and every so often in your lifetime, you're it.

I'm talking about Hamdani now, and a little *Newsweek* story I had taped to my bulletin board, because I was so jealous of the kid in the story that I'd have to gouge his eyes out if I ever met him. My eyes floated to it, and I could feel my heart banging. It was a one-column story amid news about the formation of USIC. The words glared back about an unnamed sixteen-year-old guy from somewhere in Asia: "...'The Kid is such a proficient v-spy that he could turn any day of the week into Christmas for American intelligence,' said an unnamed source."

I scanned, though I knew the article by heart. He had been the talk of my fave hacker chat room for a couple weeks. Every hacker in the country was jealous as shit of this guy. The article didn't say the Kid was from Pakistan, only that his ability to v-spy had prevented two bombings in 2000, one in London and one in Nepal. It had said that his value to our government was not only his programming skills but his skills with many Asian languages, and these languages are a problem with the American intelligence community. It had even been thought that they move people like that around all the time to keep them safe.

If I could run into Hillary Clinton in Bloomie's, could I run into the Kid in a Long Island high school?

No, I told myself. I'm a realist. I thought maybe this was some transmutation of the Real Guy, some wannabe who wasn't doing too bad. However, what I'd been watching all night was this Shahzad cache screens written in hieroglyphics of god-knows-what, and he would type out the Arabic, translate it to English, and send it to god-knows-who called Tim. How many people like that could there be in the universe?

I could never hope to work as a spy. I'd flunk a polygraph as soon as they got to the part "Is your mother an assistant researcher at KTD BioLabs?" But whoever he was—the Kid or a wannabe—maybe I could lend him a hand. In light of my mother's embarrassing escapades, I owed this country something.

But what could I do that would be most helpful? I opened all the cached screens and read them again.

Omar says this, Omar hopes that, Omar's the devil fucking incarnate, what with his red and upcoming vinaigrettes, yeah, puke. I knew enough to bet money that Catalyst knew something USIC didn't, or he wouldn't still be walking the streets, telling me his name was Raoul. Maybe it's the contents of this water poison that he's going to spew his next time online, or maybe it's the whereabouts of this Omar creep.

And here is something that's even better than drugs for me. I do stuff like this, and it makes up almost all the hours when I'm not in lust for yet another Xanax: *I bet that I can find out who this Omar guy is, knowing nothing more than Catalyst's e-mail address.*

It would take a few days, but I sat back down, put my fingers to the keypad. I headed off to places that could get me five to ten years in a federal prison if the government found out.

But they wouldn't. And besides: Jail would have to be a less deplorable address than the one I've got now.

TWENTY-NINE

CORA HOLMAN
THURSDAY, MARCH 7, 2002
9:35 P.M.

"CORA, YOU HAVEN'T met me, but I'm a friend of your mum's. My name is Jeremy."

I sat up slowly, actually forgetting my headache and jitters for a moment. Adrian and Tannis turned to the television, completely unaware that I was hitting some cosmic lottery. The man's British accent hummed so beautifully. I wanted to ask how he wasn't dead, after what I'd seen in Aleese's journal. September 10, 1996. I'd assumed it was a death date, but could it be the date they left each other? My instincts were still strapped to appearances and how not to look quite so unlovable.

The best I could do to meet both situations was give an awkwardly loud "Hi!"

He was nicer than Aleese. He laughed. "Oh dear. You know of me. What in hell did your mum tell you?"

It didn't sound like a fatherly introduction, but what made sense in my life? I tried not to let my smile fade as he went on.

"I just this morning heard of her passing. I surf online for her name every month or so. I always come up with nothing, but this time I came up with the *Atlantic City Press*'s obituary. I'm too late for the service, I suppose, but I wanted to at least see you, give you a hug, and extend my condolences."

"That's... great," I struggled happily. I needed him here, for superficial reasons, and very deep ones that I couldn't put into words. I came up with a shy and trembling "I... am excited to see you."

"I should have called before traveling, but I had a problem in London striking up a correct phone number. I've only gotten it now, by finally tracking down a live voice at the church where her service was held. The minister gave me your number. And I'm at Kennedy Airport."

That was only about three hours from here. My heart was beating so hard it was giving me an earache. "Please feel free to come now," I said.

"But I understand from someone staying at your house that you're under the weather. I'm sorry to hear that."

Don't go home to Europe now. "But... I'll wait up for you. They don't make visitors leave at this hospital."

My hand was shaking. My whole arm, actually. I felt weak up to my shoulders. I really had no proof at all that he was my father. I just assumed it. At the moment, I really didn't care what he thought. I just had a powerful, irrational wish to belong to someone.

"Any good hotels down your way?" he asked.

I mumbled a couple and said, "I'm afraid all the beds at my house are taken right now." He didn't have to know the Ebermans were forced to be there. He could think I had friends.

"Don't wait up for me," he said. "Get some rest. I'll see you tomorrow, how is that? I have to brace up for hospital visits, I'm afraid. After your mum's injuries from some of our wild escapades, I'm almost phobic of the places. But you'll be a great excuse to try once again to overcome that."

I said quickly that I would most likely be released in the morning, so to call before he came. I handed the phone back to Jon, who had been standing over me and listening with some satisfaction.

No matter how badly I felt, I didn't want to drop off to sleep with all the questions running through my head. Could Jeremy Ireland fill in the holes for me? How on earth did Aleese hurt her arm so badly that she gave up living? Was he my father? What happened in Mogadishu?

I started to tell the guys that he would come in the morning and they could leave now, thank you very much. But I was out of breath in some strange way—like I was breathing but the worsening throbs in my head were absorbing all the oxygen. My hands and feet felt tingly, but in the mess of hot chills, I couldn't do anything but lie there and huff. I knew it was Owen coming through my door, in spite of the mask, but his presence here made so little sense I just stared.

"What's up?" Dempsey asked.

"Rain's in the emergency room," he said without a drop of energy in his voice. "She's got this headache from hell, and maybe half an hour ago, this blood started running out of her ear."

I shut my eyes as he moved toward me and told myself I had dreamed it. It's amazing how a strange thought can come so clear when your mind is completely out of whack. I told myself quite plainly that I was pulling a trick on myself that I'd learned in sophomore psych, which was to take your own pain and suffering and project it on to someone else. *My* ear was bleeding.

Or maybe it wasn't. Maybe it was my eyes, because the tears that would hardly fall ten minutes ago made little tickly feelings as they streamed down my cheeks. And if Rain was in the emergency room, why was Dempsey saying right beside me, "Oh Jesus, get the nurse!"

I just needed to look good when my father showed up tomorrow. I needed to look like one of my Barbies, with my hair tucked neatly in a French twist as I searched for the perfect handbag. I needed to be *perfect.* I just needed to sleep…

THIRTY

SHAHZAD HAMDANI
FRIDAY, MARCH 8, 2002
7:05 A.M.

FRIDAY, I WAKE to a bright and sunny American morning. I do not feel tired, despite that Hodji has told me I will have incredible jet lag through the weekend. It comes to my memory immediately why I had attended school yesterday instead of resting at Aunt Alika's house until Monday. Inas. She is not shy like the girls from Pakistan, and coming from Beth Israel Hospital the day I arrived, she had talked quickly and with excitement.

"You like math, don't you? I signed you up for the math club! Friday we are taking a field trip to the Einstein Museum in New Jersey! But you have to come to school on Thursday to get permission slips from your afternoon teachers..." The rest of her rapid English is lost on me entirely, as I grow excited about seeing things belonging to this Albert Einstein. Yesterday, she spoke to my teachers for me. My permissions are ready.

I rise with my insides smiling, but as I look out the window,

I remember more. Inas mentioned late yesterday after we leave him in the cafeteria that Tyler Ping is in math club. *Uh-oh.*

If Tyler did capture my screen last night and he is a friend of Catalyst, then I want to speak to Tim before I spend a whole afternoon with Tyler. That he could be a friend of Catalyst seems very incredible. Yet I cannot dismiss that Catalyst could now know about Tim and me.

I reach for the cell phone USIC had given me. But there are no calls, no numbers for me to follow backward.

I take the easy way out. As we get off the bus to school, I simply disappear. I figure that I will explain something later—that I got called in to work or something. Tim can help me with my lies, but first I have to get to him.

I go for an extralong stroll toward what I think is work, comforted by the sun's familiar presence as I pass by apartments, then houses, then bigger houses, then huge houses. The sidewalks are smooth, white squares, and the road is black cake. I have not seen a lawn up close before today, and at one huge yard, I stop and pull some green threads and smell them. Aunt Alika has told me that in the spring American grass turns very, very green, and I have seen such pictures on the Internet. I think it is silky and tastes sweeter than the dune grass of home.

Nearly three hours have passed since I left the school, and I am elated over my new asthma medication for enabling me to walk without wheezing—farther than I have in years. As I approach Trinitron, I think I will simply wait around until someone from USIC shows up. But I don't have to wait at all. A car comes around the corner, pulls up beside me, and the passenger door opens. I recognize a woman from my brief squad meeting in New York on Wednesday. Her name is Miss Susan.

"Get in," she says.

I lower myself slowly into the passenger seat, and she is pulling away from the curb before I can finish closing the door.

"Where have you been?" she asks. "D'you forget to go to school today?"

I am confused. "You look for me at the school?"

"We told you in our meeting we don't have the manpower to watch over you," she says, putting on her blinker and turning down a side street. "We bugged your phones, though. Call it part of USIC's speedy screening process. A technician happened to catch the absentee message that came through from the school. We thought you might have, um... gotten yourself lost."

"Not lost," I inform her. "I walk to here because of a problem at the school."

She picks up her cell phone and presses a button. "It's me, Michael. I've got him. He says he had problems at school and decided not to go."

I think she has misunderstood me, but it is confusing, because her words are accurate. After Michael the Superior speaks to her, she glances at me. "You have to go to school, even if the dog ate your homework. It's the law. Didn't you know that?"

"Yes...," I say quickly. "But you see. There is a boy... supposed to go to Einstein Museum with math club. And I think he is friend of Catalyst. I want to ask Tim before I am to speak to this boy."

Her neck spins toward me, and she loses her place in the driving lane. She relays this information on to Michael as she pulls into an even smaller side street.

"His name is Tyler Ping," I continue. "He sat behind me last night at work...maybe captured my screen. He left with Catalyst. Tim is already gone."

"What'd we tell you to do if you felt unsafe?"

I squirm in frustration. "You give me cell phone but you fight about numbers."

She groans. "We're suddenly inundated with problems in other areas. Could you have stayed out of trouble for four days, at least? You gave us a good scare while taking your little walking tour. You should have stayed home where we could find you. You can't just drop into the black hole like that. Understand?"

Go home and do what? To be alone with a computer is, for me, like being a glutton left alone with the refrigerator.

Miss Susan chatters on with Mr. Michael in her brash English. I grow beyond annoyed, because if I were in Pakistan, I would be free to find out who Omar is by now. I could do what I want and find out many more helpful things. I feel like one rupee in Uncle's dirty jar of rupees back in his dirty office closet. If this is sophisticated American teamwork, then it seems counterproductive.

"He's looking into this Tyler Ping," Miss Susan says as she snaps shut her phone. "I'm dubious. I've never heard of him. He's an upperclassman?"

"Yes."

"High school kid...I'm real, real dubious."

I feel my face turning toward her, and it is hot underneath. "Maybe you underestimate him. And me. That is a shame. Maybe I go home now."

She has turned off the engine and reaches for the key, rolling her eyes a bit. "You want me to drive you back to your aunt's? I've got six places for every hour today."

"I want to go home to Pakistan... where I am free to be man."

She doesn't turn on the engine after all, but she stares, and I sense a little more humility, or more compassion, perhaps. "You're doing a *lot* for us, Shahzad. A lot more than you realize."

"That is... nice thing to say, thank you." But I wish she would not tell me what I do and do not realize. "I did much more at home. Hodji does not tell you all. That is fine. I do not want to make notice of myself. I just want... to put my fingers to keypad and feel my room to think," I try to explain.

Hodji had been very vague about my background to the Americans, saying no one on the new squad needed to know I was "the Kid" from *Newsweek*. I cannot quite understand his reasoning, but I have heard Roger say many times that with the agents, it is better for the left hand not to know what the right hand is doing. No one can betray the rest that way, he says.

So, I am surprised when she keeps staring and finally says, "You're that legend, aren't you? That track 'n' translate prodigy that the FBI turned up in the Middle East." She is asking because one squad member put two and two together during our meeting and asked the same question. Hodji was there and refused to answer. He should have lied or told the truth. Now she is curious, and I am frustrated.

"I am not Middle Eastern. Pakistan is not part of the Middle East any more than you are part of Canada." I manage not to roll my eyes at American ignorance over the rest of the world's geography. But I do confess, "I was helping my father. That is all."

She watches me more, and I squirm, feeling I will never grow accustomed to American women's unabashed gaze. "Yes, Hodji said your parents...passed away? Is that right?"

"Yes."

"I'm sorry. You must miss them."

Her tone has turned sympathetic. I try to remember if Hodji also told me not to discuss my father. We had been so focused on v-spying just before we left Pakistan that much was left unclear to me. I think that perhaps Hodji had told me that, but I cannot see why USIC should not know I am related to their great technology specialist, and I decide I will tell her what she should not glaze over.

"My father was a very important subcontractor for the FBI," I say. "He make very good v-spy, first in Karachi, then New York City. Plus, they bring him tapes of wiretaps, and he can translate the Indo-European languages for the agents. Then they understand terrorists."

"Are you talking about Ashad Ali Hamdani?" Her whisper is surprised.

I nod with more confidence.

"Ashad Ali Hamdani was your father?"

"Correct."

"You're kidding."

I don't know why she would accuse me of this. "And he die in his asleep. Of the gas—"

"Yes, we all know that name and that tragic accident. I just didn't associate you with that Hamdani. It's a common name. Wow. I've heard 'the Kid' stories. And I've heard of Ashad Ali Hamdani. I just never put them together."

"No one is supposed to know over here that we are related," I say. Then I ask in confusion, "But it is all right for the *squad* to know, yes?"

She keeps staring and does not answer right away. I feel she is searching behind my eyes for something I cannot perceive... and perhaps I have made a mistake in telling her about my father. But I cannot understand why. She snaps to alertness when the phone rings again. "Hi, Michael... Gotcha."

She hits her OFF button, and her face has changed. "Don't go back to Pakistan, Kid. Especially not today." She starts the car and pulls out of the spot, making the wheels screech. "We've had a tail on VaporStrike for four days now. He's left his house earlier than usual today. He's gone into Trinitron, and he's online with Omar. We'd like you to tell us what they're saying."

I feel my heart pick up speed along with the car. I am waiting for her to thank me for cutting the school, but she is busy trying to keep us safe as she drives very fast.

THIRTY-ONE

SCOTT EBERMAN
FRIDAY, MARCH 8, 2002
11:35 A.M.

I DON'T KNOW where the thought "Musical Beds" came from as I walked out of intensive care in the morning. My sense of humor was to the left of neg. I had just checked in on Cora. They couldn't have picked some other cube to put her in? Uh-uh. She was in the bed my mother had been in. Now Rain was in Cora's former bed, and because a "contagious" protocol takes precedence over a "gender" protocol, my brother was in the other bed. You wouldn't believe how quickly a hospital snaps into action when the USIC supervisor's daughter is brought in on a stretcher.

It was still hush-hush to outsiders, but the hospital was abuzz. By nine o'clock this morning, there was a budget for "Unknown Infectious Disease." They admitted Owen for observation. The CDC was flying a phlebotomist up from Atlanta, a specialist to study a new batch of our blood every three hours. Dr. Godfrey spent the morning doing nothing but moving from Cora to Rain and my brother and back again. I had stayed out of his way, afraid he would insist on bedding me down if he knew I was symptomatic. I would have gone nuts if I couldn't move around.

I still argued with myself about the possibility of our mystery germ being airborne, but none of Owen's friends had the slightest symptom, and maybe even I'm prone to convenient thinking. I kept reminding myself that I felt fine today, even after having been up all night with Cora, so I was probably okay. I also reasoned that if I wore gloves and sterile scrubs and added a mask, I was entitled to give in to my bad case of the look-arounds.

The hospital really couldn't argue. They hadn't declared the virus airborne; hence, I was not bound by law to adhere to their wishes.

To declare the germ airborne, their protocol would have forced them to contact the media, and for understandable reasons, they were trying hard to avoid that. One reason is the hysteria factor, which means everyone with anything from a hangnail to last night's bean farts would show up in the ER, wanting reassurance that their symptom was unrelated. You have to be relatively sure your infectious disease is airborne to create that much expense, paperwork hell, and torment for the medics.

And I figured the hospital was pretty sure it *wasn't* airborne. In my mind, USIC thought the germ was waterborne only—and the hospital was listening to them. My evidence was based on oh-so-much USIC presence at the hospital. Imperial and O'Hare showed up at eight in the morning, flashing badges at the front entrance. It must be my intuition that put my look-arounds in the lobby when they arrived. I backed into the gift store and hid behind a magazine as they were led immediately to the elevator. The doors closed, and I watched where they got off. Godfrey's office was on the fourth floor. Rain was on the sixth. The elevator stopped at four.

This had something to do with poisoned water, and if they thought it was the least bit airborne, Godfrey would have been calling my name over the loudspeaker all morning and forcing me into a containment room. But I'd been walking back and forth from the ICU to Owen and Rain for over an hour as USIC met with Godfrey. The nurses attending Owen and Rain wore gloves and masks, but the door to their room was not even closed.

I stuck my head in warily, scoping for Godfrey, but he was probably still with USIC. My brother was watching television. I looked at Rain's chart rather than at Rain, because I couldn't stand the sight of her scared shitless. Not a Hallmark moment. I looked again at the lines Godfrey had written at 3:00 A.M.: "infected right ear canal" and "ulcerated lesion." That the blood was coming from her ear and not her brain should have given Rain much relief, but she hadn't grabbed ahold of it yet.

The wad of cotton taped over her ear was less noticeable than her eyes. *You're supposed to know what to do!* they read. I laid the chart back down helplessly.

"Who's winning?" I asked my brother, thinking he'd have something on ESPN, but he had to turn the channel to tell me, "You want NASCAR stats, or tennis in the Bahamas?"

I didn't answer. Nothing had changed on his chart, either. Temperature: 102. All other vitals: normal. I finally let myself plop into the chair beside his bed, and the tension release in my legs made everything heavy, including my head.

"How's Cora?" Owen asked.

"Same."

"She didn't wake up yet?"

"No."

He hit four or five different channels. "Is she *going* to wake up?"

I hadn't made up my mind about that yet. Her brain waves showed coma, but none of her vital organs were shutting down—a good sign.

"Is she in any pain?"

"No," I assured him.

"So, what's wrong with her? I know you know."

I did but hadn't wanted to tell him, because any symptoms Cora developed ominously pointed back to us and what we could develop. He had enough to worry about.

"Because, when she passed out, I was standing right there," Owen persisted. "She shed a bucket of tears but couldn't talk—"

"Yeah, yeah." I decided he deserved the truth. "Dr. Godfrey finally concluded that it was just a delayed reaction to stress that came when she relaxed enough. The problem is, well, serious but painless. It's her blood sugar. It shot through the ceiling. And if it weren't for all this other stuff going on, they would have probably thought she was a diabetic in shock. But she had no history of diabetes. Somehow, Dr. Godfrey knew to look for a blood clot on her pancreas and found it."

He studied the remote. "So how did he know to do that?"

"Do I look like a doctor?"

Owen was in rare form—alert, with flashlight eyes, as fever victims can often be. "Don't give me that. Medical info just like...seeps in through your pores. I'm ready to hear."

The truth was, Mr. Important, Roger O'Hare, had shown up at around midnight looking disheveled, and he talked to Dr.

Godfrey for half an hour in his office. I had stayed with Cora. When Godfrey came back, he ordered the tests that revealed the clot. I figured O'Hare had brought him some sort of intelligence, probably something he had found out from the CDC about the nature of the poison in the water. I couldn't put anything else together.

I just sighed and went for the truth. "She's on enough blood thinner to keep an elephant from clotting. So long as she doesn't fall out of bed and bleed to death, I can't see anything that's going to kill her," I said, but was afraid to add, *However, this germ seems to be full of surprises.*

"I was thinking since I hadn't drunk any tap water in over two days now, that I would be okay. But today, I'm worse. My stomach feels like sludge again. How can that be?"

"Since I've got no MO on the germ, I can't answer that," I said. But I knew that all germs are a life force, and just because you're no longer adding to them, it doesn't mean the ones inside you can't turn their little party into Times Square on New Year's Eve.

Owen was quiet for a while, then asked, "Are we... bad people?"

"How's that?" I grumbled.

"I don't know, but... this happened. We're not dreaming it."

He was on to something morbid, the usual. "I don't believe in a vindictive God," I said. "If God was like that, He'd be after me and not you guys."

"Maybe not God, just... other people. *Poor* people."

His cheeks were dull pink, but his eyes were calming, finally. No delirium.

"*We're* poor," I said. "What the hell are you talking about?"

"We're broke. We're not poor. There's a difference. Lots of

poor people out there really hate Americans. They think we're rich and spoiled and self-absorbed and stupid and all. Obviously, some think it's okay to try to kill us."

Ah, a terrorist conversation. He wanted to know if terrorists could have a decent point. My brother would find it in his heart to sympathize with Jack the Ripper.

"Well, it's *not* okay...," I stammered. "When people declare war, they're not supposed to target civilians. That rule is as old as history...and besides...we're not supposed to be thinking that way yet. No one's sure that it's—"

"*You're* sure. You think the water got poisoned. I know you do. I guess maybe I'm just...starting to think about that. I'm trying to look at myself as a target. I'm wondering what someone has to feel, has to think, to look at me and you and Rain and be all 'Those evil Americans. Do 'em.'"

I grabbed the remote from him. I'd seen him pass up a lightweight boxing match six channels back.

"You think too much," I said. "I'm trying not to think about stuff like that right now. When I do? When I can't help myself? I think of how gratifying it would be to grab some guy like that around the throat, squeeze, and slowly watch his eyeballs hemorrhage. Think of that, if you have to."

"But it hurts less," he replied quickly. "It hurts less to look for sense than to be mad. And if I'm a bad person, I'd like to know it, that's all."

I rolled my eyes past Rain, who was pretending to watch her own TV, and I raised the volume slightly, just in case she was hearing this. Her dad was off playing cowboy. I wished he was here to play father, though he was probably getting better mileage by trying to catch the guys.

"Owen, you are not a bad person," I groaned. "Don't insult me like that."

"How am I insulting you?"

"Because if you're bad, I'm off the charts."

"How can you say that?" He grabbed the remote back again and moved up the channels. "You're always looking out for everybody. You don't have a selfish bone in your body. As for being bad, it depends on who you compare us to. Maybe I look and smell good next to some kids, but next to Joan of Arc or John the Baptist or Gandhi, I'm still your basic scuz wad."

"So...what, then?" I watched him in exhaustion. "Some group of terrorists decides you're not the next Gandhi, and that gives them the right to poison you? What are you getting at, Owen?"

"I don't know." He put his head back and stared at some high spot on the wall. "I just started to think about this. I just like to understand people. Then I don't have to feel all angry and tense."

"Jesus." I rubbed my burning eyes. It was a prayer, not a cuss. My brother might not like to feel angry and tense, but somehow he could put himself through the tortures of the damned to try to understand guys who might have wanted to whack him.

"Do they think that, like, I should have been taking all my money and giving it to the poor people in India, or something?" he asked.

I just sat there.

"Where would we send it, Scott? I mean, I wouldn't want to send money to the poison-making guys to help their families. That makes no sense."

"Neither do you. Take a nap." I reached for the remote. Cartoons only added to the lunacy, but he right-handed the thing and stared at the Road Runner pecking chicken scratch beside some Acme pile of explosives.

"I do so make sense," he muttered. "I just want to know what I would have to do, so poor people wouldn't think I was a bad person."

"From what I get off the telly, most terrorists are not poor."

"Really?"

"Really. They're from the middle class. This isn't a money thing."

"So then...why would they want to kill us?"

"Relax, Owen. It could still be an EID. Don't listen to my constant ranting. Maybe USIC just suspects something, and I've been wrong before—"

I made a quick stab for the remote, but he was faster. "Should we be sending all our money to the Afghans?"

I had to leave. I stood up, felt the throb returning to my leg muscles, and tried to shake them out.

"Dude. We don't *have* any money," I snapped.

"Oh yeah," he said.

I figured I should go back to Cora's cube. I could stand it for ten minutes at a time. Moran and Dempsey gave me some story when I got here last night that Cora's father actually was coming, that he had called, and they'd heard his voice, and he was a real guy. Until he showed up, she was alone, and the thought bugged me, despite that she had no idea what was what. After that, I'd go see what USIC agents I could find skulking about in Administration, and I could stand on their toes and refuse to lay off until information leaked out their sinuses.

THIRTY-TWO

SHAHZAD HAMDANI
FRIDAY, MARCH 8, 2002
12:10 P.M.

I AM NOT in Trinitron long enough to take off my jacket, but I can sense the presence of my old foe, VaporStrike. Posts flash before my eyes... *They will anoint the waters with Red Vinegar—rivers will run red in Colony One*... just as they did the night he first had posted them in November while I watched, amazed, from Pakistan. Now, he is under the same roof with me.

A message appears on my screen:

Capture terminal 26!

So, Tim is here. That terminal is behind me across the room, but I dare not turn to look. My cowboy spirit fills me as I capture the screen and see both Omar0324 and VaporStrike, finally together again. They are idling. I feel that my hair is standing straight up in suspense and that it will draw attention.

I scroll upward in their chatter, and it is plain Arabic, all about a Dr. Scholl's foot powder taking away an itch between Omar's toes. I remember from previous posts that he is obsessed with American over-the-counter products. Finally, chatter appears in Persian:

VaporStrike: What is the word on the dead woman's offspring? Has the young girl died?

Omar0324: She is comatose. If she had developed her problems at home, she would be gone. The hospitalization prevented it thus far.

VaporStrike: You think she will succumb?

Omar0324: I am certain.

VaporStrike: How do you know? You say Red Vinegar is unpredictable.

Omar idles, and so I translate and send that much to Tim. I hate to end on a question and not an answer, but Omar takes more than five minutes before replying.

Omar0324: If she doesn't die of her own accord in a few hours, I will help her along.

I send it full of typos from trembling fingers. The implication is that Omar has access not only to this hospital but also to this girl. Is he an employee there? Can he move about undetected as a visitor?

VaporStrike: You are taking too many risks.

Omar0324: No. We have invested much. ShadowStrike has earned some gratification regardless of the risks. USIC is doing its best to keep the situation a huge secret, but we have every reason to believe they have stopped the ingestion of Red Vinegar. The sixty or seventy deaths we anticipated may now be reduced to fifty or sixty cases of mild flu. I don't mind personally killing off the symptomatic ones. Our colleagues deserve that much.

I see this very big *bingo!* and send it along to Tim with the word SHADOWSTRIKE in scream. Perhaps it is the name of this terror cell. I ignore my frustration that I cannot surf for new websites launched and see if I can find any new rhetoric, knowing this term. But in a moment, it seeps away as more words post.

VaporStrike: How will you kill her? Not poison. Say no.

I flinch, sensing his sarcasm.

Omar idles. I keep waiting to hear a scuffle behind me. I think USIC will topple VaporStrike to the floor and put the handcuffs on him. But Trinitron hums, business as usual.

Omar finally posts:

Call me a weak man in this sense. I saw the girl last night around eight o'clock. She was sleeping. A raving beauty. She looks half Persian, if you're asking me, but skin like porcelain. As my favorite new substance is so disfiguring, am I to tarnish her in order to complete our mission? I am not so inhumane.

A disfiguring substance. Smallpox? Tularemia? Both terms are among the most dreaded terms of bioterror to v-spies this year. I type like mad for Tim.

A body drops into the seat beside me, and I realize it is Miss Susan on her cell phone.

She says into her phone, "Shahzad, don't look at me."

I keep my eyes on my translation.

"Tim says you're typing so loudly it could draw attention. Calm down a little."

I translate softly, mortified at my indiscretion, but my medication coupled with my thoughts leaves me feeling electrocuted. She drops something on the table between our stations, and I realize it is an earpiece. She meanders to the beverage line and I pretend to scratch my ear while fumbling it into place.

Tim's voice says, "Can you hear me?" and I nod while scratching my forehead. I hit SEND on the script about the favorite disfiguring substance and a few moments later, I hear him mutter nervous curses.

VaporStrike: My brother, you speak of a young woman's beauty, which is superfluous. Why don't you allow me to come and complete the task for you. You are a scientist. I am a trained assassin.

Omar0324: You're too important to jeopardize.

Tim's whisper comes through clearly in my ear, "What's in Red Vinegar, you devils..." We have many questions. I type steadily to keep my nerves controlled.

Omar0324: To put yourself in jeopardy would not serve the greater good. I am a ready and willing sacrifice.

VaporStrike: As am I.

Omar0324: I fear, my brother, that your willingness suggests things other than patience, such as a lack of faith in our research.

VaporStrike: I trust in your abilities to mutate an airborne agent of bioterror into a waterborne agent. I trust in your abilities to predict its efficacy as a killer. I do not entirely trust in your ability to bring it all to pass before USIC figures out our plan and stops it.

Miss Susan is beside me again. "Stay calm," she says into her cell phone. "You're doing great. I can hear Tim, too."

Omar0324: I feel that you just want to partake in the thrill of a face-to-face meeting with a victim. I will contact you by phone when I am sure it is safe. I have a detailed plan.

I almost groan audibly upon hearing of the phone. If USIC has neither located nor identified Omar, then they may not be able to hear this phone call. I pray quickly that he will change his mind and post where he wants VaporStrike to go. When he replies, however, I am disappointed, but only for a minute.

Omar0324: For the moment, take your strength in what has already been accomplished, and leave the rest to me. The Americans cannot undo what is done. Red Vinegar is slow but steady, as was its mother Q.

The post is in French, so the letter Q is its English equivalent. I think Q stands for Queen, and do not understand them entirely. I hit SEND.

Tim mutters curses and puts the translation together so fast that it leaves me stunned.

"Susan, Red Vinegar is Q fever... I'm going outside to call—" and silence follows, as if he took off his mouthpiece.

I feel victorious on this news; however, Q fever is not what I expect to hear. My readings over the past months presented it as a disabler and not a killer. However, it is a well-known airborne agent of bioterror, on the list of substances intelligence would take rather seriously. I get a chill thinking of terror scientists mutating it to a waterborne agent. If air is like adhesive tape, water is like paste, making germs stick to organs and tissue with that much more efficacy.

I flinch as a new voice comes through my ear.

"Keep sending posts," it says. "Johnny and Michael are back here. Susan, get the kid out of there just as soon as they exit."

I don't understand this wish to "get me out" as quickly as possible. I perceive that Trinitron is crawling with USIC at this moment. I want to be part of any discussions. Some chatter bumps onto my screen.

> **Omar0324:** Don't waste your energy, my brother, stewing over v-spies and traitors to the Truth. We will find them and snuff them out. Their paltry little victories will be short-lived and remembered no more.

And with that, Omar exits, off to wander Inner Space where I am not allowed to chase him. I am relieved, for once, struck with what Hodji used to call on a good intelligence day "information overload." I type the personal threat slowly, trying not to focus on it. However, it was similar to a threat left by PiousKnight last night, and it makes me wonder...*Do they think we are watching and reading?*

VaporStrike logs off, too. Miss Susan nudges me and says to her cell phone, "The subject is leaving, Tim. We'll let him exit, and then we'll leave."

VaporStrike may have a half dozen tails on him, I do not know. And if I ask, they will not tell me. Miss Susan is glancing over one shoulder with her turned-off cell phone to her ear. Finally, she folds it up with a snap.

"He's gone. Let's go."

"Where are we going?"

Before she can answer, I hear a collective sigh that seems to come from many terminals. At least six men stand up and walk quickly back to what must be Tim's terminal. I see Michael there. I stand up, and Miss Susan grabs my arm.

"Leave them alone," she says. "There are some outsiders in here right now, too. We don't need to add to the convention. Besides, they can't talk to you anymore."

I think I have misunderstood her English. I just watch as she puts her cell in her pocket.

"I don't need to hear much, thank you, but I can greet them, in honor of my father, may I not?"

But she tugs at my sleeve. "Come out to my car, and I'll tell you why you can't talk to them."

So I pass by this cluster of agents without so much as a nod. They act as if I don't exist. My face is quite hot by the time I get into her car and close the door. She starts the engine.

"We're letting you go," she says. "You can't work for us after today."

I think I am in a nightmare. I cannot right then remember the word *fired,* so I say, "You are quitting me? I do not understand you."

"I talked to Michael right after I dropped you off," she says, pulling out into traffic. "You said you were Ashad Ali Hamdani's son?"

I remember feeling I may have committed an error when I told her, by the way she stared. I cannot deny it now.

"Ashad Ali Hamdani talked incessantly about his eldest son, and four of his five FBI contacts now sit on this very squad. You're not eighteen. Michael says you're fifteen if you're a day."

I am sixteen, but do not correct her, as I perceive this as a very minor problem. Hodji's words stick under my ribs: "*Americans would shit themselves before letting a teenager spy on their turf,*" but that was said before I brought them the mother agent of Red Vinegar, a pending attempt on a girl's life, and many clues to help them find Omar.

"I will call Hodji. He will tell you the many things I have done in Paki—"

"Look, you might be able to fool Hodji Montu and Roger O'Hare about your age. They work in the field. But you can't fool us for too long. We don't hire children."

"You insult me," I mumble. "You insult my family."

She smirks angrily. "I insult you by telling you your age? It's a fact. You can't get insulted by the facts. If your age isn't enough, you have another problem. An agent picked up your friend Tyler Ping fifteen minutes ago. He's at police headquarters right now, telling us everything from Catalyst's address on Long Island to what asthma medications won't give you the shakes. What in hell have you been telling your new little friends in school?"

THIRTY-THREE

SCOTT EBERMAN
FRIDAY, MARCH 8, 2002
12:15 P.M.

CORA'S CONDITION WAS the same when I went back up to the ICU. Her body, to put it in layman's terms, was wired up like the back of a hard drive. I watched her eyes flicker once, but that's normal for comatose patients. I sat there beside her, and the heart monitor's regular bleeping got on my nerves too badly to stay.

I figured I had to get some sleep, at least for a couple of hours—the problem was where to do that. My uncles had left for their homes, almost too easily. With Owen sick, I would have thought they would refuse to leave—at least Uncle Davis, the self-employed guru of fortune. There had been no way to keep that much from the two of them. I wondered if Steckerman had confided in them, asking them to leave. I wanted to reach my hand down USIC's throat and pull out information.

First, I found a gurney on the maternity ward, wheeled it around to a side corridor that contained nothing but a janitor's closet, and I jumped on. I slept for two hours on and off, and nobody even walked by. I finally sat up, and the world sloshed sideways. Some bizarre headache slithered up my temples like a cobra.

"Just tired," I told myself, though when I stood up, I realized I couldn't think conveniently for too long. The headache was unlike any I'd ever had. My knowledge of brain aneurysm put me in a terrible position, where I could imagine some throbbing vein behind my eye ballooning. I actually welcomed the pain in case it was an aneurysm. There's less pain after one bursts, and allegedly its victims can die peacefully. I figured as long as this vein hurt like a bitch, I was okay. But I needed to find Godfrey, confess my condition, and get some meds.

The ICU was the closest place to look, and I hoped I'd find Godfrey with Cora. I fell in behind a visitor who was stopped at the ICU double doors by a security officer.

"Sorry, you can't bring flowers in there," the officer was saying, and the guy looked disappointed.

But he rebounded with a smile, saying, "A present for you then," in some weird accent that I was too sick to place. New Zealand? Australia?

I went with a hopeful hunch and asked, "Are you Cora Holman's dad?"

He turned and stuck out his hand.

"Whew, glad you're here," I said, holding my hands in the air and saying evasively, "We don't shake hands around here unless we're gloved."

"A good thing," he said pleasantly. "I understand entirely."

"She's been alone, except for me occasionally. I'm Scott, a friend of hers."

"Nice to meet you," he said, glancing around nervously. It's not unusual for visitors to the ICU to be more freaked out than visitors to other wards and feel they have to whisper. "I'm terribly sorry I didn't get here sooner. I just now heard she's taken a turn for the worse." His eyebrows furrowed anxiously, and I pushed the button that opened the double doors.

To distract from his nerves and my agony, I blathered about her condition, the cause of the coma, and how we didn't know what to expect. "I know she was looking forward to seeing you. It sounded to me like she either hadn't seen you in years or had never met you."

I couldn't help the blunt moment.

"I have never seen her," he confessed, and I studied his troubled profile as he seemed to search for words. He finally laughed uncomfortably. "Forgive me... I've just always had an aversion to places like this. Her mother was much better with, er, the harsher sides of life."

Half a smile shot up the side of my face that didn't hurt. *Then brace up, Air Mac. You're about to see the ultimate.* I imagined him off playing poker at one of the casinos this morning, trying to get his nerve up. Great dad, yeah.

He continued, "I pray that she wakes up. Of course, I have lots of things to... to say to her."

He looked sincere. It was beyond me how somebody could have a beautiful and sweet daughter like Cora and never try to see her. Her mother might have been a witch at times, but she wasn't the Evil Troll Who Controls the Universe. I could hardly look at him, my stomach being in the condition that it was. He had dark hair like Cora's, but turning gray around his sideburns.

I took him past the nurses' station and sensed somebody right on our heels. A weary glance over my shoulder revealed Roger O'Hare with another guy in a suit. I was disappointed not to see Godfrey with them, too. I needed medical expertise, not the spies extraordinaire.

"What are you doing up here?" I figured a blunt assault was not uncalled for.

"We came to see Alan Steckerman's daughter, so I figured I would drop up here to see the other young lady as well. I understand she's comatose, but it couldn't hurt."

"Nice of you," I said, and hoped my sarcasm was noticeable but not out of hand. "Meet her dad. This is Jeremy... Ireland."

I figured I couldn't be too sick, what with my memory for names functioning well. I also pulled out of my ass the concept that I probably shouldn't introduce Roger O'Hare, at least not by full name and title. Not with all the goddamn big secrets he was obviously carrying around.

O'Hare introduced himself by first name only, I noticed. They got in a dialogue about flights from overseas and how long it takes to get through security at JFK International these days. I thought my head would crack like a walnut if I didn't run off to find Godfrey, but I'd had a plan to step on a few USIC toes until information squirted out their nostrils. Jeremy Ireland looked increasingly nervous, glancing around at the nurses and all the paraphernalia attached to the patients in each of the pods.

I finally busted into the middle of Ireland's statement about a two-hour wait to get through customs, and I pointed to Cora's pod. "She's in there, Mr. Ireland. One of the nurses can go with you and explain all the equipment." I hooked him up with the first nurse to pass by and pinched the sleeve of Roger O'Hare's suit jacket so he wouldn't follow him.

Then I pulled him along with me. He was a little resistant, and I couldn't tell whether he knew I planned to drill him, or if he was just transfixed by Ireland for some reason.

He finally fell in beside me and asked, "Why do I get the feeling Mr. Ireland is not very familiar with his daughter?"

"Touché," I muttered. "Does the job give you an eye for detail like that?"

"Obviously. During an interrogation, I can tell when somebody's going to lie to me before they even start lying." He smiled easily like he had at Steckerman's when we were talking about dropping our cell phones into the toilet. "Anyway, in case I run into you around here with anyone else you know, please don't introduce me by last name or title. I sometimes work undercover, though—"

"I didn't introduce you just now, did I?" I asked acridly.

"No, you didn't. That was great."

We were almost to the door and I glanced over our shoulders to make sure no one was listening. "I'm not a child. Don't pull any head-patting routine on me. That's not what I want to hear from you."

I laid on the big, metal button, and the double doors to the ICU swung open. I stepped through. He just stood there. Obviously, he was not thrilled to detect my mood, and he glanced over his shoulder as if Jeremy Ireland might be better company. I reached across and pulled him by the sleeve.

"I'm sorry, Scott. I can't leave here right now. I'm waiting for Dr. Godfrey."

"So am I," I told him. "The only other entrance to there is the fire escape. He's a doctor. He hates knocking."

I pulled the mask off my face, and his eyebrows shot up. I must have looked like shit. But he couldn't know the full extent of it, so I told him.

"I just woke up with a fever of about a hundred. I could puke on your shoe if I dwelled on my stomach for about thirty seconds, but I won't."

He stared in concern.

No one was in the waiting room, since official ICU visiting didn't start for another couple of hours. He parked himself facing the door, so he could get up and bolt if the more important Godfrey came past.

"But even if I puked on your shoe, it would be okay, wouldn't it?" I raised my voice to keep his attention. "I mean, nobody likes getting their tassels messed up, but it's not like I'd be puking a hot agent, is it? The germ we have is not airborne. It's waterborne only. Right?"

He said nothing, only swallowed.

"Look, my mother's dead. My brother's in a bed downstairs, in case you didn't notice when you looked in on Rain. Right now, I've got a headache so bad I think my head could split into a canoe. I think I have a right to know what's eating us—"

He started to his feet. "Scott, if you're feeling that bad, you need medical attention right away—"

I grabbed his arm and made him sit again. "I'm a paramedic. I know what I need and when I need it. I need information."

"I'm sorry," he said, shaking his head, like he couldn't give up anything privy. "I don't have any answers, and we're not really sure this is a USIC matter."

I decided I'd have a better chance if I asked direct questions.

"Does the CDC know what we have? Come on, have mercy. Just answer that much."

"They're working on it. I heard Dr. Godfrey say they might have a confirmation soon. Or they might not..."

"Was the water on our street infected by a terror cell?"

"We're not sure."

It implied they were investigating the water. It was more than I thought I would get.

"How'd you know to look for a blood clot on Cora Holman's pancreas?"

He watched me for a moment, kind of amazed. He stumbled, "I didn't decide that... Dr. Godfrey decided that—"

"Yeah, based on some info that you gave him at midnight. You and the CDC must have had some understanding of how the germ would behave. You must have a particular germ in mind to predict it like that."

"Look..." He stood up, and I realized this was pointless. He was a sealed drum, and even if my brother or I died of this raving bitch, it would not change the fact that he would not breach his job. "I'm going to have Dr. Godfrey found for you—"

"I can find Godfrey my goddamn self!" I stood up, too, and the world swam. I tried not to let it show. "You goddamn bureaucrats. You have no respect for human dignity."

"Scott, we do," he argued. "I spend my whole day, every day, fighting for human dignity. It's my life. I know you're scared shitless right now. We're doing our best. And right now, I have to be in that ICU. I'm sorry."

I let out a sigh as long as California before realizing there was something in his tone that was adamant. I scoffed.

"What're you doing? Lying in wait for terrorists to come blow the place up?"

He only smiled glumly and stuck out his hand to me to shake.

I tried not to feel totally depressed. He hadn't told me anything—but he had, in what he refused to say. I shouldn't have been bothered by the sudden idea that a terrorist could visit this hospital. I mean, I already suspected they ran a discount fucking shoe store here for at least three months.

O'Hare suddenly gripped me by the elbow, and I kept myself from pitching forward by grabbing his jacket. "Let me get you a doctor, Scott."

"It's not that!" I stared at the floor, wondering if I'd just committed the ultimate of stupid moves. "On the tapes at Cora's house, her father had a totally British accent. That guy in there with her now has an accent, but I can't place it! It's not—"

I never got out "British." O'Hare took off down the corridor and I followed on his heels, barely noticing him reaching for his gun in a shoulder holster.

THIRTY-FOUR

SHAHZAD HAMDANI
FRIDAY, MARCH 8, 2002
1:00 P.M.

MISS SUSAN PULLS her car quickly away from the curb with me in it, for the second time in an hour.

"I swear to you! I do not speak of myself, anything, to Tyler Ping."

"He knows a lot about you," she says. "A *lot.*"

"He hacked into my terminal last night. Now, I am certain."

"You think he saw your IMs to and from Tim."

"Yes."

"Michael will crap. Nonetheless...did you send any IMs with the name of your village in Pakistan in it? Or the fact that you're a straight A student? Or the fact that you're an asthmatic? That is a hell of a lot to find out about someone—"

Over the years I have collected much information when the rest of the world is sleeping. I don't understand Tyler's interest in me, but I perceive he has the *Newsweek* article that Hodji and Roger leaked out when USIC formed in January. It mentioned my asthma. And Tyler has done some hacking...to where? I hope it is not to our café's hard drive in Pakistan. We have, supposedly, a foolproof firewall, an FBI gift. My thoughts jump and confound me.

"He is a hacker," I tell her. "He can hack into anything, says my cousin."

"So, why his interest in you?"

I say nothing at first, equally angry at her for thinking I would trumpet my USIC business to another student. I finally offer, "When my cousin told him I got a job at Trinitron, I perceived that he was envious. Perhaps he hacks to see how I am more qualified than he—"

She makes a dirty word and sighs. "We can't be on top of everything! How in God's name were we supposed to prevent *that*?"

I say nothing. I am only glad she does not perceive it as entirely my fault.

She continues, "We looked for him at the Einstein Museum like you said to. Turns out, he was home, cutting school. In my opinion, he doesn't need to go anywhere because he's a real trip in and of himself. First thing he says when he answers the door is 'You guys found out about me already? You're smarter than I thought.' He's a disrespectful brat."

I don't know what to say.

"At any rate, he's not associated with Catalyst. That's what he says, and we're tending to believe him. But he's all over the place...says he can give us information about these two North Korean agents posing as shop owners...he says he can give us information about Colony One...and he's got some sort of computer programs. North Korea and Colony One, we can check on. We can't figure out what he's saying about the programs—it's all too technical. We just want you to stand behind the glass at police headquarters—we're using their facility until our offices are finished. Just listen to him ramble, and see if what he says about his little v-spy programs makes sense to you. He won't be able to see you. Can you do that?"

She drives us to the police station, where Tyler sits at a table behind the big glass, being questioned by some agent. He looks disheveled, as if he has not yet combed his hair. And he needs to use this tone once in Uncle's face to learn never to use it again.

"Maybe I'm telling you all this because I'm an asshole, that's why."

"You're providing information on these two men, two alleged North Korean agents, because you're an asshole?" the interrogator parrots Tyler.

"Yes. Don't *you* be an asshole and ask me how I know this stuff, okay?"

"How do you know this stuff? And please don't call me that again. If you want us to listen to you at all, don't act like a lunatic."

"I know because I'm a hacker. I'm a scunge-wad, disgusting hacker who could rob the Commonwealth Bank if I wanted to, without ever leaving this chair. How many times have I said this stuff now? I'm sleep deprived and on a short fuse, Mac. But maybe instead of being condescending, you ought to listen to me."

"We're here," Miss Susan says into a microphone, and I flinch, thinking it would blare all through that little room. She had said Tyler wouldn't know I was here.

But the agent just flicks at a little earpiece, like mine for

Trinitron, and says, "Let's take this from the top, just one more time. About these computer programs. Okay? Maybe I'll get it this time."

"In your dreams. I need to share this stuff with a seasoned programmer. Do you have any in USIC? *Yet?*"

"Don't antagonize me, Mr. Ping."

"Don't try to lie to me. Just get me Hamdani. He's doing favors for you, and we both know it, so—"

"Mr. Hamdani helped us out for a few nights. He is not on our payroll." The agent shifts a little. "You've got bad information, Mr. Moderate Hacker."

Tyler laughs. "Just get the guy for me. And maybe I won't add ten grand to your grandmother's water bill next month, just to repay the insult."

"Oh my." I turn to Miss Susan. Hearing English so constantly, even for two days, I understand more. "Why does he speak in that tone?"

She leans up to the intercom and says, "Should I just bring Shahzad in? We've pulled him from Trinitron. His gig is off."

I let her pull me around the corner into the room. I notice that Tyler Ping does not look at all surprised as I fall into a chair beside the agent.

He flings disks into my hands, explaining them one by one. His English is fast, but many computer terms are universal.

"Hamdani, here's some programs I've been perfecting for a little more than a year. I call this program Dog Leash. You program in the log-ins you want to follow, and it searches all your favorite chat sites. Once it finds one of those log-ins, it 'leashes' and follows it and creates a record on your hard drive of everywhere that person goes online."

He tosses the disk into my hands, and he has written USIC BULLSHIT 1 in magic marker. I have a similar program. I shrug, unimpressed, because of one glitch. "After the person logs off, you have to start from scratch," I suggest.

"Uh-uh. With Dog Leash, they're *leashed.* Permanently. From any terminal. You're only screwed if they change log-ins."

I wonder in amazement if the thing actually works and try to work my head through the problems he had solved that I couldn't. But he moves on.

"These guys are already using a program to make chatter disappear, right?"

I don't answer.

"Their program is stupid. It just makes the color of the type seek out the color of the screen and change to match it. The type isn't actually disappearing."

I feel fire of embarrassment hit my face. I would have realized this myself if I'd had more time to think—and more license to think freely.

"We walked together to the train last night, and I made a few wisecracks about this program I have that, uh...prevents the computer teacher at school from seeing what I'm saying on the school's system. His eyeballs bugged out when I explained it. I wonder why? Ha...He said he'd give me twenty bucks if he can upload it—which he did successfully at 11:27 this morning, thank you, Dog Leash. It's called Blizzard. *Sucker.*"

The agent tries to interrupt, but Tyler waves his hand to ward off words. "There's a bug in the program. Anytime it's activated, on any site, it will seek out Tim's e-mail address and send him a message with a hyperlink. Not only can you capture all Catalyst's chatter, but you have an automatic tracer to any new site he's using with his cronies. He'll basically be walking around the Net with neon footprints. I'm *giving* you it." He looks at the agent. "For free. I call it Blizzard Erase."

He holds a third disk out to me, but Miss Susan intercepts it, and I watch it disappear into her jacket pocket with awe. Ping will have done huge, huge favors for American intelligence if the programs will work as he says.

I see the agents trying not to respond with too much shock, but I am shocked as he repeats a line I am quite familiar with. Apparently, it is not as original as I thought: "In the land of computers, men are the children and children are the men."

I feel the agents' anxiety. Tyler's manners are horrendous. And yet, I would not have had the nerve to introduce myself to Catalyst and present a false program concept to his face. I am a good TNT but an inexperienced mole. I wonder how good I would be with this maniac Tyler Ping for the other half of my brain.

"Maybe we could try them and make for certain they work," I tell the agent.

"They work." Tyler folds his arms across his chest. "But suit yourself."

The agent still watches him, very uncomfortably. "Why are you giving us these things? Are you expecting to be paid?"

"Any offer less than three million would be an insult, so maybe it's like I keep saying—maybe I'm just an asshole."

The agent tries to smile but looks befuddled. "How do we know, if you're willing to give them one thing and us a better thing, that you haven't actually given *them* a better *better* thing?"

Tyler smiles. "Well, I guess you don't, do you? You want to take a risk? You want to take a risk to find out who Omar is and what other tricks he's developing, before a lot of Americans turn into something resembling a smallpox victim with a short-term memory of zero?" Tyler turns to me. "Did you see that chatter last night about *new vinegars*? That ought to get some anus muscles working."

He is vulgar and very much of a "loose cannon," to use one of Hodji's terms.

"I guess we all know where Colony One is, don't we?" He continues to shock me.

I do not know that yet—thanks to this new job. The agent acts as if he *does* know the location of Colony One, which galls me.

"Did you hack into the CDC?" He points a finger at Tyler. "Because that's a very serious federal offense."

"I don't think so. I don't remember. You'll have to ask my attorney. What the CDC doesn't know, that guy Catalyst is probably willing to discuss with his friends. Oh, and he said he would take me to a party with him sometime soon and introduce me to—"

Miss Susan puts her hands in the middle of the table and beats on it once or twice to silence him. "Mr. Ping. We are grateful for anything citizens bring in here, but there is a hell of a big difference between stumbling on information while you're minding your own business, and making our business your business. Your safety comes first. Okay? So, what kind of a deal can we cut so that we don't have teenagers chasing guys like Catalyst around town and trying to sell them software and video games, for god's sake?"

"He took the software, didn't he? The guy loves me. I can make anyone love me—for a few days. Can we just say that for reasons I cannot state, I owe you? Why don't you just take these programs here, and let me help Hamdani out sometimes? Bet I could be a really, really big help."

"I'm afraid that's impossible," Miss Susan says. "Mr. Hamdani wasn't forthright about his age. We're letting him go."

I suppose Tyler Ping does not see my world falling apart in my eyes, because he only cackles more and says, "You guys found out about that, too? Took you long enough. I'll be eighteen in ten months. I'll be as old as some of those guys being trained to toss grenades in Afghanistan. If they're old enough to toss grenades, I'm old enough to... what's the term? V-spy?"

He pulls his driver's license out of his wallet, but she does not drop her eyes to look at it. "Mr. Ping, to provide an intelligence service for the Coalition, you have to be efficient in every possible way, because trust is such a key factor. I don't think anyone in USIC could work, even sporadically, with your personality."

She hasn't said it spitefully, but the honest words cut into him. Despite his continued smile I can see the sadness smoke through and completely overtake the harshness in his eyes.

He stands up. "Keep those disks. They're user-friendly. Maybe you'll discover some things by the time Catalyst's buddies come up with, uh, *green* vinegar, or black-and-orange-polka-dot vinegar... in Colony Five."

My neck snaps at his harsh words, which Miss Susan ignores entirely.

"It's not in my job description to stop you from befriending maniacs, Mr. Ping. Just leave me a phone number, okay? When we find your body hacked into five pieces outside the

Midtown Tunnel, whom do we call to collect you from the morgue?"

I'd have been more worried they would find him toxic and dead from a chemical agent. Tyler pulls on his jacket, blinking into the tabletop, and for the first time, he looks very serious. All he mumbles is "Let me think about that."

And he turns and walks out. I turn my stunned eyes from him to Miss Susan as she reaches and pulls the first disk out of my hand.

"Miss Susan." I stand quickly. "I have been helping my father v-spy since I was ten. I don't think age is a critical factor. You need me!"

"Yes, we do," she says, pulling on her jacket and studying her cell phone messages. "But there is no way in hell we'll keep on a minor. If something happened to you, every mother in America would want to lynch us. We'd be 'irresponsible lunatics' on every news channel in the world. And look at the way this played out. We work with one kid, and within twenty-four hours it's a horrendous mess of big mouths and immature people with dangerous information. It'll never happen again. Tell me, why'd you do it? Come over here and lie? You seemed to be doing great where you were."

Don't I know this? My first thought is to protect Roger and Hodji. "Having been an FBI subcontractor and not an agent, my father was not entitled to death or medical benefits. I have very bad asthma and need American medicine, which is expensive."

She looks up from her phone, and perhaps I can sense a mother's heart in her softer tone. "Well. You're here. If you give your aunt custody of you, you'll get American medicine from her insurance at work. You just can't be a v-spy over here. Go to school. Get educated until you're an adult."

She probably means this without insult, but it rings of Uncle Ahmer's "*Act like an adult!*"

"I don't think it is right for you to explain to me how I am and how I am not," I blurt. "You know nothing about me."

But it is in vain, I see, by her unmoved eyes. Americans are very organized. They are moved by policy and forfeit common sense. They would rather be huge and organized than humble and correct, and they are so self-righteous about this tradition that they feel no guilt over their losses.

"Do you want a ride home?" she asks in a sweet voice that I find condescending.

"I do not. And you treat your children like sacred cows."

"We just want them to live to be very old cows," she says, but I am finished listening to her many quick answers, and I leave through the door in which we came, heading into an afternoon fog.

THIRTY-FIVE

CORA HOLMAN
FRIDAY, MARCH 8, 2002
2:00 P.M.

AS SOON AS I could see clearly, I knew that I had not died, and this place was not heaven. There were many tubes and wires pressing on my face and chest, and the constant beeps made my ears want to shut down. I sensed that time had lapsed since I spoke to my father on the phone, and somehow, I had gotten into this other room with all these machines.

A man stood beside the bed looking down at me. He had a kind smile. He was patting my head and talking to me in one of the languages that my mother used to babble in. But it sounded pretty and poetic. *Jeremy?*

Our eyes locked, and he stopped speaking suddenly and looked stunned. This time, he spoke in English.

"You see? I woke you up. When people hear the golden poetry of the Orient, it can rouse them from death. That's how pretty it is."

My dad? The questions poured forth, but I couldn't utter

them. A tube felt like a snake in my throat. I had only a second to decide that I was breathing through it, but that I was also breathing on my own somehow. It slowed when I stopped breathing.

My throat was sore. My hand jerked awkwardly, then flopped onto my chest. A series of tubes pulled and wouldn't let me bring it to my throat, so I pointed one finger shakily.

"You're thirsty, aren't you?" he said.

He brought a bottle of water out of his jacket pocket and put it to his own lips and took several swallows. "You won't be thirsty for long."

I shut my eyes just to rest my eyelids, thinking he would get the nurse and bring her in here. I couldn't understand the meaning of all these tubes, but I sensed I didn't need them. I needed a drink worse.

But when I looked again, he was only licking water off his lips and watching me. "You're very beautiful," he said. "In my country, you would be considered a prize. A porcelain prize."

I would have liked anything kind my father had said, I supposed. But I couldn't remember how to smile.

"I'm glad you have awakened. I have a lot I want to say to you. Unfortunately, I don't have much time. And besides, I personally do not feel it is appropriate for men to talk to women. But I will tell you a couple of lovely things. First, I am sent by Omar. You don't know him, but he knows you well. He made you ill. And now, you are about to be sacrificed. Are you afraid of dying? I hope not."

The syringe he brought out of his pocket sent out a flash of alarm. I wanted to ask, *"Daddy, what are you doing?"* But I was too limp to even thrash my foot.

"I wish this were a fast death," he muttered, reaching over me, behind me it seemed, but I was too dizzy to tell. "I would like to stay and watch you leave us. But my associates, they won't have it. They want you to die melodramatically. They are right, of course. It will leave a better message for those who foster you and your kind."

The *kind* came out in a hateful whisper, and I felt the tubes in my arm giving way, but I couldn't tell if it was a pinch or a jab or just a movement...it didn't matter. My heart banging was sending me dizzily back into dreamland.

But loud noises came close—an argument.

"You *said* it was her dad! You didn't tell me you've never seen the guy before—"

I didn't recognize the voice, but I did recognize Scott Eberman, who flew under some tall man's arm. I thought he had jumped on my chest. My brain screeched as tubes went flying through the air, from my arms, my neck, my abdomen. He yanked the long snake out of my throat and a stream of something acidy followed into my nostrils and out. I choked endlessly but could hardly hear myself because of Scott hollering.

"What the hell did you just give her, you freak!"

A blond man slammed the other man into the wall. I would swear he had a gun to the man's head. This was not my father, the impression was strong. My head fell on Scott Eberman's shoulder, but he gripped my chin in his hand, staring insanely.

"Cora! Did he inject you with something?"

All I could do with my throat was gasp for air. Scott yelled down at the ground. "...empty...syringe is empty!"

He fainted. He slid off my bed onto the floor, and I only remember going back to sleep in some nurse's chest.

THIRTY-SIX

SHAHZAD HAMDANI
FRIDAY, MARCH 8, 2002
2:00 P.M.

I EXIT THE police building, and the weather has turned foggy. Tyler Ping is not ten feet from me when I realize he has emerged from between two parked trucks.

"Congratulations on getting fired."

"I have nothing to say to you." I try to keep my dignity since all else is gone.

But he walks along beside me. "Yeah, I guess I'd be pissed, too. But now maybe you can really get something done. Right?"

"I go home to Pakistan, that is what I do," I mutter, more to the fog than to Tyler. "I go back to *my* land of the free. My land do not stop me from my life."

A flash of Uncle's face shoots through my mind, and I realize how angry he will be. He will now not get his forty-thousand-dollar "cost-of-intelligence" fee for my services. Perhaps he will be so angry, he will not take me back.

"Aw, fuck 'em all." Ping makes a grin about his dirty word,

which I have heard more often in a day of school than in all my years of exposure to English-speaking foreigners at home. For all the study of poetry that is forced upon them, American students seem not very poetic.

"If you want to work for free, you don't have to go all the way to Pakistan to do that. We can fuck up Catalyst's life right from here. They're not tailing us," he says, looking over his shoulder for the second time. "I don't think they will, given that their Colony One problems are starting to hit the fan."

With that mysterious statement in the air, I cannot help but keep walking with him. I am a hopeless addict for intelligence.

"What do you know about Colony One?" I ask.

"Okay. There's a town in New Jersey—maybe three-plus hours from here—where two women recently died of brain aneurysms within twenty-four hours of each other. One got a huge write-up in the obituaries. Her name is Eberman. The other, I can't remember. I found the obits in their online newspaper. After that, around nine o'clock this morning, I found out that one of their kids was admitted to the local hospital Friday for observation of strange flu symptoms or something."

He glances over his shoulder again almost reflexively before going on. "It's a little town called Trinity Falls. What a mess that's gonna be."

"You are *sure* this is Colony One?" I ask. "You have confirmation from a reliable source? Did you hack into the CDC?"

"Let's say I can't remember." He giggles as evasively as he had in the police station. "But there's a handful of other people in Trinity Falls who have the same symptoms as the dead women. They're mostly relatives, mostly young, like, our age. They're in and out of a hospital near there. The town is lousy with USIC agents, for reasons unbeknownst to anyone but USIC, and probably the CDC." Tyler nods in satisfaction. "Trinity Falls, New Jersey, just a hundred-mile trek down the Garden State Parkway after the Lincoln Tunnel. It's not a big city. But a big city would probably be outside terrorist capabilities, and it's within three hours of New York, within driving distance of Catalyst and friends. It makes perfect sense."

"Who else was admitted to the hospital? Somebody else now, too?" I ask, his "in and out of a hospital" comment still echoing in the air.

"If you can believe this—are you sitting down?"

Obviously, I am not. I wait for him to stop cuckooing with his strained laughter. "One other hospitalized person is the daughter of the new USIC supervisor in South Jersey."

I stop dead, staring. He continues laughing.

"The South Jersey USIC supervisor lives in Trinity Falls. Both deceased victims live on his street. Do you *still* think Colony One is somewhere else on the globe?"

I walk along, trying not to burn too thoroughly over certain issues, like Tyler knowing more things than I do. Also, I don't like that Hodji and Roger are avoiding me to "appear respectful to my new squad," as Hodji had confirmed in the plane would be their stance. I cannot be the one to deliver the news that Colony One is in America, and Home Base is New York, just like my instincts had said. I have suspected that perhaps Roger believed more of what I said than he was letting on. He would have said he was trying to protect me, but I am owed some congratulations, at least. Instead, I am fired.

"How did you find this out?" I persist. "I must know."

"Various hacking adventures. But I've got something even

better than that. Do you know how to hack into a *phone* conversation?" he asks.

I figure it is probably as easy as hacking online, but confess, "I've never done that."

His laugh turns full of disgust. "You'll fit right in here in America, dude. Everybody's a goddamn specialist. I hacked into a phone line today that could turn out to be a really special phone line."

Uh-oh. "A USIC agent?" I guess.

He laughs more. "I would definitely do jail time for that, and I might end up doing it for this. Yesterday, I made myself a deal that I could find your friend Omar. Well...I got a cell phone number and a bunch of phone chatter with a guy named Omar Hokiem. The last four digits of the phone number are 0-3-2-4."

It takes me moments to believe him, because he is laughing so hysterically at what face I must be making. I am all of awed, disbelieving, and horrified.

"Why you not tell of this to USIC? They would value this more than your programs."

"When was I supposed to tell them? Before or after they told me to go fuck myself? I want to get this guy on the line so you can hear him."

This is big trouble if I am caught. But how can I resist?

He says, "I didn't tell them because, for one, I've got my little streaks of pride. I gave them programs that I'm sure will work. I don't want to give them tapes of Omar McFoogle-Dee-Doo talking about the weather in Ireland in Gaelic. I can hear him talking, but he's talking in some other language. Before I decide anything, I want to make sure I've got the right guy."

I finally break out of my freeze, tugging him along with me by the elbow, despite that we are going to his house and not mine, and I don't know the direction. I only perceive that he is right, and USIC is not tailing us yet, and I am not surprised. They have major challenges and think they have time to catch up with us later.

"I can only get live conversation," he warns me. "God forbid if he's taking a long nap..."

As I am not going to work tonight, I do not perceive this as a problem.

THIRTY-SEVEN

TYLER PING
FRIDAY, MARCH 8, 2002
2:20 P.M.

HAMDANI AMUSED ME at my house. I tried to bust on him while we were waiting for Omar to make a call, but there were two problems. First, the guy did not understand sarcasm.

When we first got into my room: "Hamdani, you gonna fire up that extra terminal or stand there all day with your dick in your hand?"

"My how?"

"Your dick. You know? Your schlong, your paddle, your parachute, penis, poetic loveliness..."

He quickly checked his pants to make sure the barn door was shut.

Second, he didn't do drugs. I laid a Xanax next to his keypad. "Here, this is for your headache."

"Thank you, I feel much very good." He gave it back.

He's got a language barrier as a built-in sobriety factor. Still,

I was glad I brought him, despite that if his USIC squad decided to show up here, they'd have fodder to deport him to Syria if they were in a foul mood.

He wondered aloud at one point if he would get a paycheck for his three days' work at Trinitron. I asked how much they were paying him and almost shit my pants. For less than three hundred smackers, USIC had gotten *a lot* of translations on *great* intelligence—especially if you want to throw my three programs into the ballyhoo that Hamdani calls TNTs. All he wanted to discuss was the pair of Gap jeans he wanted to buy. I hated to burst his bubble, but I had to.

"Hamdani, USIC is probably not going to give you a dime if you were hired under false pretenses," I told him. "And not only that: If you ever do that much work for three hundred bucks ever again, I will personally have to poison your water, you Hindu moron."

He informed me very quickly that he was Muslim. The guy has zero humor, and somehow, I don't think he understands money very well, either. It's hard to know what in hell he's thinking. Some of my acquaintances from the Middle East are not known for rubbery faces, and I had not seen him happy since he was in the food line, eating bagels and introducing himself to the Jewish persuasion. I didn't understand the guy, but I had to love him for being polite the whole afternoon to the likes of me.

Still, it was a long two hours before my home-baked program CellScan finally chirped. How it finds and records a cell convo is my little secret, but I could sell it for twenty million if I felt like it. I don't feel like it. Omar0324's phone number showed up.

"*Bingo?*" Hamdani asked with emphasis on the *go*, which tickled me. I take it that's an intelligence term fudged by an Indian accent.

"It's him." I put on the speaker phone and started to record.

I recognized this Omar's voice, but again he went off in some foreign tongue, all "*Blah blah blee blee blee blay blow blu blah blee...*"

"Is it King Germ?" I whispered, but Hamdani held up a warning finger, and his eyes were utterly bulging.

"With somebody named Manuel," he finally whispered, and I wanted to dance a jig on the roof of the house. I figured Manuel could be PiousKnight, the guy Catalyst had been talking to last night when I broke into Hamdani's terminal at Trinitron. Or he could be somebody new to follow.

"*Blee blee blee blay blow blu...*" on and on.

Quickly Hamdani pulled up to my keypad and started to type. Just a huge mess of alphabet appeared on the screen. I started to tell him his fingers were on the wrong bloody keys, but he opened his eyes for a moment, saw his alphabet soup, and still didn't switch. This Manuel cut off Omar.

"*Blee blee blee blay blo blo blu blu...*"

Hamdani continued to type with his eyes closed, whispering, "This much very big *bingo*. Tyler, you make *very* big *bingo*."

After twenty minutes of me silently pissing myself, I heard the good-bye clicks. Hamdani just stared, first at the screen and then at me.

It was the first time I had seen him where he didn't look at least slightly confused and out of sorts—despite that his screen looked like ABC stew.

He asked, "Tyler, how much do you love America?"

Don't ask me serious questions, okay? "Uh...I love my computer more, my teddy bear more, my favorite jeans less. What the fuck is up?"

"I am wondering if you love America enough that you would risk going to jail for serving your country. The agents need these words I type. Except maybe they will be too angry for the law breaking..."

I got the point despite the broken English. How many times had I said to myself lately that jail would be a better address than this one?

Which doesn't mean I could up and tell Hamdani yes, like some sapsucker. But maybe there is a God: At just that moment, my mom's Korean floated under the door...from under *her* door. I couldn't decipher any words, just a tone and a notion. She was still on her goddamn cell, fucking up my school life, my goddamn country, my whole universe, actually. It might not be *her* country, but if you come here at the age of eleven, it's *your* country. She was horrendous.

"Yeah, I'll go to jail. What do I care?"

He turned his eyes back to the screen, still stone-faced, and he pasted all his mishmash of letters that made no sense into an e-mail. He put at the top in English:

"Uncle, I care not if Hodji is in Karachi or Washington or somewhere on Long Island still. Make sure he gets this immediately." He hit SEND.

I watched him until the suspense barreled up my throat, and I laughed at the top of my lungs. A bang from the other room was followed by my mother shouting in Korean, "Keep your noise down!" And in English, "For Pete's sake!"

She had thrown a shoe or something at the door. I had a

feeling lately that her intelligence vat was in a state of drought. She couldn't take the slightest noise.

"That was my pet Saint Bernard," I told Hamdani. "The breed barks multilingually. What the hell did you just send your uncle that looked like alphabet soup?"

Hamdani went online to a site called BabylonDoo. It had a bunch of keypad icons. Apparently, its programs could make your keypad work in any number of alphabets and languages, and after a minute it showed an Arabic keypad on Shahzad's screen. I realized he had just used the English keypad to hand-script that conversation of Omar's as if it were an Arabic keypad, just by memory. After a minute, his jumbled English text appeared in Arabic. I know the alphabet but not much else.

BabylonDoo...Get it? *Babble Undo?*

"Can you read that now?" I asked, hearing myself giggle.

"Mostly. It no makes perfect."

"What the hell did Omar say?" I cut to the chase.

His English got pretty good, like I noticed it could sometimes when he didn't stop to think about it. "Today, Omar do a very bad thing. Very, very bad. Hodji told me often this truth when we would tire of wait, wait, wait to catch terrorist chatter that is not forthcoming. Hodji says that people grow careless and feel powerful and take risks, and in time, these men would do this. He is correct. It seems that Omar thinks he is so smart that he can get away with careless jokes on those he despises. Now, I have a script of his joke. *Big bingo* is in his joke."

I figured I needed to read the script to understand what he was talking about, and I had my doubts about other things. First, I didn't really expect anyone to believe us, and second, I couldn't imagine anyone reading it immediately. He'd just sent an emergency e-mail to his uncle on the other side of the world, who is supposed to find some Hodji guy who could be anywhere in the world. And it's like Hamdani is afraid of having anyone read the thing, so he didn't paste the Arabic translation into the e-mail—he pasted the alphabet mishmash of what happens if you tried to use an English keypad like an Arabic keypad. If this Hodji person turns up in OutToLunch, Mongolia, he's supposed to know how to decode the thing.

Hell, I wake up each day and go on the Internet, and I practically live there all my waking hours. I barely know what it's like to not have faith in virtual reality. But I couldn't bring myself to imagine that his e-mail is actually going to be received, deciphered, understood—and believed.

"People are dying three hours from here, and you're launching strange e-mails at Pakistan," I reminded him.

He just sat with his hands folded, staring at the screen and waiting, like a kid in the Great Pumpkin patch on Halloween.

THIRTY-EIGHT

SHAHZAD HAMDANI
FRIDAY, MARCH 8, 2002
3:30 P.M.

TYLER APPEARS TO have a chronic itch on his insides, such that he cannot sit still for three minutes to see if Uncle will send me an acknowledgment of receipt. I glance at my watch: Just after three in the afternoon.

Maybe Tyler forgets that it is the middle of the night in Karachi. But I had set up an alarm with Uncle, which he promised to have turned on and functioning for if ever I got into trouble. It would crow like a rooster and shout in Urdu, "WAKE UP FOR TO HELP YOUR NEPHEW!" at the terminal at his bedside—if he remembered to leave it dialed up at night.

Sometimes I have had doubts about Uncle's love for me. Now is one of those times. I *know* he loves money and *think* he loves me also. But as minutes pass and I receive no reply, I get a queasy feeling and wonder if Uncle is glad I am gone from him. Perhaps he does not remember to leave his terminal dialed up, because if he thinks of me at all, it is with gratitude that he no longer has to split the café's money with his brother's son. His forty thousand in Pakistan is as good as four million dollars in America, and as far as I know, he still thinks he is coming into it. Maybe all he thinks of is building a villa for himself and Aunt Hamera, and I am forgotten.

The thought drives me to pay attention to Tyler, who is itching to know what bad thing Omar did. I take my Arabic copy, run it through another program on BabylonDoo, and it comes up in English.

He scrolls very quickly. I feel that Hodji would be outraged over this breach. But what am I to do? Tyler captured the intelligence in the first place, and besides, I find myself trusting him, in spite of his bad attitude and dirty mouth. I see something behind his eyes that is not hateful and full of impudence. There is a big heart driving him, my instincts tell me, and I am tired of ignoring my instincts.

Omar0324: I sent a foot soldier over to the hospital today to finish off the girl.

Manuel: He was successful, I presume?

Omar0324: I told him not to contact me until tomorrow just to be safe. USIC is roaming the hospital. But he was an assassin in a past life...bloodthirsty in my estimation. He injected her with something unspeakable.

Manuel: Ah, one of your charming unspeakables.

Omar0324: It takes time to work, but the end results should be worth photographing. I'm sure the doctors will take pictures, and we will find them on their Web pages and download them for my colleagues. However, all this waiting brings close to me a certain level of frustration and acting out. I am not always mature and sensible.

Manuel: Oh dear. And how have you acted it out?

Omar0324: Today, I named the makings of Red Vinegar...in a roomful of thirty people.

Manuel: Not the scientists on faculty, I would hope.

Omar0324: Great god, I'm not blatantly stupid. It was only the students. America spends so much money to make them so mindless. Sixteen years of alleged education, and their laughter reminds me of the bleats of a lamb. I told them the history of Red Vinegar. I told them I was joking afterward. I am a teacher: I laugh, they laugh. It was pitiful—and enjoyable.

Manuel: Nonetheless, you are taking risks.

Omar0324: I deserve the adrenaline rush, which I certainly am not getting from USIC.

Manuel: How much did you announce?

Omar0324: The whole thing. I said there was a deserted bayside town in the Soviet Union, where formerly biochemical agents of germ warfare had been stored and cultivated. I told them that if you knew what to look for, all these years later, you could find the cultures growing out of the very tree trunks. It's inherent in the bloodstreams of the squirrels. I wrote on the blackboard how you could mutate the germ. At the third mutation, you would have a waterborne agent, whereas before you had a germ that would only pass via dust, or the saliva of an infected animal.

Manuel: Did you mention the former germ warfare agent? Did you say the exact term, "Q fever"?

Omar0324: My friend. I can all but hear you sweating profusely. Don't be so given to nerves. I did not mention the term "Q fever," but believe me, I could have written it on the blackboard a dozen times and shouted it from the rafters in there. American students know nothing about history—nothing about their own roots, not even from twenty-five years back, when their parents were scared of the Russians. So long as I don't say, "It's on the next exam," I could tell them how to use smallpox to their advantage—or how it could be used against them. They will not remember if it does not apply directly to them, in this week or next.

Manuel: Your laughter does the heart good, Omar, but please don't take unnecessary risks.

Omar0324: The only people in the room who would have suspected my seriousness are those we would want to recruit. We need a few good recruits for our upcoming meeting Monday night, do we not? I would like to see if I got at least one student of the sciences to understand me. There might be all sorts of foreign nationals in that class. It is a very mixed-looking bunch—

With that, Tyler punches me in the shoulder. I am waiting anxiously for Uncle to indicate he indeed is awake and helping us, but Tyler pulls my hair so I must look him in the face.

"Were you listening to him, or were you just type-typing away? There's a recruiting meeting Monday night at some college near Colony One. Gotta be Astor College. Omar will be there. Are you hearing this?"

"Of course," I say. It is beyond my comprehension that Tyler thinks we should go there.

The conversation ends a few lines later. Tyler has jumped onto an Astor College website and is rooting through pages of announcements using the site's search engine. He finally opens "Panel to Discuss 'The True Nature of American Foreign Policy,' featuring" several names I am not familiar with but think they might be a *bingo*—more people in this terror cell. Their names are followed by "Visiting Professor of BioChemical Engineering Omar Loggi of the University of Hamburg." Tyler continues, "Betcha Omar Loggi is your Omar Hokiem."

I nod in stunned agreement.

"Bet it'll be a lot of rhetorical bullshit and nothing hard-hitting at that meeting," Tyler mutters. "They'll just keep drawing the right guys in closer and closer, and those guys will get invited to 'private parties' where the talk will grow thick."

"Yes." I am almost certain he is correct. This is how extremists behave online before finally making friends with someone they meet often in a chat room.

Within moments, I hear car doors outside. Two of them.

THIRTY-NINE

TYLER PING
FRIDAY, MARCH 8, 2002
4:15 P.M.

CONSIDERING I HAVE zero friends, I figured the car doors and adult voices floating up from the street were a couple of my mom's goons. Hamdani merely turned and said with ridiculous calm, "That would be USIC at your door. Please answer it."

I was all "Impossible. Not in twenty goddamn minutes." I stood up and looked out the window. The cars had pulled up across the street. A guy with jeans and a huge cowboy hat was holding open the front gate to my house, allowing a man and a woman to shoot in before him. The roofline didn't allow me to get a look at those two, but I saw Cowboy Man well enough, and cowboys tend to look out of place on Long Island.

I mentioned as much, and Shahzad jumped up like he couldn't help himself. He ran, taking my stairs two at a time. The three people on my porch turned out to be Miss Susan, the guy in the cowboy hat, and another guy I didn't know.

Miss Susan introduced the last man to me only as Michael. Hamdani ignored Miss Susan and Michael, but he seemed awfully glad to see the man in the cowboy hat. *Hodji,* Miss Susan said. Shahzad tried to look tough but threw his arms around the guy's neck after the guy said something in some other language that made them both smile.

Then Shahzad went on and on to him. *"Blee blay blo blo blu blu blu blo blo!"* He sounded truly pissed. The cowboy hat guy shushed him with an attempt at a calming tone. *"Blee blay blo blo. . . ,"* he replied.

Miss Susan ignored them and smiled at me like she was making an attempt to be happy to see me. *"I don't think anyone in USIC could work, even sporadically, with your personality."* Yee. Why hadn't she said my *copped attitude* or my *impudent mouth*? Personality—that cuts to the heart of things. It sounds like something you just can't help. Something you're born with. I'd never trust her again, after she used that word to describe my inadequacies.

"Blee blee blay blo blu!" Shahzad was still on a rip-tear at this Hodji, and I invited them in, half panicked. What a cluster fuck. My mom would know to shut up as soon as she heard adult voices in the house, but she would definitely go into cardiac arrest if she knew who these people were.

"Mom?" I shouted up the stairs. Her door opened a crack. "Mom! I've got the hardware guys here. They're coming upstairs to look at my hard drive. It's way fritzing. Okay?"

And I turned to them. It was too easy a situation, considering how many things could have gone wrong. They didn't want her to know who they were any more than she wanted them to know who she was. They figured I had done that for them and nodded their thanks. I took them to my room, and we closed the door. Even at that, Miss Susan and Mr. Michael talked very softly to me while Shahzad and Hodji continued to argue heatedly in some foreign language.

"Where did you get this conversation with Omar that Hodji just e-mailed to us?" Miss Susan wanted to know.

"Uh . . ." I trusted her not to arrest me about as far as I could throw her. But the truth was too grand to patch out. "I hacked into his cell phone."

"And how did you find his cell phone number?"

It's like somebody asking you, *"And just how did you find out what was on television tonight?"* "Can we leave it that it was easy?"

"No," she said. "It's important. We really need to know."

"Are you going to arrest me if I tell you?"

Her gaze rolled sideways to find this Mr. Michael, and he said, "USIC has no interest in arresting minors, especially with many things going on. We want to work out some assurances that you will leave these men alone after this. They're beyond dangerous. You have no idea what you're tangling with."

"You mean . . . after all this, you still want nothing to do with us?" I asked.

Michael managed to look sad. "I'm afraid we don't have options. If we were soliciting favors from minors and something happened to you, *we* could end up in jail. We're going to play by the rules, all the way."

I reached over and turned up my music so my mom wouldn't catch any stray words, and I made sure it was my most irritating hip-hop, to get even with these ancient crows. Hamdani finally stopped arguing with Hodji, and the man just picked up in our conversation like he'd been listening all along. I heard intelligence agents could be trained to do that—hear like three conversations at once.

"Listen, Tyler. Susan, Michael, me, we've all got kids your age. We know you're plenty smart. We also know most of you don't have the fear factor yet."

"What's the fear factor?" I asked. I knew fear. At least, I knew what it was like to walk into my school every morning at eight and know I could have my face kicked in at any moment. I don't suppose these guys walked into their offices feeling like that.

"Fear factor is when you hit a certain age, or you have an experience that is highly traumatic, and you say to yourself, 'I could be dead tomorrow. Or the next day. I really don't know what the stars have in store, but I ought to live my life carefully, every day, no matter what.' That's the fear factor. Shahzad has it. Unfortunately, sixteen is far from old enough to work for us. We, uh, thought he was eighteen. But I understand that you are seventeen. I watched your tapes from the police station today, and you are nowhere close to having the fear factor. In fact, I'd almost say you're on a suicide mission."

I opened my mouth to argue, but there was no argument. I just smiled. *Touché.*

"These are not the guys to meet on your first intelligence gig," Michael said. "But I'll tell you what. If you can get yourself in a better frame of mind, Tyler, and give me your word that you will have no further contact with these men, I'll give you a recommendation as soon as you turn eighteen. You could get paid internships, paid college, and solid work as a media consultant until you're twenty-one. You're both extraordinarily talented, and god knows the Coalition could use that talent. I can almost guarantee you both a job, if you promise to lay off these dangerous men, leave them entirely alone, and don't make any further attempts at intelligence freelancing or curiosity mongering. None at all."

The silence was long. It was such a tremendous leap from Miss Susan berating my personality type in the cop station that I wanted to give them my word on the spot. I would be eighteen in ten months, and to work for the Coalition as an adult would more than compensate for my rotten childhood. Still, watching Hamdani squirm was not easy. They were asking him to take time off for two years. *Two years.* It would be like asking him to go to jail for two years. I mean, what is school, except that the inmates don't wear orange?

For his sake I reminded them, "We just gave you the contents of Red Vinegar, the source of Red Vinegar, the recipe for Red Vinegar, and all but the very class that Omar teaches, which, by the way, is at Astor College. And still. You're saying there's nothing you can do with Hamdani except ignore him for two years."

Hodji slumped until his chin bobbed to his chest in dejection. Miss Susan said, "There is absolutely nothing we can do with minors. But do you want a job for the future, Tyler? I know I said some pretty unkind things to you today. But I take them all back. You're an amazing programmer."

Of course it crossed my mind that they could be lying—just trying to get me to stay out of their business. And I could apply to USIC at eighteen and get a letter similar to the one I got from Trinitron: *No thanks, no explanation.*

I glanced at Hamdani. "Is she telling the truth?"

I wondered if she was the one who figured out he was too

young and blew the whistle. It was that kind of a betrayed and hateful look he gave her. But then he turned to Hodji. Hodji looked at me and said, "She's telling the truth."

And Shahzad added, "Hodji never lied to me, and he would not lie to you."

I couldn't pick out a lie in any face. So we shook hands all around, and USIC stood up.

"I'll make you another deal," Michael said. "We won't bust you for hacking, and we won't report you to the FBI. But we want your cell-scanning program moved to disk. Moved—not copied. It's illegal to use it."

I had several disk copies, and I suppose they knew that. But I went along with it, gave them a disk, and tried to tell myself to behave—forevermore. I was sorry to watch them leave with Hamdani. I guess they were dropping him at home. No point in leaving him with me. We might be tempted to break our word.

I looked at the article pinned to my bulletin board over my bed. If anyone had noticed it, they hadn't let on. "'*The Kid is such a proficient v-spy that he could turn any day of the week into Christmas for American intelligence,' said an unnamed source.*"

I lay down on my bed and wondered if Mr. Cowboy Hodji was the unnamed source. There was a knock at my door. I glanced quickly to my terminal. The screen saver was on. I wouldn't have to scalp my mother unless she came in, which she never did.

"What's up, Mom?"

She opened the door with her usual foot. "Those fix-it guys leave already?"

"They took the hard drive with them," I lied. "Could be complicated."

"Do you need my credit card?"

"I will when I pick it up, probably in a few days. Don't worry about it now."

I could see it disappear from her mind in one blink. "I'm ordering," she said. "What's your pleasure? Pizza, hoagies, or Chinese?"

I tried to remember which of The Three we had last night. I was too busy watching her. My mother was probably the most graceful grown woman I have ever laid eyes on. She's got almond-shaped eyes, but not exaggerated almond, because her mother was German. They're hazel but can look totally green in certain lights. Whatever stress she carries doesn't show up on her face, and it hasn't given her shiny brown hair a single gray strand. She looks mature enough to be sharp and responsible, and young enough not to be worn down. She's tall, taking after her father, who was Samoan. We're not actually North Korean; she and I were both born in Samoa. She met the North Koreans when she went to graduate school in South Korea just after I was born. I've put that much together.

"I don't care, I'm not hungry," I told her.

"How about a salad?" she suggested. "They make yummy ones at—"

"Why don't you take me out for once?"

She smiled, more genuinely than I would have predicted. "I will. I promise. If it's any consolation, I think every day that I *should* take my son out. He's the only son I've got!"

"How about we set a date?"

"Okay, let's do that," she agreed, and I didn't read any fakeness in her face. *Is this my lucky day? USIC is offering me a job in a year, and my mother agrees to take me out to dinner soon.*

"What night?" I asked.

"Any night. You pick it. Just not tonight. I've brought home too much work."

She pulled the door shut, and I guess she will choose between the Big Three for tonight all by herself. The word "work" echoed in the air. I shut my eyes and let my breath roll out, because I suddenly felt sick. The realization struck me that should have struck me right away, if I hadn't been too excited about my own life to remember hers.

I can't work for USIC. I can't *ever* work in intelligence. What was I thinking?

I suppose USIC isn't as quick as other intelligence agencies on grilling their employees, but it's inevitable that they get around to it. The background checks for all intelligence agencies are murder. They include a polygraph. I reflected again on how that needle would go off the charts when they asked, "Is your mother a lab technician at KTD BioLabs in Newark?" Even if I managed to pass a polygraph, they would find out about her. No one would ever believe I was against the whole thing—unless I turned her in, which I simply could not ever do. Not ever.

I was as totally fucked as I ever was. I reached in my nightstand, fumbling around for a Valium. I didn't need food—I needed a nice, long nap, where the world and all its woes couldn't bother me for about nine hours.

FORTY

RAIN STECKERMAN
SATURDAY, MARCH 9, 2002
2:15 A.M.

I TOTALLY CAN'T think, so I'm lying here crying. The nurses are already used to it, and over an hour ago, they quit sticking their heads in the door to say comforting things, or "Get some sleep."

Owen is asleep with the curtain open, so I can see him and be glad he's out of it, though it is hard. If he were awake, I could motormouth and not think about Cora and Scott and how much my ear hurts. Although my ear hardly hurts, actually. I can't decide if it hurts because I'm thinking about it, or if I'm thinking about it because it hurts. Anyway, it couldn't hurt too much or I wouldn't have that question. It hurt a *lot,* but then Dr. Godfrey said it was just an ulcer and not a whole aneurysm (it was actually my ear bleeding and not my brain), and I feel like a dumb jerk face for not being ecstatic about that. Actually my stomach hurts worse than my ear, from the silent-sobs routine. I don't want to wake Owen. My stomach hurts, and my teeth. I keep grinding my teeth together.

My thoughts keep landing on the worst memory of my life. Hildy Kirkegard was this inordinately huge chick, like, five-seven, one eighty in sixth grade. Every class has its token bully. In my class, the bully was a girl. Hildy said it a thousand times: "Do that again, I'll kick your butt." "Watch out, I'll kick your butt." She took a karate class, and anyone who had the nerve would whisper that she looked like a sumo wrestler and not a karate expert, but you could never let her hear you say that, or she would "kick your teeth down your throat" or "chew off your left ear and shove it up your right nostril." Psychobabe.

One day Owen and Dobbins and I were throwing a football at lunchtime. I threw a long pass to Dobbins that was way off and knocked Hildy's hat from her head. It was a total accident, but she started in from like forty feet away.

"What the hell was that, Steckerman? You did that on purpose! You're dead!"

And she came stalking toward me. The whole world fuzzed over until there was no one in it except me and this mastodon, huffing and snorting and coming fast. My thought was... *I'm gonna pee my pants. Unless—*

Instead of running away, I ran *at* her, and I jumped on her and sunk my teeth into her scalp. All this pent-up outrage at having to be scared all year shot out like a geyser. Before Owen finally pulled me off, I had given her a broken jaw and four loose molars, and I spit hair out of my mouth for days.

It wasn't until after Hildy was taken away in an ambulance that I had this dawning revelation: I had never seen her kick anyone's butt, and neither had anyone else in the class. It had all been flap jaw, and then, I had to listen to my dad for two weeks while he enforced my grounding to the max.

Mr. Even Keel says that people who hate are usually reflecting how they've been made to feel, and the best thing to do with a school bully is to be nice to them. It catches them off guard, and they don't know what to do.

I've spent my life since then being nice to people who are mean. Because I feel that same snatch of outrage coming over me, and if I don't spout out something nice, I get terrified. I know what anger can turn me into.

I had Mr. Kinnard's sophomore psych class, and he went on one day about your "fight or flight" mode. He said, "Most people choose 'flight' when they're terrified, but some people will choose 'fight.'"

I should say I've spent my life being nice to meanies *until now.* Now I don't have any bullies to be nice to. I don't know who did this. When I try to imagine a face, the only one I see is Hildy Kirkegard's.

So, I'm watching Owen sleep. He doesn't snore. I am kind of glad of that, though you might think it shouldn't matter to me one way or the other whether Owen snores. I mean, we're not an item. Never have been.

But it's always been this secret thought of mine, the one I never share with anybody, that I am saving Owen for when I get married. He's the type who would make a terrible boyfriend (too boring), but a great husband. He wouldn't want to have Boys' Night Out every weekend or go trout fishing with a bunch of drunken potheads every Saturday. Besides, he told me he is a virgin, and I just pretended I didn't care and all, but secretly I was all *Yah Sheenah!* Some people think that shagging a virgin is just a guy thing, but I don't think so, or maybe I'm just weird. I think it would be very cool to marry a virgin.

I wonder if that makes me more of a feminist or less of a feminist.

When I get out of college and have my job, and I'm ready to be old and start staying at home nights, that's when I'll make my move on Owen. It's all between me, myself, and I until then.

Until then. *Until* then. "Until" is just a word I've said a gazillion times. *Until* I play a sport in college. *Until* I get my first real job. *Until* I find out if I can room with Jeanine Fitzpatrick up at Montclair State University or I have to room with a stranger. *Until* is a word that links the present with the future. A transitional word. (See? I'm not so dumb. Some people think I'm dumb, but it's not true. I just don't try to be overly smart.)

But after being brought here from the emergency room last night, I realized how any time this week I used the word "until" it was like I had dropped the f-bomb. I have to be very riled up to drop the f-bomb, and for some reason it makes me strangely nervous or anxious when I do. This week, the word *until* has gotten me feeling that way.

It used to be that nothing existed between the here and now and *until*, except time. I'm starting to see what it's like for people who have challenges, like those who are in wheelchairs or have cancer, or who have Lyme disease and walk funny because their joints hurt. They have to think of all sorts of things when *until* spills out of their mouths, like the fact that *until* might be very hard to accomplish, or that *until* might never get here.

It's so much easier to think of others than me. It's probably that old psychological twitch: Like, I'm *wishing* Hildy Kirkegard was the biggest thing I had to worry about.

Owen told me something terrifying tonight, just after we found out that Scott passed out in intensive care. We don't know what happened, only that he passed out, and the nurses said everyone is working on figuring out why. But it inspired Owen to tell me this secret thing he saw outside Cora's house after I was admitted last night. The doctors told him he would be admitted, too, but since he felt basically okay, they let him go home first.

He packed some clothes, and some football mags and books to read, then walked back to Cora's for his toothbrush. There was a crowd of men out on the sidewalk and he realized it was my dad and strange people he'd never seen before. He assumed it was the USIC crew that had been holed up in our house. But they weren't dressed in business suits. They were in jeans and flannel shirts, though he saw a gun in a holster, and maybe that's when he thought *USIC*.

They had shovels and a couple of flashlights, and they'd been digging—right around that puddle outside Cora's house. He hid to watch, and suddenly they stopped digging and all froze. There had been something buried there, and one guy shone a flashlight on it. Owen said it was a muddy red box about the size of a suitcase. The guy said something he couldn't hear.

He said the guy turned and looked at my dad. And my dad started to yell wildly—to yell and curse and kick dirt—and it was all unbelievable, because neither of us have ever seen my dad curse or kick anything. And then he fell down on the ground and started to cry…cry and say my name, and curse and say my name.

I try getting a picture of this in my head, and all I can come up with is the image of Hildy Kirkegard.

Owen can't keep a secret for the life of him. And after telling me, and after me pretending the story didn't terrify me so it wouldn't terrify him, he promptly fell asleep and left me awake. Don't ask why I want to marry this guy. I can't answer that.

FORTY-ONE

SHAHZAD HAMDANI
SATURDAY, MARCH 9, 2002
9:45 A.M.

TYLER KNOCKS AT Aunt Alika's door on Saturday morning, and I let him in. I try not to look unhappy, but his arrival adds much complication.

My aunt and Inas are still upset with me for cutting the school. Inas still thinks that I know Tyler only as the boy who spoke to me in the lunch line. Neither my aunt nor Inas know I am fired from my job at Trinitron, not that they ever knew I was a USIC employee in the first place. My aunt thinks of me as "high maintenance," the word she used three times last night when she heard that the school called to say I was missing. I reminded her that it is not a law to go to school in Pakistan after age thirteen and said simply that I had become confused. I had wanted to go to work at Trinitron instead.

Beyond the complications with my relatives, Hodji and I had a huge fight over Tyler while driving from his house last night.

Once we were in his car, he changed his tune quickly, telling me to stay away from Tyler at all costs. He said that he can detect a drug taker from miles away, and that Tyler is one, and that he seems haunted by something, perhaps a molestation or abuse. I said such things are not a person's fault and he was being unfair. Hodji said that I sounded awfully American for only having been in school for one full day.

But from all this, I gathered they were not expecting to hire Tyler in a year. Hodji finally came clean with many grumbles, his excuse for lying being that they would say anything to keep a minor away from dangerous men who could hurt him. And besides, Tyler is too strange to be hired, he said.

I vowed never to speak to Hodji or anyone in USIC again. While Hodji and I had certainly engaged in many lies together to many extremists, I had never seen him lie to *me.*

It was Hodji's unremorseful confession to lying that turned me from a well-behaved person to an f-word-flinging monsoon. Hodji flung the f-word back, and I marched out of the car upon reaching my aunt's. I told him do not call me again, ever, and ended with "May you drink the Red Vinegar I just found for you for free, you spoiled ingratiate."

However, this does not mean I want to see Tyler or that I will tell him this atrocious news. I do not know what to say when he appears on Saturday morning.

Tyler reaches a hand out to shake with Aunt Alika across the kitchen table. "Hello, I work at Trinitron with Shahzad." Aunt Alika accepts his lie, and I try not to flinch.

Inas is watching cartoons in the living room, and she watches us through the doorframe, giving Tyler her big, American, unshy smile. "Wow, I didn't know you worked at Trinitron, Tyler. That's decent."

"Now you know." He turns to me. "I thought you might want to go out for bagels."

"Baggles?" I repeat in confusion. "I don't very much like the baggles."

He steps on my foot as Uncle used to when he would want me to curb my tongue. "How about doughnuts? I can introduce you to Krispy Kremes. They're beyond sadistic."

I nod. Aunt Alika's view of my feet is obstructed, but she watches my eyes.

"Can I count on you to stay out of trouble?" she asks. "I can't imagine what trouble a teenage boy could find on a Saturday morning, but I want you back here in an hour."

I look at my watch, nodding dutifully. "Again, I am sorry. About the school misunderstanding."

She waves at me with a long sigh, and Inas keeps smiling at us. I think that Tyler will ask her to go, but she is dressed in long purple snowman clothing, which I am sure he will recognize as pajamas. I pull him out the door, wondering at American girls, who will not flee to the bedroom rather than let boys peruse their purple and snowmen.

Outside, Tyler says, "Thank god she wasn't dressed. I thought she would ask to come, or your aunt would sic her on us. I want to say a couple of things to you alone, and then I'm taking off."

"Where are you going?" I ask, and he ignores that question.

"First, the deal is off. I can never work for American intelligence."

It is as if he overheard Hodji and me, and I blush. Then I detect that his meaning is personal. "Let's just say that...I wouldn't pass a background check."

"You have committed a crime?" I guess. I know of his

hacking crimes, but it seems to me that these would be quite pleasing to those hiring someone to hack.

"Yeah, I committed a crime. I was born," he says evasively.

"You don't have to tell me. But you can," I encourage him.

"No, I can't. And I didn't come to talk about that. I just wanted you to know that after we get doughnuts, I'm going to Colony One."

I reach for his wrist. I don't want him to do this thing. "Why? Omar is probably in jail by now. We turned him up."

"I don't think USIC was fast enough. I cached a bunch of chatter last night. My translations on BabylonDoo were pretty horrible, but I got the gist. That ShadowStrike assassin, the one sent to the hospital to finish off the girl, was arrested by USIC yesterday."

I freeze, terribly interested. And after my argument with Hodji, my deal is off, too. I do not want to work with people whom I cannot trust to tell me the truth.

"The assassin Omar referenced in his phone chatter with Manuel? He was arrested?" I ask.

Tyler nods. "Omar got itchy, went to the hospital, and overheard some nurses saying that a terrorist attacked one of the patients suspected to be sick from the poisoned water. The guy was taken away in a cop car. I imagine Omar's hiding now. But he might still be in the area."

"How do you know?" I ask.

"I don't. Catalyst e-mailed me this morning. He wanted to say thanks for the software, Blizzard. I was all 'You're welcome.' *Asshole.* We did a small talk back and forth, and he mentioned a party he'd been invited to at Astor College. I guess I sounded jealous in my reply. Wasn't hard to sound jealous—I never get asked to parties. He asked me to come. It's this afternoon. Maybe they'll mention where Omar is. Hell, it's a party. Maybe he'll fuckin' show up. Maybe they'll even try to recruit me, *pfwaa.*"

"These men are dangerous," I repeat, my deepest instincts alerted.

He laughs. "Find me a twelve-step for people with death wishes, and maybe I'll have more willpower. Right now, all I can picture is me calling USIC with the whereabouts of Omar. That would, uh, make up for a lot of sins in my family."

I don't know what he means.

"You could call them now," I say, but realize that he has just made a promise to them and already he has broken it. They would probably put him in juvenile jail just to keep him out of the way. He would need a bigger tidbit to soothe them down.

"Let's go get doughnuts before I take off," he says.

"I want no doughnuts," I mumble, but for some reason, I get in the car anyway.

He comes slowly around to the driver side, drops into the seat, and says, "So?"

I realize I have left my asthma canister in the house. I am wheezing already. I try to ignore it while I say, "I have longed for a day when I might see the sick people in Colony One. I have worked hard for them. I feel...connected to them. I will risk my aunt's anger, because tomorrow they might be died."

"Dead," he corrects me and laughs sadly. "Your aunt's anger will be nothing compared to my mom's. This is her Audi, which she never lets me drive. But fine. I'll take you to Colony One and the hospital. But when we get to Astor College, I want you to promise me you'll go for a walk or something—you'll let me go in there alone."

I mumble "we'll see" in Punjabi.

FORTY-TWO

TYLER PING
SATURDAY, MARCH 9, 2002
12:30 P.M.

MY MOM'S NOT what you'd call a savory character, but she has become American in one classic sense: Her car is her holy temple. I love driving it. Yet I feel like I'm falling over a cliff, because I'm doing so many things that would piss off so many people, and her anger haunts me the most. It's all in the name of being a good American. Life either makes no sense or is boring as hell.

I showed Hamdani how to change the songs on the radio, and it was amusing to see what stuff he was attracted to. He stopped pushing buttons when he came upon Eric Clapton, the Who, and the Beatles, and when I tried to tell him those people were older than his aunt, he looked confused, as if the concept of a generation gap was lost on him.

The parkway had gotten more narrow and emptier the farther south we got, and the trees had changed on either side of the road. First they had looked like plain forest, but below exit sixty it had changed to these knotty, ugly pine trees with beach sand on the forest floor.

"Pine Barrens," I told him. "You gotta be nuts to live down here."

"I like beach sand," he said. He looked peaceful, for once. Frankly, I hadn't seen him happy since he ate that bagel and shook hands adventurously with the Jews in the White Mound.

We got off the parkway right around twelve thirty, and followed signs to Trinity Falls. The place looked like it had been dropped out of a family movie. Huge oaks lined the roadbed, making arcs like canopies. There were old Victorian houses and colonial homes, and nice gardens and a few shops in what looked like a business district, only too pretty. I figured I could give up on Xanax for calm nerves if I lived down here.

I got out my MapQuest directions, and Hamdani navigated. I guess maps are universally understandable. We parked six blocks from the hospital and walked the rest of the way. Let's say I was paranoid about having my mom's car impounded if I got arrested somehow. I followed him into the hospital lobby.

"Do you want to see a patient?" the woman asked us.

"Yeah, we go to school with the Ebermans." I remembered their name from the mother's obituary and hoped I sounded convincingly casual.

"Well, you can't see Scott. He's in intensive care. Only immediate family. Owen and Rain are in isolation to prevent them from catching any other germs. You have to wear a cap and gown and stand outside their door. Right now, there are four kids up there already. You have to wait until one of them comes down. It could be a while." She rolled her eyes with a pleasant smile. I like women who prattle on in that friendly small-town way. I wished she was my mom.

She asked for a photo ID, which made my heart dance a bit, because that is unusual. I showed my driver's license and Hamdani showed his school ID, which blatantly revealed that he did not go to school with the Ebermans. It was a tricky moment, but she just made sure our faces matched our IDs and didn't write anything down.

"Sign in and have a seat over there." She handed us a clipboard.

I signed "Kim Chow," who is a guy in school I hate.

Despite my high jinks, Hamdani signed his own real name.

"They're gonna see that," I growled as we headed over to the sitting area with a blue visitor's pass, though I couldn't quite figure out what harm it could do.

"Perhaps good," he said. "Maybe USIC sees that they are big liars and I am not."

He pulled a copy of the *New York Daily News* off the coffee table and into his lap, and with a finger under each word, he read the news about our troops in Afghanistan and some remote possibility of going to war with Iraq.

It ogled my brain that the kid could know so much about so many things and bag on English. Computer geeks can do that these days because of the translation programs, but it burned my ass. I hadn't been here a year, and I knew English so well you would have thought I was born in Queens. I like words, I guess. Words don't hate me like people do.

Two strapping jocks got out of the elevator, each carrying a fistful of light blue fabric—probably a mask and a surgical cap.

One had his arm around the other, who was looking at the floor and pushing tears off his face. That must be two of the four visitors. Therefore, we could go up—if we both wanted to. My stomach is a lot less firm than I let on, sometimes. I turned to Hamdani.

"I'll stay here. This is *your* inspiration. I already have mine."

Hamdani didn't question me, though he looked at me again like he had when he asked me to tell him my huge problem. When I waved good-bye in his face, he walked off slowly toward the elevator, but with some glint of determination in his unusually deadpan face.

FORTY-THREE

SHAHZAD HAMDANI
SATURDAY, MARCH 9, 2002
12:45 P.M.

THE NURSE ON the sixth floor hands me a little cap and a mask and a blue paper robe that you have to put on backward. She leads me to a doorway. I cannot see inside because two other robed boys are standing in the way talking to the patients. They are very big, full of muscles, and I cannot see past them.

I try to think of what I will say. I had not considered this a problem until now. However, I remember I am a stranger who speaks with an accent, and I could look very suspicious simply by saying that I had heard of them and wanted to meet them.

A man sits in a chair beside the door. He reads the newspaper until his eyes gaze upward to mine. It is in my instincts now to smell USIC ten miles away. *This is an agent. He has been ordered to guard the door without arousing suspicion of visitors.* I recall Tyler's tale of this morning, that an assassin had been arrested here. I am glad for this agent.

However, I detect that he is profiling me and trying not to. I look like someone he might find untrustworthy. I step back away from the two visitors and pretend to adjust my mask, so the man can see my whole face and realize that I am not old. Perhaps he will see my sharp elbows and skinny arms, from asthma always making me too winded to exercise. He looks into my face and I see him relax slightly. But before I can put the mask back on, I run into a trouble I did not predict.

A man turns the corner way down the corridor, and two well-known eyes lock with mine, coming closer and closer. They are blue as the sky.

"Kid, my god. What are you doing here?"

If I hadn't so much to think about, I would have guessed USIC would be everywhere in this hospital. Agents often have to make their office wherever their travels take them.

When I don't answer, Roger mutters, "Welcome to Colony One."

I am thinking he will apologize for doubting my instincts about Colony One being in America. But he changes the subject instead of offering due praise.

"Hodji will be here any minute. He left me a message late last night, said he was coming at noon. He's actually late..."

"You have spoken to him?" I ask.

He pulls his cell out of his pocket and shrugs in frustration. "No cell phones allowed in a hospital. Not even by USIC. CDC got here at five yesterday, and I haven't left since. I'm only returning my 9-1-1s."

He means that other agents would put "9-1-1" into his phone pager after their own numbers, and it means that they need a callback immediately. For a moment I am deflated that Hodji did not consider my termination a 9-1-1. Then, I realize something intriguing: *Roger does not know I am fired.* I do not imagine that this could be a vast wealth of information for me. I just know instinctively to be still.

"I'm leaving messages all over the place. I need some face-to-faces. I need Michael down here. I told him so explicitly...I don't get why he would send you."

I try not to look stunned by his inference. "I only do what I am told..."

He seems pleased. For a moment. Then he shakes his head. "You're a rookie. What the hell is going on up there?"

"I wanted to come," I say, which is truthful. "I have chased the men who torture these people for many months now. It is only natural that I want to see them."

He speaks in Punjabi, which makes me long for home. "I could have gotten you a chance to meet these kids once we got out from under."

"What if they die?" I ask from my heart. "Then I will never meet them."

He digs his fingers into the back of my neck. He doesn't deny it. "I'll introduce you. Just promise me you won't get emotional," he warns. "Especially not in front of the boy."

I grow stiff with pride at the suggestion and wonder why he mentions the boy and not the girl. Aren't girls usually the emotional ones? The nurse brings him the same hospital outfit as I have, and after putting it on, he moves me over to the door. He is so very tall that he speaks over the heads of the two huge figures standing there.

"Guys. Can I introduce you to someone?"

The two big boys part, and I see the two figures in the beds. Roger tells them I am a friend from Pakistan who has come to America, and that I had helped them with a few things.

"This is Owen and Rain," he says to me.

The girl makes me stare. She has very long yellow hair, which I have only seen in Pakistan a few times. There are probably a number of such yellow-haired people in Karachi, but they don't make it to my village. She has a bandage over one ear. I wonder what element of Omar's Red Vinegar has left her thus bandaged and looking so tired.

The boy's eyes are half dead, as if all hope has left him. He is as large as his friends who took up the whole doorway—maybe larger, though he looks pale and weak. He forms a nod, but it is as if he can do no more.

A man has been sitting in a chair inside the room. He has on the same surgical outfit as mine, but his eyes, while blue like Roger's, have the intensity of Hodji's. He stares at me and extends his hand.

"I'm Alan Steckerman. Rain's dad. You're..."

I tell him "Shahzad," and I shake his hand. I keep my eyes to the floor, thinking this name will mean nothing to him. I know *his* name, surely. When USIC tested the water towers back in January, Steckerman was the main speaker at the news conference. This girl is his *daughter*. Tyler had spoken this news accurately. I wonder if the terrorists have targeted his neighborhood because of him. I imagine he wonders the same thing. But my name seems to have distracted him momentarily.

"You're Shahzad," he repeats. "*The* Shahzad?"

His voice is soft, as if he doesn't wish to bother his daughter and her roommate with this information. But he looks keenly at Roger.

Roger says nothing, which means *yes.* Mr. Steckerman squeezes my hand very tight, which screams a hundred thank-yous. I find this quite honorable given his current circumstances. And I have shaken the hand of a very important American through our sets of gloves, and now Roger squeezes my neck through his gloves. Something about this feels "not quite here."

The girl has her father's intense gaze, and I perceive she listens for things she should not hear. She absorbs the whispers and speaks soft English.

"Wait a minute. Are you that kid Scott was telling me about? He said there was an article in *Newsweek* about the Kid... and that Roger knew him."

Roger must have thought that I would never meet these people. He must have been under enough stress not to be able to "think five steps ahead," like he always preached about himself. The girl seems hypnotized by me, and a little smile forms on her lips.

"I'm bad," she mutters. "I never paid enough attention to the computer geeks in school. I mean, the computer whizzes. Come here."

She holds her hand out to me. Feeling shy, I still would like to touch the warmth of life on her fingers through the gloves and think that maybe something I have done has helped her. I am a Pakistani, but in this doorway, I *feel* American, because the presence of its victims, healers, protectors, encouragers is so very strong.

"He's not allowed in," Roger reminds her, and she drops her hand and rolls her eyes.

"This place is getting on my nerves. There's no better way to get well than to be able to touch your friends."

Her father's intense gaze implies an understanding of both the medical needs and her need. He takes me into the room by the arm, and over to the bed. The girl beckons me closer, despite that Roger follows me and doesn't let go.

I don't know what to say as the girl takes my gloved hand in hers. Her squeezing very tightly makes me squeeze back. Her fear shoots up my arm, but also her hope, which comes from I don't know where. Except that I perceive in her beautiful little town, with so many hopeful presences surrounding, that hope is part of life.

Roger mutters in my ear from behind in Punjabi, "She doesn't know exactly what you do for us, but I think she gets it. I want you to do something very important right now. I want you to deny that you are the Kid."

His words hurt my heart. Roger thinks I am still hired. I think it will hurt very much to deny who I am, but in reality I am no longer the Kid, not after yesterday.

"I am not that person of whom you speak," I say. "But I wish you well. I hope you... make better soon."

She lets go of my hand in disappointment. "Oh. Well, it was nice meeting you. Thanks for stopping by."

Roger takes me up an elevator, mumbling in tired, nonsensical English that it is fine for me to see the other boy, because he will surely not recognize me or ask me any questions. In fact, in the ICU he leaves me alone with this patient who goes by the name Scott, while he talks to another agent who is reading the newspaper just inside the double doors.

This boy is under a dozen tubes and wires. He looks a little like the boy downstairs, but he is not quite so big. He is more lean and slightly older, with golden hair instead of yellow. I cannot think of what ICU stands for, and Roger has not told me, but it is very serious, obviously.

I take this Scott's hand. He does not move, and though Scott's eyes are sometimes half opened, Roger has mentioned not to mind this. He said the boy has an aneurysm on his brain and one on his heart, also. His coma is caused by a drug that slows his heart enough to prevent the heart aneurysm from bursting. He can either be alert and quickly dead, or comatose until they can figure out what to do with him.

"I don't know how the doctors can help," I explain to him in Punjabi, "because I am not a medical person. I am a v-spy now and forever. I promise, with Allah as my merciful friend, that I will find those bad people for you. My father would want me to."

I could say much more, but Roger is suddenly beside me. It renders me unable to think, except to understand that I am in quite a predicament here. I make a decision. I will deceive him, but it is more than to get information. I will lie to get away from yesterday. I so long to be my old self—to be useful and productive and a part of important issues, to help this boy, his brother, and the girl with the yellow hair and lively eyes.

"You know what? Skip the fourth patient," he says in Punjabi. "Despite that she's under sedation, you might scare her out of her wits. You heard that some ShadowStrike whore got in here yesterday, right?"

"Yes. He tried to attack the girl." I realize he thinks my

squad told me, and my giving a detail back will reinforce this. I decide to play into the conversation as if yesterday never happened. It makes me breathe more easily to pretend as much.

"He tried to inject her with something deadly. CDC still doesn't know what it was, though they're working on it. Scott Eberman and I stopped him."

"I suppose they are not dying fast enough to please Omar," I say.

Roger nods. "Fortunately, the guy injected it into her IV bag and not directly into her bloodstream. They're growing overly confident. Omar took a great risk. This time, he lost."

He nodded at the bed. "The overexertion almost blew Scott Eberman's heart wide open, and it may yet. Anyway, we got one of their goons. We're still trying to make him, but his IDs are all false. He can rot in the can until we figure that out."

I find my voice, but can only say, "Congratulations."

"And the same to you. Not that we have time to discuss it. Maybe Michael's not being so stupid after all. Most of what I had to tell him concerned you. This doesn't end with the arrests, you know. We need evidence that will stand up legally. We don't have enough yet. We need chatter—we need them confessing to each other what they've done. That would be great."

"Any specifics?" I ask.

"Anything with new names, first of all. We got a couple because they posted a website. Did you see it?"

"No," I confess with irritation. I could have been the one to find it, were my hands not tied. "I had to settle for discovering what the 'Q' in 'Mother Q' means."

"I saw that. Good find, Kid. Actually, the CDC has suspected it was a Q fever mutation for several days now."

I am surprised but do not ask the source of this. Roger often gave me many intelligence details in Pakistan, but only surrounding those issues that he perceived I needed to chase chatter.

"We need more background confirming which guys actually poisoned the water. Maybe they're bragging between each other on how they only infected one small part of the water supply that runs into five streets. We found the device they used. It was hooked up to the sewer line in front of the house belonging to the first dead woman. A confession that links specific people to it would be a profound *bingo.*"

I nod. "And what about their predictions on how the virus will act?"

"That's not a main priority right now. The CDC predicts that the worst is over as far as very sick people turning up. ShadowStrike made a major error. They weren't considering America's bottled-water fetish, especially among the more affluent folk. Most of the people on those streets haven't drunk from a tap in years. Six people on that street have turned up 'suspicious' and were tested, but the CDC is calling them 'acute,' and telling them they have the flu for now. It acts like a flu, and it will go away with antibiotics if it hasn't reached a certain toxicity level. We're trying not to start a panic, which means holding off telling anyone anything until we have more answers."

"I have read all the panic protocols," I say.

"These four kids are being called 'chronic.' Very high toxicity levels. We haven't seen any more like that."

"Perhaps you would like for me to try to locate the other terror scientists? Perhaps, if they developed the germ, they would have developed an antitoxin in case they should infect themselves."

Roger nods. "Keep trying. Omar and VaporStrike are the only big guns we've identified so far from ShadowStrike. Omar probably was involved in designing the germ. VaporStrike, while not a scientist, is a higher-up, and possibly a trained assassin. PiousKnight and Catalyst are just puppet men. We think that they and four others worked in a discount shoe store in a nearby town for a few months as a front. Look for anything containing 'store' or 'shoe store' or 'shoes.' It appears that in the middle of the night of December 28, they drilled the water main that serves five streets—including Steckerman's. It's pretty obvious that they mapped out their plan to include his household. They buried a container filled with a concentration of the hot agent and a transline connecting to the water main. It was set to release the stuff over a period of four months. It was an experiment. If they'd had a couple of dozen deaths, they planned to repeat it other places. Now they know Americans generally don't drink much tap water—at least not enough to make it worth their while. They target the very successful—the stockbrokers, the lawyers, the doctors, the professors—but they'll go back to the drawing board."

"I will do my best," I say, though my conscience is seeping through. But now, I have to ignore its pangs. Roger would die if he knew I was terminated and he had spoken so liberally.

He goes on. "Well, they're getting a bit boastful lately, Michael says, though I haven't seen their brags firsthand. If they start bragging—admitting their actions and applauding one another—we can use that as a confession."

I nod, thinking of Tyler's captured phone chatter, Omar admitting to telling a whole roomful of students what he did. Roger will see that soon enough.

"Should Red Vinegar still be a priority in my search engines? The chatter of yesterday alluded to them maybe moving onto newer—"

"No, replace it with something else. Just 'vinegar' or 'poison' or whatever you think is worthy. The CDC probably has enough on Red Vinegar now. The germ was baptized by the CDC 'Q3 Fever' or just plain 'Q3.' The '3' in Q3 is for the mutations that their Level Four specialist went through to make it waterborne and unrecognizable to any scientist alive in this world. Q3 won't penetrate your scalp with your shampoo or bother too badly with the bug bite on your ankle or hit people in the face when you sneeze. You have to drink it—daily."

He seems to be quoting something I scripted once recently. He would be adding insult to injury, except I am focused again on these important patients, watching Scott breathe with a machine.

"You think they will die?"

"I don't know. The problem, according to the CDC, is that no one can figure out yet how to flush the Q3 virus and undo the damage. It could take time...I'm not sure if they have time. Q3 amasses in the bone marrow and eats away at the lining of the veins and arteries on its travels. At a certain toxicity, it starts to turn veins to mush. They develop weak spots that fill up, burst, and bleed out, usually in the head, but they could happen in your chest or other places, too. Many people these days live through aneurysms, but if your veins are slowly being stewed, it decreases your chances. The CDC has some drugs to try. They're optimistic, but it's tricky. A medication strong enough to kill the germ could also do damage to compromised veins and arteries."

"I will try to find the scientists, try to find an antitoxin." I draw my eyes away from Scott so as to think practically. "Anything else?"

"Yes," he speaks softly. "Michael doesn't even know this yet, so I'll tell you myself. Omar and VaporStrike are in the black hole. We're thinking they must have gotten suspicious when we hauled their flying monkey out of here yesterday. But that's not the worst. I'm ashamed to say... Catalyst and PiousKnight are among the missing, also. If any of them come online, try to get an IP address immediately."

I cannot help but show my surprise here. VaporStrike and Catalyst had been tailed by USIC. I have never heard of American intelligence losing someone they were tailing.

"We're just people," Roger says. "That's what this country doesn't understand. They want a foolproof plan. But as long as it's just people running things, mistakes can be made. PiousKnight and Catalyst went into a little boutique in the train station up on Long Island. Those things are so small that the agent didn't bother to go in with them. They never came out. We had the owner arrested, but it appears he merely took a hundred bucks to let them out the back door, and he knows nothing. We haven't picked them up again."

My asthma pulls tightly in my chest. For a moment, my heart feels torn in half, as the better half of me certainly wants to say immediately, "They are at Astor College." But the limpness that has overwhelmed me since being fired is suddenly replaced by a swelling of importance. I would not call my silence revenge, but more a clawing for the restoration of my dignity. Perhaps it is as Hodji proclaims: What goes around comes around.

Roger's cell phone rings. He looks at the screen. "It's Michael. I'll tell him I talked to you personally."

My instincts say to stop him and confess immediately. It would mean trouble, but far less trouble than walking out of here and letting him hear this truth from my irate former supervisor. But Roger dashes for the stairwell. "I can get reception outside—"

And the door closes behind him. It is too late. I break quickly for the double doors and a different stairwell. Everyone will be infuriated with me in this strange and new country—except Tyler. I jump down the stairwell that empties out near where he is waiting in the lobby. My wheezing does not help my clarity. I start to see the error of my decisions. USIC could have me put in jail just to keep me out of their business. I could stay there for a very long time—until whatever month, or year, their business is finished.

FORTY-FOUR

TYLER PING
SATURDAY, MARCH 9, 2002
1:25 P.M.

SO, WE GOT BACK to the car and Hamdani was wheezing so furiously, I thought I would have to say "Screw this" and drive him the hell right up to the emergency room door.

But a few minutes after he stopped running, his breathing started to ease up. I drove fast and turned up the radio so I wouldn't have to have a heart attack and crash my mom's Audi. But then, he wanted to talk, and minus oh so much air, I had to turn the thing down to hear him. He saw a man named Roger, a USIC bigwig, was all I could get.

"And?"

"...didn't know I am fired."

"And?" I waited, but he wheezed only. "Did he tell you anything good?"

After a stare fest out the window, he finally nodded.

Not what I expected.

"You messed with a USIC agent's head?" I asked. "Are you crazy? And they said *I* was the one on a suicide mission."

"Perhaps I am crazy," he wheezed. "I have too many things to... to feel! I do not know where my life is!"

I guessed I could relate. I turned the wheel. "I'm just pulling into a side street. You can have your nervous breakdown with some lovely view. That's the best I can offer."

I buried us between two parked cars in front of a fairly nice Victorian home with a brick walk and a willow tree. If I were new to America, I would be happy to see a willow tree and some well-kept, East Coast history. He watched the tree sway, and his wheezing cut back yet again. But he looked forlorn.

"Just get it together," I said as calmly as possible. "And then we're driving back home. We're going to forget all this stuff with Astor College—"

"Wait," Shahzad cut me off, staring at the roof of the car while banging a fist on his chest. "I could go to the jail for what I just did! Roger and Hodji love me. But they love their jobs more. Their country more."

He thumped his chest rhythmically, giving in to one new thought after another. "They could put me in... crazy hospital. They could... deliver me to the Syrians."

"You're letting your imagination run wild," I said.

He nodded finally, like I made sense. "I just... I have never defied them before yesterday. Not ever."

Three days in America, and he's already a derelict. "The worst they could do is put you in juvenile. In fact, I'd say that's a definite. They'll probably keep you there for your own protection. I've never seen a juvie, but I understand it's not a picnic."

"You must go to Astor College," he said.

I hung on to the steering wheel. "You've just misled a USIC agent into giving you intelligence, and now you want to go play freelance mole? How is that going to help anything?"

"Omar, VaporStrike, PiousKnight, and Catalyst... all are not to be found," he said. "If we can find them..."

Now he sounded like me. If Catalyst was in the black hole, and we could dig him up for USIC, that would be quite a favor. If PiousKnight, VaporStrike, and Omar were all there it would be a beyond-huge *bingo*. They wouldn't dare throw us in juvie after a stunt like that.

"Here's a plan," I said. "Pretty harmless. Let's just go see if we can find the place. Maybe we'll get lucky. Maybe we'll see Catalyst or PiousKnight hanging around outside. You know what PiousKnight looks like, right?"

"I understand he has had a tail, but he has not been in Trinitron." He shakes his head.

"But he knows Catalyst. So, maybe we would see Catalyst walk past a window, and we can tell USIC where he is without actually meeting up with him."

Hamdani looked into my eyes desperately. Obviously, it meant a lot to him to look capable to these USIC guys.

"I just don't want to risk looking doubly moronic by telling USIC before we check it out," I continued. "What if Catalyst gave me a phony address or something? People have invited me to parties before, and they think it's funny when I show up to a vacant lot in the Bronx. But it would be nice to call USIC with an address."

The MapQuest directions led me to an apartment complex four towns over, and I could see signs to Astor College buildings along the way. I imagined the campus was picturesque, but this complex must have been on the outskirts. The scenery had changed a lot since we left Trinity Falls, not that the neighborhood was ugly, per se. There were trees and little fake lakes and water fountains. Still, every apartment looked alike for endless circles and cul-de-sacs.

As I approached what I thought was the right place, we didn't just get lucky—we got extra lucky. Catalyst was standing out on a little balcony, looking down on the parking lot like he was waiting for people. He waved at me. I waved back. He ran inside enthusiastically. We got so lucky that suddenly we were unlucky.

I stammered to Hamdani, "Don't know if he saw you... I'm taking the risks! Jump out and get in the fucking trunk! Do it fast—"

But before Shahzad could even get out of the car, Catalyst came out a first-floor sliding glass door and trotted to us with a smile.

"Shit," I announced with a huge grin on my face. There was nothing to do but park and get out.

Here is something interesting: This Catalyst was the nicest guy you'd ever hope to meet. It had been so easy to approach him on the street after Trinitron that night, interest him in my computer prowess, and offer him something. It took no effort at all.

Now he smiled broadly and shook my hand with both of his hands. "I am so glad you could come. Introduce me to your friend."

"This is Shahzad," I said, remembering something I'd heard while hacking on my mother. When you take a fake name, you try to keep your first name. That way, you don't get confused easily.

"Are you a computer guru as well?" he asked. His English was so perfect, you wouldn't believe it. It was British perfect, or breathy perfect—poetic somehow.

"Um, I am okay on computer," Hamdani said, studying the guy's shoes and looking not amused. He bowed instead of offering his hand, and Catalyst bowed back. I wondered that Catalyst didn't recognize him from Trinitron. Thursday night, Shahzad had gotten up for coffee about the time that Tim figured out I had hacked into his terminal and captured his screen. Catalyst had nodded, and Shahzad had cracked me up, looking ready to shit himself. I hadn't remembered that until now, but maybe it didn't matter. Catalyst didn't seem to remember.

"Well, I hope you will be my good friend, too. A man can't have too many friends, right?" His smile almost sparkled with pixie dust. "I am Raoul. Come, and let me introduce you to my friends. We are watching football. You like football?"

"Sure," I said, and to cover Hamdani's slight wheeze, "Where do you get football in March?"

He smiled with enthusiasm. "From the satellite. It is known as soccer here! The Ethiopians are having a tournament this week. One of our friends is from there. We are helping him feel less homesick."

"Oh." I felt my guard letting down as I eased away from the revelation again: *This guy poisoned a town.* But he thought we were friends.

Inside were seven other guys. The first one we met was Manuel, obviously the same Manuel who was talking to Omar yesterday when we hacked into that phone call. I wouldn't forget his voice so fast. I couldn't place his accent, but it was proper like Catalyst's, and he looked about the same age. He introduced us to five guests and the host. The host looked midtwenties also, but the others looked like college underclassmen, and all but two had foreign accents that were familiar but that I couldn't quite place. I tried not to look like I was making value judgments. But I realized Catalyst said only first names, and I wondered if that was recruitment protocol or just normal American party behavior. I hadn't been to enough parties or been introduced to enough people my own age to really know.

At first I thought it was funny there were no girls at this party. Then I remembered tales from some third world guys at school who had just landed here. They said they would not see their wives until their wedding day and things like that. They didn't drink, didn't do drugs. I decided that maybe to these guys, this was a party.

There was a huge bowl of greasy potato chips in the middle of the coffee table, and all these guys were grabbing handfuls and munching. They drank sodas out of the can. Food didn't seem so important at a party, either, so it smelled more like a recruitment party than a regular party.

"What can I get you?" Catalyst asked, holding up a can of birch beer.

I nudged Hamdani and pointed. "You have to try that—birch beer. It tastes a lot like root beer."

His eyes kind of lit up for the first time that day, and I remembered the bagel saga when he met the White Mound. He liked trying new stuff. This could relax him, though his asthma wasn't making any noise right now.

Catalyst bowed and went off to the kitchen. Manuel was in there. They spoke in a foreign language that, just by the inflections, I took to be Arabic. Any words that floated out of the kitchen were all gibberish to me, but I think Hamdani was trying hard to overhear some of it. He kept his eyes fixed on the television, except when they muttered things in the kitchen. Then, they would drop to the floor like he was concentrating.

I nudged him at one point and just muttered the words "Getting it?" meaning their conversation.

He shook his head no, so I guessed it was too soft. I wondered if Manuel was PiousKnight and continued to wonder after Raoul/Catalyst came back with two cans of birch beer. I might have shit a small brick if Catalyst had handed me an open cup filled with soda—just considering his track record with poisoning people. But it was a cold can out of the refrigerator, and it cracked and fizzed when I pulled the top. Hamdani and I drank birch beer while these guys all shouted at the soccer match.

At a commercial, Manuel took the empty bowl of chips into the kitchen. Catalyst followed. They spoke English this time, so I got it by shutting my eyes and focusing.

"Do you think Omar will still come?" Catalyst asked.

"Didn't you speak to him on his cell today?"

"No. He didn't answer it."

"Why not? He always answers his cell."

There was a long pause and something I couldn't decipher, and then Catalyst muttered, "...cell is done for. He thinks he picked up a..." and more mishmash, but I couldn't help trying to fill in the blanks.

He thinks he picked up a phone tap...which would have been me.

I cheered with the other guys as one team fumbled, and inside I was going, *Ohhhhhhhhh god. I had been thinking the arrest at the hospital drove Omar underground. Could I have added to his suspicions by tapping his phone line? Could he have suspected?*

If you're me, and you're always in trouble with somebody, you do things right off like tell yourself how it's not your fault. I told myself USIC could have been more grateful for programming freebies at police headquarters, and I would have done anything they wanted. I wouldn't have bugged Omar's phone if they'd asked me not to nicely.

But Hamdani took a deep breath and let out some death rattle, and I had to feel responsible that I brought him here into a den of god-knows-what kind of cutthroats and soon-to-be fanatics.

I figured I would get us out of this right now, not do another single thing to piss off USIC—just go home and slice my jugular. I had to think fast, because we'd been here only five minutes.

I got up and stuck my head in the kitchen. "Do you guys know if there's a drugstore around here? My friend has asthma. He'll be fine if we just get some stuff for it. He forgot his canister."

All true, all neat and tidy, and it would get us out of here. Or so I thought.

"He has asthma?" Catalyst asked, showing concern. "I, too, have asthma."

He glanced into the living room at Hamdani, and said, "Come in here, my friend. I will give you something for it."

He opened a kitchen cabinet and pulled out one of those inhalers. My heart dropped into my pisser, though I had no clue if I was being smart or being paranoid. Some weapons of bioterror are waterborne, others are airborne. Almost all can be produced in *aerosols.* Shahzad came slowly forth with wide eyes and his quick, nervous breathing left no question. He obviously shared my thought: *Do you accept aerosol medication from a guy who goes around poisoning people?*

"Thank you, I cannot," Shahzad stuttered. "I have something specific I take."

But Catalyst held it out to him. "Don't you have an inhaler, too? This is standard medication. Please. Feel free."

Shahzad's wheeze tightened noticeably. Still he said, "No thank you."

"You sound like you might die," Manuel noted with a nervous but polite grin. "Please. Let us do something for you."

I suddenly doubted my fears because the thing had been so unplanned. The two looked absolutely lost and confused over Hamdani's refusal to inhale an aerosol medicine they had offered. They were either sincere and not acting, or they were the Antichrist. Shahzad took the canister in his hand and tried to read it. I casually bent over him. I don't know what I expected—maybe to see "Catalyst Jones" on the canister, or something else with his log-in. *Dumb wad.* I did notice the name wasn't Raoul.

"This is yours?" I asked.

Catalyst started to nod and must have realized my problem—the canister didn't say Raoul Somebody.

"Oh!" He laughed pleasantly. "It is actually my brother's. He and I share the same genetics, same asthma, same medication. Please! You will feel better!"

Hamdani stared at him so long and wheezed so ferociously that Catalyst and Manuel both stared without moving. It's like a bad devil came along and suddenly peeled a layer out of the room. When we came in, the air in the room was white with a calm party aura. It suddenly changed to red—red air from red alerts going off in their brains.

Something told me—with dead certainty—the game was up.

Their faces were red with the shock of suspicion. Hamdani's acting was for shit. *Red alert. Red alert. The game is up. Up. Up.*

"What's the matter?" Catalyst laughed, but the skin on his face had tightened somehow. He asked, laughing incredulously, "Do you think I will poison you?"

When Hamdani didn't answer, Catalyst took the canister back and gazed for what was probably another five seconds, but a civilization could have risen and fallen. *Game over. Game over. He knows.*

I just didn't know how to get us out of the house. Hamdani couldn't even run. Catalyst put the canister down on the counter, crossed his arms, and laughed to himself. "Let us discuss what is making you so afraid of a harmless person like myself," he said.

Harmless. He had enjoyed saying it. I figured I might puke on him *Exorcist* style, if Hamdani didn't beat me to it. Hamdani took a step back and leaned against the sink, finding something on the floor to stare at, not that it helped.

"You were in Trinitron the other night," Catalyst remembered. "I waved at you. I wondered what on earth was making you so nervous. *I* was making you nervous... wasn't I? Today, you showed up with my new friend Tyler."

We stood there so stupidly while he put two and two together. It was the stupidest moment of my life. But what do you say? Do you stand there and tell the truth? They already knew it.

The soccer team must have scored, because the guys in the living room came to life, and it made me realize how softly Catalyst had been speaking. Manuel walked slowly around behind us, as if blocking the way in case we tried to run.

I felt his hulking presence as Catalyst laughed quietly to himself, staring at the floor. "I must ask you this. Because if it is untrue, you will not understand me, and if it is true, it will show in your faces. Here it is: My friend Omar believes that our conversations online have been watched—that our privacy has been invaded by someone perverse. That someone would not be you two, would it?"

I shook my head no and faked confusion along with Hamdani, but our acting must have been even worse than I gathered, because he laughed even harder. He was almost hysterical for a moment. "*This* is what American intelligence drums up to throw at us? Two boys who tremble over an... an asthma medication canister?" He put his hand over his eyes like he was ashamed to even look at us, and his laughter got higher in pitch.

"You're crazy," I said, my pride buttons being seriously pushed. "I have no idea what you're talking about, but you're freaking me out all of a sudden, and we're leaving."

"I don't think you are leaving," Manuel said, with ominous politeness in his voice. He was still blocking the door.

I spotted a set of knives on the counter, and Catalyst must have watched my eyes. He was still laughing but said, "Unless you want to end up like Daniel Pearl, don't even think of it."

Daniel Pearl is now famous. He's a journalist who was beheaded by terrorists in Karachi about six weeks ago. The beheading had been taped, and the beyond-sickening clip was still all over the Internet. My head banged with Michael's words from when he sat in my bedroom yesterday: *"They're beyond dangerous. You have no idea what you're tangling with."*

I said something appropriate, like "shit," and Hamdani coughed.

"Do not try *anything,*" Catalyst said, still in a low voice. "Do not think that those boys will help you. If we were to tell them everything now, and ask them to choose between your way of thinking or ours, I am quite certain they would side with us and help us to dispose of you. They have measured up that far, despite that they know only a little about us yet. I assure you it is not our wish to harm you in front of new recruits. But you should be aware that we could kill you in less than five seconds if you try anything. Without guns, without knives, without even our fists. Though you may wish to have been beheaded once we are finished."

He stood there a few moments more, enjoying watching us squirm like two butthead guys in high school who had bitten off more than they could chew. I had a brief thought that I could get ahold of the aerosol can by Catalyst's left elbow. But Manuel loomed from behind, making that seem all but impossible, too.

It turns out I didn't need a game plan. What sounded like an explosion came from the living room moments later. The front door flew off the hinge, and bodies piled through, holding guns, screaming in loud voices. Before I could count to ten, there must have been a dozen agents in every room screaming, *"Get on the floor! Everybody on the floor!"*

FORTY-FIVE

SHAHZAD HAMDANI
SATURDAY, MARCH 9, 2002
2:00 P.M.

HODJI TOES ME in the backside and mutters in Punjabi, "Thanks."

He means that I have led him to these men. I feel more relief than humiliation, though not much more. I have my nose turned to the kitchen tiles along with the swine we had been chasing for months.

"Get your hands out of the cabinet! Get on the floor now!" Hodji shouts at Catalyst. And while I cannot see what he was trying to do, I hear triggers clicking—several of them—and believe many guns are pointed at his head.

"Frisk them," Hodji says, and I feel hands pushing and probing at my bones and try to remind myself with gladness that such would find any hidden weapons on Catalyst and thereby protect us.

With my asthma smoldering, I turn my head to the side to breathe. I see Catalyst lying on the floor like I am. Whatever he was trying to reach for in the cabinet has not worked, and he is without any deadly weapons now. The female agent over us does not object that I have turned my head to the side, but when Catalyst tries to do the same, she hollers, "Nose to the floor!"

He complies. It lets me know that the agents are aware of who I am. But what they have planned for me and Tyler cannot be good. For one thing, all people lie on the floor, and we lie with them for what feels like eternity. A few frightened cries and sobs rise from the living room, and I am reminded that these recruits are probably not versed in any ShadowStrike business. They are shocked. USIC agents begin ripping, cutting, breaking things, obviously looking for something.

I have nothing to do but lie there and study Catalyst's long hair, which is rich dark chocolate brown, like an angel's. He does not look nervous, and I try to reflect on him and his thoughts as opposed to Hodji and his thoughts, because the former in this case is far less painful. I think perhaps Catalyst is not nervous because there is nothing in this apartment to implicate him. Perhaps he does not think USIC has much on him.

My eyes fix on Catalyst's hands and at first it is because I am aware of how limp and loose his fingers are, as his left hand flops over his head. His fingers dangle as if he were asleep, and despite that this seems arrogant, I wish I had his nerve. He is less afraid of Hodji than I am.

His fingernails are cut like I have never seen others cut. Most men cut their fingernails straight across. But he has cut his on either side, so that there is a slight point in the center of each. It isn't a dramatic point, and his fingers have a nice and shiny manicure. You would hardly notice it were you not lying on a floor beside the sight with nothing to distract you. I remember earlier thinking he looked like a musician or artist, and I wonder now if he plays classical guitar and his nails help to pluck the strings better. That would be ironic, him playing a beautiful instrument. It kills time, this wondering.

The agents are being very slow and methodical. I hear tape ripping off a roll often and plastic bags rattling.

Then two pairs of boots stomp into the kitchen, kneeling above my head, and hands are pulling things out of the cabinet under the sink. I perceive one agent is opening bottles and sniffing them, and passing them back to another agent with Baggies and roll tape.

"Here's something," the female agent says, but I cannot see where she is pointing.

My birch beer can is still in my hand, but suddenly it is gone. I hear the agent above me sniffing the can. He stands very still. Hodji stands in the doorway, studying Catalyst carefully.

Tyler mutters very softly, "Oh shit, oh no..."

"Quiet!" the sniffing agent roars.

I nearly jump as he takes Catalyst by the hair and sits him up. He sticks the soda can in front of his face with a gloved hand and says, "Drink this."

My head comes off the floor. I cannot help it. I lie like a sphinx, poised in horror, recalling terrible premonitions from home—*that I could accidentally drink the very poisoned water I seek out.* I am poised in horror to see whether or not Catalyst will drink from the soda he gave me. He looks at the agent, looks at me, looks at Tyler, but doesn't raise the can to his lips.

Tyler makes two more "oh shit"s, and the agent kicks him hard in the leg.

"Drink it!" the agent demands of Catalyst, as Hodji moves slowly toward him.

Equally slowly, Catalyst takes the soda can, toasts me with it, and swallows the whole can. He wipes his lips dramatically afterward.

My head splatters on the floor like a jelly mold. All I can hear is the roar of my asthma and Tyler yelping in relief. Catalyst bangs the empty can down two inches from my nose. He is full of impudence now, and his ironically kind smile has a glint behind it.

I say to the agent, "Try his asthma canister."

They do not answer. I don't think they are pleased that I am addressing them. However, the agent who told Catalyst to drink the soda now holds out the white canister.

"Use it," he says.

I watch sphinxlike again, but without so much terror, as I had not taken any of the medicine.

Catalyst rolls his eyes to one side and then the other, and slowly he raises the inhaler toward his lips. I wonder quickly if USIC has been stupid. I wonder if they have handed him an aerosol weapon which he can turn on us. Hodji is watching him carefully, but not with any panic that I can perceive. Catalyst brings it slowly to his lips, presses down, and inhales.

Again he drops the thing in front of me, smiling, giving me no look of betrayal.

Hodji stands over my head while Catalyst sits cross-legged right beside me.

"Where is it?"

"Where is what?" Catalyst asks.

"This house is dirty," Hodji says. The word "dirty" in this

case means that USIC believes something dangerous is hidden here. "We can look at every inch of every item in here under a microscope, and you can rot in jail while we go through all that. But I know this house is dirty."

As the other two agents point guns at Catalyst, Hodji turns and looks into the cabinet right behind where Catalyst is seated. It appears to be empty now. Above it on the counter sits a bottle of blue glass cleaner. Hodji takes it carefully in his gloved hand and smells it. The cap has been removed and it has already been smelled by the agent who was sniffing everything in here.

"You were reaching for this when I came in," Hodji says, eyeing him.

"Yes," Catalyst agrees with ease.

"You were going to clean the window, I suppose?" Hodji asks, kicking at a sponge that had fallen out of the cabinet and lay by the stove.

Despite the invitation, I am very amazed when Catalyst says, "I get the impression you find glass cleaner dangerous."

Somehow, Hodji returns his smugness equally. "I'll tell ya what. I don't believe it's glass cleaner."

I stare at the blue liquid. It looks like glass cleaner to me, but I am used to reading atrocious things about terrorist germs in liquids, and I don't have the nerves of steel that Hodji has. The thing swiftly becomes to me as threatening as a bomb, and I cannot peel my eyes from it, despite that Catalyst laughs in that good-natured way I am utterly sick of.

"Mr. USIC agent," he says. "Your little monkeys asking me to drink this and inhale that, they underestimate my commitment to our goals. I am a willing sacrifice. You cannot believe that those items are not tainted, simply because I took them."

I tear my eyes from the blue liquid to find them gazing at each other, trying to seek something from the other as instinctively as jaguar cats. Catalyst is looking to see if he can dismay Hodji, I gather. Hodji is trying to read his mind, as to what in this house of millions of molecules is dangerous, and what is not.

He finally replies, "I don't believe there was poison in the canister or in the soda can. But I believe it's in this room."

"And why do you believe that?" Catalyst asks.

"Because. Death is like bungee-cord jumping, even for people who are trained not to be scared of it. There's a look on the face before a person leaps—and you didn't have it when you just drank or inhaled, my friend. Or I wouldn't have let you do it."

He pointed a finger toward the glass-cleaner bottle but did not touch it this time. "What's in there, Raoul? You can be a drama queen and rot in the can until the CDC figures it out, or you can tell me and save us all a lot of time."

Another long silence follows. I hear a handgun cock over my head. Hodji puts his hand out to warn the agent to be careful, while casting a glance at me and Tyler. Hodji does not want a skirmish wherein a minor could get shot, but he is also aware of things, I sense, that are slightly beyond my comprehension. *"They're beyond dangerous. You have no idea what you're tangling with."* Michael's words yesterday strike at my heart. USIC agents never miss. Yet I feel exposed and vulnerable somehow, and to something I know not of.

"Fine. I will be honest with you," Catalyst says, though I doubt his sincerity. "There is a very dangerous chemical agent in this house, and in fact, it is in this room."

"Don't waste my time," Hodji goes on. "Tell me where it is, or don't."

"It is under my fingernails."

I glance at his shiny nails. It is an absurd lie to annoy the agents. Still, I focus on the strange cut of those nails, into sharp points, but it is beyond my comprehension until it is too late.

Two seconds later, Catalyst is dead on the floor with at least three bullets in his head. I have been pushed around somehow, but I don't realize what Catalyst did until I see Tyler's face. He has four bloody scratches down one cheek. From the way mine burns, I am certain I've suffered the same.

I spin in amazement to look at Catalyst's pointy little nails. They are relaxed now forever, but they are pulpy with blood on his nail tips... *nails which were not manicured, but wet with something.* I jerk my gaze to the bottle of glass cleaner, which Catalyst had been reaching for as the raid started, and the sponge now on the floor... He must have wet the sponge, dug those strange nails in, and...

My asthma shuts my chest, and I drop into a dead faint with my cheek stinging.

FORTY-SIX

CORA HOLMAN
FRIDAY, MARCH 15, 2002
NOON

I TENSED, LOOKING into eyes that were getting to be very familiar. Out of nowhere, a familiar gaze could shift to something frightening, alien. I had gotten to know Jeremy Ireland rather well over these past six days and had enjoyed watching many tapes of my mother either feeding the world's poor or filming stunning violence in her attempts to stop all wars. As her cameraman, he had much to tell. But then suddenly, I would be overcome with the few memories I had of the ICU, when I first came out of my coma and thought another man was Jeremy Ireland. Then I would think, *The first assassin was caught... but is there now a second one? If this man is only pretending to be Jeremy Ireland, how would I know? Maybe he's been slowly poisoning me this week with... what?* I would totally freeze and be unable to speak.

Jeremy Ireland stood at the foot of my hospital bed and

brought a VHS tape out of his pocket. "Here it is. As requested. How are you feeling today? Better than yesterday?"

"Better today, thanks..." I kept staring at him. I was still myself in the sense that guarding my words was second nature. I had not revealed to him, not once in six days of visits, that I could often forget how much I liked him and out of nowhere suspect he was an assassin. And once the suspicion overcame me, it did not go away easily.

He came up beside me, avoiding my IV lines with a respectful pause, and reached around them with the tape. *Is it a bomb?*

"I appreciate it," I said, and forced myself to take it. Nothing happened. Just a tape. Same as yesterday.

I had given him a key to my house, so he could get beta tapes, transfer them to VHS at the local news station, and bring them to me. But on a bad paranoid moment like this, I wondered if I had been stupid.

I tried to divert myself from my fear by reflecting on what I liked about him. Jeremy Ireland wore designer clothing and had blond shoulder-length "journalism hair," as I call it, and spoke the King's English. His father was in the House of Commons, and they owned a small castle in Tetbury, Gloucestershire, where Prince Charles has a home. I was shocked at first, trying to picture him with Aleese. It's hard if I'm remembering the Aleese I lived with for four years—or if I'm wondering if he's an assassin. But as I watched the tapes I often forgot about that Aleese, and my suspicions would melt away. We watched videos Jeremy shot or Aleese shot in war zones, and I kept being introduced to this daring, courageous pirate lady, who had an idea in her head that photography and video could cancel the concepts of war and starvation on the planet Earth.

I turned the tape over absently, and saw it was marked MOGADISHU.

"You're *certain* you want to see this?" he asked.

"Yes."

"It's quite brutal. Some things are better left unseen."

Perhaps it could bring a lot of painful flashbacks to him. But I defended my stance. "I watched *Black Hawk Down* this morning. I saw the Mogadishans jumping up and down on top of the killed American marines. I saw them strip and drag that man."

"Well, the marines are not one's mother. You already know that four journalists were stoned the day your mum was injured... beaten with rocks until they were dead."

And my mother would have made five.

She'd been injured in several of the tapes I'd watched with Jeremy. She took shrapnel in her arms once, and got her back singed running from an explosion in an Israeli marketplace. This is the one that proved to be too much—the one that created her great metamorphosis, much like that of Gregor into the cockroach in Kafka's story.

He put the tape in the machine and hit PLAY. I had already decided I wanted to start my own journal, and I would write each day of this illness until I was better, and maybe it would be useful to someone... somewhere, someday. Maybe if there were ever another terror attack on a small town.

But I decided upon watching this that I could never do justice to my mother getting injured. It was a torture scene that had basically taped itself from the dashboard of a Reuters car, in which she and Jeremy were escaping the same enraged mob that was stoning four journalists somewhere in the dusty background.

Jeremy had thrown the camera onto the dashboard so he could help Aleese, and most of what was filmed was chaos, but the situation came clear. Four huge, angry Somalians broke the passenger window of the car as the driver yelled helplessly. Aleese was in the passenger seat. The car was surrounded. The men pulled her out the passenger door to do god knows what—but Jeremy jumped over from the back into her seat and grabbed her left arm. You could hear the engine screech and men screech, bones being crushed under the wheels. Jeremy refused to let go. So did the four huge men. As the driver picked up speed, the men dropped off one by one, but it took a while. The worst was my mother screaming in agony. It was endless. As one man dropped off it would subside long enough for her to gulp for breath, but it would start up again.

They were mad at her for taking pictures of a bombing site where little children had been hurt—I think. Nobody made a very clear case for why they were attacking her. But after five minutes of hearing my mother yelling, *"AhhhhhAHHHHHH-HahhhhhAHHH,"* steadily, I thought I would lose my mind.

The camera managed to bump hard once and turn to a different angle. Most of the footage had been of the top of my mother's head and on the road behind it and the back fender. The men were blurry but still terrifying, holding on to her legs, biting her in the back, biting her in the legs, clawing at her waist. And finally, the last one let go of her ankle. They didn't seem to mind getting road burn. Something big jolted the car and the camera moved to catch Jeremy's chest and a higher view of the window. He gripped my mother's arm still, and blood streamed from where he'd been gripping with his fingers. Her shoulder was right at the top, but where her head and body should have been was nothing. You would have thought Jeremy had hold of an arm ending at the shoulder.

He screamed, "Stop the car! She's losing her arm!" near the end.

The car banged to a halt, and the camera swerved again, showing nothing but the seat between Jeremy and the driver. The driver screamed madly, "Hurry! They're not done! They're coming back!"

And my mother's body flew into view—just the back of her. She lay with her face in the driver's lap and the rest of her on Jeremy. I could see bites and bruises and hear her voice, alive as ever: "Go! Go now! Jesus, Jeremy, don't you ever stop whining?"

As the driver stepped on the gas, the camera toppled into her and went to black.

Jeremy had been standing beside me, and he stepped quietly to the machine, hitting STOP. He didn't look at me. I could find nothing to gaze at but the floor.

"We did manage to get away," he finally said. I was surprised to hear him laugh, however sadly. "But we didn't get to a hospital for two days. We'd no idea how bad the damage was. I think your mum knew. But in her usual style, she only wanted to berate the loss of her oldest and best camera."

I sat for the longest time, just staring at the foot of the bed. I was having what Rain had termed a "four-star day," which is when you feel no symptoms at all. I didn't feel peaceful, however. The Aleese in the footage is starting to meld in my mind with the mother-monster who existed in my home for four years. The end result of her was starting to make a little sense. It's linked to something—something courageous, something that counted—despite that it had torn her to shreds.

Jeremy cleared his throat. "Your mother detested violence, for all that she sought after it. She watched this footage over and over once we got back to Beirut. I should never have let her see it."

I wanted to say, "Don't blame yourself," but my voice had left me.

"I think what really killed her," he went on, "or killed her will to live, was the situation more than the men. The Americans went to Somalia intent only on feeding the starving people. There was endless civil war there, and many dangerous men looking to, uh, become king. The warlords would steal the children's food to feed their militias."

My eyes floated up in horror. Life in Trinity Falls gave me no preparation to understand this.

"The U.S. militia decided that to feed the poor, certain warlords had to be done away with. It was a mistake. To fight wayward power with wayward power does not work out. The bombing inflated the mob, which stoned the journalists, and almost got your mum." He sucked in a breath and let it out again. "Many people thought after the *Black Hawk Down* business that we should not feed people in countries experiencing civil unrest. They said we should let those countries argue it out among themselves, and maybe the starvation will snap them into disciplined action. The feeling was, when we feed the poor, we end up devoured by the hands we try to feed. Feeding the poor and ending violence had been Aleese's life. I don't think Aleese could quite argue with herself as well after Mogadishu.

She'd seen violence before, but none that took away her ability to photograph. She told me back in Beirut that her life was meaningless and, for all intents and purposes, over."

"I wish I had been more kind to her," I said, and shut my eyes, but tears built under my lids, and I felt Jeremy brush a tear off my cheek.

"When I said good-bye to her, just before she came home to you, she was sharp and unruly, and I don't suppose that ever got any better."

"Did she say her good-byes on September 10, 1996?" I asked.

He thought for a moment. "I don't recall the date as much as her resolve to cut herself off from me—from a past which she had convinced herself was a failure. It *was* September."

Jeremy was sitting now, leaning into me, patting my hair. My bad moment had passed. I didn't believe he was a terrorist. At least not now. Tomorrow might be different, but it wouldn't matter. His flight was leaving tonight.

This conversation had been hefty. It seemed to open a door for what I knew I needed to ask. It was now or never.

"Are you... my father?"

FORTY-SEVEN

SHAHZAD HAMDANI
FRIDAY, MARCH 15, 2002
NOON

I AWAKE THIS morning under heavy sedation again. I absorb the view of the Empire State Building out my window and decide I am actually in my Pakistani village, downloading photos of King Kong off the Internet for my father. He loves King Kong. I am planning a surprise for his birthday of King Kong photos. And suddenly I realize this is a fanciful dream, and I am at Beth Israel Hospital and this time not for asthma, per se, though it acts up for at least six hours a day. On a far more serious note, I have been scratched in the face by a devil. I have not spent much of my life reflecting on the devil. But now, I decide that the devil is personified in a man who will make it his last ambition on Earth to threaten the lives of two people.

Hodji had made an on-the-spot decision to fly me and Tyler here, as he says Beth Israel has the best protocols in place to counter acts of terror such as mustard or nerve gas. After my asthma visit upon arriving on American shores, I did not think I would be back so soon.

Saturday night, I found myself hoping that Hodji was overreacting and that there had been nothing under Catalyst's nails that could hurt Tyler or me. For one, the scratches stopped burning after an hour or so, despite that the scabs had swelling beneath them until yesterday. For another, there is an absurdity to what happened that protects me, prevents me from fully accepting its reality.

The sedation is not a good feeling, but not a bad feeling. The only bad feeling I have is an itching beneath the scabs of my cheek and a restlessness, due, I am certain, to computer withdrawal. I have been given nothing to do but watch the television and the view while USIC, the CDC, and the doctors here have been trying to name a germ they claim to have seen in our blood. As appears to be characteristic with ShadowStrike, it is nothing they have seen before.

I notice immediately that Tyler is not in the bed next to me where he has been for six days.

I see the arm and leg restraints have been left where he lay. His thrashing about had become worse and worse with each passing day, as it appeared his mother was not coming. She had been contacted by USIC and told quite frankly that her son had been scratched in the face by a suspected terrorist bearing a yet unidentified substance under his nails. I cannot say why she chooses not to visit, but "she'll steal my hard drive" and "she'll figure out what I am" were common expressions of Tyler's after he tried to fling himself out the window on the second day.

I tried to remind him repeatedly that he is an American hero and his mother ought to be proud. But for some reason, this would only soothe him for an hour at a time. It has been like sleeping next to a rabid animal, and I am hoping that perhaps while I was under a sleeping sedative, they removed him to get some help with his mind.

The room is too quiet, such that when Roger shows up, I am relieved just for some distraction. He glances at Tyler's vacant spot and does not look bothered by it, so I do not question him right off. He seems focused. He sits and leans the laptop to face me so I can see the screen. He has not mentioned my duplicity at the hospital in southern New Jersey. Perhaps he is ashamed. Dr. Briglianni has accompanied him, but at first, the things Roger shows me are not medical, and are quite engaging. He waits as, slowly, a black-and-white photo of a laughing man forms on the screen.

"Omar," he says.

I stare, hypnotized by the picture of a nondescript man of perhaps fifty, with dark curly hair and a clipped beard and mustache. The photo was obviously taken when Omar was not concerned about hiding himself. I see a marketplace in the background that looks highly cultured but perhaps not American. The buildings are older, yet familiar to me.

"Germany?" I guess. "Taken in Hamburg while he was professor over there?"

Roger grins into his lap and lets out a breath that sounds like relief. "Don't lose your mind because of all this, Shahzad. It's a good mind. It's fantastic. It's a computer chip wrapped up in a big heart."

Whatever, as the American kids love to say. To recognize German buildings is for me no more difficult than to remember languages that I see and hear.

"Omar Loggi," he tells me. "Professor of biochemical engineering, University of Hamburg. He was an associate professor for two years—not to blame the Germans too much on this one. It's not like they could have possibly known him. Before that, he was Gustav Mojobian of Romania, and before that, who knows... A national is sometimes a person who has become devoid of a homeland, devoid of family, devoid of alliances with his people. That's one good way that you can tell a terrorist. Did you know that, Shahzad?"

I still have the droopiness from the sleep sedative, and I do not interrupt him.

"A terrorist is a person who holds principles above people. That's the first trait. If you can trace them back far enough, you often see them divorcing themselves from any people with whom most people are normally close—family, friends, neighbors, communities. People who can prey on the world's innocents are not attached to people. They have replaced people with principles. Principles become their best friends. It sounds very high and mighty. However, we live in a world still too influenced by intelligence over instinct. Thank you, the Enlightenment. But terroristic behavior is not high and mighty. It's sad, and sad is simple."

His speech makes me mindful of my father talking about coming to New York. I had told him often, in anger and frustration, that I did not want to stay alone and help Uncle Ahmer and that I wanted him to remain in Pakistan as always. And I reminded him that what he wanted to do in America could easily be done without being there in person.

"But Shahzad, if the Americans are to trust me, they will want often to shake my hand and sit in meetings where they can see me,

hear me, smell me, and look into my eyes. It's always primarily about the people, Shahzad, about the relationships."

"We discovered that four times between 1998 and 2000, during Omar's tenure at the University of Hamburg, he made trips to an obscure island in the Soviet Union, where Q fever has amassed in the systems of wild goats, birds, silver foxes...It has developed in a mushroom that has overtaken the roots of trees. Q fever was cultivated on that island during the germ warfare period of the Cold War. Though the Geneva Convention stopped further development of biochemical weapons in the late 1960s, what was in the air there continued to cultivate. It was from the cultures of this Q fever that he developed Q3. He developed the waterborne agent either in Hamburg or in a lab somewhere near Astor College. We haven't found the lab. I'd love to say Q3 didn't work out very well, but those four kids down in Jersey would find that statement offensive."

"So where is Omar?" I ask. "Have you captured him?"

Roger switches to another photo, which uploads slowly. As I wait for his answer, I try to remember what came next in my father's most memorable "people" speech, but I cannot. I am cognizant instead of a piece of a famous saying: "Of the People, by the People, for the People..."

Maybe my father had gone on to say that, maybe not. But obviously, the People is something mass killers don't feel affection toward.

"We haven't found him," Roger confesses. "We traced two credit card numbers he was using all over South Jersey since December. Neither has been used since last week. We're reasonably certain he hasn't gotten out of any of our international airports, but we can't vouch for Canada's or Mexico's."

I hold my disappointment in silence. I sense in my deepest instincts that he is gone, far away.

"Ten men are in custody," Roger says to placate me. "They include PiousKnight and members of ShadowStrike, most of whom were living in Europe. They're being extradited, and we will try them in America."

"How did you find them?" I ask, feeling jealous that he could accomplish so much when I am stuck here. However, his answer makes me smile.

"Tell Tyler his Dog Leash program is a gem. It leashed a couple of suspects and then leashed them to others. Fast and furiously. It filled in a lot of holes."

I wish Tyler were present to hear that.

"And VaporStrike?" I ask. I have wandered through the months of vague chatter and suspect that Catalyst and Pious-Knight were foot soldiers, and VaporStrike was Omar's colleague, perhaps a very ambitious and dangerous officer in ShadowStrike.

"Gone also," Roger says. "We'll find them. I promise. That's not for you to worry about. It's just that you've worked so long and so hard, I'm telling you this much as a professional courtesy."

The obvious question pours out of my mouth. "And how do you expect to find him without me?"

"Shahzad, don't goad me while I'm busy feeling sorry for you" is his only answer. I reach for the terminal and clutch it, but my grip is not as strong as his, and besides, the sleep medication makes me care slightly less.

"Fine, have your laptop." I sweep it toward him with reproach. "I would love to have your terminal and to help you search for these two men, but I am not in the habit of sacrificing my dignity. I am more concerned with 'the People' at present, namely the one who was in the bed next to me. Please tell me that you haven't lost track of Tyler, also."

"He's doing okay. He's on the psych ward, talking to a psychotherapist."

"That is a type of doctor?" I try to recall.

"Yes. Hodji's with him, too."

I feel peaceful, even outstanding for a moment, over something I cannot quite explain. It is about my primary focus being on Tyler, a person, rather than the laptop, an information receptor, which had been right in my fingers.

"And now... Dr. Briglianni is here to show you something else." Roger hits the touch pad again, and a different sort of picture comes up on the screen. Omar is gone, and in his place are roundish orange circles floating in a dark pool. It looks like a science photo.

Dr. Briglianni comes to the other side of me and points at the screen, saying, "Hodji told me to tell you the whole truth, so I'm telling you."

Tyler and I had asked Hodji to extend to us this courtesy, but I find the daily results falling somewhere between irritating and terrifying. It's not that I wish I had not said it. I just wish the results were coming out differently than they are. The picture of my blood that I was shown yesterday had, perhaps, half as many of these orange circles floating in it. From the day preceding that, they had doubled as well.

"The good news is," Dr. Briglianni went on, "that now that we have identified the germ agent, we can tell other things, such as the gestation period, and more importantly, how to quell its effects."

"You know what the germ is?" I repeat.

"Yes."

He clears his throat, which forces my words out.

"Only tell me it is not smallpox, please. I have seen images of its victims on the Internet. It is better to be dead."

"It is not smallpox," he says.

I sigh in relief, but only for a second.

"It is a mutated form of ulceroglandular tularemia."

I think of Omar's online allusion to creating other vinegars and play the terminology through my head. Tularemia is a bioterroristic agent, but not as dreaded as smallpox. I cannot remember much about it on the spot. The first term has the root words *ulcer* and *gland* in it. My stomach starts to dance and sway in upset.

"You can get rid of it?" I ask.

"We would have been trying all the antibiotics we've been trying so far, plus an antiviral, which we will start you on immediately."

"So, you can't."

He clears his throat again. "We have alerts out to drug specialists on four continents. We'll come up with something, don't you worry."

I close the lid of the laptop, so I am not looking at these ever-multiplying orange blasts. They are shaped like hearts, if we care to discuss absurdity at its finest—reddish orange hearts in a bed of dark green fluid. I am a computer man, not a scientist. I had never processed the thought before this week that photographed blood can appear dark green.

"What shall I expect?" I ask as Roger whisks the laptop away.

"Do you know what a gestation period is?" the doctor asks.

"Yes." It is the time between when one is infected with a germ and when it begins to show symptoms. I have read as much.

"We believe this germ has an approximate ten-day gestation period, and it is not my opinion that we can find an effective medication in the next few days. Hence, next week you may break with a fever, and your skin will turn bright red, and a rash will start to—"

"Never mind," I cut him off. "I don't wish to hear it."

Roger offers, "The thing won't kill you, Shahzad. The other assurance we have is that it won't affect your vital organs. The CDC believes it will go mainly after skin tissue."

"Correct," Dr. Briglianni adds.

My memory is probably more remarkable than most people's, but it is not always a good thing. One passage I read about tularemia months ago floats to the forefront, along with a picture of ulcerated skin lesions and the remaining scars. I will not look like a smallpox victim, but it could be hideous nonetheless.

I wish to ask for Hodji but remain silent. He has watched over me for days, feeling guilty to the extreme for not removing Tyler and me from Catalyst's reach, for not having the imagination to conceive of his unprecedented intentions. It had been tricky for him, and I never cease to remind him that his guilt is unfounded in a situation for which there are no existing protocols.

He has since provided the details of how he came to find Tyler and me in time. He had been late to meet Roger at the hospital the day that Tyler and I went there because he had been tailing us the whole way. Perhaps USIC meant it when saying they didn't have time to check up on us, but Hodji made the time.

Seeing our direction, he reasoned that I wanted to see the sick youths and waited in his car to see what we would do next. He called in a "hunch." After Roger took that call from Michael outside, the one that made me flee in haste, he called Hodji, telling him with many explosions that USIC would haul our bad behavior to the local juvenile detention center and book us. If Hodji had done that immediately, he might never have found Catalyst and PiousKnight, who was Manuel.

Hodji's instincts are good. He followed us again and put two and two together that we were on our way to Astor College. He was able to get a raid organized in twenty minutes. If he hadn't followed us and done all that, we would probably be walking around with scratches, wondering at our "luck," that Catalyst had tried to scratch us like a small child instead of saw off our limbs. Hodji, Susan, and Michael had said that these men were dangerous beyond our wildest dreams. And in my wildest dreams I never pictured a man who would load up his own flesh and sacrifice his life to meet an end.

Had it not been for Hodji, Catalyst might be with Omar instead of dead. Things worked out slightly better this way, but I cannot help but say my thought—about being scratched in the face, and playing host to an ugly germ in the sixth day of a ten-day gestation period.

"This entire situation is absurd," I report.

Roger and Dr. Briglianni say nothing.

FORTY-EIGHT

CORA HOLMAN
FRIDAY, MARCH 15, 2002
12:21 P.M.

JEREMY IRELAND LOOKED at me with affection, patted my hair, and said, "No."

It was not as easy as usual to hide my emotions. I had never been completely convinced he was my father, but to hear him clearly say no, he was not, sent me into some emotional freefall. My jaw trembled, my lips trembled, and I tried desperately to focus on my fingers, how my nails needed filing.

"I'm gay," he went on.

I didn't exactly see the problem with that. There were gay men all over the planet who had been married or had had kids.... The answer irritated me. It was too cut-and-dry for a complicated situation.

"What I mean by that," he said, "is that your mother and I never..."

I guess that was evidence enough that he wasn't my father, but it left before me many mysteries, the least of which was

Then, who is? I decided that if he knew, he would certainly have said as much—even if he didn't feel comfortable providing a name. Pictures formed in my head of Aleese, drunk after a hard photo shoot, flirting with one guy after another in some journalists' bar. If my roots were that loveless, I was not ready to hear it.

"But...you loved her," I said. "So much..."

"I worshipped her. I still do." He stood and put on his jacket.

He left me numbers in London where I could call him if I needed anything—anytime. I needed time alone right now, my usual diet, to digest my life under these new terms.

Unfortunately, after Scott got out of intensive care, he was moved in with Owen, and I now had Rain in the other bed. She came in, pushing an IV and grumbling. She'd become more quiet these days. She wasn't her usual vivacious self, and she even offered no opinion when her father mentioned that they were sending us to a rehab facility fifteen miles from here. I would have thought she'd collapse, but all she'd said was "I'm still going to the prom...I don't care how I do it."

"Did you see that stack of homework our teachers sent over in case we were bored?" Rain grumbled.

Before I could answer, Owen followed her in a wheelchair being pushed by Dobbins. Owen immediately dropped himself into her bed, and she said, "No dibs! I'm tired."

The room was a convention when Dempsey followed them, holding up an envelope filled with papers. He dangled it by two fingers, implying it was the dreaded homework we'd heard was coming.

"And get this, Cora," Rain grumbled on. "McIntyre sent us an essay to write for history. And he just gave us the same one as everyone else. He wants us to tell him what it means to be an American in 2002. How in the hell do *we* answer that?"

No one noticed my tears until I tried to answer. My "I hadn't heard" trembled.

She came over and lay down beside me, and Dempsey sat at the foot of the bed. I could feel Owen watching me. Dobbins took a seat beside Owen. I was utterly surrounded.

"Your dad leave?" Rain asked.

I felt like I was being thrown out of a truck. Or maybe it was that the truck was roaring up my throat. But I could feel myself snapping and cracking, and finally some sobbing alien stepped out of me and took control.

"He's not my dad. I kind of doubted he was my dad, but I wanted to find out. I have no idea who my dad is. I don't have any relatives and... I don't have any friends, either."

Their reactions amazed me, though I don't know why. It was filled with, perhaps, the last thing I would have wanted to hear them say, but I could not have predicted the amount of sincerity with which they would say it.

"... and we're chopped liver?"

"... we're your friends, Cora..."

"... your friends..."

"We're your..."

"... friends."

And on and on. I didn't know what to say, but I knew "thank you" was wrong. It was a harmony—off-key, but humming.

Owen ended it with "Come over here and I'll hug you. But you have to come over here. I'm *not* having a four-star day."

I almost went to him. But in keeping, I took a tissue from the box Dobbins held out to me. I blew my nose rather hard, and didn't realize until I tried to use two hands that Rain was holding my one hand. I didn't try to pull it away. It felt very normal.

After a minute, she said, "You know what we should do? We should all try to keep a diary. Bet we could get out of a lot of English and history homework by promising that instead."

Owen laughed at her. "*You're* going to keep a diary? I'd like to see you write more than three sentences in your life without getting distracted."

"This is serious, though," she said. "It's, um, stirring my need to be lit'rary. To keep a record, at least."

"It's a shame you can't punctuate," Dempsey giggled.

"I'll say it all into a tape recorder," Rain countered. "Don't some really important CEOs keep their diaries that way? Maybe when all of this is over, we'll find a famous editor who can type it out for me."

"I'll type it out," I said. "I'll edit." It sounded like a *me* project, and if I was to be their friend, I would long feel a nagging need to repay the debt somehow.

I sat among them, and let them do all the talking, but it was the first time since Oma died that I felt something akin to relaxed. Despite an IV, despite the surroundings, and despite an unpredictable future.

Life is a mystery, but that's nothing new to me.

FORTY-NINE

WHAT IT IS LIKE TO BE AN AMERICAN TODAY

By Rain Steckerman

HISTORY 4
MARCH 15, 2002

HI, MR. MCINTYRE. You know I hate writing essays—I hate writing anything, in fact, but I also know you are nicer than Ms. Curcio, who won't let us start our English papers with anything but a totally boring introduction. I know you won't be counting off for saying the truth from the start, right?

It is hard for me to think about being American. I am busy thinking about what it is like to be here in a hospital.

You've heard by now what happened to us, I guess. My dad held a press conference this morning. Bet you had the TV on in the classroom, like you always do, but this time the scenery and the names were a little more familiar. Anyway, these terrorists opened a discount shoe store over in Surrey and pretended to run it, and on December 28 they poisoned the water.

They only poisoned five streets, but I live on one of them, and so do the Ebermans and so does Cora Holman. The Holmans and the Ebermans drank tons of tap water, and so did I cuz I was always over at Owen's house (no, we do *not* go out, though I know that has been a rumor for some time among people who don't really know us. All I ever did over there was drink the water—honestly. Back to my story). So now, we have this germ that the Centers for Disease Control is calling Q3. We are very glad they caught those men, but I don't like to focus on them. It arouses our puke factors, let's leave it at that.

Right now we have Q3 in our blood and in our bone marrow, and they can clean it out of our blood, but it just comes back from the bone marrow. Doctors are working hard in all these very kewl cities like Vienna and Sydney and Minneapolis to figure out how to get rid of it. I'm guessing they will figure it out soon.

The worst to get hit of us kids was Scott. He had an aneurysm both in his heart and in his head. I got so scared he would die. He got lucky because there was one easy surgery they could do if the aneurysm near his heart was the right shape and size, and it turns out it was. They cauterized it with a microscopic blowtorch. If it had been a rip-open-your-rib-cage surgery, he'd still be in that coma, unable to go through that much trauma. Sometimes I wish he was still out of it, because he is very pissed and he can get very mouthy. He needs to take an anger management class.

Owen is okay, good days and bad, but he floors me. There's a chapel in this hospital, and you're allowed to light candles in there. He lit four on one side and ten on the other.

The four are for us. Get this: The other ten candles Owen lit were for the bad guys. Bob Dobbins was all "He's totally lost it. Those guys should burn in hell." I agree, but I know Owen, and even on his worst day, he will not feel good about people going to hell. Here's what he said:

"Hell is a place for..." Wait a minute, he's right here. I will let him write what he feels, because he can say it better. (This part still goes toward *my* grade, not his.)

I just don't believe in passing judgment until you can put yourself in the other guy's shoes. I don't know if they're arrogant or confused or scared or stupid or... I just don't want to eliminate any possibilities until I can understand. The thought of ten people burning in hell makes me feel less satisfaction instead of more. I believe that heaven and hell don't exist for what personally makes me glad or what personally pisses me off. I do think there will be murderers in heaven. Don't you? They can't just include "anyone except the one who came after my family," right?

I know that sounds really crazed and all, but I have to say, on the days when my head feels like it's going to explode, I want Owen near me.

It is not fun and it is not easy being here, and it is surely not fun to think that I have something that can't be gotten rid of tomorrow. I've never had anything before I couldn't kill with a good night's sleep and a couple of Advils. Sometimes I think Owen is crazy, and I want to go kill those guys myself, or at least get front-row seats for their trip to the electric chair. There's a lot of time to think in here.

But maybe this sort-of-essay does relate to the assignment anyway. Because yesterday I had the thought "Do I wish that I had been born somewhere else? Do I wish that I had lived in Sweden? Or Finland? Or Canada? Or somewhere exotic like Polynesia? Do I wish I was something other than American, so that this would not have happened to me?"

We all have times when we wish we were more interesting and from some more colorful place—but it's not the right response when some terrorists come here, trying to shake up your whole universe. That makes me even more patriotic. Somehow. Maybe it's a pride thing. I told my dad this last night and he actually smiled (first real smile in a long time). He said he was in college toward the end of the Vietnam War, and almost everybody his age had long, shaggy, nonmilitary hair, and made loud statements about hating the government, and it was kind of trendy to dislike your country thoroughly. In this year of 2002, everyone loves our country a lot. It's more like things were right after World War II. Dad says that if he and USIC can keep the terrorists from hurting anyone else over here, that this, too, will blow over, and we'll return to normalcy—with everyone here and abroad nitpicking at what's wrong in America.

I don't know why his thoughts bug me; maybe they imply that if my dad and his fellow agents do their jobs really well, their big reward is that people will return to a state of lukewarm feelings about where we live, and who's in charge, and even USIC. That doesn't seem fair.

Maybe this is what it means to be a great American: You remember the good things about your country even when everything is going *well*. When things are *boring*. When your biggest problem is that you can't get your whole college tuition together for next semester and you don't know what to do.

I used to hate it when my dad would raise the question after some complaint fest of mine, but now I might start asking it to others: "How'd you like a one-way ticket to Namibia?"

And I think that's as patriotic as I can be, considering there are bigger questions in my face right now. I can't stop asking them. So, I might as well put them in this essay and help my grade along by using them to fill in space. They're not good for much else: Will I make it to the PROM??? Will I be able to go to college? Will I live through this? If I do, will I be able to have children? If not, who will want to marry me? What would it be like for my dad to have to bury me? Why is it that I'm still glad I didn't say yes, the last time my dad asked if I wanted a one-way ticket to Namibia?

GROUND ZERO

FIFTY

SHAHZAD HAMDANI
SATURDAY, MARCH 16, 2002
NOON

HODJI AND I emerge from the cab a block from what is formerly the World Trade Center. I cannot see the disaster site from here, but I hear the echo of cranes and bulldozers even above the pitch of all that is New York.

"Need a hand?" Hodji asks.

I grip my bag, which contains a carry-along box that releases antibiotics into my blood constantly and looks like a small plastic briefcase. The tube that runs from it to my vein is almost hidden beneath my jacket cuff. Hodji has put the box in a gift bag under much tissue paper, with a card dangling off that reads, FOR GRANDMA. This was his good thinking, so that I will not appear to be carrying a device that resembles something my enemies would love to detonate.

"No help. I feel much good, thank you," I say as would befit a man.

We get out of the taxi a block away because Hodji wants me to see St. Paul's Chapel, which I recognize from many Internet photos. Its steep iron fence is consumed in a 9/11 memorial, so I can only see spikes at the top.

I can feel Hodji studying the large, square bandage that covers my cheek and the scabby scratch marks. I had asked for flesh colored, as neither he nor I want to make notice of ourselves in a place of anxiety and mourning. However, my scratches are not even itching today. It is like I cannot feel them. I don't want him fussing over me with my bandage and briefcase, and so I ignore him, studying instead the fence at St. Paul's, which is covered in flowers and pictures and colored drawings and toys and jewels and messages and every conceivable thing. I move close to this fence.

Hundreds of messages are strapped there for all to read: kind notes from a fifth-grade class in Japan, a junior high school in Thailand, the royal family in Madrid, a football team in Cairo, the nursing staff at an Ecuadorian hospital... sympathies and encouragement pour out of the many scrawls. I have seen this place so many times in pictures. But pictures have no odor. They don't blow the wind in your face. This endless fence pulsates with words that both move and confuse me.

I raise my formerly unanswered question, as it lurks at the base of my confusion. "Are Americans the tired and poor? Or are Americans the rich and ridiculous?"

Hodji says, "We're both."

His answer displeases me. It is too easy.

"It seems to me that people show up here the tired and poor. They come to better their situation, and after they become rich, they turn ridiculous. So, why bother to come?" I ask.

"Maybe it's the view of the thing. Americans working hard out on the prairie love to buy Hollywood magazines, so they can revel in the bankruptcies and ugly divorces of movie stars. But if they had the chance to become a star, most would jump at it."

"I do not understand this place," I say, and add, "I will go home to Pakistan."

He need not repeat his news of the past three days, but he delivers it into my space regardless. "Your country won't let you in, not loaded up with viral toxins."

"I am not contagious."

"No, but they're not equipped to restore you to health, and they know about you. You have to stay."

"They do not make even flattering promises here." I turn and stare across the street into the side window of an SUV, at the reflection of Hodji and me stepping out of the line of sympathizers. I don't want to cross the street and view my bandaged face close up, for fear I will also see it break out in the lesions promised by what Catalyst had under his fingernails.

My coming to America has been in every way absurd—last minute, under the cover of lies, to sneak up on men whom only one sixteen-year-old can interpret. And now my body is in an equally absurd situation, unlike anyone's in the universe except Tyler's. I cannot find words to describe—in any of the languages I speak—what it is like to be in the seventh day with a bad germ that has a ten-day gestation period.

Now, with this monument behind me and an SUV's side window reflecting clearly in front, I rub my good cheek, wishing I could keep its smoothness. I have never accepted changes well—not changes or sitting still.

Hodji has been my constant companion, except when he is with his wife and his son, Twain, and yesterday when he spent a morning on the psych ward with Tyler. He got me permission to leave the hospital today and visit this site. I look, feel, and sound like a normal person carrying a gift bag—just another Ground Zero visitor—except for the supersized Band-Aid on my cheek.

"When these lesions break all over my skin," I ask, "how painful will it be?"

"They can manage the pain. Don't worry about that."

"How ugly will be the scars?"

"Think positive," he says. "It's a mutation. The only one who knows, I would guess, is Omar."

Last night, Hodji took a call from Roger, who confirmed their fear that Omar and VaporStrike had escaped across the border. They could be anywhere by now.

As well, Omar had left a good-bye note posted in a Yahoo! thread that was brazen, in Arabic, and attached to something comically irrelevant, a Mothers of Asthmatic Children's newsgroup, I believe. So, it was as if he wanted only his v-spies to find it, and now, he was probably joking with VaporStrike and other secret associates. I had read the post several times, and while it was galling to hear him speaking so frankly and glibly, I was distracted by the impending state of my health. I did not want to think of him now. Still, I could not help but imagine him and VaporStrike on the Polynesian beaches where my father so desperately coveted a visit. I think the best medicine I could have would be to get on the Internet and find them. For now, I am forced to face my computer withdrawal symptoms. I have not touched a terminal in over a week.

"For the time being, it would be better to focus on the bright side," Hodji replies. "The thing won't kill you. And it's *never* better to be dead."

Americans always think it is not better to be dead. Other cultures take solace in the approach of heaven. Many Americans have such a nice life, I suppose, that they need not dream of perfection.

However, I spin from my reflection and stare at a memorial picture of a firefighter and a message beneath signed Margie, Talia, Joshie, and Pooey, and it has also beneath a small picture of a mother with two little children and a cat. The missing firefighter looks a bit like Catalyst, only with shorter hair. Same nice smile. This world is absurd, and no man is God. USIC is not God, either.

I have nothing to say on this complicated thought, and I turn from the drawing, needing to settle the practicalities of my life.

"Has my aunt said yet that she will take me back?"

"I talked to her again this morning. I thought a few words from me might help," he says. "She hasn't changed her stance, and she assured me again that it has nothing to do with any impending health problems."

I almost wish it was the germ that frightens her. She says that by now I am too independent and stubborn-minded, and I will influence Inas to also disrespect every authority figure, from school to law enforcement. She took my Saturday escape with Tyler very badly, especially given its outcome and timing—just one day after I had cut the school. I wonder at the downsides of having been a business owner in my teenage years.

"You said you are home for two months," I hint. I do not ask outright, but I would very much like to stay with Hodji. However, there are Twain and Mrs. Montu to consider. They know me only by name.

"Don't I wish...," he says, reading my mind. "I actually asked Alicia. When USIC told me they were on to your real age and were letting you go, my first thought was 'Finally. He won't be undercover. I can introduce him to Twain!' Christ, you're both like sons. But Alicia said, um..." He clears his throat, and I can feel mortification rising off him while he delivers her thought. "...she said that there's nothing in Twain's past to prepare him for something like this."

He cannot meet my eyes. Mrs. Montu does not want Twain exposed to something horrific, as might be my skin, as might be my state of mind, as might be the schedule for the 101 pills I may have to take for months. Of course, I do not want to impose myself on any soul, given these factors, so I resist the urge to jealously state, "*You treat your children like sacred cows.*"

"I will live with Tyler," I say. "He will gladly have me."

I have not seen Tyler since Thursday night, because he is staying on the psych ward, but I know he shares my predicament of no relatives or willing parties. I also know from Hodji that he is feeling better and may be back with me in a few days. Yesterday, he talked at length with a psychiatrist, Hodji, and USIC, and the end result is that his mother was arrested as a spy. She had run to a hiding place in Philadelphia instead of staying to care for her son, but after spying on her for so many years, Tyler came up with the exact address where she might be found, Hodji said.

Tyler's often outrageous behavior makes sense to me now,

under the stress of so much disgrace. And from Hodji I understand that he is still quite sassy, but is much calmer somehow. I don't entirely understand how that could be, but Hodji seems to.

"We will start an Internet business, and nobody will have to look at us if we become badly scarred. We will make our way as men."

"I wish you would give some more thought to what I proposed yesterday," he says.

"I don't want to live for months in hospital," I repeat yesterday's answer.

"You're not hearing me. It's not a hospital. It's a house. It's a house that's being turned into a rehab facility."

"Rehab sounds much like hospital. I came to America to eat good food, not food that makes me long for home. I came here for nice, soft mattress, like I see on fancy hotel websites, not a plastic sheet topped with—"

"House," Hodji repeats. "H-O-U-S-E. The state can occasionally own a house, and the state of New Jersey owns this one. For years, it was a historic landmark that fell into disrepair. Now, it's been fixed up and they're opening it to anyone rehabilitating from a terrorist attack in New Jersey. That includes you. A nurse will live there, too. If you need anything, *kabala*."

He clears his throat before continuing. "Uh... You can have your own computer, too."

He had not said that part yesterday. I look in his eyes, expecting to see a trick. I would say his look is "resigned."

"You trust me with computer?" I ask.

"Not on your life. But I'm willing to say that, um, well, what I don't know won't hurt me. And I often take tips from anonymous sources."

I stare into his serious eyes to perceive if I am dreaming this. His making me out to be eighteen is not an item for us to discuss, as he will not even admit to me that he knew the truth all along. I am sure he feels his job was threatened by the discovery, and since then he has been hard-lining me with "playing by the rules." But his eyes seem full of sentimentality today. Perhaps the sentimental surroundings are influencing his logic. I repeat aloud what my heart has uttered over and over on this day and those preceding.

"I am a v-spy, now and forever."

"I know," he says.

We silently turn to stare at the memorial again, but I am certain he is doing what I cannot help doing—replaying in my head that final post from Omar with all its dastardly implications. It had been addressed to no one, but I had taken it very personally:

> It appears my stay at Astor College is terminated early, which suits me fine. I am ready for a nice beach vacation before returning to work. The nature of that work will continue along the same lines as it long has been: to stand strong against the devices of Satan, especially those in Europe and North America, where mongrels have replaced the richness of tradition with the seduction of materialism. If we do not stand mightily against them, we, who are of high integrity and excellent descent, will have been absorbed into a world of meaningless, spiritless forms such as flourish in the Western world today.

I avoid the word "kill" and use the terms "stand strong against" in our rhetoric, not because I am a coward but because I am a humble man. ShadowStrike is a humble organization. We do not wish for recognition; we do not wish to make great displays of our very adept abilities to extinguish those who are errant and useless. We will meet our goals better long term without acknowledgments. We will strike without warning. We will strike with humility. We will strike and, unlike others you choose to call "terrorists," you will never be sure it is us.

A village will fall ill of a strange plague, and many will mysteriously succumb. Was it a new and unidentified strain of flu, or was it us? A vacation resort will empty as its guests suffer skin ailments and flulike symptoms from a germ that no one can pinpoint, and a dozen or two will die. Was the swimming pool water the culprit, or was it us? All attending a certain school or office building will require medical attention for sudden headaches, dizziness, and blurred vision. Many will die. Was it a gas leak, or was it us?

We plan to be around for many years. But you will never know quite where we are, who we are, and where we will turn up next. Greetings to you, my little friend...OL.

While the post reeked with madness, that last line haunts me the most, because it leads me to think he is talking directly to me, the Kid. Perhaps God has a sense of humor. Perhaps

Omar had discovered what I looked like, and now, I can chase him with a whole new appearance that I did not have to pay for.

I repeat my statement, which gives me strength. "I am a v-spy, now and forever."

"I know," Hodji repeats also. "I finally had some time to think about it after the arrests. My only other option, I suppose, is to kill you."

I share his grin. "Where is this place, this *house*?"

"Just outside Colony One."

It is far away. But Colony One is quite beautiful. I liked the willow tree best.

"The Q3 victims from Colony One are being sent there until a recovery plan can be put into effect. At least three of the four. They're not happy about it, but the medication they're taking to try to clear that up is tricky. No one thinks they can remember how to take it all on their own, and if the state is providing the cure, the state provides the hospitality and housing. There's not a lot they can say about that."

I interrupt him. "You said only three. Do not tell me one has died."

"Remember the one in the coma?"

"The one who helped capture the assassin, Richard Awali? Scott. He is dead?"

"Actually, he's awake. Scott is almost twenty, and they can't force him to go. He feels about rehab as you do."

"How did they fix his heart?"

Hodji shrugs. "I'm not a doctor."

"And the aneurysm in his head?"

"Still there. I understand their main goal is to keep him

from losing his temper. He's close to finding out the true meaning of 'blowing a gasket.'"

Hodji's last term is English, and I do not understand it.

"And Tyler could go there, too?"

"Tyler could go there, too."

"Will they hate to look at us?"

"I highly doubt this group of kids is going to pass judgment like your normal person. Like Alicia..." He rolls his eyes upon this little outburst. He has never said anything against his wife, or anything for her. But I have long suspected that Hodji enjoys working on the other side of the world because his life at home can be atrocious.

He smiles, seeing he has made me feel better. He points to the flowers and the message of God blessing the families and America. "See these? They're all for you. All these messages, they're for you, too."

He is patronizing me, I think. I am a Pakistani villager who, from natural modesty and professional need, has always diverted myself from being noticed. I deflect the feeling of mattering so much, though I do not want to turn away from it.

My eyes fall on a bouquet of purple and yellow silk irises brought by a deceased fireman's wife and children. The message reads, "To our daddy, we love you, Daddy, and we know the angels like you up there. Love, Brittany, Chelsea, and Austin." The crayon drawing is of a fireman with both pointy-toed boots going off to the left. He wears gigantic wings and carries his fire hose.

I stare, finding in this childlike drawing something that I have long been looking for—a symbol of America which endears me to it. The place is, perhaps, touched by angels, but the fractured kind with the knobby knees and the turned-sideways feet. They mean well. They shed their angel dust over the McDonald's and the Disney's and all the rows of stores. But considering their target is the tired, the poor, the results are surely not perfection. I take a sideways glance at Hodji as prime example—a dark, squat Egyptian in a cowboy hat, feeling he is the Clint Eastwood. He has watched over me for days, feeling guilty for not removing Tyler and me from Catalyst's reach, for not having the imagination to conceive of his unprecedented intentions. I cannot dissuade him from his guilt, no matter how often I say I made my own choice, and no matter how often I remind him of our life in Pakistan. Night after night for years, he protected my back, watching and calculating behind many violent extremists. I always felt safe, and I feel safe now. He is not perfect, but he is USIC. They will always watch over us, and for me, that has to be enough.

"You want to see the disaster site?" Hodji points down the street.

I can hear huge cranes and trucks moving about down there. They sound graceful and purposeful and orderly. My life is chaos. I shake my head.

"You want to go see where your family died?"

It is nine blocks away. I think I would like to walk there. But I am suddenly tired, and any new sensation, even unexpected fatigue, startles me. I walk slowly thinking about how best to budget my time of good health. Uncle is coming next week. He did not receive his forty-thousand-dollar cost of intelligence but has paid out of his own pocket to bring my aunt Hamera so they can "embrace my brother's son and be glad he still has breath." For all the wondering I have done of whether my uncle really loves me, I think now that I know. And I know he will want to see where my father died. I can see it with him, if he stays until I feel well.

I think, instead, of how to honor my father's living, instead of his death. Next week, these lesions may break out and nothing will taste good.

"Where is the nearest Kentucky Fry?" I ask in English.

Hodji turns and studies me until a grin spreads on his face. "Few blocks over."

We shift directions accordingly.

"Anyplace else you want to go?" he asks.

"Did you not mention this morning that the Yankees practice this afternoon?"

"They're practicing. The weather's awesome. Say the word if you want to go."

I say, "And I want Yankees cap. And baseball."

"Signed by whom?"

"Hmm... Soriano."

"Done."

"And then we should make to the Gap. I need the blue jeans."

"I'm buying," he says.

"You can pick out what is most good-looking. Just don't make me look like a drip," I tell him. "I cannot appear drippy to the beautiful yellow-haired female who goes to this house place."

"I take it you're ready to admit you're going there."

I admit to nothing. I am feeling a bit more powerful and, having gotten so many requests granted, I feel it is all right to ask for one more, but in a more discreet way.

"You must miss your family. You will leave me early tonight."

"Twain's going to a party," he replies. "God forbid my kid should stay in on a weekend night and hang out with the old man."

That means Hodji will stay with me once again. I have asked him to stay at nights in the hospital until I fall asleep, and I have drifted off blinking into his strong gaze. He is married to an unendurable woman, I suppose, because he has not yet refused me. I know he will be there with me tonight. I will drift off, knowing I could awake to the beginnings of a nightmare, but it is comforting to think of his presence, his gun, his badge, his watching over me. And when I sleep he will go home, as should befit any husband.

But perhaps I will get lucky. Perhaps he will come back early, and perhaps, if I sleep as long as I feel I will need to tonight, he will be there when I awake in the morning.